The Woman Who Found Grace

A CORDELIA MORGAN MYSTERY

The Woman
Who Found Grace

A CORDELIA MORGAN MYSTERY

Bett Reece Johnson

CLEIS
PRESS

Library of Congress Cataloging-in-Publication Data

Johnson, Bett Reece.
  The woman who found Grace/a novel by Bett Reece Johnson–1st ed.
     p. cm.
  ISBN 1-57344-150-3 (alk. paper)
  1. Morgan, Cordelia (Fictitious character)–Fiction. 2. Women private investigators–Fiction. 3. Ex-mental patients–Fiction. 4. Women murderers–Fiction. I. Title.

PS3560.037184W56 2003
813'.54–dc21   2003010169

Published in the United States by Cleis Press Inc.,
P.O. Box 14684, San Francisco, California 94114.

Printed in the United States.
Cover design: Scott Idleman
Book design: Karen Quigg
Cleis Press logo art: Juana Alicia
First Edition.
10 9 8 7 6 5 4 3 2 1

FOR REECE,
the man and the woman

ACKNOWLEDGMENTS

This book is not entirely a work of fiction. In fact, it was inspired by the 1931 "Trunk Murderess" case of Winnie Ruth Judd, a woman convicted of killing her two best friends in the manner I ascribe to my fictional character, Gracie Lee DeWitt. Like Grace, Winnie also dominated the tabloids of her era, was movie-star gorgeous, escaped seven exasperating and increasingly embarrassing times, and after her parole in 1971, attempted to live a quietly uneventful life in small-town California under an assumed name.

I have used a plethora of such historical details from Winnie Ruth's life, yet in spite of the factual backstory, no one should suppose this novel is not, first and last, a fabrication of my imagination. The tale told here belongs entirely to the http://www.buyhorseproperties.com/canyon-creek.htm fictional Gracie Lee—no such events ever, to my knowledge, happened to Winnie Ruth after her release. In addition, I have played fast and loose with time: the real-life murders actually occurred on October 16, 1931, not December 22, 1962. Winnie Ruth did not, like Grace, stop aging during her incarceration. Winnie's husband, Dr. Judd, died in a veteran's hospital in 1945 while she was housed at the Arizona State Hospital for the Insane. To this day, however, no one knows what really happened that October night in 1931, though few believed, then or now, that Winnie Ruth acted by herself, or that she acted with premeditation. Nevertheless, Winnie took the fall—she alone endured thirty-nine years of incarceration for the crime.

I met Winnie Ruth briefly back in 1989, a pleasant and wholly gracious elderly lady, and when I heard of her death on October 23, 1998, at the age of ninety-three, I thought of the miscarriage of justice that took so many years of her life. I thought of the longstanding and still enduring inequity toward women that stretches from long before millions of us were tortured and killed through three centuries of witch hunting, right down to the recent execution of Betty Lou Beets, the Texas "Black Widow." And then I thought of writing this book.

For the facts of Winnie Ruth's life and the events during and after sentencing, I am indebted to J. Dwight Dobkins' and Robert J. Hendricks' Winnie Ruth Judd: The Truck Murders, *and especially to Jana Bommersbach's* The Trunk Murderess: Winnie Ruth Judd. *Thanks to Retha Williams for all of those pictures and "Winnie stories" taken from her personal, first-hand, long-time friendship with the infamous "Marian Lane." To Katherine Forrest, for her wise (and tactful!) editorial suggestions. To Jude Messer and Joy Alesdatter who, for love of sushi, continue to give me good readings. And to my entourage of cats and dogs and horses—all of whom, when the sun sinks and the lights fail, are always, always there.*

Morgan

Anyone who says the past is dead never met Killer Frost, the Trunk Murderess. She carries yesterday around like a Fourth of July flag carries stars, and if there's any truth to the notion that the body takes its cue from the mind, maybe that explains why Gracie Lee Frost DeWitte quit aging thirty-five years ago when the jury sentenced her to death by lethal gas.

In a newspaper clipping of the time, a twenty-one-year-old Gracie Lee with her pale blond hair pulled back from her face stares into the camera, her eyes as wide and mesmerized as Joan's at the stake. At her side is the good doctor, "Daddy D" as she called him. His eyes are concealed behind glasses and his face is an aesthete's, fine-boned and turned slightly away from the photographer. In the half-tones of the old newsprint photo, his hair too is pale, though silver rather than blond. He wears a light-colored, well-cut suit with the stylishly wide lapels of the time. He grips his wife's left hand, his elbow leveraged against her forearm so that she is jackknifed against his side.

That was in 1962, the year Dylan was singing "Blowin' in the Wind" and Carson took over The Tonight Show *and Kennedy stared down Khrushchev over stockpiling Russian missiles in Cuba; the year William Faulkner, Marilyn Monroe, and Adolf Eichmann died, the Marlboro man sprang fully formed from the forehead of Philip Morris, and I received a Shetland pony named Sky Roy for my sixth birthday. It was near the end of that year, the Saturday before Christmas, when Gracie Lee DeWitte left the clinic where she worked in Phoenix while her husband remained in*

1

L.A., stopped by her apartment to change clothes, then dropped in on her two best friends, Mary Bess Fredrick and Jesse Ballantine. She shot them both through the head, cut up one so they would both fit together in the steamer trunk she rode beside on a train all the way from Phoenix, then seven days later turned around and rode back on a plane from L.A. between two FBI agents after her husband turned her in.

In 1963, while the Beatles landed in New York City chanting "I Want to Hold Your Hand" and Taylor and Burton went public in Cleopatra, while Robert Frost lay dying and Medgar Evers caught a bullet outside his home in Jackson, Mississippi, Gracie Lee was counting the days on death row as the governor refused time after time to commute her sentence to life by reason of insanity. In November, somewhere around the time the Presidential limousine was pulling out of Hope Field in Dallas, the gas pellets with Grace's name on them were sliding into place; by the time the limousine was on Elm Street with Jackie scrabbling out of the backseat and across the trunk with her husband's brains splattered all over her pink suit, the Pinal County Superior Court jury pronounced Killer Frost insane and sentenced her to a mental institution until "her reason is restored," after which time the death penalty would be reinstated.

It took over thirty more years of newspaper articles by Julia Simmons and the influence of heavy-weight lawyer Melvin Belli to convince the parole board, and then the governor, that not much investigating had been done at Gracie's trial. For one thing, even though Grace had admitted to being in an alcoholic blackout at the time, her only recollection of the murders an image of an amputated head as she stood with the bloody scalpel in her hand, the prosecution had never come up with a motive. And there was the question of the dismemberment itself: Belli pointed out it was a stretch to imagine that someone with Grace's nervous temperament, not to mention the strength required to quarter and decapitate the body that way, could execute such a deed without an accomplice. And the heart, it still hadn't turned up to this day. In the nineties' media-saturated inquisitions, questions like these that formerly slid by unanswered would get hit by a thousand watts, but in the sixties, justice was a crapshoot.

It was the kind of front-page trial that tossed readers selected snippets of information, a sensationalized story that kept the presses hot for weeks, yet not one reader in ten could have told you that one body, not two, ended up in pieces in the infamous steamer trunk. Almost no one recalled that

Gracie had given herself up, to her husband to be sure, who in turn contacted the police. In fact, not only the reporters but the kingpins of the courtroom paid scant attention to stone-faced, unapproachable Doctor DeWitte who sat through the trial every day at his wife's side, though not once did he visit her in prison or the mental institutions where she escaped seven times just to find him. All things considered, the newspaper-reading public had already tried and convicted Gracie Lee Frost DeWitte long before the courts ever did. She had killed her friends, chopped them up, and by God her head ought to roll right along with poor Mary Bess's.

By the time Gracie Lee's sentence was commuted to time served and she walked out of Mt. Havens Mental Facility a free woman in 1995, she was fifty-four years old, looking like she had yet to see thirty, her hair as naturally platinum as the day she walked in. She slipped with little fanfare into the hot, free sun of Phoenix, boarded a plane that took her to San Francisco, and was still able every step of the way to spin people around for a triple-take without even knowing she was doing it.

Grace Frost: a woman who is a mystery, even to herself. One who drags the past around in her bones because she was there, she lived it. But the past is more than a presence; it is also a choice. I carry it because I choose to, because I have made it my business to know, have read every word written about her—transcripts of the trial, news stories that grabbed every headline of every paper coast-to-coast, histories of the era and of Phoenix in particular—because the printed page is a powerful tool. It can give you a ride back. Anyone who says otherwise suffers from a failure of the imagination and indefensible intellectual ennui.

I am a woman whose professional life for years depended on perception, whose livelihood now more than ever requires making calculated wagers. I have never bet a loser, never lost a wager, and after researching the times and the woman, I will give you any odds you want to name that I was there with Grace Frost.

Your call.

PART I

Déjà Vu

1

E VERYONE TOLD ME YOU HAD TO BE CRAZY to live in
Las Tierras, but they were only half right. I was crazy before I
moved there, according to the official records at Mt. Havens Mental
Facility. Of Las Tierras's other 1,723 residents, all I can tell you for
sure is that they weren't at Mt. Havens. I figure it's a matter of conditioning—most of them have lived here long enough to think
having their Main Street built right over the San Andreas fault line
is normal in the way that folks down in Southern California think
breathing air with toxic levels of carbon monoxide is normal.
Sometimes *crazy*'s just another word for not being there.

It wasn't like I didn't know better. I'd studied up on the place
for so long before I ever laid eyes on it, that driving down the middle of town with Julia that afternoon in August two years ago was
like coming home.

She'd met me at the airport in San Francisco where the air had
more oxygen in one breath than Phoenix had for the whole year.
After snatching up my suitcase and a cardboard box off the revolv-
ing luggage rack, tossing them in the backseat of Julia's car, we set
sail for Las Tierras. I hadn't been caged up for so long I'd never
seen a freeway—I'd been to California, so I knew what they looked
like. But these were a whole lot wider and faster and more tangled
than what I remembered. Julia sorted them out, slipping from one

clotted strip to another with the ease of a captain setting that boat-sized Lincoln on a conquered sea. Somewhere around San Jose, when the air heated up, she rolled up the windows, torqued the air conditioning, and gave that old Lincoln some gas. She drove with her arms straight out, hands on the wheel, perched high enough on her pillows for a clear view. After a few miles, as the traffic thinned and the city fell behind us, we were climbing into rolling, sun-scorched foothills, and by the time we took the Las Tierras exit an hour later, the landscape was lush with trees and the air laced with pine. Julia took a few turns, threw back her head, and announced Main Street just ahead.

It looked exactly like the pictures in the books I'd ordered from the library: the sidewalks were shaded with dark green canopies and lined with trendy galleries and restored historical buildings like they have in these little California mission towns. But I'd seen cute canopies before. What grabbed my attention was the red bricks we were driving over. They only lasted one block, but the minute we hit them and the tires commenced humming, I felt like I could look right through to where those two rocks, the Pacific Plate on the right and the North American Plate on the left, might be getting ready this very instant to shift. When I think back on it, I swear I felt them slip just a tad as Julia drove along that solitary block, like it wasn't the bricks humming up through the tires and shimmying that old Lincoln, but those two neighborly slabs of rock starting to mumble and rub together like a cricket playing its legs, making that kind of electric vibration they say animals sense long before the human species knows that the earth is about to split and buildings fall and freeways collapse.

"What are you looking at with your eyes so wide?" Julia had said, peeping over her glasses. She nodded at folks strolling along the sidewalk. "These are good people here. They will not know a thing about you except what you want to tell them, if that is what you are afraid of."

"Who's afraid?" I said, not taking my eyes off the bricks, the way they'd been laid in a herringbone design, with the center of the street humped up a little and the sides worn smooth. "I'm just trying to figure if it'd split down the middle or take to the sides."

I had a crystal clear image in my mind of exactly how that fault line looked way down there in the dark, under the surface. I'd studied up on locked faults and creeping faults, knew about "S" waves and "P" waves, and I'd seen the sharp black lines straight as a razor on the fault-line maps. But what is science but a lot of theories with more blank spaces than answers? Take the daily weather report: for all the meteorologists showing you where a storm's been and where it's heading, there's a wind blowing somewhere going to prove them wrong. So I knew the geologists' fondness for that straight line was not just an error in cartography, it was a failure in imagination as well. The San Andreas fault we were traveling over was the kind of prevaricating fissure that you'll find on the surface of an otherwise flawless egg. A kind of elegantly splintered, lethal fracture as might appear on a human skull that's been hit too hard. I know first-hand that the earth's surface is just such an inexplicably fragile and cryptic place.

Julia was laughing in that way she has of letting out a series of ear-splitting cackles. Several people strolling under the canopies turned to stare. "You will have to find something better than that to keep you up nights," she said. "This place has been here longer than God. It has a mission built over two hundred years ago, the only one in California still in its original shape. It is perfectly safe. Don't let all that silly earthquake hype fool you."

After Main Street, we angled back in the direction we'd come, zipped past the freeway, and after a couple of miles, turned onto a narrow road which wound through dense groves of eucalyptus. They were massive, graceful trees, a tunnel of fragrant shadows that ended just before we reached a leaning mailbox faintly printed with the name JORDAN. Beside it, a narrow gravel driveway led nearly straight up the side of a steep ridge. On each side was a badly flaking three-board fence that enclosed nothing but burnt scrub brush and bare dirt. Julia stopped a few yards from the mailbox, revved the engine, and gunned the car up the driveway, the old Lincoln slipping and spitting gravel as it struggled for traction. Near the top of the ridge, the driveway veered sharply left, then leveled out just before disappearing into a thick bower of eucalyptus. Nestled at their center, nearly concealed, was a sprawling one-story house and an immense shambling barn with missing doors and tumble-down corrals at each end. Julia parked in a wide dirt space between the two structures and switched off the engine. She smiled like she'd just delivered twins.

"Home sweet home," she chirped.

I sat staring at the house that had cost me a bundle. It had seen better days, no doubt about it. That made two of us. Its shingles were sprung, its narrow front deck listed barnward, and its clapboard sides looked to be flaking at about the same rate as the fence along the driveway. On the other hand, I'd always said I didn't want to live in a house older than me, so that being the case, I figured I'd finally struck it lucky.

I followed Julia up some rickety stairs bracketed by rotting wine barrels that had once held plants, judging from the dead stalks still sticking out the tops. At the front entrance, she pulled out a set of keys, pushed open the door, and dangled the keys in my direction as I stepped inside.

I stood in a wide, dark room with tightly closed drapes, a few scattered pieces of furniture, and a mammoth fireplace dominating one wall. Beyond it, the room opened into a large kitchen. But even in the semi-darkness, it was the knotty pine that hit you in the eye no matter where you turned. Knotty pine walls, knotty pine floors, even the ceiling was knotty pine, and when you closed your eyes you were still seeing knots.

I blinked and let Julia lead the way. I made happy noises as I poked my head into the pantry, the laundry room, the closets; opened cabinets stocked with food and dishes and household essentials. We followed a mazy hallway among four bedrooms while Julia explained how she'd come across the property, the owner at first not wanting to separate it from the adjoining piece next door, and then finally relenting. I finished a dutiful sweep through the last bedroom, a large L-shaped affair with library and office written all over it, then suddenly felt myself sinking fast under the weight of the travel and the trying formalities of being released from Mt. Havens. While Julia put on a pot of tea, I migrated to the living room and opened the drapes.

That's when the exhaustion went south. The scabbing paint and ramshackle barn and knotty pine were no more important than the dust motes drifting through the sunlight flooding the room. I forgot the threadbare furniture and the dingy braided rugs, the ugly rock fireplace and the mock chandelier made out of a wagon wheel suspended above the dining table. I pushed open the glass doors, walked across a huge redwood deck that wrapped around the back side of the house. From there, heaven itself unfolded. To the east, in the distance below where I stood, Las Tierras lay spread like a miniature Hollywood set, its rooftops poking up among toy-sized trees; beyond that, extending all the way to the far peaks of the Sierra Madres against the eastern horizon, lay the emerald fields of California's Central Valley. Not to be outdone, the western view was a spectacle of redwood mountains and deep-cut canyons, with a patch of the turquoise Pacific visible through two intersecting peaks. I smelled it then: the scented coastal air, its unique perfume of eucalyptus and sea. I closed my eyes, took a deep breath. It was the smell of freedom. The gold ring. And it had been a god-awful long time coming.

I heard footsteps approaching, then the sounds of china being set on the table beside the railing. "You done good," I said, my eyes still closed, unwilling to relinquish the moment. Then I felt her beside me.

We stood together, shoulder-to-shoulder. We gazed west across the mountains at the patch of ocean, then east to where the late afternoon sun lit the geometry of bright crops and cast a wing of shadows toward Las Tierras.

"Well," she said, "it cost more than it ought to, I suppose, if you were anywhere else but California, but here, this place was a steal. Ten acres and privacy, that is what you paid for."

"I love it, Julia, I mean it." I didn't give squat about the money, never had. There was still plenty left from the sale of my parents' farm in Indiana, thanks to Julia who'd invested it until I had some reason to think I might need it. "Everything's perfect. I got nothing at all against picking up a paint brush, maybe covering over a few of those knots. It's not like I lack the time to do it."

"And I live just down the road," she said, raising on her tiptoes, which might have put her just over five feet. "You can't see it from here, but my house is just two doors over…"

There was no house visible through the surround of eucalyptus, though I looked in the direction she pointed. Watching her, I felt tears spring to my eyes. Without Julia, I'd still have been in Mt. Havens, would have died there, no doubt. In the waning August light, balanced on her toes in a pair of grimy, oversized Nikes and skin-tight leggings under a baggy knit top that reached to her knees, Julia was a sprout of a woman heading into her eighties. I'd never been able to look at her without thinking of a wren—she moved in sharp, bird-like jerks, cocking her head first one way, then another. A little engine of flapping arms and darting eyes and high-pitched exclamations. She'd been my strongest champion from the night she'd sneaked into Mt. Havens with her reporter's audacity and her spiral notebook ready to take down my side of the story. She hadn't needed a notebook for that. A matchbook would have been plenty of room.

"But you *must* remember *something*," the tiny woman had protested, dragging her chair closer to the bed where I'd been napping after the ten o'clock evening news. She'd pushed her glasses up to the bridge of her nose, and in the frail light of the television I looked into round eyes enlarged by the thick lenses. They were a crackling sapphire blue, like the tips of a hot flame. A row of fierce eyebrows that had never seen tweezers bristled above her glasses, and a frizz of hair the consistency of spider webs framed her face. But what made us sisters under the skin was what she wore: the same turquoise polyester uniform as the female attendants, complete with rubber-soled shoes and white stockings. I'd dabbled in disguises myself, and this one was not bad at all.

I scooted up to sitting position on the bed and sat cross-legged facing her. *Remember something?* Sure, I remembered something—coming out of an alcoholic blackout for just an instant, long enough to look down and see the bloody scalpel in my hand and the two dead women in the trunk, wishing the blackout could have lasted longer so I remembered nothing at all.

I contemplated the little woman perched on the edge of the visitor's chair that nobody ever sat in, her dangling legs not reaching the floor, and I thought of all the trouble she must have gone to, stealing that uniform, those shoes ugly enough to stop trains. For all her originality and determination, however, she could've saved herself the trouble and come during the day in her street clothes. Mt. Havens in the late sixties wasn't much on security, had even given me my own key after I accidentally ripped the window screen by escaping that way one time.

On the other hand, I'd asked the staff to turn away all the reporters. Not that I minded telling them what I knew, which wasn't much, but what I couldn't abide was having to repeat it—like anybody who hadn't believed you or paid enough attention to understand the first time was going to somehow get miraculously convinced or improved hearing or a bigger brain the second time around. But that request had been a few years back, long enough that when this little woman had peeped in the door, I figured five years between saying something once and saying it again was tolerable.

Plus, I like some original entertainment when I can get it. I gave her my foxy look and said, "'Remember something'? You mean, like something not on the record? Maybe something, like, I left out at the trial?" I added the secret smile to the foxy look.

She cocked her head sideways. Her solid line of eyebrows shot up, and her fuzzy hair glowed blue in the television light. "Exactly. Anything you want people to know about that you did not get to say back then." Then she paused, cocked her head the other way, stuck out her neck. "So long as it is true. I work for the *San Francisco Chronicle*, not one of those grocery store tabloids."

"Oh sure, you bet. Just the truth, nothing but the truth."

I was sitting in a full lotus with my back straight as a broom stick, just the way poor dead Mary Bess had taught me, and I held up my right hand like everybody had to do in court. Still, I was booked in as a crazy and if I wasn't that, I was dead meat. I didn't put it past the governor, even now, to try to trick me up by sending an undercover agent, so I folded all the fingers in but the middle one and gave her my widest smile.

In the end, I told her the same things I'd told the jury, all of which she already knew. Fact was, if I'd added anything, it would've been the kind of stuff that belonged in the tabloids. By the time I finished, the late show was coming on, *Bonnie and Clyde* as I recall, and I rang the bell to ask Minnie Lou, who worked the night shift, to pop us up some corn. Heavy on the butter. The three of us had a fine time watching Faye and that Beatty boy making monkeys out of the law, and before Julia left she slipped me her card with her home address and phone number written on the back, said the next time I took one of my unscheduled vacations from Mt. Havens I should drop in on her.

That was the way we started up. Julia had written so many articles about me after that, I'd lost count. I'd have to be crazier than people think to regret her championing my cause, but I couldn't help wonder now, as Julia pointed through the eucalyptus, if she herself might.

That's why I'd had a devil of a time deciding whether to use my own name or a false one for my new life. I'd finally compromised by letting Daddy D's name go and using the one I was born with: Grace Frost. Gracie Lee DeWitte was still recognized by more folks than I liked to think about, but Grace Frost, that one belonged to me alone, and even though there at the end some reporters had got a chuckle calling me Killer Frost, mostly nobody remembered it much. So I'd let go Gracie Lee DeWitte for Julia, living right next door to me and worried that if people knew the way she'd worked so hard to set a convicted murderess among them, it would darken her reputation as a journalist. After all she'd done, I'd be damned before I'd let her suffer a minute on my behalf.

But that was two years ago, and good intentions are like those strong winds the weather folks have such a hard time predicting— they don't always take the path you expect. Every day since, I'd felt more and more kin to that meteorologist watching his forecast go straight to hell. From day one I'd felt uneasy living a deception. The unease had grown into irritation, and of late into a kind of high-pitched anxiety because I know that eventually, usually sooner than later, the offspring of your falsehood is going to walk in the back door and knock you right on your ass.

Call it superstition if you want to, but when good fortune has finally come to room with you, living like you're ashamed of who you are is like telling her to sleep in the barn and mind the chores.

That's what gnawed at me today as I sat at the picnic table staring at that turquoise patch between the two mountain peaks where, on a clear evening, I could watch the sun drop into the sea. The tranquility I usually found here was gone. Anxiety had lowered its head and dug in, perverse as sin and gathering force like the fog bank creeping in from the coast, shrouding the mountain redwoods and dimming the threads of bright foliage that marked the streambeds in the canyons and left a vague nimbus where the sun had been.

The time of year probably had something to do with it, too—there's no month like October for turning a flesh-and-blood woman to nostalgic pudding. With the slightest weakening of the will I wouldn't be seeing fog any more, nor hearing the geese fussing and flapping over grain, goats muttering at their hay. In this autumn hush with its eerie half-light, neither day nor evening, it would be all too easy to step back into a different time when a child raced across dew-wet yards, chased twinkling insects through Indiana corn fields, ever farther from the porch where the elders, visiting Preacher Frost and his wife, talked at the darkening sky. Autumn reeks of such nostalgia, of burning leaves and charred dreams. I could, with no effort at all, call back any one of them, turn back to see—

A gust of wind hit the eucalyptus, set their leaves rattling, and jerked me into the present. I felt a wave of relief without knowing why. What I did know was that dawdling in the past is a fool's game. I pushed myself up heavily: there'd be no tranquility in a sunset this evening.

I grabbed a jacket from the house and headed down the driveway. I figured Julia wouldn't mind if I set out early on my evening ritual. I'd check the mail, walk down the asphalt road till I reached her driveway, follow the meandering dirt road up to her house, drop in for talk and tea, then return home using the high trail along the ridge. It wasn't a long walk, maybe a mile, but its daily routine kept my bones from turning to dust.

I crunched down the gravel beside the white fence that stood out starkly against the landscape. I'd not lacked for activity these two years: the barn still needed work, but the house and fences were painted, I'd laid in ground cover and banks of wild flowers over the couple of acres out front, reinforced the corrals, adopted two goats and the geese for good measure.

Still, I thought, shoving my hands into my coat pockets, there was something hollow about the time I'd lived here. It had the same feel you get when you walk into a room without furniture, without curtains at the windows or rugs on the floor. Empty. I said the word to the early evening, heard the square syllables touch the twilight and echo from the corners. Yet not unhappy, not without satisfaction, I thought, the gravel loud under my shoes. A stark contrast to my time at Mt. Havens. Those memories were full of people and bustle and noise. I'd had talks with folks there that filled the pockets of my mind like food settling into an empty stomach. More than once since my release I'd wondered if the mental institutions had sucked all the interesting people out of the world and locked their doors against the rest. Still, I was willing to meet an interesting person if there were any besides Julia here on the outside.

I paused beside my mailbox. Across the asphalt, a series of descending and cross-fenced pastures reached all the way down to Las Tierras. A stream ran through them, meandering a crooked path and bordered by eucalyptus and live oak. The trees had gone to orange, and the fields had already begun to take on their winter green—such are the topsy-turvy seasons here. Somewhere an invisible cow lowed. I thought I'd glimpsed a movement among the trees, the briefest flash of pale among the shadows, but when I surveyed the spot I saw nothing more.

My mailbox sat firmly on a hefty metal post that I'd sunk in concrete so that passing cars could still sideswipe it if they'd a mind to without setting it askew. I'd kept the original box, left the faded JORDAN on the side, liking the old-fashioned look of it, but on the front I'd spelled out G. FROST in small black plastic letters, the ones preferred by Millie Rains who presided over the local post office.

When I opened the door and stuck my hand inside, feeling for envelopes, my fingers closed around an object—cold, round, familiar.

I screamed and jumped back.

I have always loved them, even as a young girl. Picked them up as they slipped through the grass, checking first to make sure they were not the poisonous cottonmouth or copperhead. Mostly they were harmless ground runners, the ribbon or the garter or the gopher snakes. I would reach into the grass, lift them carefully with both hands, positioning their bodies along my arm. I would hold them up and watch the slender tongues, the gleaming eyes; stroke their cool, muscular bodies along my cheek and neck. I have ever loved a snake.

But not this—this cold, dead thing in the box, a young Western rattler with its pit viper's skull crushed, wrapped around with white lace over a piece of lined yellow note paper. I pulled the paper from the lace and read the message written in pencil with child-like printed letters:

gracie gracie, pudding and pie
kissed the girls and made them die,
after putting them in the trunk,
gracie gracie, pleaded drunk.

2

THE RATTLER'S BODY was still firm and flexible, not long dead. I took off my jacket and wrapped it around the reptile with its elegant patches of browns and tans, then examined the ground beside the mailbox. It was set far enough back from the pavement that the carrier had to pull onto the dirt shoulder to insert the mail, but someone on foot could easily remain on the asphalt and lean forward to open the box without leaving footprints. Recent rains had left the earth soft enough to show the aggressive tire tread of Garvey's old mail delivery Jeep from a couple of days ago, but nothing more recent. Whoever had left the snake must have been on foot, and probably after Garvey's scheduled three o'clock delivery. I checked my watch: 5:37.

I looked again at the trees where I thought I'd seen movement, thinking the person might have hung around to watch the fun. Nothing. Cradling the snake against me, I crossed the pavement to examine the shoulder on the far side. Again nothing, only a thick tangle of weeds that extended from the road all the way to the stream. There, the waterway being narrow and seasonal, one could easily jump across it to the pastures on the opposite side and walk the three miles to Las Tierras, concealed by trees.

I stared into the shadows for a long time, then turned back to the road. It was deserted in both directions. Farther up, north of where I stood, the asphalt disappeared around a curve. The terrain there rose steeply, with the dense vegetation giving way to a tangled forest of wild oak. There was only one house past my own, according to Julia, and then the road fizzled out beyond the curve and provided local teenagers with an ideal lover's lane. In the other direction, the grounds were scrupulously manicured, planted with long, straight rows of fruit trees fed by tidy irrigation ditches, all sequestered behind an elaborate wrought-iron security fence. Julia said a widow lived there, but beyond that I hadn't inquired. California is a heavily populated state, yet it's possible to live a lifetime within a few yards of your next door neighbors and never know their names. That had suited me just fine.

Until now. The virtues of the landscape that had appealed to me for two years, its privacy and remoteness, now struck me as isolated and sinister. The fog had thickened, entirely blotting out the sun, and the air was leaden and damp. Through my jacket I felt the contours of the snake against my breast. I shivered and turned toward home, thinking less about the hand that'd killed the rattler and written the note than where it had last enjoyed stretching itself in the sun, rubbing its belly against the earth and rocks of its particular habitat. I laid it gently under an immense eucalyptus and went to the barn for a shovel.

The old building was still an eyesore. I'd re-hung the doors and patched a few holes, but had put off till next spring the badly needed renovation and structural repairs. The light switch beside the door turned on a low-watt bulb dangling from high above that cast shadows over a large central area bordered on one side by three horse stalls, and on the other by a tack room, an open storage cubicle, and at the far end, a bunk room. The latter contained, among other things, an ancient round-topped refrigerator where I kept veterinary supplies and a carton of milk for a scruffy, mange-ridden black cat which had shown up a few weeks ago and, just now, was bounding down from the shadowy loft.

It performed an impressive series of leaps among cross beams and rafters with the expertise of a high wire artist, then landed at the center of the barn floor and trotted in my direction, its tail waving and eyes glowing. Wrapping itself around my ankles, it ushered me toward the bunk room. I opened a can of tuna, poured a dish of milk, and topped off a bowl of kibble. He was a street cat, no doubt about it—he gorged himself on the tuna, then attacked the milk. I bent close as I dared to inspect his coat; any attempt to touch him while he ate provoked a deep growl during which he flattened his ears and turned rigid until I backed off.

But the cat had remained unsightly. His coat, the scant portions that still remained between the bald patches, was matted and dull. His bones protruded sharply along his spine and sides, and because he was unusually large he struck me as something of a Frankenstein among cats—comically long legs, torn ears, severed whiskers, a tail bent at a ninety degree angle. Only his golden eyes were unflawed—generally wary and luminous, they could narrow to slits in an instant or glow a phosphorescent green that made my blood run cold. Like the time I'd tried to pick him up, and he'd done his slash-and-run number. Stupefied for a moment, the blood running down my arm, I'd considered taking after him with the pitchfork hanging on the wall. But I'd scrubbed the wound with peroxide and looked at it from his side. I guessed his weight around fifteen pounds, mine being one twenty. When I imagined what I'd do if some alien creature eight times my size tried to snatch me up off the ground, I figured he'd let me off easy. I stuck a bandage over my torn flesh and decided I could live with letting the cat walk his own ground.

Inside the house, I tossed the snake note on the table, carried in a few pieces of wood from the trunk I kept on the porch beside the door, and built a fire to take the chill off. Then I went to the back bedroom. It was the large L-shaped room I'd taken as a library, though I'd left behind most of my last collection of books for the residents of Mt. Havens. One wall was already filled, and I'd started on another. In the desk below the window I rummaged in a drawer and pulled out a packet of papers secured by a rubber band. At the dining table, I spread the items in a straight line from left to right in the order I'd received them.

There were a total of ten notes. The first three were on lined blue tablet paper, the next four on pink, the last three on yellow. All were printed in the same childish hand. All were folded into thirds and had arrived, excepting the last, in a standard-sized white envelope, and none had passed through the hands of postmistress Millie Rains. They bore no stamp, no cancellation mark, nothing but the word "grace" penciled across the front in exactly the same lettering as the note attached to the snake. They were all awkward poems, not particularly threatening in spite of their anonymity and persistence.

I'd not paid much attention to them before, but now I stared at each one and thought hard, trying to remember when they'd arrived. I knew the first had come just after I'd moved in, a simple "welcome grace / with pleasing voice / and pretty face." I'd imagined a shy boy or young man, young enough anyway to blush at thoughts of an older woman seen, perhaps, walking the cracked sidewalks of Las Tierras. Someone who couldn't know by my appearance just how old. I stroked my jaw line, the taut skin along my cheeks and neck. I hadn't thought about it at all in Mt. Havens, but Julia had called it to my attention that first day at the airport, how people still turned and stared, just like they always had.

People like Bruce DeWitte, a man twenty years my senior, impossibly obsessed with a young girl's beauty all those many years ago. Daddy D...

I stared at the last note, then at the fire. Today was October twenty-fifth. I swept up the notes, careful of the order and annoyed with myself for not jotting down the dates they'd arrived. I replaced the rubber band, pulled on my jacket, and shoved the notes in my pocket.

In the gray light of evening I headed toward the path along the ridge, the shortest distance to Julia's house. The goats reared up on their hind legs and leaned against the fence, muttering hopefully, while the geese, perennial queens of melodrama, squawked and flapped in giddy terror. At the crest of the ridge I followed the narrow, weed-choked footpath that connected my house to Julia's, with the intervening widow's property marked by the high, ornate fence. From this perspective, a view of the house was blocked by a riotous jungle of green plants which twined up the wrought iron bars and cascaded over the top. On the other side of the ridge, fog had moved in like a white wall, erasing the mountains and turning the air soupy. It was then I heard a sound just behind me.

I froze. The adrenalin hit: my heart raced and my hands shook. When I turned around, I could see nothing in the wide flat stretch of weeds that extended the length of the ridge, peppered with sporadic gnarled trees which, further up, thickened into forest. I am not generally afraid of anything I can see, but this afternoon had been the kind to let in ghosts. I could hear my shrinks back at Mt. Havens saying that ghosts were only as real as I let them be, but those shrinks had a limited store of imagination and precious little experience outside a textbook. Which is what I had told them.

The cat slipped out of the weeds and onto the path, his eyes glowing as he emitted a guttural sound that I presumed to be his best shot at a meow. A wave of relief flooded over me, and I knelt on shaky knees and called out softly. I didn't really think he'd come bounding into my arms, did I? Not without a can of tuna on me. I left him there and continued along the path that cut down the ridge to Julia's place. In the twilight fog, the security light above Julia's garage hung suspended in the air, a spot of haze. Her windows, never curtained, were lit, and she stood at the kitchen sink. I paused and watched her—the flyaway hair pinned in a knot, her forehead creased in a frown as she bent over her task.

"Well, child," she said, looking around when I pushed open the door, "I didn't think you were coming this evening." She cocked her head, eyes round behind the thick lenses. "Is anything wrong?"

There is something heartening, I suppose, but ludicrous as well about two women living side by side, growing so attuned to each other's habits and oddities and predilections that one can pick up the other's emotional climate as easily and reliably as a dog sniffs bear.

"I reckon it's about time I got your opinion on these," I said, pulling out the notes and taking a stool at the kitchen bar where we always sat. The bar looked odd. I realized all the piles of moldering papers and knickknacks had been cleared away, though the counter space didn't look neat so much as empty. I slipped off the rubber band and was about to give her a thumbnail sketch of the problem when a woman walked into the living room from the rear hallway. Dark-skinned, slender, with flashing eyes and long black hair tied back, she was probably in her mid thirties, wearing jeans and a tucked yellow cotton shirt. She looked like she could be named Rosa and dance with a rose in her teeth. She held a broom in one hand and, in the other, grasped a black trash bag by its neck.

"Ah, Natalia, you have finished then?" Julia came around the bar and into the living room, motioning the woman toward us. "This is my friend from up the road, Grace Frost. Grace, Natalia Santillanes. Maybe you know each other? This is such a small town."

I stood up and stuck my hand out, but I could tell the woman didn't much like this American custom. She set down her trash bag, though, and came over. Her grip was strong, quick, and her dark eyes were penetrating.

"I've got the water on. You want to join us for a cup of tea, Natalia?"

The woman glanced back at the bag sitting in the floor. She still held the broom in her hand. "I will finish the work. Is better," she said, moving off. She grabbed the bag, set it outside the front door, and disappeared down the hall.

I looked a question at Julia who had never expressed much interest in either keeping her own house or having anyone else do it for her.

"Wife of a local man, Rico Santillanes," she said in a low voice, going back into the kitchen and taking down cups. "Does gardening work for folks around here, just brought Natalia and his kids up from Mexico a few weeks ago. Lots of kids, the two of them. Needs the work right bad is my guess. You would not want any help with your housekeeping, would you?" She put two steaming mugs on the bar and hopped on the stool beside mine.

"Reckon not," I said, taking up my tea and sniffing. "You know if she fixes barns?" I stuck my finger in and tasted it. Sure enough, Julia had tried to slip one of her concoctions in on me. I scowled and went into the kitchen, telling her about the notes while she looked them over. I poured out what tasted like a mixture of quinine and Tabasco and searched for some tea with a label on it. Nothing was where it was supposed to be. I was peeking into round, metal canisters beside the stove when Julia spoke:

"Not much of a poet, is he?"

"Who says it's a 'he'?" I opened a cupboard and began pushing things around.

"Experience," she said, looking up. "I don't know why you cannot just try something new once in a while," she said with exasperation, hopping off her stool. She plucked a foil packet out of the cupboard and tossed it in my direction. Mint. I dropped it in my cup and poured hot water from the kettle over it.

We sat down together and studied the notes. Finally, she twisted around on her stool, leaned back, and folded her arms across her chest. She was wearing her fuzzy blue robe, and she sat there looking at me with her gray hair frizzing out of its knot. If there'd been a blue jay flying overhead, its maternal heart would have about burst at the sight. When Julia opened her mouth to speak, it was all I could do to resist looking around for something to drop in it.

"There is probably a very good reason why you have kept this to yourself for over two years," she said. Her eyes had begun to turn milky lately, and she squinted a lot. "And there is probably yet another reason why you have decided to tell me now." She glanced pointedly at the yellow note that I had kept separate from the others and now held in my hand. I took a deep breath. Something clattered from the back of the house where the woman worked. Fog pressed against the windows in front of us, and in the glare of the overhead fluorescent light, the glass reflected two women, one of them an old woman who did not need this kind of aggravation in her retirement years.

"Reckon somebody's figured out who I am," I said. I laid the snake note on the counter. "Could be thinking of making it known. Or charging some not to. Could be writing on a new poem this very minute, saying how much gold he thinks his silence is worth." I told her about finding the snake.

Julia listened, then closed her eyes and nodded. Finally, she leaned toward me, her hands flat on the counter. The skin was mottled, and the veins running over the bones were dark cords under the skin. "Well, what are you going to do about it, child?"

"Don't reckon it's up to me," I said. I jerked my chin at the notes. "I reckon whoever's working on his poetry skills here is pretty close to giving me some directions."

"Haarwwk!" she said, smacking the counter. She leaned back in her chair and looked down the spine of her nose. "So you are at last going to allow somebody to tell you what to do, are you? Well, I will just bet all those lawyers and policemen and all those Mt.

Havens shrinks would be tickled pink to hear it. I bet they would beat a path right up your driveway, still hoping you will help them fill in all those blank spaces you left behind." She gave her bitter lemon smile that knotted her face into a fist of wrinkles.

"This isn't about me, Julia. I could give a goddamn rat's ass." I drained the last of the tea and went into the kitchen, opening cabinets, looking for something besides mint. Looking for something a little stronger, maybe some Golden Seal. What the hell, maybe something really powerful, maybe some Lipton's.

I slammed a cabinet door hard and glared at her. "You got any fucking bourbon?"

"Grace, you stop this right now!" Her face was set so tight, it didn't look like a fist anymore, it looked like an asshole. She dropped her voice into low gear. I watched the struggle behind her eyes, could almost hear the gears grinding. She was making an effort, and it was costing her. "This is no time to lose control, dear. Just come over here and sit down. Let us talk this thing through."

I leaned against the stove and squeezed my eyes tight. When I opened them again, I was looking into the black eyes of Natalia Santillanes. She stood in the shadows of the hallway, and for the briefest instant I thought I saw something like hatred in her expression before a curtain fell.

Julia looked around. "Natalia. I know this place must be more than you bargained for. It is time to stop now, dear, before night sets in."

Natalia took a step forward, out of the shadows. She looked from Julia to me and back again. She started to say something, but nodded instead. Julia took money from her purse, walked the woman to the door, and returned, shaking her head.

"I offered to drive her home, but she will not hear of it. Her husband is working down at the Pattersons', a mile from here, mind you, and she insists she will catch him before he leaves. She is a good, hard worker, no one can fault here there. She has found a place for everything, you see. I am doubtful I will ever find anything now that it has been put away so well." She resumed her stool and sighed. "Now, I want to go over these with you, get this thought out straight." Nodding at the notes, she patted my hand.

"Do you have any suspicions at all who might be sending them?"

I explained to her what I'd thought, up until today. "This is the only one of them that shows the person writing them knows who I really am, calling me Gracie and that line about..." I took a breath. "...killing the girls and the trunk, it just set me to thinking of the old days. That's when it suddenly struck me—today is October twenty-fifth." Julia, owl-eyed, waited for me to continue. I picked up the last note and waved it. "Today is my wedding anniversary. The day I married Bruce DeWitte. October twenty-fifth, 1960."

"Are you saying you think it is no coincidence it came today?"

"It would be *quite* a coincidence, wouldn't it? And the others," I nodded at the notes, "I can't remember exactly the days they came, but seems like there was one around this time last year because I remember thinking it was a Halloween prank..."

Julia was hunched over the notes. "Nine, not counting the last," she said. "So they started in August, when you moved in." She tapped the first. "And you said they have come every three or four months? That would probably put that second one at October then, October twenty-fifth if we are on the right track." She laid a long, bony finger on the second note:

> *mirror mirror on the wall*
> *grace is fairest of them all*
> *with her eyes of jade*
> *and her lips of red*

"You were married in 1960, right?"

I nodded. She moved her finger over the word *jade* and tapped it. "Then this note would have come October of 'ninety-five. Setting aside for the moment that your eyes are blue and that you young folks no longer observe such things, but jade is the traditional gift for a thirty-fifth wedding anniversary." She lifted her row of brows that had gone to a wiry, grizzled gray years ago. "Another coincidence, you think?"

I felt the blood drain from my face, my cheeks grow cold. "Are you saying that Bruce DeWitte is around here somewhere, sending me notes?"

"How old would he be now?" She rolled her eyes at the ceiling. "You say he was twenty-two years your senior, so that—"

"Seventy-eight," I snapped. I didn't care if the *New York Times* broadcast my age on the front page; what I hated was every time somebody brought it up, people started looking at me funny. Some of the brave and crazy ones would ask how I got to a plastic surgeon while I was incarcerated. The sneaky ones with manners wouldn't say anything at all, but they'd take to edging in a little closer, and if I looked around quick, I'd always catch them inspecting me. Even Julia did it, like now. I leaned away from her. "I reckon he'd be about your age, wouldn't he?" I said with some acid.

"Right close," she grinned.

"Well, he stuck by me through the trial, testified how he'd been in L.A. that night when I called and talked to him, right before the...before it happened." I still stumbled over it. I would always stumble over it. "Then, after I was put away, he was gone. Why should he stick around? He was married to a nutcase, a convicted killer, and a famous one at that. I don't reckon that made it any easier for him to build a practice with that tagging along after him."

"Dr. Bruce DeWitte was not much for eternal love, I take it."

"Seemed right smitten at the time." I fanned myself with the snake note. "Anyway, we can mark him off, unless you think the dead can rise," I said, knowing she wasn't set against believing it. "He was in that veteran's hospital, just outside of Tucson. That next-to-last escape I made, that'd be number seven, he died the night before I got there. No, I'm thinking somebody's recognized me from those pictures that stayed forever, seemed like, on the front page—the resemblance still being pretty good. Anybody could go to the library, dig up an old paper."

Julia wasn't listening. She had that distant look that comes when she's about to get into some trouble. I'd seen it often enough, always on my behalf. I think she might once have fed on such tough nuts, but that was before her heart had slowed her down. She'd been one of the best investigative reporters of her day, stubborn as a bulldog when she got her teeth sunk into a story.

She squinted at the notes and ran that long, bony finger under them. "Let us just suppose," she said slowly, "for the sake of argument, that your poet has been sending you anniversary notes. Now, can you remember when the others came? Even generally."

I thought about it. They'd seemed so harmless I'd barely noticed them. It was amazing I hadn't thrown them away, would have if it weren't for my pack rat compulsion. It was all I could do to part with a T-bone after I'd eaten the meat. I stared at the notes with Julia.

"Christmas!" I said, pointing to the third one. "I remember thinking maybe this time he'd sent me a Christmas card."

> *hush a bye gracie dont be sad*
> *daddys going to love you till the day your dead*

Julia glared at me. "And that did not upset you?" she asked. Her voice fairly dripped with exasperation.

I shrugged. "It's just a kid's rhyme. Sort of. I just didn't think anything of it."

We sat for awhile, Julia staring at the notes some more. Finally she clasped her hands on the counter like she might pray. "Do you think it could have arrived on December twenty-second, by any chance? I mean, since we are talking anniversaries and all." She had moved from exasperation to sarcasm.

There's a good reason I don't keep track of days, or even months sometimes. Mostly, it's because there's more to forget than remember. That picture in my mind of Mary Bess, for example. December twenty-second. Both Jesse and Mary Bess, shot in the head. Oh dear God, Mary Bess. I put my head in my hands and pressed hard at my temples and squeezed my eyes shut. "Take it easy, dear." Julia patted my back and heaved a sigh. Sometimes her sighs were the biggest part of her. "I think we can safely say the person sending these is up to speed on your bio. We are going to let it go for tonight. I want you to be thinking about the rest of the notes, when they came, some kind of anniversary or significant day, and then we will talk some more tomorrow." Julia's hand fluttered like wings on my back. "We don't know what he is after for sure, or whether he might be dangerous. My first thought is that he wants money, though it is odd for him to have waited this long for it. That could mean he is getting some pleasure in watching you, in scaring you." She paused. "Just assuming that he *is* scaring you."

"I reckon he's not," I said, looking up. "I'll let you know when some asshole putting nursery rhymes and dead snakes in my mailbox scares me. If I was him, I'd be the one was scared."

She rolled her eyes, then glanced up at the wall clock that was moving toward nine-thirty as she collected the notes. "All right, then. So here is where we are. Being unsure just what your poet is after, let us just say that whatever it is, you tell him to get lost and he goes public. Let us just say he writes Sam Oliver down at the *Trib* and spills the proverbial beans." She fitted the rubber band back around the notes, then fastened me with one of her iron-eyed looks that will nail you right up against the wall every time. "Then everybody knows you are Gracie Lee DeWitte, the famous trunk murderess. How is that going to be for you, Grace? Is that your worst nightmare?" She snapped the rubber band and slapped the packet down in front of me.

My worst nightmare? Having my identity revealed? I choked back a laugh. My worst nightmare had already come and gone, everything else was a piece of cake. That wasn't the problem. I looked at her ancient flesh that melted away a little more each day. I saw the bones emerge as the flesh let go, disintegrating at last, like the snake, like all the dead lost things as the earth begins to draw them back. How was it going to be for her when the reporters started in, talking about how she'd got me out on the streets to commit mayhem again? She'd already had two heart attacks, and that kind of publicity wasn't going to help her blood pressure. I felt the tears rise in that prickling way they do just before they find the eyes. I turned away.

Julia wasn't the kind to let it alone, though. She never had been. She grabbed my wrist with a grip that matched the iron in her eye, and with her other hand she pulled my chin around until I had to look at her. "I need to know how you want to play this, Grace, because you must see that it makes no difference to me."

She squinted hard, and I suddenly understood, as her eyes held mine, that it had never made any difference to her, all the times she'd risked her reputation as a journalist to help free a convicted murderer. It still made no difference—except it wasn't her reputation at stake now, but her life. So I told her then. Told her that when I had moved here, I had chosen at last to do it under the easier name because of her. Told her, too, that I had been regretting it, that whoever the poet was, he could not begin to conceive that it was a favor he'd be doing me, and not the disservice he thought.

"So I reckon that in writing those notes he might have sharpened up his rhyming skills some," I said, "but if it's up to me, like you say, he won't be drawing on my bank account."

Julia clucked and shook her head. "You thought you would be harming me, after all I have been through getting your freedom? Why, child, don't you know you could walk around bare-ass naked with 'Gracie Lee DeWitte' tattooed right across your bottom, and it would not do me a lick of harm?" She cocked an eyebrow at me. "Not that you would turn any more heads than you already do."

"I don't give a damn about what people think," I said, as I rose to leave, "but I do dread it that the reporters will be swarming all over again. I just despise having to repeat myself." Which launched her into a wave of cackles.

Before I left, she told me her plan: she'd talk to Sam Oliver about doing a story on me for the *Trib*. Once my identity was out in the open, the poet would have to find another hobby to entertain or enrich himself. If that's what he was doing.

3

Morgan

Headed west down the mountain, the motorhome leans and lurches around the curves. The horse stands in the rear stall with his legs braced and his neck arched over the dutch half-door, staring straight through the bedroom, through the kitchen, into the rearview mirror. His eyes are huge and black and shining. I have often thought he has foresight, that we are connected that way in spite of our bodily differences. His eyes tell me to hurry. We feel some demon gaining on us.

I doubt that it is Cruz. I have left him and his men scouring the forests outside the gated community of El Gato where I made my escape on horseback, descended the backside of the mountain to the small town of Crystal Springs, and purchased the motorhome/horsetrailer combination I saw parked at the rear of the used car lot last week. Cruz will be on the alert for a woman on horseback, possibly one driving a vehicle and pulling a trailer. I am safe for the moment.

At first, I drive as always—watching the asphalt spool out, feeling the vibration and hum of the tires, letting my thoughts roam free in the late October air.

But some darkness sucks at me, pulls harder with each mile. Takes my breath like a strong wind. My throat constricts as though fingers squeeze it.

I pull over and switch off the engine and lean my head against the steering wheel. The horse paws, tosses his head, nickers.

I need to focus my mind.

I leave the driver's seat and sit at the table across from the stove and spread out the map. I take a yellow marker, thinking to chart our course westward, but the threads of highway blur so that I cannot see what lies ahead or what road to take next.

Unable to chart my future, I look out the window. The pavement descends steeply through the pines. In a valley far below sits a tiny village.

I feel a pressing, overwhelming need to make sense of my life, sitting here in this green and foreign spot. I attempt a retrospect, but my mind wanders. I can barely remember last week. I try a new tack. I start at the beginning, cast my life into the language of a fairy tale to force simplicity on it, to find the villain, to understand what path has brought me to this impasse. I look at my past from the outside, as though I am a stranger to myself.

She (who is I) was not always a woman on the run from The Company, a woman whose specialty for ten years was surveillance and apprehension. Once upon a time, she had been a princess. She lived at Tara (so it looks to my memory) in Kentucky and her tall, handsome father raised Thoroughbreds and her mother wore white gloves and a small hat with a veil to church. Her name was Cordelia Krevlin (born with her father's name, as little girls are), a child who rode her pony through emerald pastures, waving at neighbors as she galloped across the countryside until one day, when she was fourteen and her father had gone on a business trip, her mother called a cab and they both drove away forever. They lived in a women's commune in Indiana, and after Cordelia finished high school and went away to Chicago to begin college, the commune was burned to the ground and her mother with it.

I hear the ticking of a clock. I look around the motorhome but find none. Outside the wind had risen. A branch taps against the window. The sun angles west, its long rays stretched to me. I close my eyes and lay my head on the table.

After the fire she had gone to live with her father at the Kentucky farm, attended the races with him on weekends when he entertained important people. Like the man from Milan named Pasonombre—head of an international business called The Company. And his friend, Simon Cruz, owner of a research laboratory in Santa Fe, an influential man with whom she lived for two years, before joining Paso's Company.

She had attended The Company's School in Milan, recovered the repressed childhood memories of her father beating her mother. She had taken her mother's maiden name and become Cordelia Morgan, The

Company's "Numero Uno" Specialist. Until 1993. Needing a break, she took a "vacation" assignment, a surveillance job in New Mexico. And defected.

She has been running from The Company ever since, but mostly she runs from Cruz. He is a man with an ego. He hadn't liked losing millions when she had scuttled his development scheme during the last assignment. He especially didn't like the incriminating papers she held over his head, papers that on her death from any but natural causes would go to Paso and from there, Cruz was a dead man. She had thought this would keep him at bay. She had been wrong. With the right kind of persuasion, he felt, she could be made to tell where the papers were hidden.

I sit at the table, staring at the trees but not seeing them. Thinking that my past has not explained Cordelia Morgan, who she is, why she has come to be sitting here. Where she should go next. For all the impossible tasks I have performed for Paso, I cannot make sense of a child's story. There is some answer at hand. Near and visible as the trees. But I cannot see it.

She thinks, "I am a stranger to myself."

4

BRUCE DEWITTE COULDN'T have been a more perfect daddy if Oedipus and Freud had gotten together over cocktails and hired him for the part. I figure Herr Sigmund was close enough from the men's point of view; for women, he was pissing in the wind. For us, it's not about sex, it's about power. It's about a woman not having any and wanting to rub up against all of it she can find. And Doctor Bruce DeWitte had it in spades. He had silver hair, a narrow mustache, granite eyes, and he wore suits that looked like the angels burned the midnight oil sewing for him. And the icing on the cake: he was the head honcho of Evanston State Mental Hospital. The minute I laid eyes on him, my heart woke up and saluted.

That was thirty-eight years ago. He'd been out of my dreams long enough that I didn't count how long anymore, but he was back in them tonight—walking in through every door in that round room I dreamed in with its doors for walls, and Daddy DeWitte opening every one of them. It was a dark room, jet dark, and so I shouldn't have been able to see him, but the old Dream Runner behind the projector didn't give spit about realism. I was lying in bed, and all around me that carousel of doors was spinning and opening, hundreds of them, and Daddy D walking in like at the carnival's room of mirrors. But he shouldn't have been wearing those suits the angels made; he shouldn't have been wearing anything at all. That's mostly how I remember Doctor Bruce DeWitte.

Well, hell!

I threw off the covers and switched on the lamp. One door, four walls at right angles, one window. Standard issue bedroom, not so different from the one I'd had for over thirty years at Mt. Havens, right down to the piles of books stacked on the bedside table and towering around the bed. The big difference was not a matter of décor, but of accessibility. Now I could make a cup of tea without having to ask permission, go outside without having to cut through the screens to get there.

I brought the tea back to the bedroom, scanned the piles of books there without finding one that struck my fancy, then went into the rear bedroom I used as a library and stared at the shelves. It wasn't like I didn't have plenty to choose from. Books on monasteries, rules of poker, white-water kayaking, raising beef cattle, British Romantic poetry—I'd read just about anything that struck my fancy. But tonight I was restless, nothing sounded interesting. I thumbed through a biography of Queen Hatshepsut. Another on advances in non-invasive surgery. Beginning fly fishing. Upgrading computers. Intermediate yoga. Interpreting gargoyles.

A book wasn't going to chase away the images of the good doctor that kept jumping out at me on every page. I went back to my bedroom, slipped on a robe, and carried my tea out to the deck where a blanket of fog had covered the stars, though a spot of moon burned through. Closer to earth, the mist drifted in shreds through the eucalyptus, shutting out the lights from Las Tierras as though I were cocooned here, the solitary inhabitant on an alien planet. Me and one other, I thought, squinting at the murk; someone writing letters and killing rattlesnakes, maybe someone out there right now watching me.

Like Daddy DeWitte?

Not bloody likely. The notion of it had given me a start at first, but for all his Houdini tricks, the good doctor would have a tough time pulling this one off. I liked the irony, though, thinking of the time after the trial when I'd waited for him to visit me. It's such times as that, times of great extremities, that'll strike a match and burn you up inside with anger, so that when the fire's stopped you must look inside and see what's left. Times like that, you'll finally understand you're alone in the world, that whatever resource you'd expected to rescue you in a pinch was all a sham, some space cadet talking at the moon. Somebody that hadn't been there.

When I finally understood he wasn't coming, that's when I started my businesses: fixing the women's hair, doing their laundry, all of it to finance my escapes. Six of them, before the last. Escaping had been the easy part, easy as slitting a screen or lifting a key off a hook or just giving the attendants a little ordinary kindness. The hard part, the part I'd failed at every time, was finding Daddy once I was out. It was like I could hear him calling the minute I put Mt. Havens behind me. Knowing there was no rest till I was with him again. That seventh time, I made it two hundred and ten miles across the Sonoran Desert to the hospital outside of Tucson where I last heard he was—not as a doctor, but as a patient.

The desert is not a bad place, but it'll take a toll on you. After I'd trekked through it, I stopped off at a gas station down the road from Daddy's hospital, washed myself using toilet paper to tissue off the sweat and the dirt and the dried blood as much as I could. I opened my suitcase, took out the new navy blue dress in its plastic wrapping, the matching heels and silk stockings.

It was a men's hospital, one for veterans—even though I knew Daddy'd never spent a day in the service. He was never one to be hindered by rules. I waited through the afternoon, till the lobby was deserted. It was twilight when I pushed open the double glass doors and walked into that antiseptic smell I'd know anywhere, went to the admissions window where a woman sat with a hard white nurse's cap pinned over frizzy gray hair. I gave her a false name and explained that I was Doctor DeWitte's niece, come all the way from California to see him.

"Visiting hours are past, you know, but I'll see what I can do." She dialed a number, spoke with someone about a visitor for Bruce DeWitte, and then put the phone down. The eyes behind her wire-framed glasses were the same color as her hair. "He was taken to intensive care last night, dear. His heart, you know. I'm so sorry, I'm afraid he didn't make it."

I felt the floor slant sideways, and then the nurse was standing beside me, holding me up.

"Is there someone I can call?" she asked, helping me to a chair in the waiting room. "You just sit here a minute. I'll bring you some water."

I tried to think where I'd go now, but nothing sprang to mind as I sipped the water and made up stories for the nurse about the trouble with the train system from California to Tucson. I didn't have to think too long about where to go next, though, because after a few minutes the double glass doors woofed open and blue uniforms were walking through them. I wasn't too surprised. That happened every time I came to visit the doctor. Some part of me was glad I wouldn't have to be paying anymore calls.

And so the last time I escaped, Daddy being dead, I had it all planned out in advance, from the several months it took to knit the ladder I used to climb out the window and reach the ground, to the direction I planned on heading. The thing that I hadn't figured on, though, was getting outside the hospital grounds and standing there in that raw, free air, breathing it in and feeling the black emptiness of it: like having a full tank of gas on a Saturday night and not a place in the world to go. But it passed. I put one foot in front of the other and headed west, to California this time. I stayed out six-and-a-half years, so long that when I went back, the parole board seemed to be worn down, tired of arguing with Julia and the lawyers and putting me back again. Said they believed I wasn't a danger to myself or others.

The fog had thickened, the moon was gone, and layers of mist floated through the trees and rubbed against the deck, pale and gray. It didn't take any amount of imagination to see Daddy stepping from behind a wide eucalyptus trunk nearby, wearing one of the soft dove-gray suits the angels had sewn, almost the same color as the fog with his silver hair and pale eyes and the thin, precise mustache, his steel-rimmed glasses not even hazed over by the mist. And he was not seventy-eight, he was not a minute past forty-two and every inch the god I'd first laid eyes on when I was eighteen.

"Miss Frost?" he'd said.

He sat behind an enormous mahogany desk in an office three times bigger than any of the others I'd seen at the hospital. Its windows were covered by heavy draperies, its size undiminished by several pieces of dark, massive furniture to match the desk. After the secretary had closed the door behind her, Doctor DeWitte nodded slightly toward a straight-backed chair. While I sat and waited, he read papers inside the folder spread open in front of him. I'd only glimpsed the director from a distance, a tall elegant man at the end of a corridor, but now I was close enough to see the fine hairs on the tops of his hands, the circle of white cuffs showing inside his jacket sleeves, the long tapering fingers and the manicured nails. The empty space on the ring finger.

Hospitals are cesspools of rumor. During the late night shifts, the hallways grow longer, dim tunnels stretching from one pocket of light to another where night nurses sit waiting for others to join them through the lonely hours till morning breaks. Those are the times when the staff clusters to talk away the time, telling stories of the insane who sleep uneasily behind locked doors, gossiping about their colleagues and the doctors and especially that immaculate man under whose hand the hospital runs. The tales fly: a man whose wife ran off with a book salesman, who died in childbirth, who simply disappeared. Is, anyway, gone.

Doctor DeWitte leans forward with his hands clasped tightly across the folder. Clasped tightly except for the two index fingers whose tips meet and point like a dagger directly at where my heart beats so loudly that I'm sure the windows are shaking with it. But if they are, Doctor DeWitte doesn't hear them, for even as the fingers are aimed at me, they slowly begin to open in the way an insect's antenna opens—slowly, spread wide, exploring; closing again into the dagger point. I stare at them, hypnotized by their rhythm as they open and close, open and close…

"…that your father is a Free Methodist minister?" His voice is so low, just above a whisper, that I lean forward to catch his words, so that we're both leaning forward, the desk between us. "I expect you have had a very careful upbringing then. A very moral upbringing, was it? I see from your file that you have taught Sunday school and sung in the church choir. All this, and making good grades at the nurse's college as well." The fingers pointing, opening, closing. "Even without seeing you, Miss Frost, I would have thought you a most exemplary young woman."

His thin lips below the mustache tighten instead of smile; his tone carries an edge of accusation, mockery, of something I can't identify. Blood rushes to my face, and in my lap my hands twist and wring each other like pale, rabid snakes. In my confusion I wonder how my background is going to affect my three-month performance evaluation. I need this job if I want to keep attending the nurse's college nearby, so I've been practicing for this interview in front of my bathroom mirror for weeks, training my face to lie.

"Your review looks good, Miss Frost. Very good," he says. When he nods, his glasses reflect the light. His eyes behind the lenses are the color of twilight, the color of frost on stone, gray with dark at their outer rims. He taps a white sheet of paper lying on top of the folder and frowns down at it. "However, there is some information missing. Just routine, but the documentation does need to be finished, I'm afraid." His left hand shoots out, and he glances at the gold watch on his wrist. "I've an appointment just now, so we'll have to reschedule," he says, pushing back his chair. He circles around the massive desk, walks toward the door as I rise and follow. He reaches for the doorknob, but doesn't turn it. Instead, he waits till I stand beside him. "In fact, it would be to your advantage to have the evaluation completed as soon as possible. I wonder if you might be able to meet me this evening. Around eight, say, at the Cromwell Inn." It's not a question, and he doesn't wait for an answer. He opens the door, and as I walk past him, I catch the faint odor of lime, that and something else. A smell as familiar as my father—the odor that's not quite sweat, almost like pecans, the unique odor of a man's skin.

It's difficult, it seems to me, to look back on the crossroads of your life with dispassion. Didn't I know the director was breaking an ethics code by arranging a liaison with an underage employee? Did I truly believe he'd show up at the Cromwell Inn carrying that incomplete form in his hand, ready to fill in the gaping blanks? No matter how honestly I've answered to myself—especially to myself—an emphatic *yes, yes, yes*, doubt creeps in, hissing. But of this I'm sure: for all that I'd smelled a man's skin, I'd not known his would be so white, so hard, so insatiable. I was that young.

Around the deck, the fog shifted and churned. The passage of thirty-eight years since that first night in 1959 with Daddy DeWitte might've made me wonder at my innocence, but experience and a lot of reading had blown my romanticism straight to hell. Most of my awake time at Mt. Havens was spent inside a book, any book, and if the sixties and seventies and eighties rolled by without me in them, I kept up by reading the movers and takers. What I knew about how women can be brought to bear the guilt for acts perpetrated against them didn't need any better teachers than Daddy D on the one hand, and the firm of Friedan, Greer, and Millett on the other. Forget a woman's age and the size of her breasts; women in 1959 left their homes still children, walking out of one asylum in search of another—looking up, always looking up.

It's funny how when a man looks for something, he'll keep his eyes to the ground or straight ahead, scanning the horizon, but women will go around looking with their heads leaned back and their gaze straight up. Women'll sing hymns to daddy or god, not thinking much about how they're the same, all the time praying and aching between their legs for the very thing they're taught to call an abomination. When women looked up back then, they saw an empty sky and a statue of a man nailed by his wrists and bleeding, saw him and ached so bad for him that between the desire and the shame there was nothing left to living but guilt. For a long time I wondered how Freud could've missed so completely this fountainhead of a woman's identity, and then one day at the trial, as the shrinks took the stand one after the other, I realized that a man can no more fathom a woman's heart than he can read her soul.

"And so you've come to the big city in search of your fortune," he says, this man whose suit is the color of clouds as he glances at me over the top of the menu. He's not brought out that incomplete form yet, though I expect him to do it any time now. He slaps the menu shut, hands it to the waiter, and orders extra rare steaks for us both. When the waiter disappears, he says: "And when you graduate, a real registered nurse, do you plan to stay in the mental health field?"

I nod, reeling from *extra rare*, twisting the red linen napkin in my lap where he can't see it. We sit on one side of a large room with burgundy carpet and tables covered with white cloths and crystal glasses. The room hums: subdued voices, the tinkle of silverware, soft steps of the waiters.

"Ah, so you enjoy your job, you like working at the hospital?"

This is what I'd been practicing for in front of the mirror. I want to say I despise it, that I attend classes at the nurse's college with barely three hours sleep, that I'm repulsed at how mental patients are restrained and abused and ignored. Doctor DeWitte waits with an elbow propped on the white tablecloth, the globe of his long-stemmed glass cradled in his palm. I study his pose, his elegance, wonder if he's practiced it in front of a mirror: his head is tilted to one side, his lips compressed in a smile, his eyes soft, unfocused. I nod, still twisting the napkin. He tips his head back, sips at his drink and watches me above the crystal rim. He sets the glass carefully beside his plate and clasps his hands in front of him.

"Tell me, Gracie," he says, leaning forward. His index fingers meet in their dagger's point, aimed at my heart, then spread slowly. "What is it like to have a minister for a father? Do you miss singing in the choir?" The fingers spread wide, close. His eyes have darkened, the pupils dilated over the gray. "Tell me, Gracie, do you believe in God?"

I steady myself, grab on to his eyes as he has grabbed mine. I reach for my glass filled with the clear liquid and the olive at the bottom, like his. I lean on my elbow, the same angle he's used, tilt my head back, sip. I'm ready for the acrid taste, have tasted gin before.

"He's a man, too, isn't he?" I say.

His eyes glitter and his voice is hard. "Tell me what you know of God and men, Gracie."

I watch his fingers open and close three times, and then I do it— I close my eyes and imagine myself in the choir back home. I keep my voice low, for just for the two of us:

The earth shall soon dissolve like snow,
the sun forbear to shine,
but God, who called me here below,
will be forever mine.

When I open my eyes again, his have gone pitch black, blank. The waiter arrives with the plates and sets the bleeding flesh before us. Doctor DeWitte doesn't notice; he's still staring, not blinking. I cut through the steak; blood runs and pools in a circle around the rim. Not the thin pale liquid of cooked beef, but a thick, hot blood. I spear a piece on my fork, note the way the striated flesh hangs on the silver tines. I look across the meat at him while the blood drips on the plate. I see something move in the darkness behind his eyes.

I place the meat in my mouth, chew slowly, never taking my eyes from his.

His dark gaze probes. I feel him inside me, feel my breasts and nipples gorge with blood, the hot shooting pain between my legs.

Doctor DeWitte is a man who understands how to calm a woman. That night, after he's spoken in his low, patient voice for a very long time, after he's administered the drug he promises will dissolve my anxiety, we lie together in my bed with the traffic sounds from the street floating up through the open window like moths.

I turn on my pillow and watch his silhouette, the angle of his forehead and the straight lines of his nose and chin, the cigarette ember glowing as he inhales, the radio playing low on the floor. I ask him about his wife. After a long while, he answers: "It didn't last long. She died two years ago."

"How?" I ask. "How did she die?"

He lifts himself to his elbow and leans over me, runs his fingers through my hair.

"You're very beautiful," he says.

"How did she die?"

Back then my hair was long, like blonde silk. He combs his fingers through it, takes a handful and rubs it across his face, inhales it. "Cancer," he says, breathing deeply. "She died of cancer. She had it when we married, and we knew she wouldn't live long."

"Why did you marry, then?"

He drops my hair and lies back facing the ceiling, smoking. "I liked the way she sang," he said, his voice sarcastic, dry as a desert wind.

The fog wasn't doing anything for my insomnia. I got up and paced the deck. Overhead, the mist rolled and thinned so that a hazy patch of moon burned through, disappeared, burned through again as I continued to pace. I'd been over that first night with Bruce DeWitte a thousand times, and I never could explain to myself why I'd played at such irreverence, why I'd said the things I had and sung that song to him. There was some slapstick humor, singing a verse of "Amazing Grace," but I'd always looked back on that moment, wondering why it was that particular verse that sprang to my lips, like it'd been the one defining act from which everything else followed. Like Eve eating the apple.

I've told myself countless times that I couldn't have known the events I was setting in motion, but I'm not quite convinced. A more experienced woman would've seen in Bruce DeWitte a man uncontrollably driven by his own needs. A more experienced nurse would have looked into those dilated eyes and seen not the symptoms of passion, but of drugs. Young women and morphine—the doctor's favorite combo, and so much the better if the former had access to the latter.

The fog was very thick now; the moisture had penetrated the fabric of my robe. I felt clammy, chilled, increasingly anxious as images from the past crouched in the mist, ready to walk out and reveal themselves. I knew who was going to come next, the one I could least bear—Mary Bess, cut into pieces and holding her head in her hands, dismembered from knee to foot, from waist to...

I rushed down the two stairs and waded through the fog toward the barn. I switched on the light which shone weakly through the mist and walked quickly to the backroom where the door was still propped open with the empty cat's dish on the table. On a high shelf behind a stash of cat food, I found the quart of bourbon. Still unopened after two years. Medicinal bourbon, I'd told myself.

Tonight I needed some medication. I broke the label and twisted off the cap, put the bottle to my lips and leaned my head straight back to take a long, burning drink until I felt the fog recede and the ghosts diminish. Something touched my leg, and I jumped. The black cat leaped to the table and sat squarely facing me, his eyes round and bronze and eloquent while his tail snapped in the air.

"Well," I said, breathing deeply and feeling immensely better. I screwed the cap back on the bottle and stood looking down at him, the tatters and missing chunks in his large ears, the bald patches with the naked skin shining through. I reached out carefully, smoothing the fur around the roots of his ears, around his eyes, watching for the slightest indication that he might strike. "You better get on back to bed. No offense, big guy, but you need all the beauty sleep you can get."

He glared at me, and his eyes narrowed briefly. He looked at the bottle, then back: "In that case," he said, whipping his tail side-to-side and whacking the table with it, "I guess you ought to be thinking of heading on back to bed yourself." He stood, arched his back, turned his broken tail to me, and treated me to a full view of his rosebud. Then he leapt from the table and disappeared out the door.

All right. So the cat didn't *literally* speak. Truth is, I can read a cat's eyes, I swear. I knew exactly what that cat was thinking.

I took the bottle, switched off the barn lights, and went back to the house. The fog had cleared and left the moon in full view. Her face was shaved along one edge, waning, and if I thought she looked just a little miffed, I wrote it off to my imagination that was still waiting to be shut down for the night. I slammed the door on her, grabbed a tall glass from the kitchen, and headed back to my bedroom.

I figured I'd take Scarlett's advice and think about it tomorrow. My problem was making it there.

5

OCTOBER 26, 1997
SUNDAY MORNING

F EW THINGS ARE LESS WELCOME TO A DRUNK than
morning sun. Those strips of hot light slanting in through the
blinds you forgot to close last night mean that in spite of your
worst intentions, you're still kicking. I eased one eye open and was
hit broadside by thoughts of my last alcoholic blackout—coming to
consciousness with a bloody scalpel in my hand and Mary Bess's
head staring at me from the trunk. I lay across the bed for a long
time, staring at the floor where the ass end of the empty bourbon
bottle protruded from piles of toppled books, then tried sitting
upright, inch by inch. I made it, but jackhammers tore through my
brain, my eyes would not open beyond a squint, and I was buck
naked.

The minutes crept by, heading into the next millennium. Finally,
I untangled myself from the sheets and tiptoed into the bathroom.
I turned on the shower and breathed in some steam, thinking that
Scarlett must've had bricks for brains if waiting for tomorrow was
the best plan she could come up with.

I entered the shower, held my face up into the stream of hot,
stinging water. All due respect to Miss O'Hara, the only thing
that'd ever helped me through a hard spell, not counting a hair of
the hog, was stretching out on a flat rock under the desert sun or
standing in a shower with substantial water pressure. A murderess

in a mental institution can't always find a desert rock when she needs it, so I'd spent a lot of time in the shower. There are worse ways to pass a day.

After I'd done enough penance, I adjusted the temperature to comfortably warm, savored the luxury of a solitary shower, and waited. It took a tad longer than usual. The water was getting pretty frosty by the time my thoughts started to act like more than chunks of granite, but I knew that the one thing I could do to make myself feel better, not counting another bottle of bourbon, was to take action. I'd had my wallow in self pity, and there's not much in the world feels worse. I toweled off, thinking that even though Julia was going to drop in on Sam Oliver come Monday, take care of the part about living a lie, that still wasn't the same as finding out who the poet was.

Today was Sunday, a good day for catching people at home. I figured it wouldn't hurt to ask the neighbors on each side if they'd spotted anyone walking along the road yesterday. It wasn't much of a plan, but it beat wallowing. It'd do for starters.

When I came out of my reverie, I was staring at a vague shape lurking behind the steamy mirror. You've got to understand that I've never had much truck with a mirror, never tunneled through teenage melodrama stockpiling cosmetics and hair goop, hadn't been much one for attracting boys, seeing as how Daddy was a minister and disinclined to have them hanging around his only daughter. Folks would talk, he'd said, and that was the end of it till I moved off to nurse's training.

Those three years between leaving home and the murders, I'd fussed with my hair and picked the color of eye shadow Daddy DeWitte liked, but after that, for the next thirty-three years, opportunities for mirrors were minimal: penal institutions are leery of objects their inmates can reduce to shards. Come to these last two years, I reckon I'd just got out of the habit. About the only time I'd looked into my own face was to fish out a dust mote. So I had startled myself, standing here and catching my image unaware. I rubbed off some steam and stood looking at her—a tall, leggy woman with a soggy towel hanging from her hand, her expression as bewildered as if she'd caught a peeping tom. I leaned forward for an up-close look and gazed directly into the cobalt blues of a stranger.

I was spellbound. I examined this stranger with the same rapt attention I followed the minute elaborations of a spider pulling silky filament from within itself, or contemplating the crowds of praying mantis that appeared a few days each fall and sat with their spiky arms folded and their jeweled eyes watching my every move. With my fingertip, I touched the pale arch of eyebrow, the firm flesh along the cheeks, the neck. I stepped back to confront the entire creature, this woman, and understood the furtive looks people gave me. Their remarks. Julia's observation that I'd not changed much over the last twenty years wasn't an exaggeration. I stared at the angle of the pelvic bone and the hips, the trim flesh covering the rib cage, the full breasts. I felt dispossessed, a stranger to myself in the most intimate way, and far from feeling vanity, to the contrary—I gave myself the creeps.

The jackhammers were back. I went to the bedroom and slipped into a pair of jeans and t-shirt, put on the coffee, and by the time I'd fed the animals and was sitting on the front steps, squinting into a dazzling morning, I knew the coffee was going to fail me. I knew it because, as a mild breeze drifted through the eucalyptus, shaking the branches and sending the fallen leaves scuttling along the ground, the gray shape of the good doctor had appeared again inside the shadows, slipping from tree to tree, crouching to leap out at me with that leer on his face. I held the cup tight and squeezed my eyes together, willing him to dissolve, knowing that the only help for the day was down at Harvey's Pump & Go in a quart bottle.

"Shit!" I smacked the porch step hard with my hand.

Birds that had been nearby, chirping and poking at the gravel, took to the air. They left behind a dead silence. I folded my arms on my knees, leaned my head down on them, tried to force away thoughts of flesh that didn't age, of a woman dismembered and beheaded, of the intricacies of bourbon and how it caressed the mind. An invisible jet overhead split the sky and shook the porch where I sat. The black cat who had come silently up the stairs leaned its shoulder against my thigh. I stroked his fur absently. I had to get moving, take my mind off the bottle I'd seen Daddy

DeWitte carrying with him through the shadows. Besides, I thought, raising my head carefully and tilting it back, breathing in the sky, the past was dead, Jesse and Mary Bess were dead, Daddy D was dead. After all I'd been through, I'd be diddle-dog-damned if I'd sit here and waste a perfectly good Sunday.

"Fuckin' A!"

The cat stopped leaning on me. He sat down with his tail wrapped around his haunches and looked every bit the Cheshire as he grinned between broken whiskers.

But I regretted my outburst the minute it hit the air. I'd always be the daughter of the Reverend Frost, and if there was an afterlife, my daddy was surely listening with great distress. One more thing I didn't want to think about. I downed the last of the coffee, stood up and stretched. Before I could talk myself out of it, I went inside for my sunglasses, closed the door behind me, and headed down the driveway. When I reached the county road, looking first one way and then the other, I debated whether to begin with my northern or southern neighbor. The vulture of indecision began to descend, sucking color from the day; before it gained hold, I walked south along the asphalt toward the orchards, toward the house where I'd spied the lights last night as I'd walked home from Julia's house. Beside the driveway a tidy mailbox in the shape of a bird house topped with a tiny shingled roof had "W. Remington" stenciled in white letters. I followed the curve of smooth concrete driveway bordered on each side by recently trimmed hedges, rounding the bend to confront a high, elaborately embellished wrought-iron gate with the name REMINGTON in filigreed iron cursive across it. The gate was in two sections, fastened at the center between the N and the G with a bolt.

Nothing's ever easy with a hangover. Just thinking about walking back home, looking up the Remingtons in the phone book, assuming they were even listed, and trying for an appointment seemed as laborious a task as Hercules ever had. I heaved a sigh, turned to leave. Then I spotted the small rectangular speaker box attached to a post on the left side of the drive. I pressed a button, feeling uncomfortably like a poor relative as I stared at the tiny holes in the speaker plate and waited. I pressed again, looked at the sky. It was flat, almost white; for a moment, the concrete where I stood seemed to tilt a little under the immensity of it all. Just as I turned to walk back down the drive, the speaker box crackled to life.

"Yes, yes. What is it?" The voice was male and elderly. Cranky, it seemed to me. "Who's there?"

I introduced myself and explained to the box that I lived next door and would like to speak with the owner.

"Miss Frost. So you're finally stopping in." There was a loud buzz, and the bolt on the gate slid back. "Come right on in, my dear."

My dear? I slipped through the gate, and the bolt locked behind me. I followed the driveway through grounds that looked professionally landscaped: banks of roses, hanging plants with fountains of red flowers, glossy-leafed oleanders, patches of lawn manicured to emerald velvet. A narrow trickling acequia with a flagstone border followed one side of the driveway and disappeared into a dense, shadowy enclave of eucalyptus. I crossed a small arched bridge, then followed a walkway to the house, a sprawling one-story red brick with acres of paned windows. A heavy collar of bougainvillea trailed over the banister of the front porch, and bright flowers in redwood pots bracketed the entry.

As I climbed the steps, the door opened and a slight woman in a pale yellow dress stepped onto the porch. She had a deep tan and silver blonde hair cut blunt just below her ears, friendly blue eyes and teeth so white they were almost fluorescent. I'd not spent much time at elite country clubs, but if I had, I would've expected to see women like this, playing golf and lounging poolside, perfectly content to let their executive husbands bring home the beef. Guessing her to be in her early or mid-50s, I glanced past her, looking for the elderly man I'd spoken to on the speaker, but the entryway was empty.

"Sam Oliver down at the *Trib* told me someone named Grace Frost had moved into the Jordan house," she said. "I'm Clarissa Remington, so happy to meet you." She bent stiffly at the waist and offered her hand.

For a moment I was speechless. Her voice was unmistakably the one from the speaker box, cracked and palsied with old age. Her hand was fragile, the bones slight as a bird's, and her facial skin was stretched tight and shiny as cellophane in the late morning sun. But her smile ruined the effect. It put wrinkles in all the wrong places because after that many lifts, the skin loses its direction.

"I guess I should have stopped by before this," I said, trying to cover my surprise. "I'm a little on the reclusive side, I'm afraid."

"Well, you're living in the right state," she said dryly, withdrawing her hand and beckoning me in. I followed her down a hallway and into a living room that was nearly opulent with its pale blue carpeting, brocade sofas, inlaid tables, floral paintings in ornate frames, vases of fresh-cut flowers. But the centerpiece stood before a picture window: a full-sized ebony grand piano that was more than mere decoration. Sheets of music lay scattered on its shiny top, and behind it, through the open drapes, was spread a panoramic view of the Central Valley.

"Can I get you some coffee or tea?" she said, leading me through the living room. The smell of baking pastry hung in the air. "I'm just taking some blueberry muffins from the oven." I caught a hint of east coast accent beneath the California.

The kitchen filled the south end of the house—a broad, sunny room, probably the one I'd seen lit through the thick clusters of eucalyptus on my evening walks. Two sets of French doors stood open to a sun-dappled flagstone terrace. To one side, a waterfall splashed into a lily pond with pads floating along the edge. On the other, a breeze played through several sets of wind chimes.

"I'm so glad you've stopped by. I've thought many times of calling, but some people, well, you know, people like their privacy." She chatted on as she pulled a pan out of the oven, filled cups with coffee, piled it all on a tray. She motioned me out to the terrace, to a glass-topped table arranged next to the pond.

We sat across from each other and sipped black coffee and ate muffins. Clarissa chattered and the waterfall splashed and the wind chimes trembled and overhead the birds flitted and chirped through the branches. My head began to throb, filling with all the noise like a balloon fills with helium. The world tipped slightly again—

"...know people think it's supposed to happen on the hour of the new millennium, those Born Agains, mostly. But even the seismologists are in a buzz lately, saying it's sooner than that, maybe a few weeks, a few months, but of course they've been saying that for as long as I can remember..."

Clarissa went on about The Big One in that breathless way of lonely people who've found an ear. I scanned the landscape and waited for her to run down. The asphalt road wasn't visible from here, but if she'd been out front gardening she might've seen someone pass by. On the other hand, I didn't know how to broach the subject without tipping her off that this was more than a social call. She seemed inordinately happy that I was being neighborly.

"Looks like you've got a green thumb," I said after she'd spent herself on earthquakes. "Must take a lot of time, keeping it all up."

She lifted her saucer and held it under her cup as she sipped, reminding me of my mother's Aunt Ida, a woman whose idea of bedtime fun was hitting the sack with Emily Post. "Oh my stars," she said, rolling her eyes, "not me. I can trim back a rose bush if I have to, but mostly I limit myself to cutting flowers of a morning."

She smiled with some pride in her own lassitude. Me, I can name a few plants, tell a rose from a petunia, but it's a stretch. Mostly I scatter seed and pray for rain.

"It's all very beautiful," I said. I was still scouring my brain for a way to ask my question without giving myself away.

"I was so glad to see you working on that horror those Jordans left behind them," she said. "They had horses over there, put up those corrals and just ruined the land. A horse will eat a weed right down to its root, don't you know. If you need any help, I've a gardener who's a perfect wizard." She gazed into the shadowy enclave of nodding eucalyptus. Their branches whispered. "He's a Mexican national, lives right outside of town. Doesn't charge a fortune like those gardeners who drive in from Monterey or the Bay Area."

Clarissa offered to give me his number, but somehow I couldn't quite see a lily pond next to my barn and goat pens, though the geese would have voted it in.

"It's just as well, I do keep him busy." Her eyes twinkled, clear and intelligent and youthful. She rambled on about the garden. I waited for a pause and jumped on it.

"You mentioned the Jordans. You knew the former owners of my place?"

She rolled her eyes. "Oh yes. They were here when Mr. Remington and I moved in. That would be thirty-one years ago next month, November of sixty-six when Wally was transferred from Boston." She set her cup down and ran her fingertip around the rim. "Wally, that was my husband, he rose fast in the company, don't you know. Owns part of it now. Has a nice new wife, too. That would be his third or fourth, all about the age of his grand-daughter. If we'd ever had children." She gave me a wry smile, and her cellophane face crinkled.

People wonder why I dread socializing. It wasn't that I didn't know my cues. Right now, for example, I was supposed to make sorrowful noises at her rotten luck. But I'd be lying. So I sat there and stared back at her and thought of Daddy D saying, "For heaven's sake, Gracie, don't make a federal case of everything. You don't need to turn every word into a moral issue." But whether it was Daddy D or those shrinks at Mt. Havens working on my "social skills," as they called it, the way I figure, a lie's a lie, whether you're in a crowd of people or alone in the Sahara. Think about it: a man leaving his long-time wife for a younger one to give him a tighter fit. I say, a man like that you're better off without, and I wanted to congratulate her on her good fortune at being shed of him. I sat there speechless, caught in the crosshairs of my own candor, feeling that paralysis creeping in when you've got yourself between a rock and a hard ass, followed right close by that black fizz of adrenalin shooting through your veins, forever putting you out of step with the world. My head throbbed painfully, and I winced.

Suddenly she laughed, a sharp barking sound with no tremor in it. "Hah! So that's what Sam meant about you!"

My eyes snapped open. She wore a broad, amused smile
"Um, beg pardon?"

"Sam down at the *Trib*, he told me you had a sharp tongue. I think I hear what you're not saying." She barked again. "I can see the good of it now, but at the time it about killed me when he walked out. I wanted to die. I'd left Boston behind, along with my career and family and friends. I didn't know a soul here." She shook her head and narrowed her eyes. "And then one morning, out of the blue, I woke up and I was myself again. I thought, 'Welcome back to the world, Clarissa Reingold.'"

Clarissa Reingold. The name was familiar but I couldn't place it, not until she nodded toward the picture window with the piano sitting behind it. Then I remembered her name from the classical concerts I used to tune into on NPR, Sunday nights. She smiled as she talked about training as a concert pianist before her marriage, then returning to it after her divorce.

"You know, it's odd, isn't it?" she said. "It's like something devastating has to happen to you, just to jerk you back on the path life intended before you wandered off. I retired a few years ago, arthritis, but not before I had a wonderful time on the professional concert circuit." She looked down at her hands and flexed the fingers. "I still play a little. You've probably heard me at night, sound carries so in these hills. I guess I ought to be more considerate, but it gives me pleasure like nothing else can when I wake up and can't get back to sleep."

Yes, I'd heard her. Distant strains of Chopin sonatas floating like midnight perfume through the dark hours. She was right, her music was balm for the soul. I wished she'd have played last night. Maybe she had.

"Anyway, it sure beats Frank Sinatra by a ballpark." She looked pointedly in the direction of Julia's house. "I don't mean to carp, but I didn't even like that man when he was popular, not to mention hearing him on deteriorating plastic. There's no accounting for some people's taste." Clarissa Remington set her mouth in a hard, disapproving bow that radiated lines. I saw the old woman who lived behind the stretched skin.

"She's quite a character," I said. "I was just over there last night, and she had those old songs cranked up." I shook my head, then found I'd created the opening I'd been searching for. "I walked over after I picked up my mail, went to see if she'd played a joke, slipped a letter in my box. It didn't have a stamp on it so I knew Garvey didn't deliver it, but she said it wasn't her. I don't guess you saw anybody walking by the road yesterday afternoon?"

Alarm sprang into Clarissa's eyes, and she set her coffee cup down. I cursed myself—she'd seen through me. I can't deceive any better than I can lie. Not that there's much difference, the one being just a sneaky form of the other.

"You're receiving threatening letters? Is that what you're saying?" Her old man's deep voice spiraled up, high and frightened. I saw it wasn't my ulterior motives that'd touched off her fears, but something else. I recalled the iron fence around the property, the bolted gate, the speaker box.

"Oh no," I said. I didn't have any reason to believe my poet was a threat to anyone else. "Somebody's just been putting little poems in my mailbox. Probably some kid from town, just fooling around. I'm curious to find out who's sending them, that's all."

Her hands were trembling as they hovered like pale, frightened birds over her coffee cup. Why was she so upset? Was she just a lonely woman with imagined fears, or was there some other reason she was afraid?

"Well, no. I didn't see anyone," she said, "but I would have to go down to the orchard to have a view of the road. I almost never do that. I'll ask Rico, he might have seen someone."

"Rico?"

"My gardener, Rico Santillanes. That's who you should ask." She stroked the flesh of her neck with one finger, studying a large golden fish that hovered in a ray of sun near the pond's surface, and I thought about the woman I'd met last night at Julia's, Natalia Santillanes. In the distance, church bells drifted up from the village below. Clarissa shifted her gaze toward the town as though she were watching the notes rise in the air. Finally, after the sound had died away, she said: "So you've received poems. Anonymous poems. Are they about love?"

"Well, they might be." I rattled off one of the early ones, making a face at the awkward rhythm.

"Sounds like you have an admirer," she said. "That's so bad?"

"Well, I don't know," I said. I wasn't about to mention the snake. "I just wonder, you know, who's doing it."

"Of course." She nodded and thought a moment. "Well, I've never heard of anybody getting any poems, but we did have some trouble a while back. A peeping tom, I guess you'd call it. A year or two ago, I thought I caught sight of somebody moving around out there, late at night." She pointed her chin toward the eucalyptus. "It happened several times. It might have been my mind playing tricks, but I still believe there was somebody out there. I had Meyerson Construction put that fence up, and that was the end of it. It never hurts to be safe, is what I say." She sat back and crossed her arms. "You must have been living here by then. I guess you never saw anything or you'd have reported it." It was a question, disguised as a statement.

I shook my head, didn't mention that except for the blinds in my bedroom I didn't have a window covering in the place. If anybody was interested in looking in my windows, they had plenty of opportunity.

"Well, these days, there's so much crime and violence, just watching the nightly news will tell you that."

Maybe that explained why I didn't lock much of anything. I didn't own a television. "What about the place on up the road from me?" I asked. "You know who lives there?"

She shrugged and shook her head. "I didn't even know you till today," she said. The note of censure was loud and clear. "A house on up the hill used to belong to the Jordans, too. Maybe they sold it when they sold your place. I know they were moving off somewhere, but could be they kept it for the family. So many new are moving in as the old…"

Her voice trailed off, and she gazed out across the valley where the Sierras rose faintly in the far distance. It was that same abstracted gaze that reminded me of the elderly at Mt. Havens, how at a certain point they'd quit reading the back pages of the paper, the obituary column, and stare off across the room without seeing anyone in it. Clarissa nodded in the direction of the Jordans' house, and the sun made silver sequins dance in her hair. "That was their main house, on up the hill past your place. Used yours as a ranch house, guest house, that kind of thing."

As I was leaving, Clarissa leaned in the open doorway, looking on. I'd just reached the wooden bridge when a late model truck pulled into the drive. The speaker system by the front gate hadn't gone off. Who did Clarissa Remington trust enough to give the security code? I glanced back at where she stood, but her eyes were riveted on the truck and her lips were parted in a soft smile. It was an expression I would have known anywhere—Scarlett wore it when she gazed up at Ashley played by Leslie Howard. I once wore it when I looked at Bruce DeWitte. I had a name for it these days—the Sappy Sucker look.

I walked by the truck, and a man stepped out. I guessed him to be about thirty-five. He wore jeans and a blue chambray shirt open at the neck. He had broad shoulders, hips so slim I wondered how he kept his pants up, and large moist eyes like those Latin men who've made it big in Hollywood. The bed of his truck was piled with gardening tools.

I nodded and went on. I didn't think it was a good time to ask Rico Santillanes if he'd seen anyone walking past my mailbox. When I got home, I fired up my old battered Chevy truck and drove down to Harvey's Pump & Go.

6

Morgan

Pasonombre said, "A glimpse into the absurd is necessary. After that, you can do anything." That is why he required all students at The Company School to take the class, why he taught it himself.

It is his voice I hear as I descend from the Colorado mountains ("turning and turning in the widening gyre"); *it is his image I carry in my mind's eye, his ponderous bulk lodged on the edge of the classroom desk, the book spread open as he reads:* "Surely some revelation is at hand...somewhere in the sands of the desert."

After the mountains, the highways flatten, drawn by a steady, an unerring hand, a study in sane geometry. The motorhome no longer pitches and lumbers against the curves, cleaves instead to a fixed one-hundred-eighty-degree plane. The horse rides easy in the rear compartment. He is not tied in, wanders occasionally about his quarters, but mostly, with his neck arched over the Dutch door, we watch the highway ahead.

Or perhaps not. When I glance into the rear view mirror, I find his eyes on mine. I drive west, south, west again, without thought or destination, until the mountains behind fade away and when I look in the mirror again I see little more than rubble heaped against the eastern skyline. That and the horse's eyes: huge and glittering like pearls against a purple sky:

("a vast image out of *Spiritus Mundi* troubles my sight")

Later, in a town at the center of a flat, white circumference, I search for water, for gas. I turn off the asphalt, drive slowly into the town's heart. A deserted, silent place. Hot and shadowless under the noonday sun. Scattered adobe houses with the curtains pulled tight. Yet, a familiar place. I feel some memory stir. I feel that I have returned to some alien, forbidden place; that I have been on this street before.

(Distantly, Paso speaks: his voice is immortal, unerring as a bat's flight through sunken caverns, winding along the corridors of the inner ear: "Unreal city, he says, I had not thought death had undone so many." His thumb follows the passage of words on the page. His immense bald dome gathers the light of the ceiling bulb, his eyes hidden in deep sockets. We, his chosen few, sit pondering our exit exam, a demonstration of our new philosophy, end of this world and beginning of the other. When we look up, his eyes are on us: "a gaze blank and piti-less as the sun.")

At the center of town is a square church, white with an open spire, the bell inside it clapping: "Ask not for whom the bell tolls," it warns, "it tolls for thee."

(Paso said more than once: "When you hear the bell, it is time to stop.")

I park before the mouth of the church and consider its dazzling façade, the blinding sand. A place as familiar as doom, this treeless, birdless site on an endless plain, lying bone-dry as a carcass, sprinkled with dust. Death would come here by night and pile rats in the gutters.

I step out of the motorhome. These are not rats, merely the translu-cent veneers of insects. Hundreds, thousands, galaxies of vanquished insects. Their brittle, castaway skins crackle like broken glass under my feet, the sand hot as flames through the soles of my boots. Wind has washed the husks into great piles against the church moorings, scattered like psoriasis across the sand's surface. The horse neighs his lingering, high-pitched song.

Inside the church, the enclosed air is blue, cool, ancient. Painted on the plaster of the far wall is the figure of a bleeding man draped on a cross; below him, on a table, sits a solitary statue—a slender monolith of carved soapstone, a polished mantle falling over the woman's shoulders, a shroud to protect The Child. I walk down the aisle between wooden benches. You can hear my steps on the stone floor, against the walls, the ceiling. I could be underwater, below the ocean's floor. I could be in a womb, and outside disaster waits.

("a heap of broken images, where the sun beats, and the dead tree gives no shelter, the cricket no relief")

The rough floor bites into my knees. The soapstone is so cold that my bones ache. Suddenly, behind me, the church door bursts open. A blade of sunlight flashes down the aisle. I turn into the blinding sun. A black figure stands in the doorway, an apparition

("a shape with lion's body, head of man")

But, no. It is only the wind. The sun. It is only my imagination.

Or perhaps not...

Hundreds of miles later, I sit at a roadside park in the Sierras. The horse is tied alongside the motorhome. We have spent the night here, the horse and I, high in the pines with the smell of resin stinging the air. It is not so different from the Colorado Rockies we have left behind: the house—that breathable space inside a wooden frame, crouched against the earth's surface with my name on its title. Gone now. It does not matter. I shove the eggs around on the plate with a piece of toast. Perhaps it does not matter.

A chill lives in the mountains. You can smell the snow before it comes. In this pause between seasons, if you close your eyes you can feel the flakes on your skin before they settle. But we will be gone before then. We go west, to the ocean whose waves, their sound and smell and womb pull, has filled my mind to bursting for these days since leaving the town.

I drink the coffee I made this morning. I shove the eggs to the other side of the plate. The horse paws. His iron shoes ring against the metal water bucket. He has eaten his morning ration. Impatient now to be gone. In the pine above where I sit, a crow jumps from a high branch to a lower one, daring fate.

A crow, a man, a horse: each dares as he will. There is no breath to be breathed that does not entail risk. To remain alive is not a matter of accepting the risk or not; it is a matter of increasing one's odds, of understanding that and knowing how to do it, of knowing not only yourself, but your adversary.

Consider the crow. He sits just above me, just out of arm's reach. The crow cannot fathom me, his enemy. As many before him. He cannot glean the way an arm can flash quicker than lightning, how a bone can snap before the ear will ever hear it.

The bird turns his head sideways, an eye on my plate, on the eggs, on me. The crow's beak is long as scissors. When he opens it, I can see the sliver of his bird's tongue: va ya, he says, opening his wings. I think again of the apparition. If there was one...

...a figure, a black shape in the church's doorway inside the blade of sun: it had walked down the flagstone aisle. Soundless. Stood over me. At first I could not see for the brilliance of the sun—a wraith of a figure, an old and gnarled woman in a long black dress and mantle of ancient lace, so ancient that it is torn and shredded in places, as beyond repair as a blasted spider's web. Her face is a knot of darkness inside the light:

"Vaya," she says. "You do not know yourself." Her voice is splintered, harsh as a crow's. She raises an arm, a black bone hung with lace, and points to the door. Outside, the horse sings. "No strangers are permitted here. Aquí no está el lugar para usted."

The crow closes its wings. It aims at me a singular yellow eye, a cocked head. I see the crow. I am sure of it. I do not know if I saw the woman or not.

Days to me are no more than pennies to a blind man. Time passes. I do not count it. On a freeway close enough to the ocean that I can smell the waves, I pull off at an exit reading LAS TIERRAS. The horse's eyes glow in the rear view mirror. Ahead, just past the stop sign, just past the freeway ramp, there is a gathering of Sunday travelers at a convenience store. Harvey's Pump & Go.

I pull the motorhome up to the pumps, get out. In the distance, I hear bells tolling.

7

THE THING ABOUT A WOMAN THAT OLD AND A MAN that young, you don't want to let your imagination get started on it. That was the trouble, my imagination. I left Clarissa Remington's with my mind projecting her and Rico across the California landscape in sweating big-screen X-rated Technicolor. By the time I reached home, I'd changed reels; what I saw as I walked into my yard was that bottle of bourbon—feeling the cool, smooth torso of glass in my hand, the way the liquid tilted as I leaned my head back and watched the sunlight explode inside the liquid amber and turn it gold.

When I pulled into Harvey's parking lot, the Pump & Go was doing a brisk trade from Sunday traffic off the freeway. I eased into a slot between a dusty Jeep Cherokee and a Toyota Tercel with an elderly, blue-haired woman in the back seat. I killed the ignition, sat there gripping the steering wheel. I knew I ought not to be doing this, but knowing that wasn't going to keep me from it. I was still fighting my demon, though. Staring straight ahead through the plate glass where customers milled in the aisles and the sounds of the bustling parking lot converged: the giggle of passing teenagers, the clatter of gas nozzles being jammed into fuel tanks, a bell tolling in the distance, slamming doors, engines starting. My head was throbbing painfully from last night's bout of drinking, and the sun shooting off the plate glass wasn't helping it any. Was, in fact, getting brighter the longer I stared into it. I squinted as something moved inside the glare. It was a faint image that grew sharper as I watched, materializing into Daddy DeWitte's face.

"Gracie, Gracie. Still waiting, are you?" he said, the words rising and falling, bobbing through the Sunday clamor like a bottle tossed by waves. "But not as I told you to wait. If you had only obeyed me, all the nightmare would have been avoided. But you couldn't do that, could you? You couldn't mind me, couldn't wait till I got us a place in L.A. Because if you had, everything would have been different. I was almost ready to send for you when—"

A car door next to me slammed, sharp as a gunshot. I jumped, whirled around. A man was frowning at me from behind the driver's window of the Cherokee. When I looked back at the convenience store, Daddy was walking out of the sun, coming toward me in his dove gray suit. He had a hypodermic needle in his hand and was talking about the war. That was where he'd first taken the morphine to quiet the pain until help reached him behind the lines. And when the morphine ran out, anything would do, like the bourbon we drank together, night after night. Even after I'd found out he'd never been in the war, never been wounded. But by then it was too late.

His glasses flashed, the needle held ready as he approached, and I felt the scream rising inside my throat. Suddenly, his features went black…eclipsed by another face staring directly at me through the windshield of the truck. It was a dark, stunning face—a woman in black, walking along the concrete apron in front of the store: high cheekbones, burning dark eyes, brows flaring above them like wings…and then I was looking again into the sun.

Out of nowhere, a sound—sharp, like the crack of a whip—and the light convulsed. The plate glass shivered, splintered into a million fragments suspended for an instant of frozen time, the glass a kaleidoscope of bright diamonds, a fractured fountain of light and glass, each piece brilliant as sun in a raindrop. The earth trembles, shudders like a foundered ship. The diamonds fall straight as rain to the ground. Inside the store, the shoppers are perfectly revealed, immobile: a young boy, his eyes blue and wide, a can of soda in one hand and in the other a dollar bill; the woman behind the counter, her mouth a perfect fuchsia circle, big hair sprayed hard and rolling in a sea curl over her forehead; a young woman wearing a baseball cap with a pony tail out the back, her tanned face transfixed by the exploding window, her arm reaching out now in slow motion, off balance, groping for the display shelf behind her, falling backward against a man in a golf shirt and khaki shorts, crashing the two of them into the shelves, to the floor under an avalanche of boxes and cans.

Sound, that for a single, weariless moment was sucked from the scene, rushed back. The young woman lay flailing and screaming across the man. He pushed himself up and tried to calm her while blood slipped in long streams down her arm. Shoppers inside the store shrieked and fought to get out the door. Those in the parking lot were stampeding in all directions. I had heard a tremendous crash behind me, out of sync, so that now it was a galloping echo that finally arrived. I twisted around to see that one of the metal shelters above the gas pumps had collapsed on the rear of a spectacularly long motorhome.

Through the chaos rose a high-pitched, unearthly scream. I leapt out of my truck and looked wildly around at the scattering crowd. The sound was coming from an animal, I realized, but where? Two men and a tall woman, the same one whose eyes just a moment ago had looked into my own, were tugging at the rear door of the motor home, but the upper corner had collapsed like an accordion under the weight of the fallen overhang and wedged the door shut. The woman stopped pulling and spun around. She raced to the front of the vehicle and disappeared through a side door.

The scream seemed to be coming from inside the motorhome. I followed the woman, entering the vehicle and rushing through a kitchen/living room combo and bedroom, to the rear compartment where I could see her wrestling with a thrashing, plunging black horse. She had wrapped her arms around the animal's neck, but in its terror the animal reared back and swung her against a metal dividing grid that had collapsed and trapped it against the buckled wall of the vehicle. The woman let go of the horse and moved so fast she was little more than a blur in the dimness. She rushed to a low compartment, pulled open a cabinet and rummaged through it while the horse continued screaming and struggling ever more frantically to free itself, its hooves slipping and sliding in a pool of blood. The woman, some object in her hand, raced to the horse which had contorted itself backward. It was braced on its hind legs and thrashed at the air with its front hooves. The woman paused, ducked past the flailing hooves, and threw herself against the animal's side.

For an instant, the horse froze—its neck outstretched, its eyes rolled to white. Its mouth was open wide, but the screaming stopped. The woman jumped back as the animal's front legs began to fold at the knee, descending to the floor where the hooves landed with a thud and the legs splayed forward at a crooked angle as though in prayer. Slowly, silently, the horse slid down and fell sideways on the floor.

The bloody figure stood motionless, a hypodermic syringe in one hand, then flew into action again. I stepped back out of her way as she flew past me into the driver's cab, grabbed a phone from the console, and almost before she hung up I heard sirens wailing in the distance. Between then and the time it took the vet to arrive, I obeyed the woman's volley of commands. As she worked over the horse, I gathered blankets, found equipment, delivered utensils from the front quarters of the motor home. When Jerry Preston stuck his head through the door, an ambulance had been and gone and a work crew was cutting through the rear of the motor home with an electrical saw. The woman and I were covered in blood, head to toe. I stood panting with exhaustion across from where she knelt over the horse, pressing a fresh blanket against his wounds.

"Hey, looks like you two got things pretty well under control," Jerry yelled above the screech of the saw hitting metal. He walked in and surveyed the situation, looking like he'd just stepped off a surfboard. He was deeply tanned, wearing faded jeans and a muscle shirt. His sun-bleached hair slipped down across his forehead, and he had friendly brown eyes that nearly closed when he smiled. He'd seen all my animals at one time or another over the last couple of years, and I nodded hello as the woman edged sideways and he squatted next to her. He pressed his fingers against the animal's neck with one hand and pulled back the lid of an eye with the other. Then he reached over and lifted the blood-soaked blanket. Not pretty. The horse had been slashed deeply from its rear flank all the way to the rib cage, but the blood no longer gushed as it had. Jerry probed the injury, then leaned back on his heels.

"What'd you put him out with, anyway?" he said, staring at the woman.

So did I, for that matter. In the frantic rush to save the horse, there'd been no time for looking. Now, in the dim light, I saw that even with the blood smeared across her face, she was even more striking than when she'd looked through the windshield of my truck. Her hair, jet black, was cut short and combed back. The bones of her face were spectacular: wide jaw, strong chin, straight nose, broad forehead. But it was the eyes that grabbed you and left you breathless. She raised them to mine, and I felt a sizzle of electric energy, as though I'd touched a bare wire. They were dark, feverish, burning with some savage fire. I looked away. I'd seen eyes like that before. Lots of times. I'd spent over thirty years of my life in a place full of them.

"Xylazine and Acepromazine," she said, looking back at the horse.

"Strange thing to have on hand, but you probably saved his life. Don't see any way you could have got him out of here without him doing even more damaged to himself." He began pulling instruments out of his bag. "Lucky you got the jugular instead of the carotid. Dead horse."

The woman smiled, higher on one side. "Yeah, lucky."

As they examined the wound, I looked around the compartment. It was small, lit dimly by daylight filtered through a high, narrow window on each side. The floor was slick with blood, the air strong with the smell of it and the animal's feces. In the back, where the wall had caved in under the weight of the overhang, the aluminum siding protruded inward, forming a sharp, knife-like wedge. A straight, thin slot of daylight showed where the saw was climbing vertically up the rear corner.

"No internal damage," Jerry said. He had laid back the outer layers of flesh and begun suturing with careful stitches. "Take a while to heal, but he'll be all right to travel in a few days." The woman remained squatting beside him for a while, watching him work. I expected some expression of worry, some show of distaste, but her face was expressionless. Finally, apparently satisfied, she looked up. Her eyes met mine and flared strangely for a moment.

"Hey, thanks for the backup," she said, standing up just at the moment when the saw stopped. In the unexpected silence, her voice sounded deep, husky. "Name's Rachael." She wiped a bloody hand on her jeans before extending it.

I introduced myself. "No thanks necessary. I didn't do much but take orders," I said, shaking her hand. But the blood was thick, and our palms stuck unpleasantly together. She made a face, nodded me to follow her though the motorhome to a small bathroom off the hall.

She turned on the spigot over a tiny basin and shoved up her sleeves, talking about traveling cross-country from Kentucky as she lathered her hands and rinsed her face. When I took my turn, she'd moved on to earthquakes, how she'd never been in one before. But I wasn't listening. I was watching the way the suds boiled up my arms in a bright red foam, the way the water turned the white sink red. I was thinking how the blood had soaked through my shirt sleeves, across my chest, how my clothes were sticking to my skin just like the other time...

"Hey, you okay?" Her hand shot out and steadied my shoulder.

"Fine. I'm fine." I pulled away, tried for a smile, didn't make it. I turned and rushed past her, through the living room, out the door. I leaned back against the side of the motorhome and took deep gulps of fresh air.

By the time she walked up, I managed a weak laugh at myself. "Blood," I said, flicking my wet, dripping hands, "it's okay if I'm dealing with animals, but on people..." I shuddered and wiped my palms on my bloody jeans, which didn't help.

Rachael stood a couple of feet away, looking down at me. I'm five-eight, fairly tall for a woman, but she was taller. With her hip cocked and her thumbs hooked in her front pockets, she stared at me like people do. She'd changed somehow: where she'd appeared feverish, even faintly sinister in the dimly lit stall, here in the sunlight, though blood still covered her hair and clothes, the fire had left her eyes. They seemed lighter than before, the color of damp mahogany. She appeared, in fact, unnaturally cool.

"Hey," she said, grinning and lifting a shoulder, "blood's no worse'n anything else can ruin a suit, long as it's not your own."

Her eyes might have softened, but her words sent a chill down my spine. I'd gone through nurse's training, part of it anyway, and I'd heard people talk like that before. The ones who do, if they're not medics, they're liable to be serial killers. I turned away, toward the parking lot where people still milled about.

The fallen overhang and broken window were the only damage I could see offhand, though a nervous energy ran through the onlookers. They had collected in small groups, talking among themselves while scanning the street, the sky, the concrete below their feet. They were nervous as cats, psyched to take flight at the slightest tremble. Only the work crew sawing through the motorhome was doing business as usual. They'd jacked up the shelter and propped it on a metal support. The saw lay on the ground, and three men in gray overalls were wielding crowbars.

We watched as the trio, acting on a nod from one, threw all their weight against the iron bars, and with a terrific grinding noise, the rear portion of the motor home began to move. Heads turned. The back wall of the rig shuddered, then toppled into a dumpster positioned near the vehicle. We migrated with several of the curious toward the backside of the motorhome for a better view. Sunlight angled across the horse's stall to show a room of bloody devastation: the walls and ceiling were dented and spattered with blood, the mangled pipes of the metal divider lay twisted across one side of the trailer compartment, and the floor was deep with blood and manure. Kneeling in the center of it all, his back to us, Jerry Preston was still working over the horse.

"Jesus." Harvey Meekers had strolled up between us and was staring at the gory scene. "Horse dead?"

Rachael didn't answer, but she hit him with a look cold enough to snow. Harvey shifted his weight a little toward me.

"How about that girl?" I asked, remembering the hysterical young woman with the bloody arm. "Was she badly hurt?"

"Nah, hysterical's all. Ambulance took her off to the hospital. Little cut on her shoulder. You'd thought she was dying, way she carried on." He shook his head at the motor home, slid a glance at

Rachael, then strolled away to rejoin a group of men in front of the store. The others who'd come for a look drifted off. I followed Rachael over to the edge of the motorhome as Jerry glanced around.

"Just finishing," he said. He turned back to the horse, and after a few minutes sat back on his heels and sighed. "I'll take him on over to my place for the night, keep an eye on him, but I'm short of space. You'll need to find somewhere around here to board him tomorrow. I can give you names of a few people to call—"

"There's my barn, would it do?" I said. The words flew out like they'd been roosting on my tongue, just waiting for my mouth to open. It was too late to take them back, so I went on. "There's a bunkroom right next to the stall, too, if you want to stay there till he's ready to travel."

We both looked at Jerry. He hiked a shoulder. "Barn's fine, Grace. Put down a little straw bedding. I can drive him over tomorrow after I close up, if it's okay with Rachael." He was stuffing his equipment back in his bag, and he winked like when he comes to my place and isn't ready to leave after the veterinary work is done. "Nice offer."

I ignored him, as usual. He snapped his bag shut and glanced over by the curb where his pickup was parked with a flatbed hitched in back. He leaned over and checked the horse's pulse, while Rachael stared off into the distance like she wasn't with us anymore. Jerry paused for a few moments, then came over and jumped out. He was about the same height as Rachael, but a lot more anxious. I wondered how long the anesthetic, whatever it was she'd given the horse, was going to last before the animal began to come around. I figured that's what Jerry was wondering too.

A few minutes later, after the three men had put aside their crowbars and helped slide the horse onto the flatbed, Jerry was pulling out of the parking lot. Rachael watched them disappear down the road.

She turned to me. "Hey, looks like you got yourself a boarder. You want some coffee, Coke, anything?"

That's when I remembered what I'd come for. We headed for the store, past Harvey and his buddies who were sweeping up glass. I went through the door when Rachael held it open, though the most direct route was through the window opening. Inside, the big-haired woman was clearing fallen items off the countertop. I made a bee-line for Harvey's new cappuccino dispenser in the rear, thinking that whatever else you want to say about earthquakes, they'll take your mind right off your problems and slap you back in to a no-frills here and now.

I drew a cup of French vanilla full enough to drizzle foam down the side. When I got to the checkout counter, Rachael was paying for a quart of Smirnoff and a smaller bottle of something else. Rose's lime, I saw, as the woman rang up the items. I reckon it takes more than an earthquake for some folks. On a tiny television screen mounted over the cash register, a woman in a trench coat was reporting the late-breaking news about the quake.

"We the lucky ones, ain't we?" the woman behind the counter whined. She made a sour face at the reporter as she ran Rachael's credit card. "Nobody but us got so much as a damn quiver. They saying watch out for aftershocks for awhile, like us that live here, we don't know that, right? And who else cares?"

Rachel didn't seem to hear. She slipped the card into her back pocket and hefted the bag in one arm. She carried no purse, and her black pants were snug enough to see the outline of a wallet if she'd had one. Hell, I thought as I followed her through the door to my truck, I could see the outline of the credit card, come to that. I hopped in and waited while Rachel set the bag down on the seat and walked off, over to where the men were cleaning up the mess around her rig. I watched in the rear view mirror; she talked a few minutes, dug a roll of bills from her front pocket, and peeled off a few for the men. Then she disappeared into the side door and came out with a green nylon bag slung over her shoulder.

I pulled out of Harvey's thinking about my own situation for the first time, wondering if my house had been hit, or Julia's. Somehow, I couldn't believe it. Maybe because I had a feeling verging on euphoria, ironically enough, thinking that if an earthquake can be good luck, I'd just had some. So I drove along toward home with the window down and my elbow propped on the frame, savoring deep breaths of salty air while Rachael talked about the men taking her rig down the road to an RV repair shop. I sipped my coffee and tried to compute how many earthquakes it would take to cure an alcoholic, and the more I thought about it, the more it sounded like a bad California joke.

"What's so funny? Earthquake get you buzzed?"

"I've been through worse," I said. Which was true enough, though this was my first quake. And from what we could see so far, it hadn't done much but break a convenience-store window and topple a gas shelter.

"That'll make two of us," she said, looking out her side.

I turned off the frontage road and followed the familiar narrow two-lane toward home, cruising through the shadowy tunnel of eucalyptus and only once or twice wondering about the wisdom of offering the bloody stranger next to me a room. She had lost her chattiness, was riding quiet and watching the scenery slide by. And me, I'm not one for small talk. Still, there was something more than a little peculiar about my passenger. Sure, she'd said she hadn't been in a quake before, hadn't she? But that wasn't it.

I'm not much scared of people. I've been locked up with some that would curl your hair, the acts they committed to get incarcerated in the first place. And I'd escaped Mt. Havens enough times, I know the ropes, had plenty of opportunity to meet folks from the wandering way of life along the highways and alleyways. Far as that goes, I reckon my own background would keep right up with most people's view of what makes a good scary movie. But the woman sitting next to me was a different brand of strange. She had all her ducks, anybody could look at her and tell that. They might not all've been the same make of duck, but there were plenty of them there. No, the thing about this woman was the way the air around her seemed to be electrically charging, like her energy was all damming up without the words to siphon it off. The truck, even with the sea air whipping in, started to feel the way air does after a lightning bolt has struck, even to carrying that little scent of sulfur in it. Or maybe my imagination was still giving me trouble, and nothing but that vodka of hers to medicate it with. Or maybe it was all that blood covering us both, smelling up the truck.

Just thinking of the blood got me started on thinking of the shower and fresh clothes less than two minutes away. I leaned on the accelerator a little more and stuck that shower and clean clothes right up there under oxygen on the list of things I needed to finish the day. I was just penciling in a nap under that when I flew up my driveway and nearly rammed into the back of Bill Hammersmith's car.

It was sitting right where I always park my truck, with Sheriff Hammersmith behind the wheel, reading on a book, while that red light revolved and pulsed on top of his black-and-white.

8

IT WASN'T LIKE BILL HAMMERSMITH had never been parked in my driveway before. But that had been a good while back and he hadn't been in his black-and-white, he'd been on his purple Harley. Hadn't been on official business, either, which is what I figured that red light meant. I could have been wrong, though; Bill Hammersmith is always doing one thing or another to keep people off balance.

Still, for anybody with my background, flashing red police lights in their front yard is enough to send them right over the edge. I felt the hysteria hit with a little jolt just below the stomach. I tried to stay calm. As I pulled my truck up beside the police car, I glanced around to see whether the earthquake might have brought him here—a broken water main, downed power line, a fire? Everything looked as it had when I'd left. The hysteria cranked up a little more. I turned off the engine. Rachael was lounging with one arm thrown across the back of the seat and the other propped in the window. She raised an eyebrow at me, glanced around at the sheriff, then leaned back so we had a clear shot at each other.

"Hey, Grace."

He was wearing the mirror wraparounds, like the ones he said the cop in *Cool Hand Luke* wore. A leathery scowl, deep baritone voice. Willie Nelson pigtails tied in purple at the ends, and a blue T-shirt with writing I couldn't read, though I was sure it advertised some fitting blasphemy. He looked just like when he used to come by evenings—except off-duty he tied a rolled bandana around his head and removed the star dangling on his T-shirt.

According to Julia, he was part of a trend. Ever since Clint Eastwood on down the coast had taken up Carmel's mayoral duties back in the eighties, elected offices in small-town California had attracted unlikely types. Bill Hammersmith had been an astromony professor who commuted every day just two years ago to teach at a Bay Area university. I voted for him because he didn't look any more like a university professor than he did a sheriff, but I reckon that didn't explain why he won, except people in Las Tierras are known for having a dark sense of humor.

"Hey, Bill," I said.

He switched off the red light and got out of his car, walked around to my side. He took off his glasses and bent over and squinted into the cab of the truck, first at me, then at Rachael. He was close enough that I smelled the leather from his holster and saw the splash of bronze around the pupil of his eyes. They were the kind of eyes that could go slightly out of focus without much reason, like they were looking on past whatever it was they were aimed at. Right now, they were traveling down my chest, and I blushed until I remembered that both Rachael and I were covered in blood. He stepped back a little and opened the truck door. I glanced at Rachael before I got out.

She shot me a penetrating look, like her eyes were drilling right through my forehead, into a mindspace where she had no business going. The same look the shrinks used to try on me, except Rachael was getting somewhere. And I think she knew it: she lifted one brow, while the corner of her mouth smiled sideways, the way a poker-player smiles holding five aces to everybody else's empty house. I felt like she'd just read everything written on that ticker tape scrolling through my head, and that didn't help my hysteria any.

I set my coffee on the dash because I was shaking so bad it was splashing out over my hands. I tried to keep my thoughts running in a straight line, but they were about as manageable as nutcase bats, smashing and wild and made hopelessly frantic by the last thirty-two years—by two trials, eight appeals, nine months on death row, another trial and a death sentence finally commuted to insanity with only minutes to spare; by the parole board's countless refusals to consider incontestable new evidence of a cover-up; by the thirty years I'd spent in a mental institution for the criminally insane. All this for an act which I could not even remember comiting because I never did recover those lost hours when two women were shot, when a blade sliced through flesh and then inexplicably hacked through bone, when the bodies were forced into the space of a single trunk. So of course the mad, raw things behind my eyes were diving frantically, refusing to hold a straight line.

But I couldn't tell Hammersmith that. In spite of the few months we'd tried to push something into being that didn't want to be, I'd not confided my background. We're talking *sheriff*—no way did I tell him I'd been in the nuthouse for murdering my best friends. And I thought more than once that might have been what kept me from relaxing and enjoying myself when he spent the nights, devoting most of my energy to acting like what I thought normal women acted like from the movies I'd watched and the books I read. I thought I made a pretty good show of it, but Bill and I weren't going to happen. And what the hell, on his part, I didn't think somehow he was all that torn up about it. Looking back, I knew what my problem was, mostly anyway, but I never could get a handle on his.

We'd kept up a friendship, and I wasn't above keeping that in mind as I hauled myself out of the truck and squinted up at him with the sun setting just to one side of his head. The light did more than make me squint, the heat of it increased the rank odor of stale blood on my shirt, and I felt the stiff fabric rub unpleasantly against my bare breasts. Suddenly, a wave of such revulsion struck me that I could barely keep myself from rushing into the house, stripping, and standing under the shower.

Rachael came around the truck. She'd at least washed her face and hands, and her black outfit offered a camouflage of sorts for the fountain of horse blood. At the scene of the accident, our gore was predictable, expected, a kind of heroic badge; here in my sun-lit driveway with the sheriff looking us up and down, I saw the image of two bloody women as he must have seen us: if we were not guilty of whatever it was he had come here about, neither could we be entirely innocent.

"The earthquake," I said, plucking at my shirt. "There was a horse...at Harvey's...we had to...I..." My voice cracked, wheezed, coasted to a shambling halt, and died.

"Rachael McKinley. Just passing through." Rachael's words rolled out like ripe plums dipped in midnight chocolate. She leaned forward, her arm held straight as a sword, and shook hands. "Earthquake shook things up at the gas station, roof over the pumps caved in, fell on my rig and injured my horse. Grace here saved the day." She turned her smile on me and laid her arm across my shoulders.

Bill's eyes weren't fuzzy anymore. They were hawk-like, taking Rachael in as though memorizing details against the wanted posters in Millie Rain's post office. I hadn't known the sheriff in any official capacity, but if I had, I thought this was the kind of look he'd use on the job. Maybe all that blood had put him on the alert, but I didn't think that was it. Rachael was spellbinding, but I didn't think that was it either.

"...Preston trailered him over to his place, but he's short on space. Grace offered to let me board him here, use her bunk room. Guess I'll be here a week or two, till the vet gives the nod to travel."

Rachael was talking nonstop, like she had in the motorhome as we washed up, and again in the truck when we'd first started out. It was Peterbilt talk, a semi on a downhill roll that wasn't stopping for gas. She went from the quake to her horse's loss of blood to his expected recovery to the damage at Harvey's to the beauty of the Las Tierras countryside. She was animated, smiling, nodding. Vivacious. I had to give it to her, the woman was an Olympic-class talker and nodder. But my anxiety was creeping back, fluttering around my knees, flying in bat shapes inside my head. I longed for some peaceful place to lie down. Rachael, still talking, still with her arm draped around my shoulders, gave my arm a little squeeze. That's when I realized that she was drawing fire to herself, giving me time to gain control. But how did she know?

The bats receded. I came back into the world where she was segueing into a description of her cross-country vacation from Kentucky, her destination Baja, her plans now delayed. Bill stood with his hands in his pockets, waiting for Rachael to take a breath.

He wasn't having much luck. Not until she gave my shoulder a pat, dropped her arm, and stepped back a little.

"...so I've got to find some straw, get a stall fixed up for my horse. You don't happen to know where I could find some straw bales around here, do you?" Rachael stopped talking.

The sheriff looked a little startled by the sudden drought. "Well, I, uh, I guess Jerry Preston could help you on that. Or Grace. Don't you use straw for your goats...."

I said that I didn't, as I shifted my gaze to Bill's T-shirt: in yellow letters across the front was written REACH FOR THE STARS. The sun turned the fuzz around his braids golden, and the tips of them grazed his shoulders as we stood, the three of us, facing each other in the driveway where birds stopped chirping and no plane soughed overhead and a breeze had stopped playing among the narrow leaves of the eucalyptus. In that vacuum, I felt the hard black seed of my scream quicken, find wings, rise a little at each passing second, toward the light. Up into my yard where the sheriff stood, poised to reveal something just like all those years before. I didn't know what it was this time, didn't remember doing anything wrong, but that didn't make any difference, did it? The law was here, come to arrest me, come to take me—

"So," Rachael said. "What's up, sheriff? Any problem? I think Grace here is dying to get inside and have a shower, put on some clean clothes. Me, too, for that matter." She laughed a little and looked down at herself.

"How about we go on inside, Grace? Maybe have a cup of coffee?"

I gazed up into the amber heart of Bill Hammersmith's eyes where a circle of golden petals unfolded. Exploding suns around black holes. A universe lay inside there, held some dark thing that he had come here to tell me, and it scared me to death. I turned and walked toward the house as he continued speaking, but I couldn't make out his words. They came from a distance, from behind a wall of rushing water that splashed over me, ran through my hair and down my face, washed away the blood and the horrible stench that clung to me, hot and putrid and magnified by the sun...

"Grace was pretty upset by all the blood."

Rachael McKinley's words were close, smoky. Her arm was wrapped around my waist, and I leaned against it, up the stairs. I imagined being her horse, how her hand must feel stroking his neck, how the voice sounded to his ears, the words caressing. Calming.

"Easy, Grace," she said.

We were standing at the door of my house. It wasn't locked, except at night. Inside, the room was cool. A yellow rod of sun cut across the oak table in front of the patio. The sheriff took a seat on one side, Rachael pulled out a chair for me on the other. She left, and I heard water running in the kitchen. She returned and pressed a cold glass into my hands. I took it, propped my elbows on the table, and stared through the water where the sun struck it. Bubbles smaller than salt grains rose to the top. Through them, I saw the sheriff watching me. His features were large, distorted. His hands were clasped in front of him on the table. When Rachael offered the sheriff some water, offered to make coffee, he shook his head.

"Grace," he said. "I had a call earlier today, before the earthquake struck. It was an anonymous call, a prank is my guess, but I need to check it out."

I nodded at his shirt, its brilliant royal blue shimmering through the glass. I wondered what black leather would look like through the water; that's what Bill had been wearing the last time I'd seen him, a black leather jacket. That was several weeks ago. I'd been driving by the Blue Pig one night, and I'd seen him ease his Harley into the parking lot, park it on the back side, rev its engine up loud and lean back, staring up at the sky in the spiraling roar of the mufflers before switching off the ignition and disappearing inside the town's only nightspot. For one thing, the leather wouldn't have shown the dark circles blooming under his arms like the blue t-shirt was doing. The same dark circles that used to appear there months ago, back when we used to sit here over coffee, waiting till it was late enough to go into the bedroom.

"Go on, Sheriff." Rachael's voice.

"Well, I don't think there's any problem. Like I said, it was an anonymous call. Said...well, said Grace had a body in that trunk out there on the front porch."

I lowered the water glass and stared across it at the sheriff.

"Grace, listen to me." Rachael's voice had changed. It was stripped down. Where there had been a rolling bluegrass softness, a moon behind floating clouds, now each word was scraped to the bone. "You do not have to permit this, Grace. You can insist on a search warrant. You can have a lawyer present."

The sheriff and Rachael stared in silence at one other across the table. Behind him, past the glass of the patio door, the wind rustled through the eucalyptus.

"That's right, you can do that, Grace," he said, turning to me. "I'll go on back to the office, try to track down Judge Thompson, get a warrant. You can call Vernon Higgins, or whoever it is you have do your legal work, have him come over."

"I don't..." I glanced at Rachael. She sat elaborately straight, gazing past the sheriff's shoulder, through the patio glass. "I have nothing to hide. You can look in the trunk or anywhere else you want to," I said, thinking too late of the mess in my bedroom, the scattered books. The empty bourbon bottle. I'd drunk the whole thing, had passed out and woke up to the sun coming in. I'd only passed out, fallen asleep, hadn't I? Did I...could I have...? I gave myself a mental slap. This reeked of the same kind of aggravation intended by the person putting the snake in my mailbox. Another attempt to frighten me. My terror evaporated and left the rage. I wasn't scared, I was pissed. Seriously pissed.

"Go on, look wherever you damn well please," I said, pushing my chair back and standing up. There was no law, far as I knew, against drinking a bottle of bourbon and keeping a messy house. This wasn't the fifties. "I don't have a thing in the world to hide, though I think there's somebody around here making a bad mistake thinking I do."

Rachael folded her arms over her chest and leaned back, her long legs crossed at the ankles, head cocked to one side. She gave me that odd, crooked grin pulled high up one side, then glanced at Bill Hammersmith. Her grin crept up a little higher, along with that one eyebrow.

"Now, Grace," said Hammersmith, frowning, "if you're saying somebody else is involved here, maybe Ms. McKinley's got a point."

"Man's telling you something," Rachael said. "Your call."

"Shit!" I stood there before them, covered in blood—my hair matted with it; my shirt, my jeans, my tennis shoes covered with the drying, stinking stuff. I walked over to the screen door. The trunk sat where it always had, right beside the door where I kept firewood, where just last night I'd taken out a few sticks to make a fire. "There it is," I said, pointing to it. "My wood box. Help yourself. I'm going to take a damn shower."

And then I left them there and walked down the hall.

It was a long, hot shower. I wasn't thinking about the sheriff's call at all; I was thinking about how to track down that snake killer and what I was going to do when I found the son of a bitch. I stayed under the stinging water till it ran cold, and I scrubbed so hard my skin was red and boiled-looking by the time I stepped out and toweled off. I ran my fingers through my hair, pulled on a pair of old jeans and a wrinkled t-shirt, and returned to the living room.

The sheriff was on the porch kneeling over the trunk, Rachael had her back to me, holding open the screen, but even walking down the hall toward them, I sensed something haywire. It could've been the rigid set of Rachael's shoulders, maybe the way the wind switched from blustery to stone-still. Maybe the way they both turned to me in one movement, the sheriff looking up with his face expressionless, while Rachael twisted her head around, glancing over her shoulder.

I sighed and steeled myself. I figured whatever somebody had planted in the trunk—another snake with a note, or maybe not a note, maybe an old newspaper with my picture under the headline, GRUESOME TRUNK MURDERESS GETS DEATH—was going to take a lot more explaining than my present store of energy or patience could handle.

"Grace."

The two of them spoke in one voice. That's when I knew.

PART II

The Matrix

9

Morgan

The old woman in the trunk, her dead eyes were open. Filmed over, dulled to the color of snow clouds. Even now, with the sheriff and the coroner gone, the platinum woman sedated, the eyes still haunt the shadows.

I sit near her bed, wait for her to wake. I sip vodka, and in the silence of the early morning, the ice chinks like faint bells.

Piles of clothing and books litter the bedroom floor, though I have removed the empty liquor bottle and hidden it in my satchel. A sweater hangs sideways across a chair, shoes piled helter-skelter in the open closet.

The clutter is a confusion of space, an irritation of mind. I lift my eyes above it, to the flat neat space of wall above the bed, and try to backtrack the days since leaving the Colorado mountains. My thoughts are cracked and splintered. My recollections, brief snapshots.

Near where I focus my eyes, a picture hangs slightly crooked. The shade over the lamp in the corner is off-center, casting a skewed cone of yellow light against the wall. The old woman's dead eyes trouble the shadows. Anarchy lives here. Chaos creeps like spiders through the rubble on the floor.

I set the glass of vodka on the bedside table and put the room in order. After the floor is clear and the crooked straight, I resume my vigil. The woman still sleeps: her breasts rise and fall evenly beneath the sheet. The polished edges of her cheekbones gleam in the meager light. Her lids are faintly lavender.

I close my eyes, lean back my head: one's future depends on the past. I assemble the fragments of recent memory, force them into a configuration.

I recall each one like pieces of a puzzle—anchor it, measure its relative kin and color, fit one to another, force a coherence. An intelligible, plausible improvisation without locusts or old women in spiderweb lace. When I have finished, I have assembled a credible journey from Colorado to this place, a necessary fiction that will bear yet another chapter.

It is painstaking, exhausting work, this rabbit's run from lunacy. This reconstruction of days. One's life accumulates in rag-tag hours, heaps of sand on a calendar, slipping down the polished page and through an invisible corner hole, leaving behind not a trace.

I have parried madness, its flukes of circumstance and accident. My history (anyone's history) is but a convergence of events in the absence of angels. Mere surface ornaments strung together with cat gut and hubris. The past—a ramshackle construct of insignificant gestures, less discernible than the halitosis of a dung beetle. (History is more often shaped by a glance than a gunshot.)

Take this afternoon. Behind the glass of the old truck's windshield: the platinum woman. Her hair is ash, her eyes the color of washed denim. A familiar, nameless face. Through a trick of sunlight and reflection, my own face is superimposed across the windshield, and I am shaken out of this universe, into the one which runs parallel to it, the one in which a person confronts her opposite, her double: my dark features, a negative image fitted exactly over her pale ones.

I walk on, with the woman wedged in my brain like a splinter of glass. Even as the earth tilts and the window shatters beside me, even later as I work frantically over the horse, my mind throbs, rummaging to identify the platinum face.

It is only when the danger has passed, when I have relaxed and am squatting beside the veterinarian as he works, that I look up at her, covered in blood that suddenly reminds me of where I have seen her before…

Milan, 1984. Between classes at The Company's school. I am sitting at a coffeehouse, thumbing through an American newspaper, when I come across a story citing new evidence in the 1972 FBI burning of the Indiana women's commune that killed eighty-three women and children. One of them, my mother. Following the attack, the FBI contended that the commune was a cover, a hotbed of terrorists amassing an arsenal of firearms, though none had been found among the ashes and the bodies. Despite the public outcry and rumors of a cover-up, nothing had ever been proved. Till now, twelve years later—someone had the goods on the FBI.

I stare at the story, then the by-line. Julia Simmons. I walk the several blocks to the city library, read the other American papers with similar coverage. It says that Julia Simmons had discovered an FBI memo which established conclusively that they had acted before fully checking their sources, but no further information could be found concerning the identity of the informer.

While I am at the library, I read up on Simmons. She is an outspoken vigilante of the press with a list of investigative exposés that read like a Who's Who of crime and corruption: Watergate, the Hearst kidnapping, the Manson family. The Trunk Murderess. In the microfilm room I read all her stories, including those about Gracie Lee DeWitte, "Killer Frost," pictured in countless grainy snapshots, beginning with her incredible evasion of a nationwide dragnet, her voluntary surrender, the trials, the death sentence, the appeals, the insanity plea and life sentence. Simmons, querulous and indefatigable, had written articles for years, citing new evidence and arguing that Gracie Lee was not the killer—but that time she had found no proof.

Gracie Lee DeWitte...

I recognize the face behind the blood, and then recall the epilogue to her story, one that was at least as astonishing as the story itself. Following her incarceration in the mental institution, how many times had she escaped, simply walked past locked doors and barred windows as easily as a ghost through walls? As I watch her, our eyes meet. Suddenly I experience such an obscure feeling, such a rush of kinship, that I feel off balance, reach out to the horse and steady myself.

I watch her now in the bedroom's dim light, her face in repose. She could be a statue. A Biblical icon, a priestess on a mission, immune to laws of time and gravity. When I lean toward her, the ice dances against my glass and fills the room with bells. I softly touch her cheek, her forehead. Her skin is firm, youthful, cold. The flesh of a woman who has never walked across the translucent skins of vanished insects, who has never been denied sanctuary by an old crone in black lace. There is no madness in her.

I sit back and close my eyes and feel the exhaustion dragging me down toward a place without calendars, without time or continents; into a dark river where no one knows my name, where there is no friend, no lover, no square of earth to rest my foot. I see Paso's head, disembodied and floating like a pale specter in the dark waters:

"Ah figlia," he says, "you have chosen a profession wherein flux and danger are the staples of your existence. Yet, if you outlive your youth, you will enter a time when your worst enemy is the shifting current of the present moment. Remember always that for human consciousness the present is only illusion, a necessary illusion, created and sustained, on the one hand, by the past which can be recalled, and on the other, by the future which must be imagined. It is each of us, by the sheer imposition of our will and vision, who weaves the two together, who fashions an identity that bears our name. Your strength, your very life, depends on the authenticity of the identity you create. And remember this: without the past, there can be no identity who knows itself. And without that, there is no future worth living."

So I follow Paso's instructions. They are all I have. I say my name like a litany. I say it over and over, grasping for the chronology of my past as though to anchor myself in shifting waters.

"I am Morgan," I say, though no sound disturbs the room. I am Cordelia Morgan Krevlin, daughter of John Murray Krevlin and Rachael Genevieve Krevlin, née Morgan, born 1956, in Richmond, Kentucky...

I recall the past, year-by-passing-year, its images perfect as pearls on a necklace. The Kentucky horse farm. The rolling green pastures. The miles of white fence stretching as far as the eye can see. Horses grazing. Myself, a child on a pony. My father: charismatic, carrying a glass of amber liquid. My mother: anxious brown eyes, two vertical worry lines between her brows.

I am fourteen again, seeing my mother's hand tremble as she dials the phone. She and I, in the cab, paying the driver from the grocer's bag of laundry change she has been accumulating for a long time. Standing together at the ticket window at a bus station which smells of urine and diesel fuel, two tickets to Louisville. Using a tattered phonebook hanging from a chain beside a wall phone at the Louisville depot, looking up the phone number to the battered women's shelter. The grocer's bag is empty. We stand in front of the depot, holding hands, my mother and I, until a woman pulls up to the curb in an old car and drives us to a gabled, three-story house beneath a spread of oaks.

Later, traveling to the women's community in Indiana. A dirt driveway off a remote gravel road, marked by an enormous wood post carved with odd symbols and the single word: GAIA. A small trailer among other trailers in an apple orchard, living there with my mother and, later, a woman named Claire. I see my mother in the orchard, the way the sun warms the waves of her hair, the way the lines have gone from her forehead, the way she leans her head back when she laughs. Until I leave that summer before the orchard is burned along with every woman and child in it that day when Claire went to town and did the weekly shopping.

In the darkness behind my lids, I see my mother standing before me: Rachael Morgan. The darkness stops rushing. I feel the floor turn solid again beneath my feet. I open my eyes and see an old woman watching from the high ceiling shadows, her eyes the dull gray of snow clouds, materializing and then dissolving behind dark lace.

I look down where I grip the vodka glass between my hands. The ice cubes have melted, the bells have stopped.

10

OCTOBER 27, 1997

MONDAY MORNING

I WOKE UP TO SHREDS OF FOG PASSING across a moon leering through the window. A woman in a terrycloth bathrobe sat in the chair next to the bed. She had her head laid back and her lips moving, like she was talking to someone on the ceiling.

I've had a long history of being fed sedatives, so I didn't fight it. I figured that was the reason I couldn't hear what the woman was saying, so I watched her for a while from under my lashes, and the next time I woke, the morning was breaking gray through the window. My mind had cleared a little, but my thoughts were sluggish. Someone had stuffed me under the sheet still wearing my T-shirt and jeans, the room was spit-polished, but I still couldn't quite place the woman in the bathrobe who was staring straight at me, except now she was wearing a black turtleneck and jeans and looked more familiar than before. I struggled to remember who she was, what she was doing here, why I was in bed with my clothes on. And then the floodgate rose, and memories came rushing back. I sat up.

"Julia. What happened to...where is she?"

But I knew, that was the problem. I knew. Last night, I'd run to the trunk and looked in before they could stop me. I'd seen her, folded inside, her head twisted at an impossible angle, her eyes staring up at us. Just like...

"Shhh," she said. "Try to stay calm. There's nothing you can do now. I'm afraid your friend's dead."

"No, she can't be! I just saw her last night...night before last. I don't...what happened? How did she—"

"Nobody knows anything yet," the woman interrupted. "The coroner examined her, no marks on the body, no way to know much more than that till the autopsy report comes back." She'd been reading, and the book rested in her lap, marked with her finger.

I lay back on the bed, squeezed shut my eyes, but the tears came seeping out the corners, sliding silent down the sides of my face. They came gradually at first, then harder, gathering force and pounding like a summer storm. I felt the bed move and opened my eyes. Rachael—I remembered her name, her horse, the earth-quake—was stroking my forehead as the sobs began to subside.

"I want you to listen to me," she said, "try to be calm and listen. Can you do that?"

I nodded, but I wasn't at all sure how calm I could be. She explained that she'd recognized my face, that she knew who I was. Gracie Lee DeWitte, she called me. I didn't care, and I didn't know why she was telling me this now, but I nodded again.

"I know the woman, Julia, was your best friend. She was discovered in the trunk on your front porch, and anyone who knows your background is going to assume you did it. Open and shut. But for whatever reason," she said, pausing, "the sheriff doesn't seem entirely convinced. He wants you to come by and see him. I'll go with you if you want company." A smile passed across her lips like a shadow, not quite reaching her eyes.

"I'm under suspicion?"

"He didn't say that."

"I don't understand." My thoughts had hardened into knots. Grief-stricken and confused, I could make no sense of what was happening. "He thinks I might have killed my best friend, my only friend if it comes to that, put her in a trunk on my own porch, and then had somebody call and tell him?"

"I don't know what he thinks. I can make a good guess, though. Someone knowing your history killed Julia, put her in your trunk to throw the blame on you, then called the sheriff. On the other hand, if it was you who did it, you could have been hiding the body until you had a chance to dispose of it, maybe dig a grave. Possibly someone saw you do it, called the sheriff."

"*If* it was me? Why would I do that? Why would I kill my best friend?"

"It happens," she said. She gave a flat-liner smile. "But here's another option. If my memory serves me, you were judged insane, right? Let's say you were, let's say you still are. In which case you wouldn't be acting on any rational plane, no coherent motive or course of action. It reads both ways, doesn't it? And your friend Julia's body, wasn't it placed something like your friend's back then? Staring up, I mean."

I swallowed and leaned on a tactic I once used to escape from the moment. I projected myself out of my body and onto the ceiling, then looked down as though I were a stranger watching the scene below. There were two women there. The blonde one nodded.

"Yes," I said. "Mary Bess. It was Mary Bess who was cut into pieces, but— No! Oh no! Not Julia! You said— She wasn't—"

"She wasn't touched," the dark woman said, laying her hand lightly on my shoulder, easing me back down on the bed. "No marks, no blood. Not like the other, Mary Bess was it? Who'd been dismembered with…"

"A scalpel, that's what they said. That's why I…why the crime got so much attention back then."

Several moments passed, and the woman merely stared down at me. She had large velvet eyes. I picked up a whiff of gardenias. I edged down from the ceiling, back into my body.

"Are you saying," she said slowly, "that you did not do it?"

How many times had I been asked this question? How many times had I given the same answer? It always came back to this, didn't it? So I told it again. I'd left work, gone home and dressed, had a few drinks, walked over four blocks to Jesse and Mary Bess's place. On weekends we often had dinner and played cards afterwards, drank quite a bit, but that night I'd had too much and blacked out. The only thing I remembered was regaining consciousness that one brief moment, just long enough to look down into the blood-soaked trunk and see Mary Bess's head, her eyes and her mouth wide open, staring at me as I stood over her with a dripping scalpel in my hand.

I shut my eyes so tight that stars burst behind the lids.

"Did no one at the time ever suggest hypnotism to you? The memories are still there, you see, all you need to do is—"

I quit listening. A freight train was crashing through my head, whistles blasting and engines cranking. I curled up, pulled the sheet over me as the tears racked my body like a hurricane had broken loose.

"Hey, it's all right," she said. Her arms were around me, pulling me from the sheet. She held me in the way that mothers hold children and I let her. Over and over, she patted my back, said everything was okay, so that the words were a lullaby in her deep voice, a litany. I clung to her with the desperation that only a terrified child can know. When the sobbing had passed and I could speak again, my head lodged in the hollow of her shoulder, I told her about the day following the murder—it was the only part of the horror I could recall. I'd been terrified then, too. I had to get to my husband in L.A. The bodies were already in the trunk. I knew what was inside because that one terrifying image was beating through my head. I'd booked passage on the next train out of Phoenix, had the trunk taken to the station, and ridden with it to L.A. But by then there was an odor. While the baggage clerk called the police, I slipped away in a cab and spent the next few nights hiding in a department store supply room until I'd finally had a chance to call Daddy D. Who'd called the authorities.

"'Daddy D'?"

"Bruce DeWitte, my husband."

"Ah."

Suddenly I felt awkward. Where my cheek lay against her breast, my tears had left a wet spot on her sweater. I felt the warmth of her skin beneath the fabric, the rising odor of gardenia blossoms, the hard muscles of her arm which still held me. My heart was pounding, and I pulled away. She wore a vague smile, her head tilted sideways. She bent over and pulled something from her green satchel lying beside the bed.

"I hid this before the sheriff had a chance to see it," she said, holding up the empty bourbon bottle, "so you can tell him about it or not—it's your story."

She placed the bottle down on the floor as though it were a priceless object. I stared at it, felt my face burn, mumbled something about not drinking, about this being the first time since that night. It sounded lame, even as I was saying it. She took my chin in her hand, pulled my face up, and stared at me so hard that I felt her eyes invade me.

"I want to make sure I've got this straight," she said. "The night of the murders you were in an alcoholic blackout, but you came to consciousness for a moment, just long enough to remember seeing Mary Bess's head. Then, after all these years, you just happened to feel the urge for a drink, you tie one on, and bingo, another body appears in a trunk. That's quite a coincidence, Grace." She let my chin go and waited for me to respond, but I didn't. "You want to tell me what it was got you in a party mood all of a sudden?"

"Not particularly." I untangled myself from the sheet and scooted past her down the bed, swinging my feet to the floor. For all the tidiness of the room, I couldn't see my Nikes anywhere. I eyed the bourbon bottle. Bone dry. "Shit."

The seconds ticked by.

"Must have been a real special occasion," she drawled. Dryly.

I sighed. What the hell. I sat there with the morning getting lighter by the minute and told her about the notes, the snake, my decision to confide in Julia. I told her of Julia's theory, that the notes arrived each year on special days, though we'd only isolated two anniversaries of the possible four.

"But that's not entirely why I went to see Julia," I said. "That snake and the note, they just got me moving in the direction I'd been wanting to go anyway. You see, I've never given a rat's ass if people know about me or not, but when I moved here, I was worried about Julia's reputation, not to mention her bad heart. I thought if people here knew a convicted murderer was living among them, knew it was Julia who'd helped get me released, they'd give her a bad time about it. But last night, when I realized she didn't care beans what people thought either, well, that was the best news I'd had in awhile. She was going to talk to Sam Oliver at the paper on Monday. She figured he'd jump at the chance to have her do the story, and that'd be the end of it. No more reason for whoever was writing the notes to keep it up. You can't blackmail somebody that doesn't have any secrets."

"Assuming, of course, that blackmail was the motive." She stood up, walked over to the window and looked out across the eastern mountains where the sun was about to rise. She wore the same black clothes as yesterday, but the blood was gone. She leaned a shoulder against the wall. "Okay, so you left Julia's relieved, you were feeling good. Why come home and get drunk?" I didn't say anything. "Look, Grace, I don't know what happened to your friend Julia. I don't know who put her in that trunk or why. But I want to tell you something, and I want you to pay attention." She walked over and sat in the chair facing the bed. She bent toward me slowly from the hips, like they rolled on ball bearings. Her eyes were flaming, as they had been when she'd walked past my truck, right before the earthquake hit. Our faces just inches apart, the light burned at the center of her pupils as she whispered one slow, deliberate word after another: "Guilty or innocent, I can help you."

The way she behaved, it gave me a chill, but I knew I needed all the help I could get to stay out of the room at Mt. Havens that probably still had my name on it. I didn't want to talk any more about it, didn't know how to explain it if I did, but I gave it a shot. I did my best to tell her about ghosts, about waking in the lean hours and seeing them coming at me from all sides. I tried to tell her something about being a minister's daughter in the Midwest, something about the way Head Honcho DeWitte appeared to a young student nurse at the Evanston State Mental Hospital. But if you've ever tried explaining something you're a little foggy on yourself, you'll know why my disjointed monologue was about as coherent as a plate of chopped worms. I gave up.

"Just call it a bad night, real bad. I had this awful feeling, like there was something up ahead in the road just waiting for me, something bad, so bad I couldn't stand thinking about it. I kept that bourbon out in the barn, for medicinal purposes is what I called it.

I never had a temptation for it before, never expected to, but I had to get out of my head somehow."

Her eyes were glittering like mica, her jaw set tight. She would have fit right in with those men on the parole board gathered around one end of the table with me way down at the other, them staring hard and waiting for me to sit up like a dog and beg. My lawyer said they liked to see women shed some tears, but I figured they'd get over their disappointment. I'd always suspected they were measuring me against some private notion they carried of how a woman was supposed to act. I hadn't liked that hard-eyed look then, and I sure as hell didn't like it now.

"And I don't want any shit about it, either. If you want to know, I went to Harvey's today to get more, and if it hadn't been for the quake and your damn horse..." I glared at her, but she was looking out the window again, like she'd left the room. When she turned back, she grinned that crooked smile and laughed. It was the first time I'd heard it, a deep, vibrant sound like a piano chord. Even after she stopped, it hung in the air awhile.

Then the sun broke over the eastern ridge, and light flooded the room. Rachael raised her hand to her eyes and squinted. I went back to looking for my tennies. There was not much to be found on the vast, alien plains of my bedroom floor. The books that had been strewn around my bed were arranged around the walls in neat piles, their spines so evenly aligned they looked like they'd been stacked with a ruler.

"You do all that?" I nodded at the books, the floor.

She put the book she'd been reading on top of a nearby stack. Precisely aligned with the others. Bachelard's *The Phenomenology of Fire*. "I did. Anyone ever mention you have unusually broad interests?"

"Not in those words. More like, 'Anybody ever tell you you're a fruitcake?' to which question, the answer is already on record." I was starting to feel mean. All that open space on the floor wasn't helping my mood. It looked like Texas down there. Empty, boring, perfectly useless. "I don't suppose you'd happen to know where my tennies might be?"

She went to the closet and opened the door. My stash of shoes which I kept in an snappy heap according to my preferred method of organization, most recent on top, were in a tidy line, toes kissing the wall.

"What, you're a housekeeper by profession?" I felt unreasonably cranky. If I'd been a dog, I'd have bit her. I got up and grabbed a pair of Nikes, sat on the edge of the bed to pull them on.

"I've been known to restore order."

Her words were stripped down to the bone, not an ounce of inflection. I quit fussing with the laces and glanced up. Rachael had leaned back against the wall and watched me with the dead-eyed stare that people use when, according to Mickey Spillane, they're holding a finger on the trigger and hoping you'll say something stupid. Hey, some people are very sensitive about being considered common laborers, I can understand that. I swallowed, mumbled a hasty thanks.

"My pleasure," she said.

Her tone was friendly again, but that smile carried enough high octane smart-ass to tweak a whole lot of silver belt buckles those good old boys like to wear. A woman traveling alone, smiling like that, she was asking for trouble. Or maybe, I thought, glancing up at where she stood with her weight thrown on one hip, that's what Rachael McKinley was looking for. I let it go and made a mental note: she was sensitive about her profession, whatever it was, and she got a little spooky when pissed. Sure, and speaking of spooky when pissed, who was I to throw stones? She probably didn't take up a scalpel and dismember her friends, either. Probably.

I finished tying my shoes and stood up. The clothes I'd put on yesterday after my shower were still clean, and Bill Hammersmith probably wouldn't notice the wrinkles. I didn't know what time he opened up, but I wanted to get it over with, get an early start.

Rachael agreed. "Then," I said, motioning her to follow as I headed for the kitchen, "we'll look into getting you some hay, go check on your horse. You interested in breakfast? Coffee?"

"Coffee, black," she said, following. "Maybe take a look at those notes you've been getting before we take off? Sheriff wanted you to bring them along."

11

RACHAEL SAID, "BLACKMAIL RULE NUMBER ONE: Find a victim with a secret to die for. Your snake killer got that wrong. Strike one.

"Blackmail Rule Number Two: Never, ever, blackmail someone with a history of mayhem. Strike two."

"So where'd you happen across those rules?" I asked.

"Public domain."

Rachael sat at the table, her chin propped in her palms, the notes lined up in a razor-straight row in front of her. While I'd explained the sequence of their arrival and Julia's theory of anniversary dates, she'd copied a duplicate set on corresponding blue, pink, and yellow index cards and arranged them in a row below the originals. I sipped my coffee and looked over her shoulder while she studied the poems. Finally, she picked up the original snake note by its outer edges and held it next to each one of the others, one by one, then laid it back on the table at the end of the line. She adjusted its alignment. I watched her with the same fascination I used to watch the obsessive-compulsive inmates at Mt. Havens.

"That one." She indicated the snake note and folded her arms, leaned back in the chair. Her neck, even with the black turtleneck, was spectacularly long, and her hair very short. "It wasn't written by the same person as the rest."

"Sure it was, that's the one that came Saturday with the snake. Same paper, same handwriting. Same terrific ear for language." I leaned over her shoulder and read it again:

gracie, pudding and pie,
kissed the girls and made them die,
after putting them in the trunk,
gracie gracie, pleaded drunk.

"Not a chance." She pointed to the ends of the lines. "Commas here; no commas, not one, in the others. No periods in the first nine poems, but one in the last. You think that's insignificant, but it's not. The original writer wouldn't have done that. And something else. The original writer, not counting the first note, started off with a children's nursery rhyme and mucked it up. Maybe got tired messing with it, didn't care, had a tin ear. Who knows?" She tapped the snake with her fingernail. "But this one. We're not talking Pulitzer, but see how the entire rhyme imitates and sustains the meter of the original children's poem from beginning to end? Listen." She pointed to the words of the note as she recited the original poem: "Georgie Porgie, pudding and pie, kissed the girls and made them cry, when the girls came out to play, Georgie Porgie ran away."

Call me suspicious. At Mt. Havens, I'd read plenty of poetry, even some literary analysis right at first to get a handle on it. I knew how those university professors writing criticism liked to manufacture a mountain out of a hill of beans. I still didn't know Rachael's profession, but if she'd spent some time behind a university podium, it wouldn't have surprised me. Either that or maybe she was in politics—they can talk you out of your false teeth, those folks. But I let it slide.

"Another thing, notice the difference in tone," she went on. "For two and a half years someone's been sending you these little ditties that seemed so harmless you barely took notice of them. But this last time, notice the menace, the specific references to the murders. You yourself even mentioned how odd it is—if blackmail's the motive—that suddenly the poet cranked up the volume and added a dead animal. See what I mean?"

Sure enough, the more she talked, the more sense it made, but the critics could do that too. Besides, even if she was right, what difference would it—

"Finding the person writing these notes could be very important. Two writers means the second one imitated the first one, used the same notepaper and nursery-rhyme model. Means the two must know each other. But the person who wrote the last note has a different agenda. The ante's been raised, or maybe it's a different game altogether. Escalated from a childish prank to…maybe blackmail, maybe something else. There's a chance Julia's death was the second writer's attempt at communication with you, not a note at all, in which case—"

"No! Stop." I couldn't talk about Julia's death yet, not in that impersonal way of reducing it to a criminal act. I couldn't bear to picture her at the morgue, either, though I knew there were funeral arrangements to make. And since Julia had no living relatives, I'd be the one to make them. I walked over to the patio and looked out at the birds thrashing around in the water caught in the old statuary under the eucalyptus. I could feel Rachael's eyes boring holes in my back. Silence hung uncomfortably over the room.

Finally, she said: "You've got to be able to talk about this, you know. The sheriff's going to ask you questions, important questions. You may have been the last person to see her before—"

I turned around. "Please, stop. I know you're right, but not right now. I need more time. Bill will understand."

"Bill." Three beats. "I see."

More beats.

"It's not what you're thinking."

"You don't know what I'm thinking."

"I mean…We're…It's old news. It's been over for months now, didn't amount to all that much even when it was going on." I walked over and sat across from her, looked into my coffee cup. I jiggled it and watched the surface spin. I didn't know how I'd gotten into this discussion, why I was explaining, why it mattered.

"So what happened?"

"Not much. Nice guy, just sort of fizzled out. Lack of interest seemed like."

"Yours or his?"

Our eyes met above the two perfect rows of notes. She was leaning back in the chair, head cocked, smile crooked, like the only straight line she'd ever give you was there on the table between us.

"We're still friends."

"Nothing wrong with friends," she said, "if that's what you're looking for."

"I'm not looking for anything." I took a sip of coffee. It was cold and bitter.

"Maybe that's the problem," she said.

I was about to try for a snappy comeback, but she leaned forward and went back to messing with the cards, moving them around on the table, slowly at first, then with both hands like a shell game, trying one combination, then another, occasionally writing something on the cards. When she finished, there were three columns—the first pink, then blue, then yellow.

"Okay, let's go with Julia's theory that your poet sent notes on a particularly significant day each year. You've been here 1995, 1996, 1997." She pointed to a vertical column for each year. "You get four notes a year, and you've already nailed down two dates—the murders, December twenty-second," she pointed at the bottom row, "and your wedding anniversary, October twenty-fifth," the row above. "That leaves two dates still not accounted for." She indicated the top two rows and tapped the first card in the first column:

welcome grace
with pleasing voice
and pretty face

"Nineteen ninety-five, the year you moved here. Your first note, right?" I nodded. "Remember how long you lived here before it showed up?"

I gave it a shot, came up blank, shook my head. "Wait." I went to the back room and grabbed the old calendars from my desk drawer. At the table I opened the 1995 Sierra Club model to August and scanned the boxes, leafed through the following months as I tried to jog my memory. Appointments scheduled for the contractor, reminders for animal immunizations, a dentist appointment. I felt a twinge of embarrassment at the empty boxes and slapped the calendar shut. "I can't remember exactly," I said irritably, "seems like it was just there early on. I didn't even think about having a mailbox for a week or two. You get out of the habit of collecting your mail when you're locked up. Besides, who was going to be writing me?"

"You say it was there 'early on'? Could it have been in your box even before you arrived?"

I thought for a minute. "Could have, I guess, but nobody except Julia and the realtor she bought the place from knew I was here."

"Somebody knew. Maybe the realtor passed the word around. Small towns, word travels fast. Or maybe somebody's been keeping close tabs on you through the years. Wouldn't have taken much to find out your review was coming up again. Maybe someone followed you here. It's possible."

"But...who—"

"That's the question, isn't it? Anybody taking that much interest, the day of your release might be a kind of holiday. Your own personal Independence Day. If so, you probably get a note in August about that same time each year."

"Now you mention it, I think I might. But that would still leave one date unaccounted for." I glanced at the top row with the remaining two notes, the first under the 1996 column:

gracie was a little lamb
with hair as bright as frost
and everywhere gracie goes
i will follow her

and the other in 1997:

gracie gracie quite contrary
i love to watch you grow
with silver hair and sky blue eyes
and happy days

"I kept them filed in the order I received them, so those must have come somewhere between December twenty-second and August fourteenth when I arrived here. I can't remember getting them, though."

Rachael flipped open the 1996 calendar to January and shoved it toward me. "Here. Browse through to August. Look for any significant date, anything at all that comes to mind."

The dryer had stopped, and while Rachael left to attend the clothes, I looked through the calendar. Not without feeling a certain irony. I'd spent thirty-odd years blocking out important dates like the kind Rachael wanted me to remember because when you're locked up with the truly deranged for that long, you're too busy snapping at the heels of your thoughts, keeping them marching forward in a straight line, to go digging up bones in the past. Your sanity depends on omissions; every day is an exercise in sustained annihilation. Forget the day your father took to his bed with the cancer eating his entrails, the day your mother walked alone into the nursing home and lay staring at the ceiling until her death. Don't think about the last time your eyes touched theirs without knowing it would be the last. The very days of their deaths must pass unmarked, their funerals unattended.

You must keep every one of those brittle-boned skeletons locked away, buried in the mind's basement as far down as you can get them if you ever hope someday to walk out of internment, into the light of the free world and recognize that you are seeing the sun up there in an open sky, and not that blinding white-light nutcase variety from the land of New Age loony tunes.

I sat at the table, turning one empty page of the calendar after another, knowing I wasn't going to find anything important enough to build an anniversary on. Even if I climbed to the barn loft and retrieved the thirty-two years of calendars from their Mt. Havens storage box, their infrequent notations would reveal not a bone of truth about me, because keeping hold of your mind depends on leaving all those boxes empty. And thirty years of empty boxes is a tough habit to break.

Rachael walked through the room carrying a stack of clothes and said something I didn't catch. I had turned a page and was staring at April, feeling the earth start to move somewhere in the basement, feeling the same terror that had driven me last Saturday night to the bottle of bourbon. I clasped my hands and laid them over that one glossy square of April. I heard a shower go on somewhere in the house, water hitting the walls. A memory was turning, trying to rise up from some dark grave. I squeezed my eyes shut and tried to force it back, heard the water splashing, the clank of a shower door closing.

I spread my palms against the cool, smooth paper, heard the shower door clang again, opening this time, felt the tears leaking down the sides of my face.

"Oh Mary Bess," I whispered. "Dear God, Mary Bess."

She had broken through, had climbed up out of the darkness and was walking toward me, just as she had that night. Her bare feet padded softly across the bedroom floor. Through my tears, I could see the towel wrapped around her, even the water dripping from her auburn hair and sliding down between her breasts.

"Hey, you all right?"

Rachael stood wrapped in a towel, her dark hair wet and combed sleekly back.

"I...I..." I blinked hard. I shook my head and moved my hands from April 21, unable to think of anything except that Saturday night in 1962. A lifetime ago. I wiped away the tears and glanced over at the two notes at the head of the second and third columns, read them again. I hadn't noticed before, but now I saw that in both poems, the poet had substituted my name where, in the original nursery rhymes, the name "Mary" would have occurred. Mary Bess. That night with her was not marked on any calendar in the world, not known to anyone except myself and one other, and she was dead. So how could the note writer have known about it?

I stood up and went outside. I sat down at the picnic table in the same place I'd sat two nights ago, watching Daddy DeWitte sneaking among the trees with his bottle, the same night I'd gone to the barn and gotten my own, the same night Julia...A cloud had drifted across the morning sun, deepening the green shadows beneath the eucalyptus. The statue that'd probably begun as a shapely Venus in the mind's eye of a novice sculptor was little more than a lumpy torso, without arms, lower legs. Without a head. Her knees were planted in the ground while sparrows gathered on her rough shoulders, waiting their turn to bathe in the hollow basin where her head should have been. I'd spent many hours of pleasure here watching the birds, listening to their song, not thinking much about the misshapen concrete, a woman decapitated—

I laid my head on my arms. After a while, I heard the patio screen slide open, felt Rachael sit beside me. Her arm was cool around my shoulders. I remembered the way she had circled me with it yesterday, facing Bill Hammersmith. And last night, when I'd told her what I remembered of the murder. She'd smelled of gardenia then, but now I caught whiffs of soap, a just-showered smell.

"Might help if you told me about it," she said. Her voice was mellow, cut from a dark night. A place where secrets would be safe.

So I told her mine. I described that weekend when Jesse had gone to Oregon to attend her sister's wedding, when Daddy DeWitte had unexpectedly canceled his plans to visit. It was just Mary Bess and me, alone for the first time, sitting there over the dinner I'd planned for the doctor.

"It was my first experience with…with a woman. It was like walking into a new world, one where you belonged all the time and never knew it. I knew I was in love with Mary Bess, that before that night I didn't even know what it was like to love, but I didn't tell her that. I think she felt the same way about me, though. But she was with Jesse, and I was married to Daddy D, and there was…well…the stigma…"

She didn't say anything, so I turned to her. Her hands clasped on the table, she stared off through the trees. The breeze had gone; the cloud had moved on and left the morning bright again, but without sound. I glanced at the concrete figure; all the birds had disappeared. I had the eerie sense of being in a painting, a still life. Not quite real.

"We never mentioned that night, me and Mary Bess. But it was always hanging right there between us. I could feel it. We didn't look much at each other. Every time I tried, I'd see her the way she looked across the table from me in the glow of the candlelight that night, and then the two of us washing the dishes shoulder-to-shoulder, putting them away. I guess it was inevitable that as time passed Jesse picked up a change in the air. That's when the disagreements started, just small things, then incidents at the clinic where Jesse and I worked. All the time, I told myself I was being silly, that any day the doctor would find a job and call me to move to L.A. But by December, I knew that too much had changed. I couldn't bear the thought of going back to living with him. And things had gotten very tense between me and Jesse, so I went out and rented my own place. I'd been living there three weeks when..." I stopped talking and watched the headless statue where several small, fat-chested birds had landed.

Rachael hadn't moved, but the sun sifted through the leaves, and a passing breeze made the light dance like bright lace over where we sat. It glazed her cheekbones and forehead and chin. She still had the towel wrapped around her, and her skin was moist from the shower. I wanted to touch her, run my fingers along her cheekbones, deep into the grooves of her collarbone.

"I know it's painful, going back to the past." Her words were almost a whisper. "The dead ought to have whatever peace can be found on the other side. But sometimes it is as if they are moved by some great turbulence that will not let them lie down and sleep." She turned to me and her eyes glittered with small flames. "I believe their suffering over some injustice moves them to call our names, and at such times we are their only hope of retribution." She laid a hand across mine. "It's not so strange, is it? Our past is part of us, and those who've shared it are alive in us. Isn't it natural that their pain is ours, and that in order to soothe the pain, we must take up their cause, right the wrongs that have been done them so that we, as well as they, can find peace?"

I knew she must have her own past that led her to say such things. I did not understand the dark philosophy that inspired her, though I sensed its blasphemy to my father's religion. But as strange as her words were, I could feel the truth of them, see how they fit exactly over Mary Bess and me. I could hear the ghost of Mary Bess calling, just as she described. I felt my heart race, as though after all the years since Mary Bess's death, someone at last had heard my story and understood.

"Nothing had prepared me for the way I felt about Mary Bess," I said. "You see, all my life I'd done the right thing, the things my daddy'd taught me were right. After that night I felt like I'd lost all control, like the world had turned upside-down. All the familiar truths, either they were a lie or I was damned." I looked at the estuary without seeing it, closed my eyes, but Mary Bess walked out of the darkness toward me, headless. I looked away. "It's a sin, you know, what we did that night. I was sure any minute I'd be struck down, but when I wasn't, I just waited for the memory of it to fade, like everything does if you give it enough time. But it didn't fade, it got worse, even after I'd moved into my own place. That day—it was on a Friday, December twenty-second—Jesse had blasted into the clinic in a rage. I didn't know it then, but she'd found out about me and Mary Bess. It came out at the trial how she'd been in a temper that day, but nobody knew why. And how could I sit up there on the witness stand with my mother and my daddy watching, and tell all the world I was...that Mary Bess and I had...I couldn't, I just couldn't do it. And what difference would it have made, anyway? It wouldn't have changed anything." I closed my eyes and wished for the world to end.

"Go on. Say it. You have to say it all now."

"Yes. It's true I don't remember what happened. But I know enough about psychology, going to nurses' school and working in the mental hospital with Daddy D and all, to know the mind protects itself from the unbearable by forgetting. Like it's doing you a favor and you had better let well enough alone. I believe that's what happened, that and the alcohol. When I went over there that night, Jesse must have attacked me—she had a violent temper. To protect myself, I shot her with that gun she always kept by the bed. And...Mary Bess...she..."

"Go on."

"...she saw me do it, she must have, and she must have hated me for it." I was out of breath, as though I'd been running a long way. It was a while before I could speak again. "She must've said horrible things to me, so horrible I can't even imagine what. So horrible that I shot her through the head like I shot Jesse. And then took the scalpel, Jesse always kept one in the bathroom in a first aid box, and...and..." The words came in gasps. I struggled for breath. "...because how else could I have done that to poor Mary Bess?"

There was a long silence, and then Rachael spoke: "Go on."

I nodded. I was calm now. "I've always thought it was God's punishment, visited on the three of us for our sins."

When I looked at Rachael, the flames in her eyes had disappeared. She sat very straight, with a faint smile and a kind of sadness around the mouth and eyes. I hadn't seen her look that way before, like she might be carrying around as many burdens as me. I couldn't say why, but it scared me a little. I wanted the smart-ass smile, the way it said she was self-contained and had all the answers. That was about the time she leaned toward me.

I felt the softness of her lips as I had only felt the softness of one other's. And then she stood and walked back into the house.

• • •

When I went back inside, the towel was gone. Rachael was leaning over the table, studying the notes, dressed in the same black clothes as before. Her green nylon bag lay on the chair beside her.

I walked up and stood uncertainly. She wasn't going to help me out any. "I don't know what you're thinking," I said, searching for words, "but I'm not..."

She looked around, still leaning on her hands. She wore the Mickey Spillane look.

"I'm not...you know, a...a lesbian."

She kept her eyes hard. "Hey, you think I won't respect you in the morning? I won't even *be* here in the morning. I'm not looking for anything, either." She eased into a grin before turning back to the table. "Give it a rest, Frost. Just a spontaneous gesture of affection, one human being to another."

I wasn't going to make an argument out of it. What was to argue? I pushed my confusion aside and forced my attention back to the table where the calendar still lay open to April. That's when I remembered what had touched off my memories of Mary Bess to begin with. I pointed to the two poems at the top of the columns and told Rachael my theory, the way both notes used "Gracie" to replace the original "Mary."

"Could be. Sounds pretty sophisticated, though, given the rest of them. And like you say, who would know about that night?" She began collecting the original notes by the edges and fitted them neatly into a plastic sandwich bag. She slipped the green satchel over her shoulder and tossed the notes to me. "Guess you'll have to decide if you want to share that theory with *Bill*," she said and headed for the door.

I stared after her, then shoved the notes in my pocket, and followed her out. On the stairs, she stopped abruptly.

"By the way, Frost, when's your birthday?"

It's funny how you can look at a calendar and wipe yourself right off the face of time. My birthday was April seventh.

12

FORCE OF HABIT: I HEADED FOR THE BARN to feed the animals. Then stopped. Barely eight-thirty, and Rachael had not only done the laundry and nailed down the dates of the notes, she'd fed the goats and geese as well. Probably the cat, too. He came streaking out of the barn, wrapping himself around her boots as she walked. She leaned over, lifted the cat in mid-stride, and slung him over her shoulder. Speechless, I watched her march through the barn, the cat leering back at me. She snapped a padlock onto the bunkroom door, using a fixture that hadn't been there the last time I looked. Rachael McKinley was not a shy girl.

"Hope you don't mind," she said, slipping the cat to the ground and walking back into the sunlight. "My laptop's set up in there. Easy to walk off with."

I shrugged. Empty rhetoric. I didn't figure it made any difference if I minded or not. I popped open the truck door and revved the engine while Rachael settled in the passenger side, her green bag on the floor beside her. She stretched out in a diagonal lounge-lizard position, one arm draped across the back of the seat, the other holding up the window as I headed down the driveway. At the mailbox, I stopped and nodded toward Clarissa Remington's rows of fruit trees, gave Rachael a quick sketch of my visit yesterday, my idea of checking out the neighbors, thinking someone might have walked down the road and inserted the notes. I started to turn right, toward town.

"Wait," Rachael said. "Who lives on up that way?"

"Don't know, never been there." I followed her gaze to the north where the pavement climbed and narrowed before disappearing into the trees around an uphill bend. "Clarissa didn't know either. I meant to take a walk up there yesterday, after I got back from Harvey's, but..." A shiver crept up my spine, whether from recollecting yesterday's events or from the creepiness of the isolated road, I couldn't tell.

"I vote we take a quick drive up. Call it a hunch."

"You mean *now*, right *now*?" My evil, anal-retentive twin raised her head. "The sheriff's going to be expecting me."

"He wasn't specific, said any time today."

I stared up the road at the dense wilderness, thought about it for a minute. Then two.

"Hey, relax. Live a little." She leaned over and poked me with her elbow and nodded up the road, like she was used to giving directions and having them followed. Maybe she was a Teamster.

So I turned left, but I didn't like it. The road was bad, and after we rounded the curve, it turned to gravel, then dirt. We were pushing through a dense tangle of trees, their branches scraping the sides of the truck, reminding me of those cartoons I used to watch as a kid, the ones where tree branches turned into twisted arms reaching out to grab passersby. The incline grew more steep, and the truck struggled uphill. Clarissa said the property had belonged to the former owners of my place, but we saw no driveway. Just as the road came to a dead end, I spotted faint, overgrown ruts on the left, closed off with a rusted chain and padlock. If anybody was living up there, they had their groceries dropped in by helicopter because no vehicle except maybe a tank was going to make it through that underbrush. It didn't take a genius to see no one had gone that way for a good while.

"Wasted trip," I mumbled self-righteously. Just ahead, the road leveled out into a small plateau where the forest thinned on one side. I pulled into the space to turn around, looking out through the trees to a view of Las Tierras below. Beer cans and broken bottles and a motley of trash dotted the underbrush. The local Lover's Lane.

"Hold on," Rachael said. She opened the door, signaled *stay put*, and leaped out.

"Hey! Wait..."

This long, lean-legged woman—I've seen deer move that fast, but not people—streaked out the door, crossed the clearing, and disappeared into the forest in a blink of the eye. I sat alone in the wilderness, staring at the place where the vegetation had closed behind her. I felt suddenly out of sync, derailed, unsure what to do next: follow or not? Easy—not. My flimsy cotton T-shirt was fine in the sunlight, worthless here in the penetrating chill. But I needed to do something, so I finished turning the truck around, pointed it down the road, set the parking brake, shut off the engine. Looked around. Locked the doors. Shivered. Started the engine again and turned on the heater.

I pushed back the seat and stretched out behind the wheel and stared into the dark mass of trees. Rachael was probably checking out where the old driveway led, so she wasn't going to be gone too long. Probably. I kept my eye on where she'd disappeared, but thoughts of her expedition soon gave way to thoughts I'd been pushing back. For over thirty years, as a means of retaining the sanity I was not supposed to have anyway, I'd honed repression to a fine art: when it came to squashing unwelcome retrospect, I was Attila the Hun. I must have lost my knack, though, because here they came—thoughts of Julia's death, the upcoming visit to the sheriff; of Mary Bess, of Rachael McKinley and what had happened on my patio less than half an hour ago.

"Shit!"

Plowing through the wilderness couldn't be any worse than this—all I needed was a jacket to be on my way. I twisted around on my knees and rummaged behind the seat: jumper cables, a grimy umbrella, several half-empty bottles of Pennzoil. I flipped around, bent over, felt under my seat, then Rachael's, staring finally into the crotch of the only remaining possibility. The green nylon bag. She was a woman who seemed prepared for emergencies, probably had a bag full of jackets.

I hesitated. In spite of my past, I'm not much of a criminal; a murderer maybe, but not a thief, not a snoop. I considered that bag—its sage-green color, its glossy nylon texture, its multifarious and alluring array of zippers. I popped my head up, scanned the wilderness. No Rachael. I heaved the bag onto the seat, tugged at a zipper. Lots of plastic-sealed containers, no jacket. I slipped open another zipper, then another, working my way without success through the bag. The contents ran the gamut—odd electronic devices, cords and straps and wires, a money pouch with lots of bills, a neatly rolled black turtleneck and jeans, a collection of floppy disks and CDs, a dog-eared paperback copy of *Living Down Under* by Anna Lee Stone, a bottle with something yucky growing inside, a huge bundle of checkbooks held together with a rubber band. No jacket. I pulled out the turtleneck. Fairly heavy fabric. It'd do. I started zipping the pockets back up.

At the last one, I paused. Odd, wasn't it? All those checkbooks? I mean, I could understand a couple, maybe three. Different accounts here and there. A business account, a personal account, a savings account. Sure. But...I counted them. Twenty-seven? Maybe she sold banking supplies. I glanced up. No Rachael. I slipped one from the bunch and sneaked a peek.

I can tell you, if I had it to do again, I wouldn't. I'd have gone into the forest in my T-shirt. Hell, I'd have gone without any shirt at all.

The first one I looked at, it was a checking account all right, but not Rachael McKinley's. It was brand new, never drawn on, an amount of $200,000 available to Sarah Hodgkist. In the pocket behind the crisp, unused check register was Sarah's VISA card and a current Louisiana driver's license, complete with a picture of a red-haired Rachael, 201 Pascal Avenue, Shreveport, Louisiana.

I glanced up at the forest, glanced down at another: $200,000, Marilynn Hayes; Fairfield, North Carolina; Rachael with long, dark hair. I glanced up, then down; up, down; up, down: Benita Ramos, Silver Sands, Arizona. Samantha Wilkinson, Jasper, Wyoming. I quit looking somewhere around number fifteen. All of them had a picture of Rachael in some camouflage or another.

My hands were shaking. I zipped the pocket and stared out the windshield. The pine forest seemed darker, dotted with an occasional wild oak in autumn orange, the leaves thinning and the branches turning gnarled and spidery. I shut off the heater, killed the engine, rolled down the window. The silence was ominous: a sporadic birdcall, an owl, then nothing. Rachael McKinley was out there somewhere. Probably, though, her name wasn't Rachael McKinley.

I sat still as a stone, trying to think what to do, waiting for something, I didn't know what. Then the voice:

What to do, Gracie Lee, you dumb shit, is get the hell out of here. Do not pass Go. Do not collect two hundred paltry dollars. Go straight to the sheriff.

Hammersmith. Had he run a check on Rachael's identity? Why would he? And I couldn't just drive off, leave her here.

Are you out of your fucking mind? Why can't you?

For one thing, I had her green bag and—I paused for a minute, math not being my strong suit—and over five million dollars, give or take. Plus, my home was just down the road, a twenty-minute walk, tops. And for someone like Rachael, say fifteen minutes, say ten. She'd show up, and she'd be pissed. What would I say? What if she's dangerous?

What if she's dangerous? Are you kidding?

Okay, say she is. She's not going to mind breaking a window to get back her five million dollars. Then what?

The sheriff, you idiot, go to the sheriff.

I took a deep breath, closed my eyes. Maybe I was letting my paranoia get the best of me. I knew something about being on the short end of snap judgments. I remembered this morning on the patio, the sadness I saw in her eyes, the tenderness—

Get a grip, Gracie. This isn't some sappy romance. This is serious shit.

Okay, but even if she was a criminal of some sort, what reason did she have to harm me?

None, not until you opened her bag. Knows you're on to her. Maybe give her away to the sheriff today. And there has been a killing here lately, hasn't there? Maybe she's some psycho roaming the countryside, killing for kicks. Some escaped mental patient...

That's when I quit. I draw the line at stereotyping mental patients. The best tactic was to tell the truth—"fess up" about going through her bag, apologize. Mention, in passing, I'd seen the checkbooks. She'd have a perfectly reasonable explanation and that would be the end of it. Before I could talk myself out of it, I jumped out of the truck and pulled on the black turtleneck, thinking that whoever she was, she wasn't much for variety in her dress code. Maybe she was a night watchman.

Or a cat burglar…

I locked the door and set off up the mountain. I pushed through underbrush until it became dense and impassable. Then I reminded myself the mystery woman had gone this way: I had an image of long, lean Rachael lying down and slithering through, but I was wider and shorter, not to mention older, so I lowered my head bull-style, folded my arms across my face, and leaned all my weight into the bushes, forging ahead until, near the crest, the vegetation thinned. At the top, a long, flat stretch of weeds was dotted with occasional oak and scrub brush. No neighbor, no Rachael. I waded across to the opposite side, to a spectacular vista of rolling mountains and the ocean beyond. The ridge below where I stood was decidedly less vegetated than the other side. I spotted a path zigzagging down toward a chimney poking through an enclave of wild oak.

I followed the path to a long, narrow house butted back against the mountainside with a flagstone walkway leading around front. I went cautiously, "yoo-hooing" and entertaining images of blood-thirsty Dobermans. At the front of the house, a wide gravel driveway sparkled in the morning sun and ended at a double-sized garage. The other end of the drive, amazingly, descended to a broad, two-lane highway about three hundred yards below where I stood.

Even so, the place felt deserted. The garage doors were tightly shut, the windows of the house bare. Gnarled oaks crowded thickly around the old house and dotted the brown, weedy grounds. No sign of landscaping or habitation. A flagstone porch ran the length of the house. I knocked at the front door, waited, looked around uneasily, then walked out to the driveway. On an impulse, I followed it down to the highway. A mailbox much like my own had neatly printed letters on the side: ZOLOMAN 2075 CRYSTAL OAKS LANE. I could look up the name in the local phone directory when I got home; if there was a listing, maybe give a call. Who knows, maybe the Zolomans had just gone off to work like some folks do on a Monday. Still…I glanced around quickly. Deserted as the moon. I sidled up to the mailbox, opened the door, took a quick peek.

"I have always wished to find exactly the right dog who would do that. It would save me the trip down here every day."

I jumped into the next century. My heart pounded like it was going to need an emergency room. I whirled around, found nothing, whirled again. He was leaning against a tree with his arms crossed, watching me commit a federal crime. The dappled shadows camouflaged him as perfectly as a leopard. Nearby, a camera sat perched on a tripod, aimed at some dark clouds hovering over the ocean.

"Jesus Q. Christ! You scared holy hell out of me!" My heart kept hammering, but I was angry now, past surprise.

"I have always admired a woman with a strong sense of religion," he said.

His voice was low, but the words were distinct. He pushed himself away from the tree, strolled my way with his hands in his jacket pockets. He was tall, deeply tanned, wearing a moss-colored sweater under a jacket and slacks of a slightly darker shade, custom fit by the look of them, and as he moved out of the shadows, the sun caught the gray in his hair, the square jaw line, tawny eyes both tranquil and amused. I figured late thirties, early forties maybe, walking like he had the whole day to do it in, an easy, nearly feline gait that tickled some memory in the back of my mind, though I couldn't recall it.

He crunched across the gravel in leather loafers, no socks, and paused with the door of the mailbox gaping obscenely between us. There was something about him, standing there against the backdrop of gnarled trees and flat white sky, something as utterly and totally familiar as the air that moved softly with the ocean and pine resin and the inevitable tang of dust living in it. His eyes, as though committing something to memory, lingered on me.

"Do I have any interesting mail?"

The blood rushed to my face. I leaned over, stuck my hand in, pulled out a couple of envelopes. "Sorry." I handed them to him. "I was just trying to find out who lives here."

"No harm. You are a great improvement over the dog I had wished for. You may pilfer my box any time. I give you a standing, open invitation." He dropped his head slightly, almost like he might bow. He slipped the envelopes in his jacket pocket without looking at them and lowered his eyes to my chest. "However, I am puzzled about the route you chose."

I looked down to see that Rachael's black turtleneck had acquired a thick layer of tiny, wedge-shaped stickers. I began pulling at them, but they were sharp, with small quills like tiny cacti.

I gave it up. "I'm Grace Frost, from down the road. I've been meaning for ages to drop in and say hello, be neighborly, you know." I realized I'd not given the first thought to what I'd say, how to explain why after two years I'd decided to pay a call. Telling him I was investigating murder and blackmail didn't seem like the best ice-breaker. I slipped past it and explained how I'd looked for his road on the opposite side of the ridge. "I saw that old driveway and followed it up, looking for a house."

He couldn't seem to pull his eyes off my stickers. "I am afraid it has cost you a sweater," he said. His English was scrupulously perfect, no contractions. I thought I detected the ghost of an accent, but I wasn't sure. He stuck out his hand. "By the way, I am Willis Zoloman, and there was once a driveway from that direction, but it was quite steep, not to mention the highway on this side is better maintained." Nice smile. Good teeth. Firm handshake.

I walked up the drive beside him, feeling like I was on a nature hike. He pointed out various plants, identified them by their Latin names, starting with the culprit bearing the stickers, an innocuous-looking bush with a list of virtues to its credit. I pretended interest, nodded, scanned the landscape for Rachael. Nothing. I reasoned that if she'd returned to the truck and found it locked, she'd either wait there for me, come looking this way, or else hoof it back to my place. It didn't seem to be all that serious a problem, so I let it go and turned my attention to Zoloman. He was praising yet another species of indigenous weed.

His approach to landscaping was at the other end of Clarissa's spectrum. Where she'd shaped hers to fit, he'd deliberately preserved the original. I was betting this yard looked today about like it had when the first settlers arrived centuries ago. The house, too, was a well-preserved, historical adobe that seemed to have been transformed since I passed it by just minutes ago: the abandoned derelict was actually a homestead perfectly adapted to its setting. Its center portion was adobe, the smooth rolling shapes of the large bricks visible under an outer layer of flesh-colored stucco. Two extensive wood additions had been built onto each end, with no attempt to cover them over in faux adobe to match the center. The effect, though stark, had an uncompromising authenticity, the wood portions glazed rather than painted so that the grain of the amber wood glowed through.

Zoloman caught my look. He nodded at the adobe center as he opened the screen door. "According to the literature I found at the local library, this central portion was built in 1878, using a method called 'board-on-end' construction." He pushed open the interior door, standing aside for me to enter. He bowed his head slightly, smiled. "Which basically means that in this room there are no studs."

I shot him a glance. He gazed back with the serenity of a fawn. I looked into the dim interior, then back at the stark terrain. No Rachael. No one on the planet knew my whereabouts. I reminded myself of my long history of gullibility. I reminded myself that I didn't know this guy. I reminded myself that my best friend was dead, and I'd come here looking for her killer.

And then, what the hell, I walked in.

13

Morgan

I watch this man through the window and see the other. He has that same look of pewter about him—a man smooth and polished, lethal as a gun barrel.

"Cord."

I stand facing the window, my back to him, looking down through the rain at the parking lot below. The carpet muffles his footsteps, but I know when he stops, just behind me. I see his reflection against the gray pane, his hands are raised. They mean to settle on my shoulders, but they hover instead. They fall to his sides.

"Cordelia." His breath grazes my ear. "This isn't necessary, you know."

"Yes. I know." Something moves in the parking lot, two stories down, but it is too soon for the cab. "It's not a matter of need, Cruz. It's a matter of desire. You've always confused the two." I feel his muscles tense, hardening the slender air between us, even though he is not touching me. Not quite. Not yet.

If I had looked around, if I had turned to face him, his jaw would have been rigid as steel. If I had turned, so much would have changed.

"You can't be serious. You'd go all that way, to Naples, to a place you've never been, to a man you know only from a race track? You must be mad."

I smile. How can I not? It is the finely addled logic of a desperate man.

"Paso, your good friend? Are you going to speak ill of him, then?" I could keep the smile out of my voice, but I don't. One takes pleasure where one can.

He is silent, just as he should be: a word against Paso will always reverberate. Count on it. Pasonombre is tuned to any whisper, any place. The air of our planet is too thin, too translucent, to hide in.

Nor is it true, as Cruz implies, that Paso is a stranger to me. Such knowing between Paso and myself, it does not come in increments of time, though I have known Paso for years, as my father's associate, his benefactor, an owner of race horses. For the six years I lived with my father after my mother's death, Paso was our eccentric Italian visitor whom we escorted to the tracks—an enormous, ivory-suited continent of a man, whose private jet descended each month or so with no more plan nor warning than a moth on an unlit night. He came to immerse himself, to scrutinize the feverish crowds of an American racetrack. He purchased Thoroughbreds from my father; they won, they lost. None of this interested Paso. It was the mutation of time and space he sought.

Those such as we, Paso and I: we are never strangers even should our paths never cross. Our kinship makes folly of the blood.

At the track, we dined with the others, waited for my father to take his bourbon, stagger through the lobby, ascend to his room alone. And then, to appease our hunger, we talked the night away—he, a man in search of kin; I, a woman in search of a soul. In his wide, thickly fleshed body, the blood there is more nearly mine than that volatile brand which fuels the charming, black-haired man whose name I bear.

"It's ridiculous. I'll not have it." Cruz pauses, waits. The silence stretches. The rain taps at the window. Finally: "Why?"

He has come to it at last, knowing even as he asks that it is the wrong question, the one which puts the end to us, for such answers are ever moving just west of where we stand. I speak the truth, knowing he cannot hear it.

"Why not? It's time."

Truth, the one which grows mountains, is an elegant, simple construct. Its strength is its utter, uncompromising simplicity, too complex for language—it is that singular thing, of one piece. It cannot be multiplied, divided, distilled, pulled apart this way and that; cannot be raveled, picked apart; not dissected, explicated, castigated.

Truth: it is simple as a marble.

"You bitch."

Yes, of course. His hands rise, as though the bone, the flesh, the weight of them has gone. They rise, then fall light as birds on my shoulders.

"Cordelia."

I turn to him then. His eyes are gray, pale, the color of ice. No color at all. His hair, the frames of his glasses, his suit—all pewter. The color of rain against an afternoon window.

"It's not coming. I phoned." He does not speak the words, he breathes them. His hands are on my shoulders again, hard this time. He pulls me to him. His voice carries authority, the father voice, the voice of the Director of the Lab. His Lab, his and Paso's. "Stay a day, talk this over. You're behaving like a child."

I pull away. "And you're behaving like a bully."

His jaw tightens. He glances at the window behind me. "I doubt the planes are even flying in this mess. Even so, it's not safe. A day isn't going to make any difference, and you'll see—"

"I'll see tomorrow exactly what I see now." I go to his desk and pick up the phone. There is no dial tone.

"Look, Cord. You don't understand who Mr. Pschari is, what he does. He's…"

I whirl at him, the dead receiver still in my hand. "And you do? What is it Paso does, then? What is it that you do for him at the Lab? Tell me, change my mind."

He cannot, of course; it would be the end of him. No matter. I suspect, have long suspected, even before I met Simon Cruz at Churchill two years ago when he joined his friend Paso at the track. Paso's Company is an enterprise which does not bear talking about. I do not know the specifics, but I know enough. I am bored. I itch for diversion.

Cruz looks away. He is twenty years my senior, two years my lover. Cruz is history. Still, no woman should underestimate such men as these—fueled not by love nor habit, but by a tyrant's sense of lawful occupancy. I smile at him, inhale the odor of him, step out of my shoes and drag my toe across the mauve carpet where we have lain many times in the sun, behind the locked door where the secretary sits guard in the outer office.

"Maybe you should tell Frieda to cancel your afternoon appointments?"

In the brief time he confers with her, I slip his spare MG keys from the file cabinet into my pocket and later—some time later— saying I will wait in the lobby for him, I drive the MG to the Albuquerque airport. A simple thing, really.

1982. Fifteen years ago. Time melts as easily as flesh, leaving this dried and wrinkled hour. I watch the man through the window and understand he is such a one.

14

I'VE BEEN IN THE SOUTHWEST, I've seen enough adobe houses they don't give me jitterbugs anymore. But walking into Willis Zoloman's reminded me of my first time in a house pulled right up out of the ground, made with dirt bricks stacked one on top another. I stood looking around at the whitewashed, wavy walls and rolling corners, thinking that what it came down to was a matter of disposition. If you're from the Midwest like me, your first adobe is more likely than not going to set you running back to those straight rows of corn and that white frame house with every corner measured close enough to fit a T-square. But if you've the temperament to stay awhile, not minding the occasional centipede or scorpion, you'll find the two-feet-wide dirt adobes will keep you cool on a scorching day, warm on the coldest night. You'll come to stroke those walls when the mood takes you, feeling like the earth's reached right up and cradled you, holding you easy in her own rhythm. I've known folks who'd rather swing in trees than live in a house with square corners. For those like me who can't abide a straight line, an adobe house is made to fit.

Zoloman and I stood in a large, sunlit room that was sparsely furnished with a few Adirondack chairs and small tables. A white-washed kiva fireplace with its arched opening occupied one corner, surrounded by an acre of glowing Saltillo tiles that reflected light from the windows. But the austerity of the open floor space was more than compensated for by the walls. They were crowded with Indian weavings, textured prints, charcoal rubbings, objects inside niches, and hundreds of old yellow photographs in antiquated frames. As I followed Zoloman across the room toward a door near the rear of the house, he pointed out the ceiling of tiny polished *latillas*, some original lath and plaster construction, along with tidbits of the house's history. But then the light was behind us, and we were moving along a narrow, dark hallway with our footsteps echoing off the walls. In the meager light, Zoloman's moss-colored jacket swayed ahead of me.

Jesus Christ, Gracie Lee, you need to be put away you're so gullible, walking right into a man's house where you've come looking for a killer...

I tried to silence my paranoia by focusing on the corridor. On the left was a series of closed doors; on the right, a solid wall—the backside of the house, I realized, butted up against the ridge. On both sides, the wall space was hung with row after row of the faded sepia photos, a long cloistered gallery of pale, dead people. Or maybe not. In spite of the gloom, I noticed that all the prints seemed to contain a blonde woman. I glanced uneasily back, toward the receding doorway of the adobe room, then faced forward just in time to avoid bumping into Willis Zoloman's shoulder as he stopped. Then he stepped aside for me to enter.

We stood at the threshold of a huge country kitchen—open-beamed ceiling, brick floor, large fireplace flanked by a rocker and a spindly table piled with books, papers, pencils. A wall of small-paned windows looked out over a terrace and grape arbor. Next to a door leading to the terrace sat a broad kitchen table. It was an oddly archaic kitchen, the kind that might have belonged to somebody's grandmother. Round-topped refrigerator, gas range with double ovens and blue ceramic handles, open-faced cabinets with neatly stacked white dishes, battered wood countertops. Not an electric gadget in sight—no can opener, microwave, not even a toaster.

"Cream? Sugar?"

Zoloman had gone to the stove and was setting a tray with cups, pouring coffee from a battered aluminum percolator with a glass knob on top. I nodded and sat at the table while he hummed and smiled placid as a hausfrau. Maybe it was seeing him this way, harmless enough, that set my anxiety on a different track, imagining Rachael returning to the truck, finding me gone, Rachael who was not Rachael—

"I'm a photographer," Zoloman said. He had glided up to the table and eased the tray down while I stared blindly at the wall where more sepia prints hung over the table. He sat across from me, and with his elbows propped on the table, cup in both hands, Zoloman talked about photography and computer splicing, about freelancing for *National Geographic*, his shows in Chicago, Mexico City, London. His recent semi-retirement. He talked easily, without pause, like he'd been wound up with a key and set loose...like he didn't notice the person across from him was maybe going into cardiac arrest.

Because suddenly the photos had come into focus. What I'd taken as old pictures were actually modernist compositions. In all of them, a blonde had been costumed in period attire. In one, she wore a knee-length swimming suit and aimed a beach ball at the camera while behind her a well-endowed Bay Watch hunk surfed a wave wearing nothing but a G-string. In another, she stood over a stove in a housedress and frilly apron, unaware of the faces peeking in through a dark window, the nearest with the unmistakably mad eyes of Charlie Manson. At the center of the arrangement, in the largest of the photos, the blonde sat in profile, wearing high-heeled shoes with bows, her legs crossed at the ankle with their lower portion cased in shiny silk stockings. Her narrow, calf-length skirt matched a jacket with wide lapels, a bow at her throat. Her pale, nearly white hair was brushed back in deep waves after the fashion of my mother's time. On her knees, a chubby baby grasped her index fingers with its tiny hands. The woman and child smiled into each other's eyes. Clouds hovered above a background of winter trees. No, not trees. Looking closer, I saw that what I'd taken as a wintry landscape was actually a napalmed battlefield, littered with corpses and the nearly dead who crawled along, dragging torn or severed body parts behind them. In the lower right corner of the photograph was penciled neatly, ZOLOMAN.

My paranoia was back on track one, shooting up to critical mass. I eyed the terrace door behind Zoloman: was it locked? how fast was he? could I make it back down the hallway, out the front door...

"...tired of traveling. I thought I would try something new, live in one place for longer than a month." He stopped talking and smiled at me over his coffee cup with the euphoric, vapid expression of the very young or the feeble-minded.

I wanted to get out of here, but what could I say? *Well, hey, this has all been very interesting, Willis, but you're too weird for words. You're scaring the holy shit out of me, Willis, and you don't have a clue.*

We looked at each other as the silence stretched out. My smile felt etched on. Not that he noticed. He had begun to gaze around the room with that blissful sheen in his eyes, like the old guys at Mt. Havens used to get in the last stages of Alzheimer's. When his eyes came to rest on the pictures, he said, low and almost to himself, that photography was not only his vocation, it was also his passion.

"Life is meaningless, is it not," he said, his gaze drifting down to me, slow as autumn leaves, "without passion?" His lids hung nearly closed, but beneath them, his eyes stared into mine with such intense and unconscious longing that I suspected he was still seeing the woman in the photos. "The woman. You noticed nothing unusual about her?"

I looked up at the pictures again, studied the pale hair, the remote eyes—a stunning woman in that glacial, bloodless way of some blondes. An edgy quality, too. Some tautness of the spine? The way her lips didn't quite meet? I shrugged and shook my head. Which seemed to amuse him.

"Well, of course, she was a woman of a certain age in the early fifties, so she would be quite elderly now if she were still alive, which she is not. However, I would hazard to guess that most people, not knowing that, would..." The vacant expression gave way to the amused look I'd seen at the mailbox. "They would take *you* as the model. Without the twigs, of course." He glanced up at my hair.

Twigs? I swept my hand over my head. Or tried to—my hair was a rat's nest of snarls and sticks and crispy things.

"Damn!" I shook my head violently, sending out a cloud of forest confetti that floated into my coffee, across the table, down to the floor. He laughed. I figured that meant he wasn't all that upset about the mess in his kitchen. And then I stopped shaking my head. I looked at him, and then at the pictures. It was true, the blonde woman and I could be twins. Only someone whose sole use of a mirror was to floss her teeth would have missed it. I'd been known to look at a plate glass window without recognizing my own reflection. To Julia's great amusement. I could hear her ear-splitting laugh, her cackle filling the kitchen.

"What's wrong?"

Without warning, tears stung my eyes. I squeezed them shut, clenched my fists. When I felt his hand on my arm, I pulled away. He'd put down his coffee and was staring in total bewilderment.

Nutcase: I can read a man's eyes when I have to.

"It's just...my best friend, she's...Julia Simmons, you might have heard about...about her death."

He shook his head, and I remembered how oddly empty his house was of modern fixtures. No television, newspaper, not even a radio, though I figured somewhere there must be a computer, given his eccentric photos. I told him about Julia, that she'd been found dead yesterday. I left out where she'd been found and that I was the prime suspect in a murder investigation.

"I am sorry to hear it," he said. "The newspaper woman, yes. I have heard of her. I knew she lived nearby. I knew her by reputation, of course, a person of great passion to have pursued such truths as she wrote. I am very sorry for your loss." He reached out and put his hand on my arm, and this time I let him. "A true friend is indeed a rare blessing."

Whatever fears I'd felt about Zoloman had passed. So the guy took weird photos, so what? They weren't nearly as weird as those melting clocks that Spaniard had painted. Still, a cloud of depression had descended. The anxiety nagging at the back of my mind returned full force. Rachael must have returned to the truck by now, wondering where I'd disappeared to. Maybe she'd hiked back to the bunkhouse, worried about her horse and eager to contact Jerry. Then I remembered the stack of IDs, and the anxiety cranked up another notch. And the sheriff—had he called the house, sent out a deputy, discovered me missing? Did he think I'd left town? Had he issued a warrant even as I sat here over coffee?

I pulled my arm away from Zoloman and began wringing my hands in my lap hard enough to hear the knuckles crack. I stood up quickly, startling Zoloman. "I'm really sorry to have barged in on you like this," I said. "I only meant to stop for a minute, introduce myself...I really have to be going." I edged toward the door. Feeling awkward, I stuck my hands in my pockets, and the right one fastened around the plastic bag with the notes. I recalled why I'd come here and felt my paranoia shoot up again.

"Certainly, certainly, I understand," Zoloman said in the placating tone used for overwrought children. He rose and opened the door. As I passed by him, I paused and glanced once more at the photos.

"That woman," I said. "Who is she?"

Zoloman, who had had been smiling benevolently into a shaft of morning sunlight, seemed to darken, recede. "My mother," he said. "She died shortly after my birth."

"I'm sorry."

"*Es la vida.*" He bowed his head slightly and followed me across the terrace. "It happens. She was from Mexico, where I was raised. It was a very long time ago, many years have passed, but..." He stopped and stared into the shadows of the grape harbor at a redwood table scattered with books and papers and a mug of coffee. "There are occasionally events in one's life which do not dim with time. Such events, they become our obsessions, do they not?"

From someone else, it might have been a rhetorical question; for Willis Zoloman, I didn't think so. We had that in common, anyway. I knew about obsessions, about how some memories, say the scent of a woman's hair, were so fragile you stored them away like pressed flowers, wrapped carefully and hidden deep in a secret drawer. But there was another kind of memory, caught in the click of a camera in the mind's eye, some accidental, horrifying image burned in the retina, made of iron and impervious to time. I wondered which kind of memory was driving Zoloman.

We stood shoulder-to-shoulder as he pointed out a path that ran along the other side of the house and back to the road where my truck was parked. I could smell the sunlight rise from the fabric of his jacket, see the quixotic mix of light and shadow that slipped across his face as he gazed toward the path. Some chord of memory, some ancient and long-lost refrain rose and dissolved so quickly that it was not much more than a catch in my breath, gone before I could recognize it.

"*Vaya con Dios,*" he whispered, lowering his head slightly as I turned to leave.

Leaving the terrace, I passed the redwood table, glanced down to see *The San Jose Mercury* spread open, its pages weighted under a coffee cup which sat just beside the bold-faced heading: REPORTER DEAD AT 83. I kept walking and didn't look back.

The path was well-traveled, cut into the ridge with sloping switchbacks, and I hurried along it, eager to put distance between me and Willis Zoloman. It dropped me into a canyon and then paralleled a stream rustling through a thick band of trees. When the path forked, the left side veered west, across the stream by means of a narrow bridge, while the right, according to Zoloman, would take me to the road where my truck was parked. I headed east, then stopped.

I admit to curiosity. I considered the bridge, wondering who walked this path and why the bridge was there and where the path led on the other side of it. I went over to the bridge and watched the stream rush along just inches below my feet. The bridge was surrounded by dense trees, and the air was damp and chill and loud. The foliage shut out the sky and blocked a view of whatever lay on the other side. I thought I caught a movement in the vegetation farther down the bank, but squinting into the shadows, I saw nothing. The hair along the back of my neck began to rise, and I turned and walked a quick clip back down the path. I followed the right fork and, with more relief than I wanted to admit, shortly broke into a clearing with the dirt road and my truck just ahead. Rachael, however, was nowhere in sight.

I walked along considering what to do next. Enough time had passed that I'd calmed down about all those driver's licenses. In fact, I thought, there wasn't any particular reason to bring them up, was there? Didn't I have enough on my mind? Whatever the woman was up to was her business, and—

She stepped out of the shadows on the other side of the truck, grinning and matching me step-for-step so that we reached the vehicle together. She was a long, tall woman, thin as a willow, and all that black she wore from head to toe was unbelievably sticker-free, her hair conspicuously twigless. Looking over the cab of the truck, she looked at my hair, grinned and lifted a brow. Then her eyes dropped to the turtleneck. *Her* turtleneck. Her grin disappeared. My hand shook as I fitted the key in the lock, opened the door, scooted in and reached across the seat to unlock the passenger side—leaning right across the green bag I'd left on the seat. Rachael didn't seem to be bothered. She set it on the floor, got in, closed the door.

I leaned forward to start the engine.

"No."

15

I'VE HEARD THE WORD *NO* BEFORE; I've heard gunshots before, too. They'd never sounded this much alike, though. I eased my hand off the key. She wasn't lounging in the corner anymore; she was practicing her posture, her spine arrow-straight, eyes hitting mine like an electrical charge.

"Okay." She glanced down at the ruined turtleneck. "So you don't like waiting. I can understand that, neither do I." Her voice was hard. Each word came out perfect and shiny as a silver bullet, no trace of the rust and dents and strums a human being's language picks up by misuse through the years. "You decided to follow me, but you were cold. You found a sweater in my bag. You put it on, took off uphill. Am I calling it right so far?"

I nodded. "More or less."

She wore the kind of tight, mean look I've known some shrinks to have, that Daddy DeWitte had when he was on a roll. It was a look that made your mouth turn to cotton. It said you were safer to tell than hide whatever it was you were thinking of hiding. So I explained about looking for a jacket. Finding the checkbooks. Every word I said, she looked tighter and meaner. When I finished, she kept her eyes aimed at me a few seconds, then turned away. She stared out at the trees for a long time.

I stared at them too, what else was I going to do? We sat there like that, the two of us, looking straight ahead like we were at a drive-in movie, watching something too good to bear talking through. I knew all about this kind of waiting. I'd been here before. It was like the time I'd stood up and waited for the judge to read the verdict, to tell me whether I was going to live or die. Or like the time on Death Row when the guard brought my last meal while I was still waiting to hear from the governor.

When Rachael broke the silence, she kept watching the trees. "Here's the deal, Frost," she said. Her words had no inflection, like she'd trimmed them down to bone. "I could give you a story about the IDs. I could make up something you would believe because I can be very convincing. But mostly you would believe it because you want to. Because it is easier to believe it than to believe the truth. There is not much to telling a good lie if you know what the other person wants to hear." She paused, and I watched the way the cord of muscle tightened right behind her jawbone. When she spoke again, she put in some highs and lows the way a normal person will. "But this morning, you told me some hard truths about your own story. That took a lot of courage. If I lied to you now, I'd be mocking that courage. I'm not going to do that, so we're doing it the hard way." She looked around at me. "We're going for the truth, Frost."

My nerves were shot. I didn't want to go for the truth. I wanted to do it the easy way, like she said first. But she didn't ask me what I wanted, so we sat there while she talked and I listened.

She started off telling a story about a kid. At first I thought she was fooling around, spinning a kind of "once upon a time" yarn about this poor little rich girl, Cordelia Krevlin, raised on a Thoroughbred bluegrass farm in Kentucky. As she talked and I pictured rolling green pastures, I started getting that sappy Jello feeling like you do watching those old movies, say *Life with Father*. That's the one where the family's chatting over dinner, mom's sneaking the pup a snack under the table, dad's pretending not to notice and reaching for the mashed potatoes, his smile and his cufflinks flashing. The kind of family where the little girl goes to bed, slips under the covers in her nightgown and reads a few pages of *Nancy Drew* before she switches the light off. So then you're sitting in a dark theater, the screen black a second or two, feeling sad and a little sorry for yourself because you didn't have a family like that.

But they don't make movies like that anymore. Today's directors are truth junkies. You watch a movie and find yourself getting that sappy feeling, you've been set up by somebody like Oliver Stone. A sliver of light will suddenly cut across the black screen, door opens a crack, you see a hand on the doorknob, a flash of cufflink, the blade of light on the bed. Then the door closes. It's dark again, but a different kind of dark. The kind that's too big, the kind that lasts too long and is shattered by the sound of Daddy's zipper, the bed squeaking, the pumping noises that would make it X-rated if the lights had stayed on.

I digress. That wasn't Rachael's story. In her version, it was the mom, not the little girl, that was having trouble being beat nearly to death by the daddy.

"I didn't remember that part till many years later, though," Rachael said to the trees. "After leaving the shelter in Louisville, we ended up living in a women's commune in Indiana with a woman named Claire. Those were good years. Till the FBI burned the place down in '73."

The FBI siege against the women's commune. I knew about that, me and the rest of the country. Eighty-three women and children went up in flames that day. I'd watched it on television with everybody else at Mt. Havens, but I'd also heard about it firsthand from Julia who'd been there to investigate the official version of what happened. It was a sad story and a bad story, but what did it have to do with all those driver's licenses?

"After the fire, I was alone. It seemed natural enough to return home to my father. Like so many abused women, my mother never uttered a word against him, never talked about why she'd left, just that she had to leave and to trust her and not ask questions. So in my mind, he sat on the same shelf with the saints and Clark Gable and Tara. He was still raising and selling Thoroughbreds, still partying at the track on weekends, rubbing elbows with all those people he sold horses to. People high on money and low on ethics, whose net worth as human beings was equal to the balance of their checkbooks. I didn't like them much. I was luckier than my father—I didn't have to.

"It didn't take long to see he was not only a drunk, but a tyrant with a nasty temper. I went to the track with him because I was bored and restless and I loved to watch the horses run. That's where

I met Pasonombre. He was an Italian tycoon who flew in one day a month from Milan to see the races. He'd arrive in his private jet on a Saturday morning, a hulking Buddha of a man dressed always in white linen suits and lumbering down the stairs from his plane with this beatific smile on his face. He was someone..." She stopped and closed her eyes. A sliver of sun had slanted into the cab, slipping through the tree branches, touching her lips, showing her nostrils widen as she took a deep breath and opened her eyes. "He was someone I felt an immediate kinship to, like we shared the same mind, the same blood. He and I, we were spiritual doubles," she said, staring at the trees, "father and daughter. We both had..."

The sun had heated the cab, and I rolled down my window, felt the relief of the cool, woodsy air, the bird sounds. I don't think she noticed. She was all wrapped up in her story, like she'd gone back in time.

"It's hard to describe, there's no word for it." She frowned. "Call it intuition. Paso and I both have an overdeveloped intuitive sense. He was a fascinating man to talk to. I lived for his visits, for that one Saturday night a month when the two of us talked into the dawn about the nature of this world, the meaning of it all, the possibility of a spiritual dimension. That's when I first began to understand some extraordinary things about myself. That the flashes of...insight, yes, call it that...the flashes of insight I'd always had since I was a kid were not available to other people. Or rather, available to them, but ignored, discounted, even ridiculed. And then I could understand why I'd always felt that odd sense of isolation from other people. Because when talking to Paso I was, for the first time in my life, no longer alone, and I could look back from where we sat, see my former isolation, understand how I had come to be so solitary.

"One day Paso showed up at the track with a colleague, a man I found irresistibly attractive. I'd been fairly sheltered, I guess. I'd never met anyone like Simon Cruz—a polished, arrogant man with something lethal about him. Simon played life with absolute concentration, no attention to anything but winning. Like his chess game, his every move was calculated, every word a strategy. I lived with him in Santa Fe for two years, and he taught me a great deal—

once he'd recognized that faculty Paso had made me aware of, a 'hypersensitivity to my environment,' as he referred to it. He became obsessed with competing with me, making a game of everything, pitting his rational approach against my intuitive one. With Simon, it was all about control. He taught me how to get it, how to use it, how to keep it.

"But it's ironic, isn't it? You get the knack of stacking the odds in your favor so you win every game, then you're so bored with winning you don't even want to play. When that happens, you're in serious trouble, because it's the nature of the mind to deplore monotony. Who doesn't secretly despise an effortless win? So the mind will jazz things up a little, raise the stakes. It'll start sending its midnight henchmen out to sabotage you every chance it gets. Count on it—the minute you start believing you've got a handle on something, you'll be left standing in the middle of the road every time holding nothing but a cup in your hand. So one night, I'm in bed, lights out, staring up at the ceiling and feeling dried out, flat, needing a change. I wasn't all that surprised when the phone rang. Paso was on the same wave length, offering me a job. He'd told me often enough I was a natural for his Company. I left for Milan the next day."

"His *Company*?" She'd said it like it was in capitals letters, so I fed her the obvious question. I didn't mind. She had a story to tell, and she was going to tell it. She grinned at the middle distance.

"Paso, he's like a general contractor. Like the guy building a house, calling in the subs, lining up the right plumber, the best electrician. Except Paso's a world-class contractor. No specialty. Any service you want performed, he provides...the subs, customized professionals to do the job. Satisfaction guaranteed. For the really challenging work, he trains specialists in his own school. A required two-year education for those of us with unusual..." She smiled, "intuitive abilities."

It was the smile that chilled me right down to where my white knuckles gripped the steering wheel. Not the smart-ass smile, but a cold, flat-liner cousin. She looked around, speaking in her husky voice, letting the words hold meaning like storm clouds hold rain. "I was one of Paso's specially educated professionals, a 'Research Specialist' according to my job title."

Research specialist? I looked at Rachael and saw her wearing glasses, a pencil stuck over her ear, working in a carrel in the entrails of university library stacks. But the eyes and smile didn't fit. I doubted any university research assistant packed that kind of expression. Maybe kamikaze pilots. Maybe sadists working the electrocution controls.

"Basically," she said, turning back to the trees, "I gather information. I can put together more data on you than you know exists, read it and digest it and know you like you can't believe anyone could ever know you. When I'm done researching you, I can look at the world through your eyes. I can see it the way you see it. I can tell you what car you'll rent at Avis, what hotel you'll stay at, what dinner you'll order, what movie you'll watch afterwards. I can tell you what route you'll take home on any given day, how you'll dress for bed that night. I can hum a tune before you know there's a song in your brain." She turned and hit me dead center with her gaze. "I can be in your dreams, or I can be your worst nightmare."

The old heart gave a mean thump. It had been a bad-news morning right from the start—a sedative hangover, followed by an adrenalin roller coaster ride compliments of Willis Zoloman. But the heart is a muscle, isn't it? The harder it works, the stronger it gets. Up to a point. I suspected I'd passed that point.

"Not to worry, Frost," she said, and I felt myself relax like a discarded puppet. "You're safe. I'm not working for Paso now. A few years back, I walked off an assignment, a serious breach of contract for a Company employee. I may not be Numero Uno anymore, but I still rank high on Paso's most wanted list, though he'd probably let it pass if it weren't for the bad example I set for the others. Paso aside, your worst enemy is always going to be the guy whose ego outweighs his dick. When I defected, I left my old buddy Cruz holding a whole bag full of hot potatoes. It's Cruz who wants to nail my ass if he can find me." She shrugged a shoulder, lifted an eyebrow, glanced at the green bag by her feet. "Never hurts to have a little spending money and a few phony names when you're playing the game."

A little spending money? Five million dollars?

"Hey, I was a pro, the best there was. You think I work cheap?" She flashed a smile before turning back to the trees.

The morning had faded. The slip of sunlight had widened, hitting the windshield and washing over us. Rachael didn't seem to notice. When she spoke next, her voice was iron.

"Listen carefully, Frost. I've spent more time than I should thinking about guilt and absolution and who's pulling the strings and divine intervention. I'll lay you five to one any day of the week including Sundays that the only afterlife for our rotting asses is what we can push up in a seedbed through a pile of seasoned horse shit. That being the case, you can see that the whole game board is in the here and now, all up to me and you and the next dude to figure out whether the prize is worth the penalty you pay if you get caught. And if you play the game well enough that your odds of getting nailed are nil to zip, you can do anything you want without penalty. That's a win, Frost. Any way you look at it, that's a win."

Her words chilled my blood. "You sound like that guy you mentioned. Cruz."

She turned her head slow, without moving a muscle on the rest of her body. Birds can do that. Snakes too. Her gaze reminded me of what I'd read about the Medusa, and I looked away, into a blinding ray of sun. I couldn't see, and all I could hear were her words coming out of the brilliance.

"You've something about you, Frost. I can pick it up like radar. Some scent coming off you that reeks of virtue."

That's when I knew Rachael, or whatever her name was, was just one more whacked-out nutcase hauling ass on a California freeway, stopped in her tracks by an earthquake. Even on the outside chance she really had been some hotshot "Specialist" with hyperactive intuition, it needed an overhaul, because I'd lived with a man of god, my father, long enough to know I was not a woman of virtue. It was odd, though, the way she'd spit out the word. *Virtue.* "You make it sound like a disease," I said.

"It could be an incapacitating handicap in some circles."

Maybe, but I didn't want to know about those circles. Mostly, I wanted to get the hell out of here. Out of this remote forest. Out of this truck with this very spooky woman. I shielded my eyes against the sun and reached for the ignition. "Guess we don't run in the same circles," I said, turning the key.

"The thing is," she said, clamping her hand like a vise over mine, "you don't know yourself very well, Frost. That's an even bigger handicap. In any circle. For example, let me ask you a question." Her arm pressed against mine, her skin felt warm, and her grip was the kind that cracked bones. Our faces were inches apart. "Let me ask you a perfectly ordinary question, and you give me a simple, straightforward answer. Nothing fancy. See what you come up with. Deal?" There was sarcasm in her tone, and her eyes that had been brown before had gone shiny and dark, almost black. "You're a very beautiful woman. You married a man twice your age. Why did you do that, Frost? Why did you marry Doctor Bruce DeWitte?"

I jerked away from her violently enough to wrench my hand from her grip. I drew back. Pressed myself into the corner of the truck. My heart was thumping hard, and my skin was clammy. Yet even in the hot spotlight of sun, I felt the ice begin to crystallize inside me. I struggled to take in great gulps of oxygen, but my throat had closed.

"Easy, Frost." Rachael was leaning over me, gripping my shoulder, but I was frozen in place. I couldn't speak, could only watch her lips moving: "I'm trying to tell you something, something I don't think you know. What's happening here, think of it as a kind of matrix of events—your discontent about your identity, then the notes coming, the most recent one tied to the snake that drove you to talk to Julia that night. Julia's death. Being at Harvey's yesterday, the earthquake. My horse being injured." She paused. She was so close her breath grazed my face like some tropical breeze. Her hand on my shoulder was a point of warmth that I focused on, feeling its heat penetrating the ice that had been spreading inside me. "And me," she said, "my presence here, right now…"

"I don't know what you're talking about," I said, still focused on the heat of her hand. On the idea of the heat she must have inside her. But my thoughts were cold, clumsy things. They were indifferent toads, lumbering through caverns of mud, climbing their long way up toward the light. "I thought…I thought you didn't believe in that kind of thing…you made your own rules and there was no punishment, no meaning.'"

"Okay, call it an arbitrary sequence of events, then. Pieces in a puzzle. There may be a maker of the puzzle, I'm not talking about that. I'm saying it doesn't matter if there is or not. I'm saying what matters is that we see the pieces, we put them together. We see a picture or…"

Her black eyes glittered. Was she some kind of tuned-in prophet? Or merely mad? How could you tell the difference? "Or?"

"Or we don't," she said. "That's my point. The pieces are always there. It's up to us, it's our responsibility, our *burden* to see them, to explore the matrix. You want meaning, that's meaning in spades."

Her eyes had lost their feverish gleam. This close to her, I recognized the faint gardenia scent I'd noticed before. Except now it wasn't gardenia. It was some other older bloom out of the past. I couldn't place it—but not gardenia, not quite…

"Why?" she said. "Why did you marry him?"

…yet some flower of the night, all the same. Some vaguely female scent, a stolen night, a woman stepping from the shower, her hair damp with that white blossom smell. Oh Mary, oh my god Mary Bess…

Suddenly my thoughts, those sluggish frogs, cleared the mud, broke through the surface and into the brilliant light of the truck.

"A matrix?" I said. My throat was dry, and my voice was so hoarse the words seem to come from someone else: "And you? What about your matrix?"

16

Morgan

"...what about your matrix?"

It must have been that thunder cracked in some silent, parallel universe, and its lightning chose here to strike. That would explain why, as I stare into the eyes of Killer Frost, the sunlight suddenly ignites her hair, sending flames pinwheeling around her face. And why (her features dark inside the glare) the past stares back at me. I see the old woman from the desert church.

Was it yesterday? The day before? Last week? Have I only imagined that desert place? Contrived the locusts, their translucent skins cracking underfoot as I crossed the sand, pushed open the church door? Only my imagination dreaming an old crone inside a blade of sun, a crow stretching its wings, pointing west: vaya!

("Oh yes, Morgan, my child," says the darkness inside the fire. " What about your matrix?")

I am ungrounded, thrown off balance. Some mystery charms the darkness, sucking at me like a vortex, a whirlpool. I grip the woman's eyes: I am not lost, not yet. I feel the hard bench of the truck pressing against my thighs. I smell the old oil smell that lives in vehicles past their prime. I hear the drumbeat of my heart. I see in my mind's eye a map, the North American continent, myself an infinitesimal dot located 36 degrees latitude north, 121 degrees longitude west. My name is Cordelia Morgan, and I am a woman in transit, staring at the one called Grace. Yet it is as though I see her for the first time, seeing her darkness spread inside the flames, reconfigured into the old crone's face, reconfiguring again into another face so familiar it is not unlike my own, though framed with fire and set with screaming eyes. A face distorted by pain, immortalized on the old newsreel I have played countless times: the burning figure running toward the camera, her arms reaching out, her hair aglow, her mouth a perfect flaming O. How many times those years following the fire did I hit the stop frame button, zoom in, magnify the face until it filled the screen? Examine every frozen melting pixeled pore to reconstruct how flesh must once have fitted on her bones, what shape the eyes till shocked from their sockets? I measured this face against my mother's with the mindless urgency of an addict, driven to know if it were she, yet paralyzed by some nameless dread from probing the mystery of her death. Obsessed nevertheless until that day, all those years ago, when Paso, taking pity, had silenced the screams...

"Mystery occurs, does it not, when what resides in the mind and what lies in the heart do not match?"

The year is 1985, a few days after my graduation from The Company School. Paso studies the glossy photograph included in the dossier of a Venezuelan despot whose regime is predicated on terror and drug trafficking, though the man fosters a public image of beneficence. A newspaper clipping beside the photo shows him dedicating a new children's hospital.

"This conflict is at the heart of every mystery. It is the passionate counterpoint between appearance and that which lives below it that creates a fine and delicate suspense, almost sensuous if you but pause to savor it."

We are in Paso's office: white walls, white floor tiles, white metal file cabinets covering one wall, white Venetian blinds throwing strips of sun across the ceiling. We sit at a long conference table in the center of the room, the two of us. The last course in the two-year Company program was the one requiring psychoanalysis and self-hypnosis sessions where I have recovered the childhood memories which now torment me—the screams of my mother, the sound of her body being thrown against the walls. Those screams—so like those of the burning woman in the newsreel. For days before this meeting with Paso, I have measured their pitch, one to the other. A duet of horrors shrills through my brain and through every waking hour. Fills this room to bursting.

Perhaps Paso, sitting so near, hears them as he explains my first assignment, running his finger along the Venezuelan's thin, cruel lips while he lays out the man's background. I watch Paso from the corner of my eye. He had never met my mother, yet how could he discern this despot's cruelty and not have detected my father's? Had he known all along?

Paso stops speaking, looks into the middle distance. His eyes are heavy-lidded under the immense bald dome of his head. After a long silence, he sighs.

"Your past has found you, figlia. It calls to you, does it not?" He considers the Venezuelan's portrait again. "Left unexplored, your past will harbor events which, like a tiger crouched in the jungle, can spring at you, be used against you by your enemies. It is crucial, therefore, that every Employee retrieves the past before receiving an assignment." He looks at me. "But you, figlia, you have an unnatural, sometimes maddening, penchant for shining light into every forbidden crevice. You do not yet understand the virtues of darkness, of the unknown. This naiveté, coupled with your other abilities, will make you a superb research specialist, but one who quests so ruthlessly for truth will travel a solitary and difficult path" In the glow of his eyes, I sense the warning, the slightly sulfuric odor of admonition: "A dangerous path."

But my mind will not still. It swarms with women's screams. My own story so fills my head that words burst into the room, describing the new memories, sounds of my father hitting my mother, how her screams recall those of the burning woman in the newsreel. I must know, I tell him, I must know if it is my mother Rachael who screams to me from inside the flames. A dead sea of silence spreads across the room. At last, Paso directs me to visit his villa the following evening, bring the newsreel.

The night of my visit has no moon. I approach his study in darkness, from the rear, as always. Somewhere a fountain fills the night with water sounds. The French doors stand open; backlit by a dim lamp in the corner, Paso waits behind his desk. My steps are too loud on the polished wood floor. I lay the video before him and take the chair opposite. I cannot see his face. He is but a great hulking darkness against the meager light.

"Did you know?" I ask.

My question is not a non sequitur to Paso, as it might have been to any other. Nor is it a question, quite, with its edge of criticism. For a long time, the only sound in the room is the water from the invisible fountain. At last he picks up the video, pushes himself heavily from the chair.

He turns and walks away, into an adjoining room which is dark save for the ghost light of a computer monitor. He sits before it, inserts the cassette into a player, and the video of the burning woman appears on the screen. We watch the image running toward us. He freezes the screen, magnifies the woman till the face alone remains. He saves the image to clipboard, switches to another program, pastes the face onto a white background. He presses several keys, and suddenly the face is electrified, flashing blue as though jolted by lightning, then transformed into a tangle of swirling wires. He minimizes the program, switches to another blank screen, then opens a manila folder lying beside the keyboard. Inside is a picture of my mother I recognize from the scrapbooks of my childhood. I do not know how he has acquired the picture; I do not ask. He places the photograph in a scanner beside the computer monitor, presses several keys, and my mother's face appears on the screen. He applies to it the same electrification process, the same tangle of wires as before. And then the screen goes black with a line of pulsing dots racing across it, replaced in a few moments by flashing red words: NO MATCH!

Later, after I follow Paso's lumbering shape through the darkness and he opens the door to my car, he says: "You have your answer, figlia. A piece to the puzzle. You are young, susceptible to appearances. You will understand someday that every picture is an illusion, only the pieces are real."

...we see the pieces, we put them together...

I stare into the flickering darkness of the Frost woman's face and see there not the old crone or even the flaming woman from the newsreel, but a host of women gathered behind the flaming one, eighty-three dead souls who had fled their homes, forsaken their histories to collect in a women's commune in the Midwest, where that day the fire burned so long and hot that their incinerated remains were little more than piles of ash among the rubble. I cleave to the darkness, hold fast to it, as though to relinquish it would be to give up my very life. Yet the screams of the burning women batter me like an angry sea, great punishing waves of sound that pierce my ears, my heart, imploring the air for retribution.

And then the blinding sunlight is gone, and the woman before me is no longer in flames. No crone in black lace. No gathering of women screaming their singular outrage. She is Grace Frost, daring to throw my words back to me:

what's happened here is a matrix...Julia, her death...Julia...

Her eyes touch mine, wide and hazy as the eyes of the dead, as the eyes of Julia Simmons staring up at me from inside the trunk.

I lean forward and examine the fine, encrypted fabric of her flesh, see in its reflective surface how we both have dragged our past behind us, have strung the years together like an entourage of rusted boxcars, pulled along on a shambling journey without destination or design. If the Frost woman has been manipulated and tricked out of time, I have been my own trickster, yet fooled all the same. It is easy now, from this unique perspective, to recognize that point where one wrong turn led into a labyrinth of lost years, each more meaningless than the last. So quickly, so easily, between one heartbeat and the next, I see my sojourn with Paso's Company, with Cruz before that, as adrenalin-drenched diversions, the mind's perverse way of betraying the screams that bide their time to be heard again. See, further, that life abides no waste, no loss—that even such amoral distractions as The Company's assignments have served their purpose: to hone my rough gifts into the polished instruments of my trade.

I plumb the surface of this woman before me, and know that though we are unlike in appearance as day and night, as sun and moon, yet we are both, I and she, hermetically sealed, preserved like plums, peaches, apples, plucked from our prime and sealed away from life. Stored in some subterranean vault until one day a hand gropes our darkness, pops the lid. Embalmed, resuscitated, returned to the world of the living, we are come at last unto this day, this moment.

I feel the planet slowing. It grinds to a stop on its axis as the platinum woman leans toward me, and our lips meet.

PART III

Mirage

17

THIS WASN'T LIKE KISSING MARY BESS AT ALL. Not even close. This was more like the antelope consorting with the tiger. Hot. Fast. Dangerous. And, most of all, stupid. Very stupid.

She sat back and draped an arm over the seat, crossed her legs, torqued up the grin on one side. My face was hot. I felt confused and uncertain.

"Look, I…if you think—" What I wanted to say was that I wasn't attracted to women, that I just happened to fall in love with a woman once, so many years ago it probably didn't even count anymore. But I didn't get the chance.

"Forget it, Frost. Say you're stressed out, say you've had a bad day or two, not in your right mind. Say whatever it is you've been saying for the last thirty-five years, and then let it go, because right now I need to know how you want to play this. You told me your story, I told you mine. You're in some trouble. I can help. Or I can disappear. Your call."

"Sounds to me like you've got troubles enough of your own without taking mine on. You're running from those people you used to work for, right? Why bother stopping here, helping me out? What's in it for you?"

Her look was penetrating. "I guess that's still the missing piece, isn't it?"

I avoided her eyes and started the engine. This time she didn't stop me. At my driveway, I pulled in. I figured I needed a pit stop before meeting the sheriff. While Rachael went to the bunkhouse to check her email, I changed clothes and tried to drag a comb through my hair. No way. The more I pulled, the tighter the tangles. Finally, as a last resort, I grabbed the scissors and began cutting. It took awhile. I cut out twig after twig, then snipped at what was left to even it up. All the while, I tried to push away thoughts of Rachael by focusing on my upcoming interview with the sheriff. I wasn't having anymore luck with that than with my hair—I remembered the way her lips had felt on mine, the quick hard press of her hand pulling me against her, the sharp adrenalin surge that turned on lights where none had shone for so many years I'd figured the lines were down and forever dead.

When my hair looked like rats no longer lived in it, even if they'd been chewing at it, I headed for the front door. On the table where Rachael and I sat this morning poring over the poems, I spotted her stack of colored note cards. I shoved them in my pocket. The dates and anniversaries we'd come up with might help the sheriff find who'd been sending the notes.

Rachael was already in the truck, slung back in her lounge lizard number. I slammed the door, started the engine.

"Cool," she said in authentic Valley Girl dialect, as she eyed my hair. "Like, you know, all it needs is purple dye."

I ignored her and pointed the truck down the driveway. But something was bothering me. When I came to the asphalt, I let the engine idle and wheeze while I turned to her, looking straight at her, but seeing that stack of checkbooks with all the different names. Then I saw the sheriff standing on my front porch yesterday afternoon, staring down into the trunk.

It seemed to me, sitting here in my old truck on this particular October morning, that the world is surely a most confounding place. That what you see in front of you, in plain sight of your own two eyes, holds more mystery than a person can rightly stand at any given time. Sometimes we forget that. Maybe that's why things happen the way they do, to remind us. To make us wonder about whether the universe operates on the laws of coincidence or cause and effect.

"What?" she said.

"I need to know something."

"Yeah?"

"What's your real name?"

She shook her head. "Jesus, Frost."

"You're the one talking about truth. Why tell part and not all?"

"That's not it. There's no advantage in knowing. Plus, there's a high probability you'll slip, use my real name, draw attention. People will wonder. I don't need that." I didn't respond. "For Christ's sake, Frost, it's just a name. Let it go."

I couldn't do it. "A person's name, it's part of them. You can't really know someone, you can't trust them, not without knowing their name."

After she told me it was Cordelia Morgan, "Morgan" would do, I pulled onto the road feeling an unreasonable relief, like we'd passed some hurdle, some bend in the road, and now we had a connection we hadn't had before. I began telling her about my visit to Zoloman's, but as we passed Julia's driveway, she interrupted.

"How did you come to know her?" she said, nodding at Julia's mailbox.

I kept my foot easy on the accelerator while my fingers tightened around the steering wheel. I could feel the tears, so I forced Julia's death into a secret room in my mind and locked the door. That way, for that short while, I could pretend she was alive, sitting up there in her house at the end of the driveway. That way I could drive along and tell this woman, Morgan, about the time all those years ago when Julia first sneaked into my room at Mt. Havens, the long string of years following as she kept writing articles and trying again and again to negotiate my release.

By the time we reached the state highway leading to Las Tierras and I'd finished my story, I was back in the present. The morning sun had headed west, and the only shade was minimal, not much available for the construction crew to eat their lunches in. The dozers that'd been busy the last few weeks removing every trace of plant life and scraping off the tops of hills for a new subdivision, were shutting down, the drivers jumping from their high cabs with lunch pails in their hands. Near the freeway ramp, a sign the size of a football field advertised Wild Oak Meadows, Country Living at Its Best. To one side, a smaller sign read Meyerson Construction, followed by a phone number. Several homes already perched on a flattened hilltop were near the final stages of construction, an uneasy mixture of Cape Cod and English Tudor, painted purple, green, and yellow, surrounded by raw red earth. Behind them a sprawling three-story condo complex completed several months ago had a line of residents' cars sheltered under a long row of carports.

"So how did you end up here, the two of you next door to each other?"

"It just happened, kind of on its own," I said. "Julia's folks had lived here for years. They died, left her the house. She'd use it when she wanted to get away from the newspaper business. She'd tell me about coming here, years before I ever got out, ever believed I would get out. She'd always figured to retire here." As I rounded a curve, Harvey's Pump & Go came into view. I edged into the left-turn lane. "Her retirement just happened to be close to the same time my sentence looked like it was finally going to be commuted, so she said if I wanted to live out here, she'd keep an eye out for a place. From the money my folks left. They died while I was inside. Well, it wasn't like I had all that many options. The property back in Indiana was sold, even if I'd wanted to go back there, which I sure as hell didn't. Daddy DeWitte, he'd died years ago. Julia was the closest thing I had to family."

I sat in the turn lane with the signal ticking, trying not to give in to the loneliness that'd just blindsided me like a cold wind. The sky wasn't blue anymore, it was that dead white like it gets in California when the air gets heated up and quits moving. Across the street, Harvey's Pump & Go was still doing a brisk business, in spite of the plywood nailed across the broken window. The collapsed overhang was gone, leaving two supporting uprights straight as obelisks at each end of the gas pump island.

"So Julia retired here, but wasn't she still working? You said she wrote a column or something for the local paper?"

"It was in her blood. Couldn't stay away from it," I said, turning left on Tierras Way, past Harvey's, heading into Las Tierras on the only street that will take you there from the freeway. It is a street that brooks no prevarication. It has no side streets segueing off it, no turnarounds for the faint of heart. Once you have taken that left turn, you're headed for Main Street with its layer of brick covering the fault line. It'd always struck me as a little odd, a little arrogant of whoever planned it, maybe somebody's idea of a joke. More likely, it was the Chamber of Commerce's plan to get some business downtown. Anyone wanting to meander around the outskirts, rubbernecking at the old historic buildings and the rambling mission, rummaging through the quaint galleries and strolling the narrow back streets, would first have to drive across that brick surface of the San Andreas fault.

"Sam Oliver, editor of the weekly here in town, he was tickled purple when she volunteered to be on his staff. She didn't have any ego about it. She'd do everything from covering 4-H shows to playing around with a gossip column. She wasn't the kind to think any story was beneath her, even though she'd broken some of the hottest stories of the century. Said her biggest regret was that she'd missed Watergate, couldn't stomach the DC scene, but she was right there when the SLA kidnapped Patty Hearst, and the Manson family was on their rampage, and the FBI was burning down that women's commune—" The words were out before I could stop them. I glanced around quickly.

"I recall seeing her byline. She ever talk about it?"

"Just what she wrote for the papers," I said. I slowed as the street narrowed into a tree-lined tunnel and the Sheriff's Office sign came into view just ahead. "But I know she really sunk her teeth into that one, even after all the hoopla had died away. She said once that that one had just about got her killed, but she'd stuck with it till she somehow got access to the FBI records, found out what she and a lot of other people had suspected all along, that the FBI knew that collective was just a bunch of unarmed women and kids and not a cover for a militant arsenal like they said. But that was a good while later, and she never did find any motive for the FBI's raid. Without that, it was hard getting any excitement generated. You know how it is—public's been saturated with it, heard all they want to hear. Even after Julia broke the story of the cover-up, it only got a few days TV coverage. People had had enough, they wanted to go on."

I turned into the dirt parking lot that'd once been somebody's front yard, set in front of the sheriff's office that'd once been somebody's home. It was a small bungalow, painted a dark russet color with bright turquoise trim around the windows. The scrub oaks around it had been left, so in spite of losing its front yard, the little house was set into a nest of deep shade. The parking lot was empty, and the office looked deserted.

What now? We could always sit and wait for the sheriff to come back, he'd probably gone off for lunch, but small towns keep odd ours. It was possible Hammersmith had closed up for the day...

"Frost?"

"Yeah?"

Big silence, and then: "You ever feel like what's past is past? Like in a few years, you're going to be dead anyway, nobody's going to remember something from twenty, thirty years ago that's not been made right? You ever feel like you're the only one walking the earth that remembers it, and pretty soon there won't even be you? Like the best thing to do is not just go on, but forget what's happened and go on?"

Her eyes burned into mine. I could feel the heat coming off her, like all the oxygen was being sucked out of the truck.

"You ever feel that way, Frost?"

I didn't want to think about it, but I did, sitting in the noon sun with the engine gasping and the truck wheezing and the dirt parking lot with not even a live ant crawling in it that I could see. I thought about the long string of yesterdays I drag along with me. Thought about the Doctor, the way he made love and the way he took to morphine and then heroin and then any other kind of mind-numbing substance he could lay his hands on. I thought about that night with Mary Bess and the way she looked with the water streaming in that gully between her breasts and down her belly when she stepped out of the shower. I thought about how people are alive one day, dead the next. I topped it off by thinking about Mt. Havens, all those long hallways of rooms full of folks who mostly were there not because they were crazy, but because somebody somewhere for some reason wanted them to be. And I thought about how Julia had believed in one of them.

"Nope," I said, "I can't say as I have."

Her grin made a spectacular climb right up the side of her beautiful face, all the way to her cheekbone. Her eyes were glowing. She let some seconds tick by, then nodded once. "Glad to hear it, Frost. That makes two of us." Her voice was deep and low, almost a whisper.

I was about to back the truck and head out.

"You're not going to check that note on the door?"

Sure enough, under one of those cardboard clocks where you move the hands to the time you'll be back, was a piece of yellow paper. I set the emergency brake and went to have a look. The clock face had both hands straight up, but since it was past noon, he could have meant midnight. Hammersmith was that kind of guy. In pencil was written: *I'm at 1210 Benton.*

"Well," I said, back in the truck, "he's on a case over on Benton. I guess we'll try back later, maybe go by the vet's first—"

"Where's Benton?"

I thought a minute, then reached over, opened the glove compartment, and found the town map. With some effort, I located Benton on the far east side. Boondocks.

"Looks like you need to get out more, get to know your hometown," Morgan said. "How about we take a drive? From the note, I'd say the sheriff's open to us finding him there."

All the time I'd lived in Las Tierras, I'd kept to the business strip or the main drag. I wondered what kind of street Benton was, why the sheriff had gone there. If he hadn't wanted to be found, he wouldn't have left the note and address, would he?

We wound through side streets with restored two- and three-story homes with lots of trees, well-tended lawns, and tidy hedges running along the sidewalks. Built as it is in the foothills of the Coastal Range, Las Tierras has lots of twisting streets, but as we burrowed east toward the valley, the terrain leveled out and trees gave way to scrub brush; the well preserved streets turned into cracked asphalt with potholes, then gave out altogether. Soon, we were on a narrow dusty road, flat as Kansas and not a tree in sight. Small houses, most of them unpainted, lined each side of the road. There were lots of broken windows, lots of trash and old, battered cars angled on the patches of dirt fronting the houses. Occasionally we passed groups of men walking alongside the road or talking in groups.

"Benton?" Morgan asked, taking up the map.

"Haven't seen a street sign since we left Topeka," I said. I'd already decided to get out of here. About the time the asphalt had quit, so had the signs. Up ahead, three brown-skinned men lounged beside a vehicle with its radio blasting a Mexican dance tune. As we drove by, they ceased talking and watched us pass.

"Hey, hold up." Morgan gestured for me to back up.

I didn't like this at all, but I hit the brakes, locked my door, and maneuvering backward to where the men were standing, tried quickly to explain the escalating violence between the Mexican and Anglo population in Las Tierras. Not that she listened. She was rolling down her window, sticking her head out.

"*Venido aquí, por favor,*" she yelled over the music.

They stared at us from dark, suspicious eyes until finally the tallest shoved himself away from the car and ambled over. He had lots of muscles under a black T-shirt with the arms ripped out and eagle wings spread across the front. Below the wings was written *águilas de la muerte.*

For all Morgan seemed to notice, he could have been a Wall Street broker. She grinned up at him. "*Donde está la calle de Benton?*"

The man stared at her for a moment, and a faint ripple of animation passed between them. He began talking to her in rapid Spanish, gesturing as he spoke. Finally she nodded, thanked him, and pointed to the road ahead.

"Take the next right," she said.

After a series of turns, we were bouncing along a rutted road that dwindled to a path and finally dead-ended at a row of three shacks topped with rusty metal roofs. Like the other houses we'd passed, their yards had no grass, but someone had tried to mask the stark face of poverty that lay across the community. Recently planted oleanders sprouted alongside the little houses, hiding the foundations and softening the square lines of the buildings. Several small trees were staked out around the yard, surrounded by a border of rocks painted bright pink. A late-model white truck sat beside one of the shacks, but the sheriff's car was nowhere in sight. As we pulled up, a rag-tag swarm of children shot from behind the buildings, the front-runner clutching some object as the others gave chase with high-pitched shrieks, a pack of barking dogs bringing up the tail. When the leader spotted us, she hung a U-ee in our direction. She slowed to a trot, then stopped a few feet from the front of the truck. The others lined up behind her. Five Mexican children regarded us with the same smoldering expressions as the men we'd passed. Their leader, a girl of maybe ten with a mouth set into a hard line, still clutched the object in the crook of one arm. When she took a step forward, the smaller children behind her followed suit.

"Ever read *Lord of the Flies*?" I said under my breath.

"Well, I wouldn't want to offer them any matches," Morgan said. She leaned out the window again. "*Su madre, donde esta?*" Nothing. "*Habla ingles?*"

The girl didn't respond except to glance past us to the truck bed where I'd piled some old, broken furniture to haul to the dump. She looked around at the others, and I caught a flash of white teeth. She took another step forward; the others followed. The object she carried in her arm, I could now see, was a grimy pillow wound tightly with orange twine. A homemade ball.

"Maria!" A man in a brilliant white shirt and tight jeans appeared in the doorway of one of the shacks.

The girl glanced once more at the truck bed before spinning on her heels and racing off with the others in hot pursuit, followed by the pack of dogs. The man was headed our way. He had Maria's eyes and firm jaw, and with a start I recognized Clarissa's gardener, Rico Santillanes. He'd locked eyes with me, and I saw the flash of recognition, the warning. I didn't know what I was being warned about until I saw a woman step from the same door and follow him across the yard.

I recognized her, too: Natalia Santillanes, but she looked a lot different than she had when I met her cleaning Julia's house. She was barefoot and bare-legged, and her black hair was now falling loose across her shoulders. She wore a blouse tied in a knot above a stretch of naked brown skin and a knee-length skirt of some see-through gauzy fabric. She walked toward us with the easy, sensual grace of a jungle cat. I looked at her and thought of Clarissa Remington's brave face, the sappy look in the old lady's eyes as she'd stood on her porch yesterday morning watching this woman's husband drive up.

I was explaining to Santillanes that we were looking for the sheriff when his wife arrived and stood beside him. Her expression hadn't changed; it was etched with the same inscrutable hostility I'd seen at Julia's. It struck me that here was an angry woman who, for whatever reason, was concealing her anger. I didn't dwell on it, though. There are a lot of women like that.

"The sheriff, he has been and gone," Santillanos was saying. "The meeting is over."

"Meeting?" Morgan leaned forward.

"Our community is asking for protection from the law, for the safety of those who live here." His wife clenched her jaw and looked away. "We wish protection against the Americanos who come by night against us."

I recalled the broken windows in the neighborhood, the dark looks we'd encountered. "Are you saying Hammersmith's been doing nothing about it?"

"The sheriff is a good man," Santillanes said, "but punishment is not a solution, no?"

I could have talked some on that topic, but I didn't get the chance. Santillanes was a man with a mission who obviously seized on any audience. He launched into the politics of illegal immigration, the desperate risks his people took at the Mexican border, the inhumane practices of immigration officials, the illegal smuggling of his people into the States, how they were charged large sums and then herded into cattle cars; how men and women too sometimes suffocated in the oven-like interiors. He talked about the unscrupulous ones who transported his countrymen across the border, only to drop them off in the Arizona desert where many died of heat and thirst in summer, froze to death in winter. Natalia's expression grew blacker. I could sense tension in her like a thunderstorm gathering force, waiting to break. She crossed her arms tightly over her breasts, and the sun glinted off the wide gold band on her ring finger.

Santillanes warmed to his subject. He was a man of passionate conviction. He pointed out the need for equitable employment laws. He spoke of his countrymen who must work for pitiful wages rather than starve, of the local whites whose jobs were dwindling away as a result. "It is all very complex," he said, looking up at the sky as though he expected help from that quarter, "but this much is clear. We must have the law behind us. That is why Sheriff Hammersmith came to our meeting. His very presence is a statement to both communities. My people must understand that in order to bring about change, we can no longer ignore the American laws of immigration which protect the rights of human beings, no matter their race. Everyone must be told—"

Natalia could restrain herself no longer. "Aaiii! My husband, such a fool!" She stepped away and lowered her head at him as though she were a bull, about to charge. "*Usted idiota estúpido!* Do you not know these are white laws, made *by* white men *for* white men! You join them! *Traidor! Cómo puede un hombre ser tan estúpido?*"

Santillanes blinked in the afternoon sun as though he'd been struck. His face, which had been lit with vision, grew dark. He clenched his fists and turned on his wife.

"*Cállate!*" he thundered. Natalia froze. She seemed to wither before him. "I am sorry," he said, turning back to us with a sigh. "My wife, she does not understand these things." Santillanes sighed again and gave us directions for the best way back to Las Tierras, cautioning us against stopping.

"My people, we are good people," he said, "but these are bad times. We must all use caution until I...until some way can be found to bring peace between our communities."

I drove back down the bumpy road pondering Santillanes' last remark. It was not unlike those of other men through history who wanted the same thing. Gandhi, Lincoln, Martin Luther King, JFK.

I was thinking it might be true that we don't learn from history. Look at what happened to them.

18

M AYBE IT WAS THE RAMSHACKLE neighborhood and its grim poverty. Maybe it was the way the woman beside me stared out the window without talking. Whenever I glanced at her, thoughts of Mary Bess rushed in. Thoughts of that night long ago, lips smooth and soft, opening to mine, so different from the way Morgan's had felt, hungry and demanding. Whatever the trigger, anxiety was creeping in and smothering me like a cloud of doom. The morning was gone, and I'd accomplished nothing. I was in big trouble, the worst kind of trouble, and though I'd set out hours ago to see the sheriff, I was getting nowhere. Panic began to seep like acid through my blood, humming and throbbing and building up to a drum roll. If I'd been alone, I'd have headed for the freeway and bid adieu to Las Tierras in my rear view mirror. Why not? What was to stay for? A few ducks, a couple of goats. Add to that, I was an escape artist of the first rank—this was a piece of cake. But I felt caught, trapped, tangled up in events and people and circumstances. The main reason, though, was that I wasn't alone in the truck.

I sneaked another peek at the woman in black. She looked deep in thought, oblivious to me, with that self-possessed quality about her like you find in some people, though it's rare. Like they're utterly autonomous, not affected a hair by anybody else's presence. The totally insane have that about them. Who knows, maybe she was trying to figure out the matrix, maybe she was right about how events conspire to bring us to some fateful, telling moment. If so, I wasn't having any luck knowing what to make of it, what to do next. Not a clue. She sat with one knee crossed over another, a long pale hand resting on the black fabric of her jeans. A sizzle of adrenaline hit me. That's when I knew I was scared. There was something about her that wasn't right, not like other people. All smoke and mirrors. In spite of what she'd confided, what did I know about her, really?

Come to that, what do you know about anyone? All I had to go on was what I'd always had to go on. Instinct. Nearly paralyzed by panic and fear, I took a deep breath. Jumped.

"Okay," I said, "you offered to help me earlier, and I want to…I want…" This wasn't easy. I took another breath, deeper. "I'd like your help if you're still willing."

If she heard me, she didn't show it. She kept staring out the window, let a block or two slide by.

Finally, she said: "You that desperate, Frost?"

The sarcasm was thick enough to slice. I didn't know where it came from or what to do about it. It caught me off guard, and it hurt like hell, so I did the only thing I knew how to do—I pretended it didn't. I told her everything I could think of that might hold a clue—my visit with Zoloman, dropping in on Clarissa. Santillanes coming up the drive as I left. The sappy look on the old woman's face.

"Whatever else Rico Santillanes might be doing in her garden," I said, as we approached Main Street, "I don't believe for a minute all his tools fit in the back of his truck."

"Hey, wait." She sat up straight. "Pull in there."

She indicated an empty parking spot in front of the *Las Tierras Tribune* building. I eased in, saw Sam behind the storefront window, sitting behind his desk and talking to someone out of view. Morgan slid out of the truck and came back with a *Trib* from the rack beside the open door.

On the front page, Julia's face stared out below the banner headline, LAS TIERRAS REPORTER DEAD. I fought back the tears while Morgan read. I was relatively dry-eyed by the time we arrived at the sheriff's lot. Still empty. I couldn't have said why, but I wanted very much to see Bill Hammersmith just then. It would have helped.

Morgan glanced up at the dark office and handed me the paper. "Tell you what, this editor Julia worked for?"

"Yeah?" I said, scanning the article. It was one of those vacuous stories that Julia used to fuss at Sam for writing. She'd been found "near her home," it said. No mention of me. No mention of the trunk. No cause of death. I was very interested in cause of death.

"Sam Oliver. What about him?"

"How well you know him?"

"Mm, pretty well, I guess." I folded the paper and laid it on the seat. "Julia used to fuss at him being so conservative. She felt he played it too safe, avoided controversial issues. We'd planned to go see him today before she...before she..."

...died, Grace. Before she died. Say it. Julia's dead. Murdered.

I swallowed. "...before all this happened. Julia was going to write up my story, put it in the paper, but—"

"Listen, sheriff's still gone, we've got some time. How about you drop me off at my motor home, then go have a little chat with Sam Oliver. You up for that?"

Alarm bells started going off. "What for? It looks like the sheriff's holding back information. Like where exactly the body was found, just for starters. I probably ought to touch base with him first before—"

"This isn't about your life story, Frost," she said impatiently. "Forget your life story. I want you to find out what Julia was working on. Doesn't matter how small. Anything at all. And do it, you know," she squinted at me, "do it sideways, so you don't get somebody standing across the door you're trying to get through. Hammersmith's probably already been there asking the same thing, but you'd be surprised what a person will tell you when he's relaxed, shooting the breeze, not talking to the law." She grinned and pumped her eyebrows a couple of times. "How about it, Watson?"

I felt uneasy. I despised sneaking around. "Are you thinking Julia came across something that..." That what? Somebody didn't want printed, so they killed her? I felt silly, like I was reading a bad script for a James Bond movie. Even now, after all that had happened in my life, I had a hard time believing murder happened to people you knew. On the other hand, I knew from the stories Julia told me that the world is full of people who consider premeditated felony about as remarkable as breathing.

"Look, Frost, this isn't a game. Julia's dead. She might have been stepping on some toes. Or about to. Think about it—a woman with her background, living on the edge with the kind of reporting she'd spent her life doing, wouldn't she have been maybe a little bored around here writing about the county fair? Especially working for a conservative type like you're saying Sam Oliver is. Julia Simmons was a world-class investigative reporter, she'd have smelled things other people didn't. Add to that, she was apparently not only tenacious, but fearless as well. Dicey combination. The kind you can count on to keep something stirred up all the time." She leveled one of those long, penetrating looks at me. "What is it exactly you're scared of, Frost? Do you know?"

"Yes. I mean, no…I mean, I'll do it, I want to do it." It was true, I'd started to feel the excitement. The way she put it, it made all the sense in the world, didn't it? I pulled out of the sheriff's lot, toward the commercial strip. "I'm only sorry I didn't think of it myself. After all those stories Julia told me, all the tight spots she got herself into, not to mention the help she gave me, seems like the obvious thing to do, now you mention it."

Morgan smiled. "Good girl."

I hung a left at Harvey's, drove the two-mile stretch of frontage road sprinkled with the usual doldrums of fast food chains and discount houses and convenience stores. Dave's Paint and Body was the only auto repair place in town, a metal Quonset eyesore sitting back off the street, flanked by razor wire above a chain link fence. I spotted Morgan's motor home parked behind it. I pulled in beside the only car in the lot, a lime-green Dodge Dart with a faded racing stripe and lots of rusted-out metal along the bottom. The triple-sized garage door on the Quonset was rolled up, and inside were several vehicles hoisted in the air or parked with their hoods raised. Morgan shouldered her nylon bag and disappeared inside.

I drove back toward downtown feeling pretty good, like I had a game plan for the first time all day. The sheriff's lot was still deserted, though a few shoppers wandered along the shady sidewalks nearby, on the trendy block of boutiques leading into the main drag. Situated in old, restored houses, the shops had catchy names in keeping with the town's reputation, names like the Split Infinity where you could buy New Age books and crystals, or The Wise Crack which sold refurbished old furniture too young to be called antique. There were shops selling handmade leather dresses, custom footwear, equestrian tack and riding apparel, quilts, ceramics, used books, gourmet coffee, Tarot readings.

On Main, the truck jazzed a little as it hit the bricks. Tourists strolled along the sidewalks, pausing to peer through shop windows. That's how I knew they were tourists. Everyone who lives in Las Tierras knows nothing much ever changes in those windows—clay pottery, gauzy tie-dyed skirts just long enough to brush the tops of your Birkenstocks, handmade candles, regional oil paintings with price tags high enough to send you to your optometrist. I noticed what I'd been too preoccupied to notice before—signs that an earthquake had struck. The damage seemed minimal enough, considering the town's reputation. A couple of plywood boards were nailed across the windows of the No Fault Cafe, and shoppers skirted a wide crack in the sidewalk, buttressed on each side by wooden horses.

The *Trib* took up the ground floor of one of the old eighteenth-century historic buildings carefully monitored by the City Council so that portions of the original adobe peeked through where the exterior stucco was allowed to scab off in aesthetically-convincing patches. From what Julia had said, it cost a small fortune in city taxes to keep the building looking as bad as it did.

The office was a cavernous, wooden box of a room made of rough-cut barn wood and perpetually gloomy because Sam Oliver didn't like lights. He was behind his desk, legs propped up, drinking a ginger ale and talking to a man who sat with his back to me. Sam usually wore jeans and plaid shirts, but today he had on a black T-shirt and black jeans. A pine-cone wreath spray-painted black dangled by a string in the window, turning infinitesimally.

"Hey, Grace," he said. He was an anxious man with abrupt manners and bristling red hair. He smiled ear-to-ear, showing an Olympic-sized overbite, a beaver surveying a choice cut of seasoned pine. Then he did a double-take; his eyes bulged, eyebrows shot up. "Wow. New hairdo, eh?"

I'd forgotten about my haircut. "Reckon it'll grow," I said, running a hand through it.

The man in the chair turned. Pandy Meyerson, the contractor who'd replaced my leaky roof a couple years ago, the only general contractor in the area. It'd been awhile, but he was an easy man to remember. You could picture him in a magazine-ad—selling a man's cigarette, a tough truck, a no-nonsense pain remedy. Faded jeans, jacket to match. Expensive boots, no dust. Expensive gold watch, no ring. He was in his late fifties, early sixties, with a soft webwork of facial lines that were eloquent: he smiled, he knew how to enjoy life, he could build you a house to show you how to enjoy life too. His eyes were Paul Newman blue, sparkling with good humor and intelligence. His easy laugh had probably charmed more than one client into hiring him. I thought the same thing now that I'd thought when I first met him a couple years ago—he was that rare kind of man, put together precisely right, running smooth and easy as a Swiss clock.

Sam was chuckling. "That's the truth, it'll grow, sure enough, and anybody can carry it off, it'll be you, Grace, wouldn't be surprised if half the women in town go over to Wanda Jones and ask her to give them a haircut just like it." Then Sam's expression vacillated between a smile and scowl, like someone was flipping a switch somewhere. "You know Pandy here?"

"You bet she does," Pandy said, standing up and offering his hand. For a man in construction, his skin was smooth and his grip light. "I probably met Miss Frost before you did, Sam. You ever get around to having that barn of yours overhauled?"

"Not yet," I said. He'd pointed out all the weak supports and rotting beams, but the price of renovation was prohibitive.

"You'll be wanting to get that done. If this earthquake didn't take it down, the next one just might." He put a little extra wattage in his eyes and gave my hand a final squeeze before sitting back down. I'd heard rumors about Pandy, married but single.

I waited for the men to finish talking and wandered around the old office. Shoulder-high cubbyholes ran along one wall, stuffed with office supplies, paper, back issues of the *Trib*. One section was set aside for the employees' personal items, but Julia's cubby was empty. Several gray metal Army-issue desks were shoved along the rear wall, all topped with outdated computers. Julia's was the last, in the farthest corner of the office.

Except for the computer, her desktop, unlike the others, was clear. Maybe the sheriff had collected whatever might have been here of Julia's, but my guess was there'd been precious little to collect. Julia used the office to socialize—to network with people, make her business calls, chit-chat with Sam and the staff. Most of her actual writing she did at home because Julia liked state-of-the-art technology, and Sam was a hopeless skinflint. Julia might have looked like an old woman, but she was an electronics guru, kept her home office stocked with a cutting edge computer and all the bells and whistles.

I sat down in the old swivel chair behind her desk. The springs creaked, just like they had when Julia sat here last week and we'd shared lunch. The sadness came, and I let it. It came with memories rolling out of the past, and that was all right, that was just fine. Because the past was the only place I could find Julia now. She'd sat here last week, leaning back in this old creaking chair, tilting her bird's head one way and another. Took a wrinkled brown bag out of the bottom drawer, unrolled the top, handed me half a sandwich. I'd noticed the computer monitor was lit, thought it odd. What was it she'd said? She was "backing up."

She'd once told me at Mt. Havens, years ago, that she always kept a backup folder of every important case she worked on. She'd dropped in to visit, entertaining me, relating details of her detective work, the interesting people she'd come across, her methodology. "You just never know, if it is a story that somebody is worried about seeing in the paper, how serious they are going to get about stopping you from printing it. I cannot even tell you the times I have been threatened, had my file cabinets broken into, even had my office set on fire one time, so that is when I started keeping a photocopy of every important piece of material I am working on. And never," she said, "never, ever keep the originals and the copies in the same place."

But this was the era of computers, not file folders, not photocopies. I glanced at the far end of the room where the two men were still talking.

"…some people on the City Council got a little worked up over it at the meeting last Friday," Pandy was saying.

I reached over and punched the power button on the old hard drive, and it hummed to life. The screen flickered.

"…probably going to drop in on you, bleeding liberals wanting you to do a story on hiring practices, wages, insurance. *Insurance*, for Christ sake. Can you believe it? I mean, we're not talking skilled labor here, you know. Most of those wetbacks, they can handle a hammer, but you have to hold the nail for them. If they didn't have these jobs, they'd be starving in the streets, robbing our stores to get money. Way I look at it, I'm doing them a favor letting them work for me, and it's the business community, all of us in the long run, that profits, keeping the cost of housing down so regular folks can afford a home."

"I wouldn't lose too much sleep over it," Sam said. "They come in, I'll talk to them. Right now, that quake's got everybody's attention. They go on till they're blue in the face about The Big One, then when the little ones come along, everybody goes into a panic for a few days…"

It took a while for the dinosaur to load. Finally the old Windows 3.1 screen appeared. I began scanning through folders, looking for Julia's personal files. There wasn't much. The only recent ones were titled "ctyfair97" and "rodeo97." I turned off the machine, pulled out a drawer. Receipts, outdated pink phone slips, notes on upcoming events, brochures and flyers from local businesses.

"That's the way most of us look at it," Meyerson said, standing up. "Glad you're on our side. I think we can all get together and agree on this, maybe call a town meeting, show the bleeding hearts some figures, what would happen around here in the business community if we didn't have access to cheap labor. Believe me, they ought to be counting their lucky stars instead of making trouble."

I was rifling the shallow, middle drawer, my arms shoved in up to the elbow, certain she'd have kept copies of whatever she was working on at home, thinking her office here would be the obvious place to store them. Or would that be *too* obvious? Wouldn't someone—

"Hey Grace, how about you give me a call, let me come on over and talk you into that barn?"

My hands froze inside the drawer. I looked up at Pandy. I forced a smile, nodded. "You bet. Will do."

While he and Sam chit-chatted toward the door in Parting Male Ritual, I quickly scanned the contents of the other drawers. Not much. Matchbooks, pens, paper clips, an AOL floppy disk, rulers, bookmarks, tape, erasers. *An AOL disk?* I picked it up and looked at it. It was one of the old ones, issued years ago. Still, why would Julia have an AOL disk here? I was certain that frugal, conservative, old-fashioned Sam wasn't online. No Internet site, no email address. Nor had I seen an AOL icon on the computer. What I did remember seeing was a disk like this one at Mt. Havens, that time when Sheryl in the office was telling one of the other secretaries not to throw them out, to erase them and use them over.

Well, now, I thought, smiling at the disk, "backup" indeed. I slipped it in my pocket, glanced up to make sure no one had seen me. Looked straight into the Paul-Newman blues of Pandy Meyerson who was at the door, shaking hands with Sam. He grinned, threw a parting wave, and was gone.

"Damn shame about Julia," Sam said, as I walked over and took Pandy's chair. His voice didn't sound like the same one he'd been using on Pandy. "I can hardly believe it, can't say I was surprised though what with her heart, she'd had, how many, two operations for it, hadn't she…"

Sam had a predilection for the rhetorical question. A nod now and then kept him going. As Julia once put it, he had a great store of commas in his oral repertoire, few end stops.

"…told her and told her not to get herself in a lather, to just relax and keep her cool and not make waves, but I don't believe Julia could do that, didn't have a cool setting, just ran hot and hot, didn't have a thermostat…"

I heard without listening, all the while trying to think how to ask about Julia's assignments without appearing to. Anyway you looked at it, it was sneaky, it was manipulation, even if it was on a small scale and serving a good cause, and damned if I could come up with a thing.

"...starting a human interest section, interviewing local residents because, like she said, we have a lot of interesting people living here, some not even knowing their next door neighbor, so she was going to do that, was planning on starting it in our next..."

"What? Wait, what'd you just say?"

Sam paused. His eyes bulged. "What's that?"

"About Julia."

He blinked. "What about Julia?"

I'd forgotten the exasperating peculiarity Sam had, like those people you hear about who can't count from seven to ten, but have to start all over again with one. I dredged up a clue for him and tried to keep the impatience out of my voice. "You said Julia was going to do a new section, human interest?"

"I was saying that she worked too hard, that I'd told her time and time again—"

"No, no. I mean, what was the new human interest feature going to be about? Something about people not knowing their neighbors?"

"Oh." He sucked on the ginger ale and stared at the can before setting it back down on his desk. "Well, I guess she was deciding on who to do first, don't know if she'd made up her mind about that, but she'd mentioned, let's see...said something about kicking it off with one of her own neighbors, you know, like that lady with the silver hair, plays the piano?"

"Clarissa Remington?"

"Yeah, yeah, that's the one. Then there was some photographer guy, lived right close too, said she might—"

"Zoloman?"

"What's that?" he snapped. Sam Oliver wasn't the type to hide his impatience. He hated to be interrupted, and people interrupted him a lot.

"The photographer. Was it Willis Zoloman?"

"Dunno. Didn't give me a name, but anyway, she was going to come in today, talk to me about a story she wanted to break, called around eight-thirty and said she'd..."

I knew all about it. She was coming in to talk to Sam today about me, get his approval on doing my story. I had planned to come in with her, but now I was sitting here talking to Sam just as we'd planned, but Julia—

"Wait. What was that? What'd you say? She called at *eight-thirty?*" Sam still had his mouth open. He snapped it shut and his whiskers flared.

"It wasn't later? You're sure it was that early, that it was eight-thirty?" Because if it was, there was no way Julia was talking about my story. I hadn't arrived till after nine. It had to be something else she was working on, just as Morgan suspected.

"No way in hell. Everybody knows I'm an early bird, never get calls much after eight or so, anybody calls me after nine, they better be dying..." Sam Oliver's brain caught up with his voice. He leaned back and looked up at the wreath dangling on its string. His eyes glistened, and his mouth was jerking sideways. "She was a good woman, Julia was."

"Yes, yes she was." We both watched the wreath turn slowly in one direction, then the other.

Outside, a family walked by and stared at us though the window. The cracking sound of loud mufflers drifted in from the street. The wreath stopped moving and hung perfectly still, the black spiny tips of the pine cones backlit and splayed against the sky, looking faintly evil.

"Damn, a heart attack, and just getting into her retirement years." *A heart attack?* "What are you talking about? Who told you that?"

"Bill Hammersmith," he said, looking at me curiously, screwing his face into a frown and setting his lips so that his whiskers stiffened. "I mean, what in hell else do you think happened to her?"

"The sheriff's already been here? When?"

"Yup, come and gone," he said, lifting his eyes above my head, "and come again."

I twisted around to see Bill Hammersmith walking through the door, a purple bandana rolled and tied around his head, matching purple bands around the pigtails, and a set of wraparound reflective sunglasses over his eyes. A fluorescent purple motorcycle helmet dangled in one hand.

Looked like he was going to miss making the cover of *GQ* again this month.

19

W HAT I KNOW ABOUT MOTORCYCLES, you can stick in Barbie's thimble. That's if she ever gets old enough and smart enough to use one. But I didn't have to be an expert to know the sheriff rode one serious hog.

Parked in front of Marsha Davis's Crack and Cleavage Lingerie Shoppe, the machine leaned streetward on its kickstand with the sun shooting off the long sprawl of Harley-Davidson chrome and fluorescent purple trim. I walked the length of it a couple of times, squinting and sifting through my store of motorcycle superlatives. Finally, I stood beside one sleek, purple haunch, folded my arms across my chest, threw my weight on one hip, and leaned street-ward with the hog.

"Wow," I said, wondering about Hammersmith's transforma-tion. Back during those few months when we'd tried each other on, he drove a Toyota Corolla.

He strolled up, a slow smile spreading across his face. I stared into his mirror-lenses and saw twin images of a blonde woman with wild shocks of hair standing on end.

"We need to talk," he said.

I nodded, explained I'd been trying to find him most of the day. "Even went out to Benton Street. Missed you, but got Santillanes' nickel lecture on Mexican-American labor politics in Las Tierras, met the wife and kids."

"Yeah?" A frown crossed his face briefly. "Well, I'm off duty now. How about you follow me in your truck?"

He was wearing knee-high black leather boots over faded jeans and a Grateful Dead tank top, toned down a little under a black leather jacket with lots of silver studs. He went to the Harley, strapped on the purple helmet, grabbed the handgrips, and threw a leg over. He settled himself into the leather saddle and grinned at me.

"Unless you'd rather climb on back," he said, then stomped something with his foot and the machine blasted to life, its long chrome mufflers vibrating and sounding a lot like cars without any. People who'd been strolling along the shop windows turned to stare. Marsha Davis's head popped up over a display of lacy, open-tipped bras.

I followed Hammersmith as he roared down Main toward his office. And passed it. Passed Harvey's and the freeway on-ramp. Passed Pandy Meyerson sitting in his truck talking to a workman while his dozers pushed around dirt. Passed the road to my house without so much as a glance. By the time he turned onto a road a couple miles later, I'd quit trying to figure where he was headed. I just followed Bill Hammersmith hunched over the handlebars of his bike, elbows poked out on each side as he leaned into the curves of the narrow, winding road.

Several miles into a remote canyon, he turned on a gravel road that became dirt, then crossed a crude wood bridge that rattled as I drove over it. We wiggled downhill along a stream and through tangled deciduous trees where the sunlight turned green and the air was loud with the sound of running water. When the road grew rutted and bumpy, Hammersmith gunned the engine and maneuvered the machine forward, following a narrow driveway that suddenly curved, became crushed white granite, and ended abruptly at a lush, rolling lawn studded with landscaped patches of wild flowers and native shrubs.

At the center sat a stunning hacienda-type home made of textured white stucco with dark red trim, topped with scallops of brick-red ceramic roof tile. I got out of my truck as Bill Hammersmith swung his leg over the motorcycle like he was dismounting Trigger.

"Wow. This your place?" Back a couple of years ago when we'd dated, he'd had a two-bedroom condo in Morgan Hill.

"Lot closer to work," he said, taking off his helmet and sunglasses.

I followed him along a walkway and into the house. Through a long hall of glossy tiles. Up several flights of stairs and landings. Into an upper-story solarium on the backside of the house, a bright, airy room with a balcony overlooking a canyon and rolling hills extending all the way across the valley to the faded imprint of the mountains in the far distance. A very large telescope was bolted to the deck on one end of the balcony where there was a clear shot of the sky. An astronomy professor. Of course.

I figured professors probably make more money than first-grade teachers, but I didn't think they made enough to afford a spread like this. Besides, he wasn't teaching anymore since he'd become sheriff, which didn't pay beans in Las Tierras. How could he afford this place?

"Had lunch?" He tossed his gear on a table beside the door and headed for a small kitchenette in one corner. He poked his head into a dorm-sized fridge and studied the interior. "Sandwich, something to drink?"

He pulled out a loaf of bread, several jars, plastic bags, storage containers, and two bottles. He kept the Heineken and handed me the strawberry-flavored sparkling water. Good choice. I wandered around the room sipping strawberries while he put the sandwiches together. I peeked into an adjoining room—a studio-sized bathroom with picture window and green slate lining the walls and floor.

"Nice place. Been here long?"

"A while."

"Sell your condo?" This place was in the boonies. Maybe he sold the condo and—

"Renting it out."

Okay, so maybe somebody died and left him a pile of money, maybe he'd won the lottery, maybe he was a cat burglar on the side. No way to tell. Hammersmith was a very private guy; even while seeing him those few months, he'd told me very little about himself. Which had worked out just fine, because I hadn't told him much about myself, either.

While he stacked wafer-thin mystery meat on top of green stuff, I gravitated to the windows and stood looking out across the distant valley, wide and endless as an ocean. I felt suddenly tired, dislocated. I leaned against the window frame, thought back over the day which seemed hopelessly long and complicated. If Morgan's theory of the matrix was right, that we had to interpret the events around us, I'd need to be Einstein to figure this one out. I wondered what she'd made of Santillanes with his feverish vision of an integrated community. What had he said about the sheriff's presence at their meeting, that it was a "statement to the community"? Some people wouldn't like that much. I remembered Pandy Meyerson's mellow voice, his friendly camaraderie with Sam Oliver, scoffing at labor rights for "wetbacks."

How did Bill Hammersmith fit into all this? It was obvious Santillanes considered him an ally. By attending their meeting, Hammersmith represented protection by American laws. That was fine and dandy for Rico Santillanes, Mexican visionary, but what about the sheriff, how did he explain his support of the Mexican community to the City Council and influential people like Pandy Meyerson? Had Meyerson known about the meeting on Benton Street? Could the sheriff have attended Santillanes' meeting with a hidden agenda? Pandy Meyerson was a very wealthy man...

"Hello?"

I jumped. Hammersmith was standing beside me with a tray of sandwiches in one hand, a beer in the other. He nodded at me to open the door to the balcony.

Outside, the air was crisp, but the afternoon sun sifted through the trees and warmed an edge of the deck furnished with a picnic table scattered with notebooks and a jar of pens and pencils. I sat down and lifted a slice of rye: odd sprouts, tiny green leaves that looked like they belonged on a dandelion stalk, crumbles of purple and white cheese, some kind of purplish meat I couldn't identify.

"Prosciuto," the sheriff said, an eyebrow lifted quizzically at me. "Smoked ham. You'll like it."

He was right. We both chewed and let time pass. I figured there was some reason he'd brought me here instead of his office, and I knew him well enough to know he'd get to it as soon without me asking as he would any other way. I kept chewing and waited him out, thinking that whatever he had on his mind might be making him as nervous as me. He finished half of the sandwich, took a long swallow of beer, and set the bottle carefully beside his plate.

"Okay, let's talk about Julia's death," he said, taking a pencil from the jar and opening a notebook. "Jim estimated time of death between nine to midnight Saturday. I want you to tell me, step by step, what happened that night. Anything out of the ordinary."

I tried to decide where to begin. "I guess it started with the snake. Usually, I get my mail in the late afternoon, then walk on down the road to Julia's for a visit. But Saturday was different. When I went down to get the mail, I found a dead snake in my box with a note attached to it." I took myself back to Saturday afternoon, standing by the mailbox. "I thought I saw something moving in the trees across the road, so I walked over to get a better look. Never did see anybody, though, so I went back home, buried the snake—"

"You buried a *snake*?"

"Sure, out back of the barn. You want, I can show you."

He gave me a look. "Never mind. Go on. So you went back to your place instead of going to Julia's?"

"Right. I wanted to compare the snake note to the others I'd been getting since I moved here." I pulled the crumpled notes in the plastic baggie out of my pocket and handed them to the sheriff. "They seemed harmless enough, kid stuff. I didn't think much about them, not until the one came Saturday."

Hammersmith shook the notes out of the bag and, handling them gingerly by the edges, scanned each one as I described my visit with Julia.

"You went to her place using the back path," he said, fitting the notes back in the bag and laying them aside. "Remember the time?"

"I remember it was nearly dark. Sam said Julia called him around eight-thirty, so it had to be after that because she didn't make any phone calls while I was there. I showed her the notes, we talked for awhile, then I left around ten or so." I skirted the issue of Julia writing my story. I knew it was time, long past time, to tell Bill Hammersmith about myself, but I had kept my past hidden so long I didn't know how to talk about it.

"You didn't see anything unusual going back to your place?"

"No, nothing. Natalia was there doing some housework when I arrived, but she'd already—"

"Santillanes' wife?"

"Yeah, I met her again today out at—"

"What time did she leave? Did someone pick her up?"

I thought back. I remembered Natalia lurking in the shadows. She could have used a phone in the back of the house to call for a ride, but I hadn't heard a car pull up. "I don't think so. She left about a half hour or so after I came, so maybe nine o'clock, must have been on foot."

The sheriff made a note. He tipped his head sideways, squinted an eye at me. "Okay, so you left by the back path, got home around ten. What'd you do then?"

Uh-oh. I studied the faint imprint of the Sierras and saw the ass-end of that empty bourbon bottle floating in the clouds above the mountains.

Get a grip, Gracie, you knew he was working up to this. It's the question you've been dreading, slipped right across the plate, hard and fast. Be cool. He'll never know you were in an alcoholic blackout that night unless you're stupid enough to tell him. Unless, like last time, you're stupid enough to believe the truth is going to get you anything but trouble. There is only one hero, only one person with the power to save your ass—and you're it.

Hammersmith was waiting, watching me with that fuzzy, far-away look in his eyes. Much as I hate lying and liars, I'd have to deal with my conscience later. I shrugged, trying for nonchalant. "You know, the usual. Made a cup of tea, grabbed a book, hit the sack."

The seconds ticked by. I could almost hear the gears grinding before he finally spoke.

"All right, Grace. Here's the way I look at it: there are two choices. You did it, or you didn't. If you did it, then you either did it consciously, hid the body in the trunk expecting to get rid of it the next day; or else you did it while you were drunk, or crazy, or in some way or other not in your right mind, and didn't even know that body was there. No matter which scenario you choose, somebody saw you do it and made that call to me."

I had put my sandwich down and was staring at it. I could feel his eyes on me.

"But I don't believe you did it, in your right mind or otherwise. I've got no proof, nothing to go on but instinct, but I believe someone else did it and planted the body on your porch. If so, it had to be somebody who knew your background, the murders back in '62, which would explain why they used the trunk. Then that same somebody called me, said where to look and what I'd find. That person intended you to be arrested for Julia's death. Case closed.

"Now here's where it gets interesting. Let's talk motive. Two choices again. One, Julia was into something, don't know what exactly, and someone killed her to keep her quiet."

I waited for him to go on, but he didn't. He was staring at me, hard; I could feel it. He wanted me to look up at him, so I did.

"Or?" I had gone hot all over. My face was burning.

He frowned at the notebook. "There's something out of kilter about this whole thing," he said. He picked up his beer and turned it around in his hands while he talked. "I think there's at least one other motive the killer might have had."

I braced myself. I wasn't going to like this.

"I don't know how likely it is, but it's at least possible that whoever killed Julia might have done it for no other reason than causing you trouble. Planted Julia's body in the trunk on your porch to throw the blame on you, have you put away again."

I stared at him.

"That's why I wanted to talk to you alone, here at the house where nobody can walk in on us. Because I have a plan." His leather jacket creaked, and his chair scraped the floor as he pulled it closer to the table. "I'm not going to divulge to anyone where Julia's body was found. There's only the four of us—me, you, your friend Rachael, and the coroner—who know about the trunk. Whoever made that phone call and is waiting for me to arrest you is going to have to make another move to get what he wants. A note, a phone call. Something."

The quiet curled around us. A wavering splinter of sunlight found its way through the branches overhead and lit the bronze splashes around the pupils of Hammersmith's eyes. The hills to the west rolled away in undulating waves of brown and shadow, a world removed from this balcony, from this strange man in his fuzzy pigtails and his weathered face, and me—a woman who had killed her best friends, dismembered one of them, and now another friend dead...

"Grace?"

Hammersmith was kneeling beside me, stroking my mutilated hair. He smelled like juniper berries, like leather from a saddle fitted to a white horse. His fingers were calloused, awkward, scratchy as they wiped my cheeks.

"Grace, it's all right. It's going to be all right." His voice cooed in the lullaby rhythm a mother uses to soothe away nightmares. He had one arm around me, patting my back.

"How long have you known?" I asked.

"Known? About Julia? I told you, someone called—"

"No. About me. The murders."

He stopped patting my back and stood up, leaving behind the lingering scent of leather. He was tall as a mountain, a thousand feet tall.

"Grace..." He started to say more, but changed his mind. He sat back down across from me and drained his beer. Sighed a deep one. Looked me in the eye. "Grace, everybody knows. They always have."

If thoughts were snow, I was in a grand-daddy of a white-out. Bewildered. Lost. "But how...why didn't anyone say anything?" All that fretting I'd done over my identity. And Julia. She must have known what everybody in Las Tierras knew, so why had she agreed to write my story? Why not just tell me? Easy, she was sparing my feelings, letting me think it had been a secret. But if everybody knew my past, what was the poet threatening me with? Could it be that we were the only ones who didn't know what everybody else knew?

"...not the kind of thing people are going to come right out and talk about, is it?" the sheriff was saying. "You don't look all that different from your pictures in the newspapers, in case you didn't know, and there are plenty of people here more than old enough to have been reading them back in sixty-two when your face was plastered on front pages coast-to-coast..."

How could he have known, how could anyone have known, how much I'd yearned to tell people, keeping it back for Julia's sake? Or so I thought.

"Hey, Grace, uh...take it easy."

But the laughter kept coming, and the more I tried to quit, the more it came. It was like opening a jar of marshmallow cream, that sticky mess rising up and overflowing in spite of anything you did about it. Finally, I got a lid on it.

"It's just...Oh God, I've been hiding it so long, not wanting to." I filled him in on Julia's plan to reveal my identity. "When I left there that night, it was like I was coming alive again after all this time, like a rock had been lifted off me."

The sheriff leaned back and crossed his arms. "Are you saying you *wanted* people to know your background? That it was all right with you that Julia was going to reveal it in the newspaper for everybody to read?"

"Well, sure. Isn't that's what I just said?" Hammersmith had never struck me till now as a dense man.

"Who else knew Julia was writing this story with your authorization?"

Hammersmith was getting dumber by the minute. "Well now, how could anybody else *know*, if she'd just decided to do it that night?"

The sheriff was still as a rock for a long time, then said, "The murderer might have."

He didn't look dumb anymore. He looked like a sheriff, like somebody who could arrest you and toss your ass in jail. He looked like a long string of devious lawmen I'd come up against and didn't want to think too much about right now. He'd set the trap, and I'd walked in. I heard Sam Oliver telling me he'd talked to the sheriff, had undoubtedly told Hammersmith Julia had called him that night before she died, said she was going to break a story, and hadn't I just told the sheriff I thought I was incognito and that Julia was writing an exposé of me? I was the only human being alive that knew she was doing it at my request, but who would believe that? What they'd believe was the evidence: a body in a trunk, yet another friend inside, one who was going to reveal what I thought was my secret past to the community, to the world.

"You invited me out here to trick me, didn't you? Acting like we're having a friendly lunch for old time's sake?" I peeked under the table. "You're probably taping this, aren't you?"

"Settle down, Grace. I meant just what I said—I don't believe you did it. But you're right to think the evidence looks bad. Another reason to keep it out of the papers. Once you're arrested, whoever put Julia in that trunk is home free. Chances are slim we'll ever scare him out. But now…well, we've got a shot at it if you're willing to play along."

"Don't seem to have a whole lot of choice."

"You haven't said anything to anyone about the trunk, where she was found? Didn't mention it to Sam Oliver?"

I shook my head.

"Good, don't. Not a word to anyone. By the way, why'd you drop in on him?"

For a person who hates lying, I was having a tough day. I wasn't about to tell the sheriff that his prime suspect was conducting her own investigation, that I'd gone to the *Trib* to find out what stories Julia had been working on. I certainly wasn't going to tell him I'd been sent there by Rachael McKinley AKA Cordelia Morgan who carried a bank-sized pile of cash and a stack of phony ID's, or that she'd been a "specialist" for some international honcho who free-lanced incidents I didn't even want to think about. "I'd taken, uh, Rachel over to her motor home and was waiting for you to show up. Force of habit, I guess, going to the *Trib*. Used to hang out there a lot with Julia. " It sounded plausible.

"Ah." He nodded and studied the empty Heineken. "Well, be sure and caution Rachael not to discuss the murder with anyone, not to mention the trunk."

"You're calling it 'murder.' You're sure then?"

"Autopsy came back this morning. Heart attack, technically. But there's evidence of suffocation. She apparently went into cardiac arrest, and somebody helped it along."

"I didn't—"

He held his hands up. "I'm telling you again, I believe you. Okay?"

"But why? I don't get it. You're taking a big risk, aren't you? What makes you so sure I didn't do it?"

"I'm not *sure*, I'm just more trusting of my gut than most folks are in the law business. Plus," he paused with a smile playing at the corners of his mouth, "we're not exactly strangers, are we? I think I know something about you. The kind of something that comes of being around a person, knowing how they take their coffee in the morning. And I think the best way to find Julia's killer is to do exactly what I'm doing. Besides, what's the worst that could happen? You going to run off and leave me holding the bag?"

"Maybe that's not the worst. Maybe I'll run off and somebody puts you away as an accessory. Maybe I'll run off and...and kill somebody else."

Bill Hammersmith narrowed his eyes. "Look, Grace. I don't know anything about the murders in your past. No vibes at all on what happened that night. But whatever it was, it's past, you've served your time, and that's the end of it, far as I'm concerned. You're going to kill again? Get over it. Not a chance in hell." He stood up and came around the table. He pulled me up out of the chair and held me at arm's length. "Gracie Lee DeWitte. Wife of Dr. Bruce DeWitte, head psychiatrist at Evanston State Mental Hospital. A young student nurse who married an old man. You've spent most of your life locked up, not counting all those escapes. I did some checking when you moved here. I know your family name, I know where and when you were born, and in spite of anything you can do to your hair and the way you cover yourself up in old clothes, everybody laying eyes on you that doesn't know your background, thinks you're straight out of Hollywood." His hands tightened on my shoulders, and he fastened me with that intense, probing stare that people use after they know my age. "You're an astonishingly beautiful woman, Grace. Astonishingly."

I was no more comfortable being held by Hammersmith now than I'd been two years ago. The difference was, I'd stopped pretending. I pulled away and went to stand at the edge of the balcony, watching the invisible point where the mountains faded to sky.

"So what is it you want me to do? You're thinking he's going to contact me again?"

"I want you to take common sense precautions. Lock your doors, keep an eye out for anything unusual around your place. I figure whoever put the snake in your box was watching you open your mailbox Saturday. He wanted to see you find it, maybe watched your place after that and followed you to Julia's. Maybe he waited till you left and paid a call on her. Something must have happened that sent Julia into cardiac failure. We might be looking for some nutcase wanting to make your life a misery, someone willing to kill other people to do it."

"You think—"

"I think there's a killer out there. We don't know if it was Julia or you that was on his mind when he killed her. I want you to go over everything you can think of that might help me nail this guy."

That's when I remembered the duplicate note cards. I pulled them from my back pocket. "Once I started thinking about the notes, I realized they'd been coming around the same time every year, so Rachael and I spent the morning brainstorming." I gave him an overview of the anniversary dates we'd come up with, leaving out Morgan's hypothesis about the two writers. At this remove, it seemed far-fetched, an over-elaboration of an already ornate theory. "So Rachael made up this duplicate set, copying the originals and adding the anniversary dates with our comments on back. I thought they might help."

I handed him the packet of colored cards, held by a rubber band. He slid the top one out, read it front and back, returned it.

"Nice of Rachael, helping you out," he said. He laid the cards by the originals and stood up, collected the plates and bottles on the tray. I followed him into the house.

"This Rachael," he said, scraping leftovers into a pail beneath the sink, "she seem a little strange to you? You say she's staying at your place, her horse too?"

"Guess so. Jerry's supposed to bring him over today, still got to get a stall ready. I should be getting back to Dave's. She's probably wondering where I am."

I followed Hammersmith across the room, into the hall, down the staircases, struck yet again by this pricey house, the way it added up to way more than a sheriff's salary. The way he'd deliberately avoided talking about it. What was he hiding?

"She mention what line of work she's in? Tell you anymore about herself?"

"What I know's what you know," I said. A veritable mistress of deception, I was. Maybe I'd missed my calling. I heard Morgan's husky voice: *if you play the game well enough that your odds of getting nailed are nil to zip, you can do anything you want without penalty.* "She's vacationing from Kentucky, isn't that what she said? Why?"

"Just wondering." The front door stood open ahead of us, and the afternoon light played on the tiles. "Single woman, traveling around the country with a horse. There's something strange about her."

"Strange?" I asked, as we walked into the brilliant California sun.

"Just a feeling. Thing is, since she's staying at your place, I checked her out. Got the license number off her rig. She bought that setup in Colorado about a week ago from somebody by the name of Eva Blake. Like she said, home address, Fairfield, Kentucky. Has a horse ranch there, clean as a whistle. Talked to the manager, said she was gone on vacation, so I guess she's not some traveling nutcase going to break in and slit your throat in the middle of the night."

We had come to the driveway where the sun reflected in a million tiny points across the crushed white rock. My battered truck sat beside Hammersmith's motorcycle, sun flashing from its chrome strips and twinkling inside the purple trim. My thoughts were whirling—*What was it Morgan had said about that stack of ID's she carried, "a few phony names"? How could Rachael McKinley check out if she was just a phony name made up by Cordelia Morgan? If there was an actual Rachel McKinley who lived in Fairfield, Kentucky, then where was she?* Everything was moving too fast, too bright, spinning around. I put my hand up against the dazzle of light and leaned against the truck.

"You okay?"

The sheriff had on his mirror glasses again. My double image nodded back at me. In the distance, I heard a train coming our way, growing closer. I climbed in my truck and banged the door shut, rolled the window down. The sheriff was looking off down the driveway.

"By the way," he said, digging in his jeans pocket, "don't know if you were aware of it or not, but Julia left her house to you in her will." He pulled out a chain with three keys attached to it. "And she had your house deeded in your name, title to it in her deposit box, along with her will. Some might see that as a powerful motive, I guess."

I stared at the keys. "She left her *house* to me?"

"Car, too." He nodded at the keys, and I took them. "I knew Julia pretty well. In her line of work, we had reason to cross paths a bit. And I know that as far as a motive goes, the way I see it, nobody in their right mind, I'm including you in that category, would kill the only close friend she had in the world. Especially when Julia would've put both those houses in your name if you'd asked her to. Now the car," he said, holding back a smile, "that car is a different story altogether. Don't think she'd have given that to you or anybody else. On the other hand, I don't figure anybody would've wanted to kill her to get it, either."

I stared at the keys, stupefied. What would I do with Julia's house, not to mention the old Lincoln? My thoughts were interrupted by the sound of the train coming closer—then I suddenly remembered that the nearest railroad tracks were over fifty miles away. I twisted around to look down the drive.

"What the hell—?"

Blasting toward us was another motorcycle, a long low-slung confabulation of chrome and iridescent red, a close relative to the one the sheriff had been riding. It slowed, drifted up on the other side of my truck with a crunch of gravel and great pulses of sound like beating wings or the convulsions of an enormous heart. The sheriff was bending over, gazing through the cab of my truck, across where I sat behind the wheel, with that hazy look on his face and the kind of sappy smile that was a dead ringer for the one Clarissa Remington had used yesterday on Rico Santillanes.

We both watched the rider on the motorcycle, large and chrome-heavy as the sheriff's, a machine sized for an Amazon. The figure leaned down to switch off the engine: a ballet of movement in black leather—black leather gloves, jacket, skin-tight pants, boots, all sprinkled with enough silver studs to satisfy a Las Vegas showgirl.

A long, elegant leg stretched up and high over the saddle, smacked the kickstand with a black silver-toed boot, and gripped the iridescent red helmet with gloves edged in twinkling silver studs.

I could have sworn the breeze nudged the trees, carrying the voice of Neil Young singing "Unknown Legend," but if I'd expected to see the woman's hair cascade down her black leather back in a long fall of golden cornsilk, I was going to have to take up reading romance novels: the helmet came off and the head that turned toward us, looking through my passenger window at the sheriff, resembled the singer a whole lot more than his lady legend.

"Grace," said the sheriff, a wide grin across his face, "meet Wayne Harris. My house mate."

20

I DROVE BACK TO DAVE'S Paint and Body thinking about the sheriff's lifestyle. It made sense, now, why we hadn't struck gold together. My guess was that Wayne Harris must have been as big a surprise to Hammersmith, back when they'd first met, as he was to me today. I was glad to see they'd moved in together and hadn't let public opinion stand in the way.

I was feeling pretty good, driving along and thinking how the earth can still bear walking on as long as there's some few among us who can stand up and be proud of what they believe in, but my mood was short-lived. Suddenly I remembered what Hammersmith had told me of Rachael McKinley. And how Cordelia Morgan fit into the picture. I'm not scared of much, nothing you can point to in daylight anyway, but I'm not such a fool as to fly into the face of trouble either. And I knew that woman was trouble, I just wasn't sure how much and what kind. That's maybe why I felt relieved when Dave gave me the news.

"Come and gone," he said, backing out from under a hood, wiping his hands on an oily rag. "Hung around hour so in that motor home. Week for parts, week to fix it, what I told her. Took a shine to my little Dart. What the hell, sold it to her." He grinned a span of yellow teeth the size of piano keys.

I headed for home, keeping an eye out for Morgan and the Dart broken down alongside the road, wondering at the stupidity and desperation that could drive a person to buy such a pile of junk. But she must have made it to my place because I didn't see her anywhere. I wasn't all that sure I wanted to. I kept hearing the sheriff's words: "...checked her out...Fairfield, Kentucky...clean as a whistle...gone on vacation...slit your throat...." This Rachael McKinley, she was a real flesh-and-blood woman, not a made-up name on a phony driver's license like Morgan said. So Morgan had her driver's license, but where was the real Rachael McKinley? I could come up with only two possibilities: either Morgan really *was* Rachael McKinley and had lied about being Cordelia Morgan, which made no sense at all, or...

Or what?

Or the real Rachael McKinley from Kentucky was...missing. *Missing? Like missing how? Like kidnapped? Like—*

I was passing Julia's driveway at just that moment. Her place was where I'd been used to coming with my problems, and though Julia wasn't there, her spirit was. I believe places are like that. Suddenly, without knowing I was going to do it, I turned in. After all, I had her keys in my pocket, and the house was mine, wasn't it?

I parked beside the garage where she kept her old Lincoln safely locked away and switched off the engine, sat looking around. No crime scene tape, no posted notices. I got out. No Hitchcock shower music, no saccharine violin strains. It looked like it always had. The difference was in the feel of the place—an unrelieved, desolate silence, the kind that hangs in the air of a place when its owner has gone for good.

And there were other changes. The front door was locked, though it had never been when Julia lived. I fiddled with the keys till one fit, walked in.

Nor had Julia ever closed a curtain that I knew of, but they were closed now, making the rooms gloomy and dark. That's why I didn't see her at first, not until I'd walked halfway into the living room. She was sitting by the old phonograph at one end of the sofa. A shadow among shadows. A file folder lay beside her, pale sheets of paper scattered across the cushions, the coffee table, the floor. A record was spinning round, the needle scratching intermittently. She switched off the phonograph.

I found myself sitting in a chair without knowing I'd sat down. I gripped the arms, felt helpless and cast in stone as surely as if I'd been facing the Medusa herself.

"What...how..." I said, fumbling for words. "Who are...the sheriff said..." I couldn't seem to match my thoughts to language, so I gave it up. It didn't matter. She talked like she knew what the questions were. She told me she knew I was coming, that she'd been waiting for me. She handed me a sheet of paper, the familiar yellow, lined notebook paper. The grainy, childishly printed letters. But this note made no pretense to poetry:

> *Gracie Lee, you have certainly outlasted us all. Like the queen said though, its time for heads to roll. Remember Mary Bess—an eye for an eye, a head for a head. ITS TIME.*

I stared at the words, mesmerized, dimly aware that someone was talking, but from a very far distance, barely audible.

A good deal of time must have passed as we sat this way. But I don't know, will never know. I only remember walking into the dim room, seeing her there. Remember an interim of electrical humming. And then she was standing over me, then kneeling at my side. She took my face in her hands, turned me to her. She was close now, looking into my eyes, talking low.

"You must listen now, listen closely. I can help you, Grace. I can say the words, but you must listen, you must do exactly as I say and follow me with your mind. I know how to find out what happened that night, December twenty-second, 1962. The night of the murders. It is the only way to find the note writer, the killer perhaps. I can hypnotize you so you will see it again." Her hand settled on my shoulder. "It's time to—"

And that is all, that is the end of my recollection.

21

Morgan

Nature is a numinous teacher. Study her well.

To wit: the next time you cross a footbridge, pause a moment, consider the stream. Note the direction you face. An easy call. By instinct, you will turn in the direction of the water's flow. With careful practice and observation, you become the water.

Thus, when I walk into Julia Simmons' home, before anything else, I switch on the old Victrola. Load the stack with Sinatra. Enter the back room where, as Frost has told me, Julia wrote. While the old crooner spins in the living room, I sit in her office chair and turn on the computer.

All this, exactly as Julia would have done.

It boots quickly. I see that her word processing program is Microsoft Word. I run a search on the hard disk for *.doc files dated October 25. Nothing. October 24. Three files. Password protected. I remove a floppy from my green bag, and in less than two minutes, open the files. Only one of the three could be the one I am searching for. I save it on a spare floppy, print out a hard copy, shut down the computer.

Two file cabinets along one wall. Old files stored in bottom drawers. A thick manila folder marked FBI BURNING in faded letters. I put it in my bag.

The old crooner has just begun his third song when I return to the living room. I sit in her place, beside the Victrola, my body fitted into the worn declivities made by her body over the years. I read the essay I have printed out, the one Simmons had been writing just before she died. It tells me what I need to know. I lean back, close my eyes, segue into the flow of the room.

Rooms are concave structures, and as such, like ships and caves and storms, they are distinctively female. Unique as any human being whose sum total of lived days is an accretion of happenstance creating that ineffable, singular oddity called personality. Some rooms, particularly those inhabited for long periods by an individual, are as cerebral or sensual or uncomfortably offensive as the human being who stripped their floors or chose their furniture or set their clocks to ticking in just such a way. Whether one enters such a room at the invitation of its owner, as a guest, or enters otherwise as a trespasser, the very introspection of its interior is an act of unqualified violation, the inquisition of another's most intimate and sacred space.

In this enclosed darkness, my eyes shut, I review the research I have accumulated through the years on Julia Simmons—the investigative reporter who, alone, attempted to penetrate the cover-up of the events leading to my mother's death. I have learned much about her before now, though in fact there is little enough outside her writing that is remarkable about her life. An uneventful childhood in this very town, a typical college sojourn, followed by her entry into journalism, and then her groundbreaking stories. No education, no money could have bought what Julia Simmons possessed: a sleuth's instinct for cover-ups, a perceptive curiosity, and most of all, an obsession for truth which more often than not put her on the side of the underdog against formidable opponents. The Indiana burning. She eventually discovered proof that the FBI had engaged in a cover-up, but she had never penetrated the why of it.

The why of it...

*All this runs through my mind like fire following a trail of gasoline. Like water coursing along a streambed. I no more choose these thoughts than water chooses its direction. I am merely a medium, a vessel inside this room, inside Julia Simmons. My senses, engorged, open themselves as pores to rain. The room is drenched with her: the odor of lemon polish, chamomile, autumn leaves, a cloistered fragrance of life fully lived and spiced with the crooner's hazy words...*poured sweet and clear, it was a very good year...

Julia Simmons. I inhale her, am light as air, nonexistent, borne along inside the flow of her resident spirit as surely and naturally as one is drawn in the direction of the water's flow beneath a footbridge. That easy, that natural.

I think of Grace Frost and sense what Julia must certainly also have sensed, given her long years of studying the murder case: her understanding of psychosis and how a history of abandonment can trigger—

In the distance, I hear the crunch of gravel as a vehicle climbs the driveway, coming closer. Outside the window, an engine idles, stops. And still I sit, waiting in the cool, gray light.

(There are sometimes these moments, spots of time, during which worlds can change; for time, as any medium, is malleable. One need only be acquainted with its defining properties and idiosyncrasies, and being acquainted, seize the propitious gift, flung without warning, sizzling with opportunity.)

I take out the note, the one I've removed an hour ago from Frost's box, and lay it on the table. Her poet has escalated his approach, danger is eminent. Close enough to feel.

But not here. Not now. Not in this room. Not yet.

Here, Julia's spirit flares a moment in the meager light, a candle flickering before the coming dawn, just as the door opens. She pauses there. Shuts the door behind her and walks into the darkness, a platinum nimbus stopping now at the room's center in a brief prologue before her eyes find mine.

And I see the fear rise like fire, burning away the mind.

I have seen this fear many times. It has been an invaluable ally, but at this time, at this place, it is a great impediment. I watch it possess her, extinguish her, take her over like some ravaging fever. It is a pure and naked fear, not only of me, but of something else I cannot yet identify.

I begin to talk her down, distract her with the poet's latest installment. I talk for a long time, watching the flames inside her eyes. I speak quietly, slowly, in the soothing rhythm I would use to lull a terrified horse. I understand that the sheriff has checked my background, my identity as Rachael McKinley, and so I explain to her, as I had not before, of my process of selecting ID names—accessing DMV files, running searches that call up drivers who match my physical description, researching each and selecting those who have interests and backgrounds with some similarity to my own, and then, when deciding on which to use at a given time, calling those on the list until I've reached one who is out of town, on vacation, gone for some unspecified amount of time. This is how I chose Rachael McKinley just last week. She comes from an area familiar to me, we have horses in common, and she is on vacation and unreachable till Thanksgiving. Using this process is neither difficult nor even time-consuming, but it is necessary to avoid detection by local law enforcement, as the sheriff has just proved.

I watch Frost calm as I speak, though I am not certain she understands the words. No matter. The meaning is less important than the tone. I simply tell her stories. My own stories, telling the most recent first. I describe my sojourn in Colorado under the alias of Eva Blake, of my friendship there with a woman called J. S. Symkin. I tell her about the subdivision in the Rockies and the killer who threatened us both, another killer who used his remote cabin as a place to dispose of young women's bodies, and yet another man who sexually battered women so brutally that he drove one to suicide. I tell her how the last two were beyond prosecution by the law, of the punishment I custom tailored for each.

Whether Frost understands or will retain any of this is not certain, but when I see the fever has gone from her eyes, I approach where she sits gazing into space. I kneel beside her chair and reach up, take her face between my hands. Her skin is cold to the touch. I turn her to me, anchor my gaze to hers.

Without warning, she bends to me, presses her lips against mine, and then I am leaning to her: a kiss for all those I have denied myself over the years. And another, deeply, for love of this moment and for hope of tomorrow.

And when this storm has passed, I sit back on my heels. Her eyes are still closed, waiting, but I must first solve the mystery of her past because there will be little enough of a future without that. And so I tell her to relax, ask her again to follow my words with her mind, to create the images as I speak them. I tell her that this is the only way for her to retrieve her past, to perhaps identify her tormentor and Julia's killer. I tell her that it is time—

Suddenly her eyes fly open, sky-blue doll's eyes, and in their incomprehensible stare, I see the fire has gone within her and that beyond that, behind the eyes, there is nothing at all.

When I try to rouse her from the trance, she is absent, conscious neither of my voice nor my presence. I watch her for some time and examine the options. I decide against calling the sheriff: Frost is already a suspect, and her present state would only increase suspicion. A hospital, then. That is no place for a woman who has been incarcerated with the smell of medicine and the onus of supervision for the bulk of her adult life. She needs a caretaker, a nurse, someone to watch over her in a friendly environment. I recall what she has told me of her next door neighbor, the lonely Clarissa. I smile to myself.

The lonely are the world's most unacknowledged samaritans.

22

I HAVE BEEN SLEEPING WITH MY EYES OPEN. A "fugue state," my doctors used to call it. The woman in black and Clarissa Remington stand over me, Santillanes leaning against the door frame. Clarissa is talking:

not much to do but wait The words slip out one-by-one from between her lips, firm and hard as children's marbles. Mere sounds without meaning. *might pass and it might not*

The woman in black, Cordelia Morgan, leans over me. At first I think she is going to kiss me, but she doesn't. Her face is so close I can feel her breath. Her eyes are pushing into mine, but I resist her, like Daddy said to do when somebody tried to interfere with his instructions, so I make her translucent, see right through her to the ceiling which is white and vacant as a desert, rolling miles of white sand where a soul can find some peace *(though now, Julia said, it is a Kubla Khan of a city with buildings that are castles, hotels that are casinos, lights which never stop flashing, spinning wheels with balls traveling around their gutters)* and where, if you travel long enough, due south, walking beside the road that just ahead is wavy with heat ripples and maybe a car passes every four or five miles, you can hitch a ride and in a day or week or however long it takes, you'll come to the town that calls to you like a siren out of the ocean, like all that sand has gone to water and you have to listen, you have no choice, because every step of the way you can't help but hear it and see it: that face rising up in the heat in front of you, rippling behind the furnace of hot air. Calling you to him.

("It's time now, Grace. It's time.")

Mesmerizing, this face. It hangs right there in front of me, between me and the desert. I wonder who chiseled the lips and got the cheekbones too high and sketched the eyebrows into the shape of black wings, why the eyes needed to be that deep and exotic and why they glitter like a knife flashing in the dark.

The green nylon bag hangs over her shoulder, the driver's licenses and checkbooks in a rainbow of different names hidden inside. I wonder at how much time has passed since I first saw them in my truck. Opening that bag, looking at all those photos. I call them back from memory as easy as grabbing the bag and taking them out and pasting them in a halo around her head. I compare each one to the original. I see now, as I hadn't then, that each has a single feature that's been changed, minute but critical—in one, green eyes; in another, auburn hair; in others, an enlarged nose or deep-set eyes or fuller cheeks. I understand as she bends close over me that Cordelia Morgan is a woman in hiding, but strangely—playing it like a game, more out of whimsy than fear.

Thoughts ebb and flow, waves on a beach. I surf their crests and gullies. When I return to the room, I am alone.

Somewhere in a far part of the house, a door closes. A car engine starts, revs, disappears. Clarissa Remington's old man's voice mumbles in the distance, fluttering sounds that grow faint, joined by a strong male voice, the two of them twining and muffled together. Bedroom noises: a man and a woman finding each other.

In the expanse of white sand across the ceiling and the soft wings of bedroom sounds, I get up, pull off the ruffled flannel gown somebody has put me in and toss it over that camera's eye they've set on me. My own clothes are freshly laundered and neatly stacked on top of the dresser.

The bedroom door stands ajar. I stick my head out, check the hall—empty. I tiptoe along the plush carpeting, across the living room with its gleaming ebony piano, the brocade furniture scattered with small pillows, sunlight coming through the acres of paned windows. I ease out the door, onto the patio, and squint against the light. I follow a path through banks of profuse plants whose dark glossy leaves are shaped like giant hands that shake and applaud as I push through them to the wrought iron fence. It is a high, barred affair, twined with iron-leafed ivy that serves as a stepladder. I climb up, vault myself over the top spikes, land in a squat on the other side. I push through the scrub brush to the crest of the ridge and the path to Julia's house.

The place is still locked up, of course. I fish in my pocket for Julia's keys, but they're gone. Doesn't matter. I know every loose door, every rattling window on the place. Including the garage. The side door pops open with a turn of the knob and an easy shoulder hit. I punch a control panel button inside the door, and the garage door slides up so that sunlight floods across the old Lincoln sitting under a skin of dust. I reach up, run my fingers along the top lip of the panel where Julia always kept a spare ignition key. I find it, furry with accumulated grime and dust.

Mostly, the art of evasion is a simple matter of common sense. They didn't call me The Fox at Mt. Havens for nothing—six escapes, not counting the last, so I know how to get out and stay out if I want to. After the first time or two, they suspended the punishment, solitary confinement and worse, just shrugged it off like it was an amusement for them, but they never could stop me from doing it, nor would they have caught me either if I hadn't always been headed for that same place where they would sooner or later show up.

This time, it's different. When Clarissa finds me gone, not too far from now most likely because Santillanes will have to get home to his wife and kids this afternoon, she'll call the sheriff. Hammersmith will come looking at my house. Now I figure this Lincoln is as much mine as my truck, because if I'd take the truck, I wouldn't even make it to San Luis Obispo before getting spotted and brought back. This way, by the time the sheriff thinks to look in Julia's garage, I'll already be where I'm going, and by then it won't matter anymore. It never did. Somehow it was just the getting there, like he told me to do, that inspired me.

The car starts up on the first try, engine running smooth as honey in hell. I back her out, hit the button on the control box clipped on the visor to close the garage door, and guide the old boat down the driveway, heading for 101 South.

I drive all afternoon and all night, and the trip seems like it could just as well have been one of those times in 1970 with the countryside sliding by, not much different than it had ever looked. So I'm not all that surprised when I pull in the parking lot and the dawn is just starting to break, the sky fading to that lead color when the air is damp and the birds still asleep. A few cars are in the staff lot under the light, just like there used to be, though before this I'd always been hitching and I'd ask to be dropped off down the road at a filling station where I'd use the toilet and change into my good clothes I'd carried in my suitcase. Use some paper towels to scrub up some, wash the blood off where I'd come through the cactus and hid when I spotted a patrol car. I'd slip on the silk stockings that'd cost me two months of doing the ladies' hair at Mt. Havens, put on the high heels, then the good dress that'd taken some time to come by, watching from my window during the midnight hours when the interns or shrinks would have a girl in, using one of the empty rooms; waiting till one showed up about my size, maybe even then having to do some alterations on the fit.

I drive on past the staff cars and back to the far end of the lot where the light doesn't reach. I stop the old Lincoln and maneuver her backwards into the parking slot so I'm facing the hospital to watch the front entrance and figure the best time to enter.

That's when I got the first surprise.

The building that'd once been two stories is now five. And behind that first building is a whole city of them, building after building, far as I can see in the dim morning light. But the words etched in gray stone at the front entry are the same: *Tucson Veterans Hospital*. And the voice whispering out from somewhere is as omnipotent and compelling as it ever was:

"Gracie Lee, you must listen to me. It's time, now. You must know that I'm only trying to help you, don't you? If you are to get through this, you've got to pay attention to me just like you have always done when your nerves have failed you. It's the only way, you understand that, don't you, Gracie? I want you to lie back, now, and close your eyes. Listen to me, trust me. Will you do that, Gracie? Lie down, put your head back, and relax. Close your eyes, Gracie. It's time."

I feel his hand on my shoulder, pushing me back on the bed, the sofa, the floor, the bathtub, anywhere at all, as his other hand pushed my legs apart.

"Grace."

But even as I turn and look up through the Lincoln's open window and see the long lean black lines of her, it is the gray man I see standing there.

"I've come, Daddy, just like you said." My voice sounds funny, disembodied and high, like a child's. "That's right, isn't it, Daddy?"

"Sure, Grace." The door opens and the hand on my shoulder pushes at me. "Why don't you just scoot on over and I'll drive for awhile."

And so the countryside slides by again, backwards this time, going in the direction I'd just come with the two hands in the driver's seat gripping the wheel and the words spinning out in the air we are whipping through at a speed a lot faster than I'd come. The voice is talking about how time can spool backwards just like forwards, how if you thought about it and counted backwards while you were moving forward the way you'd just come, you'd find some peace there. It got my head to spinning, and I did just what I was told, just the two of us moving backwards through the desert, our voices counting backwards together.

"...ninety-nine...ninety-eight..."

Close your eyes now, Grace.

"...ninety-seven...ninety-six..."

You're tired, aren't you, Grace?

"...oh yes, ninety-five..."

Just lean your head back against the seat, Grace.

"...Gracie, ninety-four...ninety-three..."

...sure, "Gracie" then...

Just me counting now, listening to the voice talking about the desert we're driving through, and me with my eyes closed, still counting while I listen:

I've heard that even in the desert there are canyons, very deep canyons where the earth has split and where you can find a path that will take you down inside them, and you can descend—

"...yes, that's right, eighty-seven, because I've come across such places myself during my escapes through the desert. Eighty-five. I've found them and hid in them, eighty-four, till the police cars went on and even liked it so much I stayed in a cave behind a sunny ledge above a rock canyon, eighty—"

Good, Gracie, that's good. You found a place you liked then, in the desert? A peaceful place you could hide and relax—

"Yes, and, seventy-seven, stretch out on a ledge in the sun, naked. The way you always liked me to be, Daddy, and I'd lay on the rock, seventy-three, with the sun warm on my skin, and I'd pretend like I was a snake, like there was nothing more in the world to want than to be in exactly that place at that time—"

Good. Okay, Gracie. I want you to keep counting backwards when you think of it, and picture that cave now, as we're driving. Can you do that, Gracie?

"Yes, Daddy, I'm seeing it, seventy-two, lying right on that smooth, hot stone."

Good. Now is there a path anywhere around, Gracie, one that will take you on down to the bottom of the canyon? A safe one, so you can climb down to maybe where there's a stream along the bottom?

"Yes, a stream. I can hear it, and a path, too, going down around the rocks. I can climb down it, just like you said—"

Good, Gracie. You're doing it exactly right. You're going to climb down into the canyon, Gracie. Going lower, deeper, keep counting backwards, you have all the time in the world. As you go down, I want you to be calm, listen to the birds, the stream, your feet walking along the path, the touch of the sun and the air on your skin, and you're still counting. When you get to sixty-two, that's where I want you to stop and rest.

"Yes, sixty-three, sixty-two—" I am tired, real tired. I wipe sweat from my forehead and then sit on a boulder, watching the hawks circle in the sky, waiting.

"Sixty-two, Gracie. Is there a comfortable place to lie down, let the sun warm you? You're going to lie down and rest. Look up at the sky and tell me what you smell, what you see, what touches your body."

And so I talk, I say how the sky's a clear blue. I say how it's the same thin, pure color of my daddy's eyes on those Sunday afternoons when my mother stayed late after church to watch over the cake walk and the clean-up after daddy was finished preaching and we came home to the empty house, just the two of us. I had been seven years old the first time he'd climbed the stairs and come into my room and said I was old enough to start praying from my heart, using more than the bedtime rhymes my mother had taught me. We had kneeled down together on the floor, and after I'd closed my eyes and repeated the long Biblical sentences after him, he'd explained how I needed to rest, that such praying must be followed by a reward, just like a good meal needed a dessert. He had lifted me up and laid me down on the small bed, then he had lain down beside me. With my head nestled in the crook of his elbow, he explained about fathers and daughters, how a daughter was the fruit of her father's loins, his creation, and how she must learn to be obedient and to repay him for the care and support it was his duty to give her while she lived under his roof. I understood, too, without him even saying it, that this was something between the two of us, something that only he and I, and God of course, were entitled to know. What he did next hurt at first, so much that I had screamed out. But he hadn't stopped, he had covered my mouth with his hand and told me I would get used to it, because what he was doing was every man's right, and every daughter's duty. It was so bad that first time, but the pain wasn't as bad as the months and years went by. But he'd been wrong about one thing—I had never gotten used to it. I have forever dreaded the coming of a Sunday afternoon, even now getting agitated by the memory of how the bed had knocked against the wall and how the springs had creaked in that singsong rhythm till he had finished with me.

And that same sky blue, the color of Daddy D's eyes, too, after he had calmed me down that first night in my apartment, after he had used his words to make me be still and stop crying, words to take away the pain, or the memory of it he says, and the same words every time after that because it's the only cure, he says, and then after awhile, after I'm used to the words, all he has to do is come into the room any time and touch my shoulder that certain way and say it (*It's time*, he says), and then time stops. There's nothing, no memory, nothing in the world but a wide vacuum of darkness until I wake with his semen running from inside me, seeping out between my legs.

The car is stopped and my face is wet, and where I thought I'd heard the skreeing of hawks circling the sky, now I hear my own hysterical crying. My eyes are still closed, squeezed shut, and the voice outside is saying:

"Grace, stop. It's all right. Let that image go, Grace. Let it go. You're alone on the rock, warmed by the sun, and you're absolutely safe, very safe. I promise you that, Grace. You're safe now. It's a private place, your rock. You can think any thought, see any image, and no one can see you. You are a secret woman in a secret place. You can see others, but you're invisible. You can see without being seen, do you hear me, Grace?"

I nod, feel the sun and the breeze stroke my face.

"All right, you're going to open your eyes now, Grace, but you're still invisible. You will see everything around you, but you can't be seen unless you allow yourself to be seen. You are very safe, very strong, in control. You're wearing a crystal bubble that protects you. Not even a bullet could go through it, nothing in the world can touch you, Grace. Do you believe me?"

Yes, oh yes. I open my eyes and look around. We are in some kind of public park. The Lincoln is pulled into a sandy roadside pull-in verging off a deserted asphalt two-lane. Around us—nothing but desert, the bristling scrub brush extending as far as the eye can see in all directions.

Sitting at a picnic table across from me is Cordelia Morgan, and above us, a shelter made of pale, narrow poles. The sun is not up yet, the morning is still gray. A nearby trash barrel overflows with litter, tatters of it blown by the wind and caught in the surrounding brush and cactus. Morgan is watching the far western horizon, her eyes narrowed. I feel some trouble boiling inside her, and though I know she can't see me, has no idea I am sitting across from her, I smile, reach out and cover her hand with mine.

"This is an absolutely safe place," she says. "There is no one around, nothing and no one to be afraid of here. Look for yourself, see that you are safe. See that there is no one here to hurt you, and when you are certain of that, I want you to close your eyes again."

No one here to harm me? I'm not seeing the stretch of brown desert any more, I'm seeing Morgan. I look at her for a long, long time. Then I close my eyes.

"Good. We're going to go back there, Grace. We must." The voice is anonymous, disembodied, words carried by the wind from another place. Where spirits live. "You are going to see things that will frighten and upset you, Grace, but always remember this: I give you my promise—they will never hurt you again. You are an invisible observer, and even when you see the body you recognize as your own, it is not really you. It is only a shell, an illusion separate from who you are now. You, the real you, is sitting right here at this table. I'm going to hold on to your hand so you know I'm beside you, the two of us going back in time now, to the number sixty-two. Nineteen-sixty-two. December twenty-second. I want you to go back to that day, look at it like you're watching it on a movie screen. Watch it and tell me what's happening there without any worry of being hurt. You'll remember everything you've told me, you'll know all about what happened once you tell it to me. Can you do that, Grace?"

Sure, I can do that. It isn't like I haven't been there a million times, can still see it like yesterday. I feel the strength of her hand squeezing mine, and I re-enter that day like I'm opening the door of a too-familiar house. It's still that real.

23

B UT IT WASN'T ME WHO CAME THROUGH THE DOOR, it was someone else.

"Jesse Ballantine," I said, as the sun peeked over the mountains and the day's first brilliant light slid across the desert, casting black shadows behind the saguaro cactus. "She's the first one I saw that morning. I was already typing at the receptionist's desk at the clinic where we both worked when she burst in like she had every morning for the ten months I'd been there, hitting the door with one shoulder and charging in with her head down like an angry bull."

As I watched Jesse coming at me against a backdrop of the vast, sunlit desert, I was suddenly reminded of that play Daddy D had taken me to at an open-air amphitheatre a long time ago. We'd seen a play about Medea, and all around us rose high red cliffs that the actors voices echoed off of and hawks circled overhead. I'd felt exposed, like I needed to find cover, but I'd forced myself to sit there and do my best to pay attention to what the actors were saying, even though their words bounced and multiplied and overlapped so I couldn't figure out the meaning at all.

I squeezed my eyes shut, remembered what the woman sitting across from me had said about being safe, and knew that even though I couldn't see it, there was that bubble around me so nobody could hurt me, even while I was talking inside the bubble and hearing my own words echoing and bouncing back.

So I told her the story I'd played a thousand times, a million times. I'd played it forwards and backwards and sideways, and it didn't make any more sense the first time than it was going to make now. But Cordelia Morgan didn't know that, she hadn't been there. She'd never laid eyes on the players, on Jesse or Mary Bess or the Doctor, so I described them as best I could, looking out across the endless ocean of sand and wasteland where I saw it all happening again right in front of me, just like *Medea* at the amphitheatre.

"Jesse, she's a big, wide woman, very formidable in her nurse's uniform," I said, squinting against the sun. "Even at seven a.m., I'd known something was a little sideways, because for every morning Jesse had hit the door like a charging bull, that Friday she hit it twice as hard. She'd given me a nasty look as she stomped past toward the examining rooms, but I shrugged it off. During the seven months I'd been living with her and Mary Bess after Daddy went to LA looking for work, Jesse's temper had always been unpredictable, but since I'd moved into my own place two weeks ago, it'd gone off the charts.

"I didn't have a lot of time to think about it, though, because that day was hectic, the last one before we closed down the clinic for the two-week Christmas break. When Jesse finally stormed out a little after five, complaining about being late to pack up so she and Mary Bess could leave for Oregon that night, she slammed the door hard enough to shake the building and rattle every window."

I remembered sitting there in the hushed, empty office, feeling numb and bracing myself against what had to follow. I put off thinking about it for as long as I could, busied myself with closing up the place, especially checking the x-ray machine that Jesse had twice left set on high so that if I hadn't noticed it, whoever stepped in front of it would have received a lethal dose.

"In fact, that's exactly what had started the argument a couple weeks before, as the three of us ate dinner. I'd mentioned finding the machine left on again, reminded her to turn it off. I suppose that was my first mistake, if you don't count moving in with her and Mary Bess to begin with after Daddy left and I needed a place to stay till he sent for me. Because in addition to having a nasty temper, Jesse couldn't bear being wrong. What followed was vintage Jesse, a hysterical tantrum that ended with her throwing dishes across the table at me and then tearing out of the apartment."

I smiled at the wasteland, not seeing it, seeing me and Mary Bess after Jesse had stormed out. "We picked up broken dishes, mopped the floor, wiped down the walls, working shoulder-to-shoulder, both of us thinking about that one night we'd had together, even though we'd not talked about it. Then there was that point in time when we suddenly stopped working and turned to each other. Mary Bess's dark blue eyes were swollen and red from crying, and I felt like a thunderbolt had struck me right out of the ceiling, because in that moment I understood with every cell in my body, sure as I was breathing, that I loved Mary Bess like I'd never loved anything before and probably never would again. When I'd asked her if she'd move into an apartment with me, she'd smiled and said that was just what she'd been hoping I'd ask her to do.

"That's all I'd needed to set me moving. I found a place the next day, just four blocks away and still close enough to the clinic to walk to work. Mary Bess agreed to tell Jesse she was leaving, but I knew how she hated confrontations and would have a hard time doing it. So I told her if she hadn't given Jesse the news by that Friday, when they were supposed to leave for Oregon, I'd come over and do it myself."

Mostly that was what I had on my mind as I closed down the office that afternoon. That and the phone call I'd let Daddy bully me into making. Before leaving, I sat down at my desk and stared at the telephone. I'd been dreading this almost as much as the showdown with Jesse. Even if Mary Bess hadn't done her part yet, I'd done mine—called Daddy D after I'd found the new apartment, told him Mary Bess was moving in with me, that I was in love with her and wanted a divorce, that I wouldn't be coming to LA. That had set him off laughing, but when he understood I was serious, he'd tried to talk me out of it, then gotten very quiet. Finally he made me promise to think about it some more and call him Friday before I left the office for Christmas break.

I gritted my teeth, picked up the phone, dialed the operator to make a collect call, and gave her Daddy D's number. The phone rang several times before a voice answered.

"Hello." A woman's voice.

I had stared at the receiver like I could see right through the black plastic, all the way to L.A. and whoever was standing there at the other end of the line. I listened while the woman accepted the collect charges, and the operator left the line.

"Yes, hello?" It was an anonymous voice, not young, not old. No accent I could detect.

"Uh, is Daddy, uh, is Doctor DeWitte there?"

"No, he's not, but I can take a message. He said to make a list of anybody that called and he'd call them right back soon as he got home. You want to leave your number?"

I stared at the mouthpiece again and hung up.

• • •

It was still early, but the morning shadows had grown shorter, the air hotter. I was tired, abysmally tired. All I wanted to do was go to sleep, but when I put my head down on my arms, a voice roused me, called at me to go on describing the movie I was watching. It wasn't a movie, it was a play, a tragedy, but I wasn't going to argue the point. I lifted my head up and stared out into the desert sun and saw myself shoving the key into the lock of my apartment I'd been living in for only two weeks, the one I'd rented for me and Mary Bess.

"Well, I went home, took down the bottle of whiskey I'd got accustomed to since I'd been married to Daddy, had a few drinks, then a few more. By the time I left and was knocking on Jesse and Mary Bess's door, I was primed pretty good and ready for anything Jesse was going to throw at me. This time, though, I wasn't planning on ducking; I was going to fight back."

At first no one answered. The lights were on inside, the curtains open, and from where I stood on the porch, I could see the living room with the television in one corner and the old couch sitting in front of it.

Then the yellow porch light came on. Jesse opened the door, standing behind the screen in her jeans and plaid shirt. I looked past her, to Mary Bess in the bedroom, holding a stack of clothes in her hands, an open suitcase on the bed. She looked very scared.

"You lost your mind, DeWitte? What're you doing here? We're not going dancing tonight. Me and Mary Bess, we got to pack for Oregon, for Christ sake. I told you that today." She was mad, but something else, too. She had a smirk on her face, almost a smile.

"I've got to talk to you, it's important," I said. I pulled open the screen, knowing they never latched it. "It can't wait."

"What's this? You been drinking again?" Jesse stepped back, followed my gaze to Mary Bess who seemed frozen in place. Her auburn hair was twisted around in a knot with flyaway strands falling around her face. Her eyes were wide as a deer's. Even with Jesse at my elbow, I felt an overwhelming rush of love for her.

"Jesus Christ, DeWitte. Get a grip. What in hell's wrong with you?" Jesse slammed the door hard and walked over to stand in the doorway of the bedroom, shutting off my view of Mary Bess. "We got a million things to do tonight, so let's have it. What's so important? I forget to turn off the x-ray machine again?"

Her face was purple, the way it got when she was closing in on high rage. I ignored her and stood on tiptoe, talking directly to Mary Bess. "You didn't tell her yet, did you?"

"Tell me what?" Jesse said. She glanced behind her to Mary Bess. "Okay, Mary Bess. It's time you leveled with Grace and cut this shit out." She tilted her chin up, folded her arms over her breasts, stepped aside so I could see Mary Bess, and glared at me. "You think I don't know how you been bothering Mary Bess, thinking you're going to talk her into leaving me for some sorry shit like you. Let me tell you something, DeWitte, you couldn't no more keep Mary Bess happy than you kept that good-for-nothing, dope-addict husband of yours happy." Her eyes narrowed, and her lips drew back in the closest thing to a snarl I'd ever seen off a dog. "You don't think I heard you two when he come here visiting? You two in the bedroom and him having to *hypnotize* you and give you *drugs*, for Christ sake, before you'll even let your own husband fuck you?"

I felt the blood drain from my face, and Mary Bess looked away.

"I been telling Mary Bess ever since you moved out and kept calling her that she's got to tell you to leave her alone. She says she don't want to hurt your feelings, but since you're here, I'll tell you,

DeWitte." Jesse took a step forward, so close I could feel her body heat. She jammed her fists on her hips. "I don't mind one bit hurting your feelings. Sitting behind that desk all day, all the doctors kissing your ass. Me having to listen to them going on about how you look just like Marilyn Monroe, what they'd like to do to you in the sack. You think that's funny, don't you? You think you can have anything you want, but you can just take your frigid ass on out of here, 'cause Mary Bess knows what she wants, and she's coming to Oregon with me. That right, Mary Bess?"

The room had gone stone quiet, but Jesse's words rang in my ears and tears stung my eyes. Me and Jesse—both of us watching Mary Bess standing there holding that stack of clothes and looking at the floor, me seeing her through a wet blur, how she brought one hand up to push back the loose hair around her face, then raised her head so slowly that I was thinking how we all seemed to be caught in some slow motion movie. It was then, as I watched the unbearably slow passage of tears sliding down Mary Bess's cheeks, that I realized she was moving her head from side to side—so slowly, first to one side, and then to the other side.

She looked me straight in the eye: "No, Grace. It's not true, I didn't...she listened in on the phone at work when you called—"

An ear-shattering scream came from beside me, like the ones I'd heard at the movies when the Indians launched an attack on the cavalry, a high-pitched, long scream that tore the air.

That's when something snapped. The camera flew into fast forward, images coming fast, jammed together. Jesse's face, dark purple. Moving fast, her head down, charging. Going for Mary Bess who still had her mouth open, saying something I couldn't hear. Mary Bess's dark blue eyes, impossibly large as Jesse caught her in the stomach, drove her backwards with the force of a football tackle. The clothes flying from Mary Bess's hands. Mary Bess hitting the dresser backwards with a sickening thud and a crack. Her body sliding down the dresser, reaching the floor, sliding like a limp rag until she lay stretched at Jesse's feet.

Jesse still screaming, the words mangled. Swinging her foot back, like she was going to kick a football right over the goal line, swinging her foot forward where it smashed into the side of Mary

Bess's head. And she lay there, her mouth still open, moving, her eyes wide, straight up at the ceiling. Blood began seeping in a crooked thread from her ear.

And another sound, loud. What was it? Screams coming from my own mouth as I watched Jesse run to the nightstand beside the bed, grabbing the gun from the drawer, shoving it at me and shouting vowel words that had no meaning. I tried to shove her away, tried to grab for the gun. Among the screams and the vowels: the gunshot. And silence.

• • •

"Go on, Grace."

"That's all. There is no more." I put my head down on my arms. Closed my eyes. I wanted to sleep more than I'd ever wanted anything in my life.

"No, Grace. There's more. The movie isn't over yet."

"Not a movie. A play."

"A play, then. But this is only Act One, Grace. You have mistaken the end of the act for the end of the play. You've had your intermission now, haven't you? You've rested."

I felt her hand on my forehead, stroking my damp hair back. The hand was cool. A gentle breeze across the desert. I lifted my head, but the amphitheatre had gone dark, silent. There were no actors there.

I shook my head. "No, it's over. There's nothing more after the gunshot. You don't understand...I'd...I'd had too much to drink before I went...a blackout—"

"No, Grace. Look, they're coming back on stage. You see them, the actors? Mary Bess, she's still on the floor isn't she? And Jesse, where is Jesse?"

She was right. The lights had come on, the brilliant sun hitting the stage where Mary Bess lay staring at the ceiling, her mouth moving, though I couldn't hear the words because...*because why, Grace, why?*...because, because Jesse was screaming, lying on the floor, curled into a ball with her hands holding her head and blood streaming between her fingers. Lots of blood, oceans of blood. So much blood that the stage swayed in front of me. The darkness began to fall again until the cool hand held mine and the bubble fitted itself around me.

"Good Lord, Gracie, what in the world have you done now."

I twisted around to see him leaning against open doorway of the bedroom—

"Who, Grace? Who is standing in the doorway?"

It was Daddy, his arms crossed over his chest as he watched us. His silver hair was immaculately combed, his soft gray suit elegantly pressed. I felt such an overwhelming surge of relief that I ran to him, knelt, hugged his legs and cried like the tears would never end. I knew Daddy would make everything right, that he would save me.

"Stop that."

Daddy D leaned over, shoved me backwards hard enough to break my hold. He went into the living room and closed the drapes, locked the front door. I felt something brushing against my shoe and saw Jesse crawling toward me, her arm searching a wide, blind arc across the floor. I screamed and scrambled backward into a corner, screaming in terror for Daddy to come. But he was still in the living room. He was stepping out of his trousers, holding them up by the seams, hanging them neatly over the back of the sofa. By the time he returned to the bedroom, he wore only his briefs. He walked past where Jesse lay and stood over me, slapped me until I quit screaming.

"I want you to be quiet, Grace. There is nothing more you can do here, so shut up."

He went to where Mary Bess lay and squatted over her. I tried to push myself up, but my legs were rubber, so I crawled toward Mary Bess who stared at the ceiling with her mouth moving soundlessly. I stretched out my arm, had almost touched her when Daddy glanced around. The light flashed off his glasses, and he swore to himself. He stood up, grabbed my arm, and began dragging me out of the bedroom, but not before I'd seized Mary Bess's hand, gripped it so tight that as Daddy D pulled me past where Jesse lay jerking and on across the living room, into the spare room which had once been mine, Mary Bess was dragged along in my wake.

As we made the turn past the bedroom door, Mary Bess's shoulder caught on the frame, and Daddy D stopped. He looked back and swore some more, grasped my wrist in both his hands and gave a tremendous jerk, breaking my hold and wrenching my shoulder so badly I shrieked in pain. By the time we reached the bed, I was screaming without pause, kicking out as he grabbed me under my arms and lifted me up, threw me down hard on the bare mattress.

"Goddammit it to hell, I told you to shut up, didn't I?" He gripped my shoulder and slapped me hard. "Gracie! Stop it! You're making yourself hysterical. You have to calm down now. I want you to just lay here and be quiet, that's all I'm asking you to do."

It wasn't that I didn't want to stop screaming, I couldn't, so Daddy straddled me, pinned my wrists with his hands, the veins of his naked arms standing out and the sharp male odor of his body burning my nostrils. Through the thin fabric of his briefs, I saw that he had grown hard, and I struggled even more frantically. I glanced over at Mary Bess where she lay near the doorway, staring at us. *Oh my god no, not now lord, please not now,* I thought, becoming so frenzied that he let go my wrist and hit me hard in the stomach with his fist.

"Now shut up, goddammit. Just shut up and lay still." With one hand securing my wrists, he grabbed my face with his free hand and forced me to look at him. "It's time, Grace," he whispered, letting go of my face and touching my shoulder, "it's time."

I lay still then, very still, like he'd taught me to do when he said those words. He left the room, stepping over Mary Bess without looking at her and her long auburn sprawl of hair across the floor where it had come loose from its knot, and when he returned, he was carrying the black physician's bag in his hand. He sat down on the bed and fished in the bag until he found a hypodermic. As he sank the needle into the small, clear vial, I took off my clothes until I lay naked, my eyes closed while I counted backward the way he said, riding the elevator he described as it plunged down, deeper, to a dark place in my mind. Felt the needle being pushed through my flesh and entering the vein.

I opened my eyes then and watched the ceiling, savoring the first exquisite rush of the chemical singing along my nerve endings and warming my blood. I became weightless. My pores expanded and opened to the air. My nipples became engorged with a tingling sensation, and my womb was swollen and throbbing almost painfully with a hunger that seemed to increase with every passing second. I spread my legs to ease the ache, feeling my vulva expand like a flower's petals opening themselves to the morning sun, wanting Daddy. He was kneeling over Mary Bess again, saying: "...not fatal, but that tackle Jesse threw her has broken her spine, might as well be dead for all the use she is now."

I smiled to think how it wasn't important, not at all—I would care for Mary Bess, so there was nothing to worry about...and now the Doctor was coming back to me, saying what he always said as he took off his glasses, folded them, laid them neatly on the table, whispering: *It's time, Gracie. It's time.* Peeling off his briefs, kneeling between my legs and rubbing his penis against my body, between my breasts while Mary Bess watched and called out for help. But the Doctor was here, wasn't he, surely Mary Bess ought to know that she was going to be all right with the Doctor here. I held her eyes with my own, looked deep into her and tried to reassure her as the doctor entered me and the bed rose and fell like waves ebbing and flowing on white sands...

"Grace? Go on. And what happened then?"

I heard the voice from the desert, but I couldn't speak, could I? The Doctor didn't allow it, and anyway it was too pleasant floating this way, receiving that thing which quenched the body's yearning, so I waited until the rocking had stopped and Daddy D had emptied himself and was pulling himself out of me, my eyes still on Mary Bess's eyes, loving her.

"You're a good girl, Gracie," Daddy D said as he drew on his briefs. "A very good girl." He sat on the bed and held my face between his hands, directing me to look at him. "But tonight, something very bad has happened. Because you're such a good girl, I'm going to help you, just like I always have. I'm going to talk to your subconscious mind now, not to your conscious mind, but to your subconscious that will protect you from shock, exactly as it is supposed to do.

"You are going to forget everything that happened here tonight, from the time you heard the gunshot until the time you wake in the morning in your own bed. Do you understand? Everything in between those two points of time will be erased, as though none of it ever happened, though you will harbor a residual sense of the evening such that you will forever understand that woman is not meant, ever, to be with woman. But you will not remember that I was here, that you ever saw me or spoke to me tonight. You will remember that the last time we spoke was on the phone around five this afternoon, do you remember that? You called my number from your office, didn't you? And you will remember that I answered the phone, that we spoke briefly and hung up, is that right, Gracie?"

I clung to the lightness still glistening inside my body and nodded. Tears gathered behind my lids, tickled my cheeks as they streamed down. I took them for tears of joy.

"You will sleep for awhile, and when you wake up, I'll be gone. You will find this place a great mess. You will think of it as someone else's mess, and it will not upset you in any way. You will only be concerned to clean it up, to leave the place tidy because you have always despised a mess, haven't you, Gracie? You will get out of bed, and in the living room, you will find a large trunk beside the front door. I want you to pick up whatever is lying on top and then open the lid. What you see when you look inside will be the only image you will keep from this night here after the gunshot. Your mind will take a snapshot of it like a camera, but it will be an isolated snapshot, not connected to any event. Then you will place the utensil you found inside the trunk, close the lid, and lock it. Do you understand what I've told you, Gracie?"

I nodded.

"Now, Gracie, after the place is tidy, I want you to clean yourself up, wear some of Mary Bess's clothes. When you are ready to leave, call the number beside the telephone and have the trunk picked up, have it delivered to the train station. Then you will go home, to your own place where you will sleep for the rest of the night. When you wake, you will not remember anything after the gunshot, but you will know that there is a trunk at the station that I've asked you to bring to me when we spoke on the phone this evening. You will go to the train station, book passage for yourself, and ride on the train with the trunk to Los Angeles. I will meet you there at the station. All this will be behind us then, Gracie, and we will be happy. Would you like that, Gracie?"

I smiled and nodded. When I woke, Daddy D was gone.

24

"THAT SON OF A BITCH! THAT DIRTY, ROTTEN, LOUSY…"
The blinding rays from over the Santa Catalina mountains shot under the roof of the campsite, straight into my eyes. I blinked, held up my hand as a shield, and tried to see the woman's expression across from me, but she was only a black shape inside the blazing glare.

I looked around. We were the sole occupants in the last of a long line of campsites, each with its pole roof, picnic table anchored to a concrete pad, and a brick barbecue grill. In the sandy pull-in space sat Julia's old Lincoln under a jacket of dust that just about hid its oxidized turquoise. It fit right into the surroundings: a bleak landscape of burnt desert and barren mountains that extended north to Utah and south into Mexico. I recognized the place—the northwest section of the Saguaro National Park, just north of Tucson. You bet I recognized it.

I was wide awake now, memory intact. I stood up with the voices still echoing and images still clawing inside my head. I walked away from the woman and the campsite, out toward the open desert that was without shelter or any visible sign of human trespass. A sandy path zigzagged into the cactus, leading east, toward the barren Catalinas, but it was soon swallowed by prickly pear and cholla. No matter. I was heading into the heart of the

Sonoran Desert, more home and sanctuary to me than any confabulation of wood and glass had ever been. One hundred and twenty thousand square miles of the largest desert in North American. July, it would have been closing in on a hundred; today, it was nudging sixty and not yet nine o'clock. But it wouldn't have mattered what month it was or what time it was or even what temperature it was: I walked without knowing I walked. I walked till I was panting for breath, and then I walked some more.

Because there's solace in movement, in being free to set your foot in any direction you've a mind to. And if you can stand it, there's a grim comfort in the solitude and integrity of a hostile terrain. I marched into the heart of it, walking fast, with my head down, but with caution—wading through sagebrush and mesquite to avoid the cacti and Spanish bayonet and the hard shiny leaves of creosote—until I felt the tranquility of the place begin its magic. As it always had—all the times I'd escaped from Mt. Havens and trekked the hundred miles of desert to Tucson, in pursuit of Daddy D. I'd found shelter in rocky caves, sucked the prickly pear and eaten its bright flowers long before California chefs began tucking them in salads. I'd befriended coyotes, watched a rattler bear her live young, discovered the undistilled contentment of sleeping under a canopy of stars.

I stopped walking then. I closed my eyes and turned my face to the sun.

The silence of a desert is intense. It is the kind of sacred quiet that will take the greatest human calamity in its fist and squeeze it to dust. I felt myself in its palm and opened my eyes, surrounded by the vast and alien and desolate forest of towering saguaro cacti. The sun cast their shadows in long columns across the desert floor, while the saguaro themselves jutted up at the sky like spiny obelisks, some as tall as fifty feet and rooted in this sand for two hundred years.

I walked among them as though I were walking among giants, heading toward a rocky incline that still lay in the morning shadows of the eastern foothills. There, I climbed and watched for rattlers as I went—not that I minded a rattler, but they don't like being stepped on any more than anybody else, and just then I had other things to do than suck venom. I found a good spot a couple hundred yards up—a rocky lip with some back support, a smooth patch for sitting, a panoramic western view—and settled in.

I leaned back and watched the sky where a couple of hawks drew slow, perfect circles. I followed the easy tilt of their wings, so much like yearning, and felt my thoughts begin to calm enough to let that one, solitary, clamoring image rise to the surface so that I could try to reconcile it with the other more familiar one. Both were of Mary Bess. The image I'd carried for so long and through so many years: her head propped dead center in the trunk, her lifeless eyes staring at me when I opened the lid. And the other, newer image that had lain dormant and concealed: of Mary Bess alive, her eyes wide and terrified, watching me while the Doctor—

"Hey."

I snapped upright. Morgan stood below with a hip cocked and her head to one side, squinting up at me. She was in black, of course, the green satchel over her shoulder. Only someone who's not spent over thirty years incarcerated for something they just found out they didn't do would be surprised that I'd forgotten her.

I waited.

She climbed for a while.

"Okay, Frost," she said, pulling herself up on my rock and breathing harder than I'd expected, "the one thing I didn't know about you was that you're a world-class walker. Not a bad climber either." She put the bag down carefully and stretched out on the rock beside me. The silver tips of her boots caught the sun and winked.

The one thing she didn't know about me?

"I had an inkling before today about what might have happened that night in December. Mostly just simple deduction based on what I'd read and what you told me." She crossed her ankles and leaned back on her elbows. She squinted one eye at the sky where the hawks had risen to high, tiny specks. "But also, I did a little phone work the last couple days. Found out where you always went when you escaped the mental hospital. Figured I'd find you at the same spot, VA hospital in Tucson. Also tracked down an old doc that DeWitte used to work with back in Phoenix, before he met you. Found out something interesting from him."

She glanced over at me. "According to his description of the first wife, she could have been your twin sister."

I stared at her. Her skin was flawless, the color of that café latte stuff like they sell in *The Riven Bean*. The merciless desert sun must have hated her. Come to think of it, right now I wasn't as fond of her as I could've been.

"Have I missed something here? Is this your business?"

"Well, I didn't think you'd mind. Under the circumstances," she said.

"The *circumstances*?"

She watched the sky: "Yeah, well, the sheriff was probably thinking his vibes had really been out of sync when he called this one, you going comatose all of a sudden. By now, in light of your disappearing act, he's probably thinking his intuition is about as good as his chances of getting re-elected. Probably figures you rigged the whole zombie business to set up your disappearance. Probably."

"It's real interesting the way you read minds. Go on. And?"

"Hey, you're doing your Sleeping Beauty number there in Clarissa's guest room, taking in the ceiling. Getting a few answers seemed like a good idea at the time. Beats television."

"Maybe you ought to take up reading."

Morgan looked down from the sky where the birds had disappeared. She hit me with a look, lifted one eyebrow. "Now you mention it, that's mostly what I did do. Got a knack for research. My specialty."

"Ah, research." I thought about that for a minute while I studied her green bag and the collection of driver's licenses and checkbooks I knew were inside. I remembered her telling me at Julia's, before I'd zonked out, about how she'd researched the names. "Okay, so you found out he was married before me, I knew about that. Well, not what she looked like, but I knew he'd been married, that she'd died of cancer or something."

"Try *something*." She looked back to the sky where the birds had reappeared. They were closer now, so I could tell I'd been wrong. Hawks don't have rubbery red heads, and they like their meat warm and moving. These were vultures. "*Something*," she said, "like morphine."

We looked at each other.

"Apparently DeWitte had a taste for it himself. Fellow I talked to said he hadn't known about the wife, Maria Elena her name was, indulging, as he called it. Said something else maybe the good doctor didn't tell you. Said he was acting like a basket case there at the end, just before the wife OD'd and was found dead. She'd been getting ready to leave DeWitte the next day, going to her folks' ranch in Mexico where she'd first met him when he was a doc there for the silver mines. This old guy I talked to, he had some suspicion DeWitte might have figured a way to keep Maria Elena from leaving. Figured he'd rather see the wife that looked like you dead than running around loose for some other man to pick up. Said that part of it, thinking of somebody else having her, was what was really driving DeWitte around the bend. He tell you that, Grace?"

"I don't...what were...why are you doing this?" My thoughts were humming, tuning up for a shot at critical mass. I could feel them exploding and flying around and bouncing off the inside of my skull like ricocheting bullets. "Why were you calling around about him?"

"Maybe I'm the Good Fairy." She smiled, but without conviction. Her voice was husky, and the words were slow and lazy, like the sun had zapped them. She shrugged, still leaning back on her elbows. "Just trying to help you out. Or maybe I was just bored. Seemed to be a lot of unanswered questions hanging around you."

"Well, that explains it, then. You get bored, you run up long distance charges." I was getting ready to make some comment about teenagers and arrested development, but she turned her head slow, in my direction, just enough to throw me a long look, then stretched out on the rock in the sun like one of those snakes I'd been careful to avoid. I changed my mind.

She went back to watching the sky like there was something there worth seeing. All she needed was a straw to suck on, she'd have fit right in with the geezers that used to hang out around my daddy's church.

"Call me curious," she said. "What I found most interesting was the other part, that she was just about your twin."

"And you're thinking that's why he married me?"

"You're thinking it was a coincidence?"

I wasn't going to open that can of worms. Anyway you want to look at it, coincidence is a dicey contraption. It can turn a hard-line rationalist into a crusading Christian in a New Jersey minute. So I tread real cautious around coincidence because once you get started looking too close at why things happen like they do, you are as liable to go looking for an M16 as a bible. I gazed out over the immense stretch of desert and giant saguaro below, the sky overhead turning white as the sun rose higher and ate at the bit of shade we had left on the rock. I tried not to think too close about thirty years ago, when I'd walked this same desert like most people walked their backyards, even lived in it a couple of months, not all that far from where we were sitting. I turned my thoughts to a more comfortable image—Julia's old Lincoln back there at the campground, thinking how I'd like to be behind the wheel, pulling in my drive. Going to bed for a week or two of sleep. Just for starters. But Morgan was on a roll.

"I figure DeWitte for a case of classic psychosis. Borderline personality triggered by abandonment. Think about it. His first wife tells him she's leaving, sends him over the edge. He kills her. If he'd go to that length to keep his first wife from leaving him, why wouldn't he do the same with the second? In your case, setting you up for the murders so you'd be behind bars, thinking no one else could have you if he couldn't."

I closed my eyes, not seeing the sky anymore, but seeing those two birds I'd thought were hawks, their wings stretched wide, circling around inside my head like they lived there. I thought about how hawks mate for life, and then I thought about Mary Bess. The next thing I knew, it wasn't the hawks, it was Mary Bess's eyes staring down at me, her face shaping itself in the darkness behind my lids. Her eyes were wide and terrified, her mouth moving without any sound coming out of it. And then the eyes filmed over, dead eyes staring from the trunk. Mary Bess had been alive before I'd lost consciousness from the drug Daddy had given me. Daddy D had been the only other person there. Had Mary Bess died of her injuries or had Daddy—

"...one thing I can't figure is why, having the brains to conceive and carry through all those escapes, even one time having the key and walking right out the door, why you kept coming back to Tucson, walking that hundred miles of desert to get there? Knowing the police were going to be there at the Veteran's Hospital. It's hard to figure why you'd do that, isn't it?"

If I'd had any other answer than "yes," I'd have said it. But the sorry truth was, it didn't make any more sense now than it had then.

I said, "Did you ever think maybe it was love?"

"I have to admit, Frost, that didn't cross my mind." We watched the birds circle for a while. "So that's what it was, huh?"

One of the things I'd learned crossing the desert all those times was that a little irony will carry you a long way. I slipped a peek at Cord Morgan, still leaning back on her elbows and considering the sky, and that reed of straw I'd imagined stuck in the corner of her mouth seemed for all the world to actually be there, rising and falling as she chewed on it. Maybe she saw me seeing it, because she grinned, and my heart suddenly soared like a barnstormer in August heat, just about like it had that night when I was washing down the walls and turned to Mary Bess.

She rolled over onto her side and looked at me. Her fingers stretched to my hair, my face. Over her shoulder I saw the hawks moving lazily in the sky. Her thumb felt along the line of my jaw and she leaned into my hair and I felt her lips move across my temple and down past my ear and she closed her teeth softly on the hinge of my jaw and moved her body onto mine. She was light and she fit me and I closed my eyes and heard my name in her mouth as she kissed my neck and her fingers found the side of my breast. I held the back of her head, the hair soft in my hand.

"Cord."

She raised her head. I looked into her eyes, she into mine, and what she saw there only she could say. She leaned into me, and I kissed her with all the longing in my soul.

I lay back against the rock, closed my eyes, let myself be carried on the wings of the hawks. It was a journey long in the coming. There on that flat rock, the two of us spread for the sky and its creatures, I saw in the reddening darkness behind my eyes an old

Indian sitting cross-legged on a skin, beating a drum whose regular, heartbeat rhythm recalled a time spanning the birth of life itself, echoing down through the ages as surely as water runs from mountain rivers into oceans. I saw a procession pass before me, ghostly shapes, dancing in an endless row to the beat of the drum, and there was the figure of Medea herself, plucked up as I watched and set down into a promised land, a place that satiated her great thirst for love. I suddenly realized for the first time as I watched her step down from her skyborne carriage, the both of us staring up into a white sky, why I'd felt such elation that day at the amphitheatre, seeing the *machina ex deus* swooping down and carrying her away—a woman who, in spite of all odds and all crimes committed, was snatched from the jaws of doom in one life to be reborn in another. I thought this as though I were soaring into the sun with the hawks, brought at last to such ecstasy that I had only dreamed could come through induced hypnosis and intravenous narcotics.

When I opened my eyes again she was lying quietly in my arms, her hand still cradling my breast. The sun had passed the noon matrix, the birds had gone.

"And so what was it, Frost, that's kept you so long from a woman? Do you know?"

I did, but I didn't know if I wanted to tell it.

"It was Mary Bess and Jesse, wasn't it?"

I looked away.

"You thought their relationship wasn't an improvement over the one you had with Bruce DeWitte? That Jesse's violence equaled the doc's?"

I nodded.

"Lot of women feel that way. Expect our own gender to behave above the laws of human frailty. We're human, Frost. It's as simple as that."

And then it was my turn.

By the time we'd hiked back to the car and headed northwest, stopping for the night in Kingman, we still had a couple hours of daylight left when we pulled into Julia's drive Friday afternoon.

And were greeted by Sheriff Hammersmith.

PART IV

Killer Frost

25

MORGAN PULLED THE LINCOLN IN FRONT of the garage, next to where Hammersmith was parked on his bike. His black leather jacket was draped over one of the handlebars, and he was leaning against the backrest reading a book. I got out, and Morgan hit the garage door opener. She pulled the car in, and the door whirred back into place.

"Hey." The sheriff swung a leg over the bike and put the book down on the saddle. I would've guessed something in the vein of *Zen and the Art of Motorcycle Maintenance*, but it was Louis L'Amour's *Broken Gun*. "Serendipitous happenstance, if ever I saw one." He walked toward me with a lazy smile, his fuzzy pigtails seeming to vibrate a little in the late afternoon sun. I relaxed a bit. It was hard to believe I could be arrested by a guy on a purple hog, wearing a purple T-shirt with a big white star circled by the words STARS AND STRIPS. It was the name of Las Tierras's only X-rated club. Given his housemate, I wondered if this was some kind of camouflage for the benefit of the community. Hard to say. The sheriff was an odd guy. Maybe he really went to the place. Or maybe he liked the humor of being sheriff and wearing that white star on his chest.

He angled off toward Julia's front porch, nodding for me to follow. I hesitated, waiting for Morgan, but when she didn't appear, I reluctantly followed Hammersmith up the steps to Julia's door.

Which was locked. I held open the screen door, trying to remember when I'd last had the keys—they'd been in my pants' pocket, so they'd be at Clarissa's...

The sheriff slipped them from his pocket, unlocked the door, handed the keys to me. "After you, m'lady," he said, making a small bow.

It was dark inside, just as when I'd last been here with Morgan, but the air was unbearably stale and damp. I made a beeline for the living room, pulled back the drapes, pushed open the windows and the sliding glass door until the place looked as it used to, sunny and airy. All the while, the sheriff stood in the entry with one shoulder leaned against the wall, his arms crossed and his head cocked sideways. I walked past him to the kitchen.

"You going to tell me why you took off from Clarissa's?" he asked, following along and settling himself on a stool at the counter. Julia's stool.

I pushed open the window above the sink, inhaled deeply, and turned to face him. "I just sort of woke up, lying there in bed and staring up at the ceiling. I recognized it as Clarissa's house, just been there the other day. Found my clothes folded nice and neat on the dresser. There were, uh, noises coming from down the hall." I gave the sheriff a sheepish look. He nodded and looked down at the patterns the sun threw on the bar while I set about making a pot of tea as Julia used to do. "Well, you know, I had an urge to get moving, just decided under the circumstances it was better not to bother anybody. I guess I ought to have left a note or something, but I wasn't thinking altogether straight. What I remember is wanting more than anything to get off by myself somewhere. Take a drive. Think."

I filled the kettle with water and searched for something herbal, all the time wishing I'd spent some time thinking about what to tell Hammersmith. I hadn't figured on seeing him so soon. All the way back from Tucson, when I wasn't sleeping, which was most of the time, I was filling Morgan in on my meeting with Sam Oliver at the newspaper office and the sheriff at his house, trying to digest the new information I'd discovered in the desert about Daddy D, feeling my insides sizzle whenever I looked over at Morgan behind the wheel. I was trying to make some sense of my life, but I hadn't made much headway through the confusion and excitement and anxiety that crowded in on all sides.

"You wanted to *take a drive*?" Hammersmith said. "After being in a *coma* for two days?"

I tried to explain something to him that I wasn't all that clear on myself. About me and the desert, how I'd crossed it so many times during my escapes I'd come to know it as a place of comfort, a safe harbor. "So I lit out on the freeway without even thinking, reckon I just gravitated there, like some folks would gravitate home."

"In Julia's car."

His voice had an edge I hadn't heard before. I glanced at him, and his eyes lay on me cold as a Fargo wind in December. He was frowning, and his lips had set hard enough to turn white around the edges. That's when I knew that for all the sheriff's easy-going manner when we drove up, Morgan had been right on target about his state of mind.

"You're the one told me it was mine," I said. I turned the gas on under a pan of water and stared at it. "I just wanted to drive it. Being in that car, it was like being close to her, to Julia. Not to mention, it's a sight more reliable than my truck." I could have added that I'd also taken it to avoid being arrested, but I didn't. Because I was standing there in Julia's kitchen, looking at the water just like she always did, and I could feel my throat close and the tears inching up. I didn't want the sheriff to see them.

I walked hastily out of the kitchen, through the living room and down the hall toward Julia's study where I waded through the familiar clutter of books and folders and scattered papers, entered the small bathroom and closed the door firmly behind me. I was far enough away from the sheriff that he couldn't hear me. I leaned back against the door and let the tears come till there were no more. When I opened my eyes again, I was looking into the mirror above the sink, staring directly at the infamous Killer Frost in my dead friend's bathroom.

She was quite a sight. In the vague light from the tiny window, she stared back at me looking not much different from that night when she'd stared from the mirror in my Phoenix apartment as I prepared to leave for Jesse and Mary Bess's place. True, her hair no longer fell to her shoulders in platinum waves, no flattering sweater showed the curves of her breasts and hips, and she was missing the glint in her eye that a few glasses of whiskey will put there, but for all that, even with the massacred hair and the tear-streaked face and the dirty, wrinkled clothes, she was so shockingly the same woman, so indelibly immune to the passage of thirty-five years, that I gasped as though I were seeing an apparition.

I thought of Clarissa Remington, the effort and expense she undertook to reverse the effects of gravity, but at that moment I'd have paid as much for the opposite effect, to have the surgeon carve in the lines and sags that would mark me as nothing more than an ordinary human being. As it was, I felt myself an aberration, grotesque and without kinship. A woman whose adult life had been lived among the insane and dispossessed, who was a freak of nature without blood family or the comfort of friendship.

I closed my eyes and took a deep breath. This wasn't getting me anywhere. The sheriff was waiting, probably wondering if I was lapsing into another fugue state. I shoved my head, hair and all, under a surge of icy water from the basin spigot and washed away the tears, scrubbed at my face till it burned. When I returned to the living room, rubbing the water from my hair with a towel, the sheriff stood in front of the patio windows with his hands clasped behind his back, looking out across the deck to the descending hillside and Las Tierras below.

I walked over and stood next to him, the two of us watching a ripple of wind pass through the autumn trees. I could feel the nearness of his shoulder, the heat of him, even though we weren't touching, and I nearly smiled to think how we'd once explored each other intimately, lovers who'd remained strangers. Of course we'd botched it, how could it have been otherwise? I glanced over my shoulder, through the screen door, searching for Morgan, turning to go look for her when he stopped me.

"Listen, Grace," he said, "I know this is a tough time for you. You've lost your best friend. Then there's this other business with whoever's been sending those notes to you, but...well . . ."

The edge in his voice was sharper this time. Alarmed, I suddenly realized he was working up to telling me something. Something ugly.

"What is it?"

He kept watching the wind ruffling the trees. "It's Clarissa," he said. "I went over there Wednesday after she called to tell me you'd disappeared. I didn't take it as an emergency. Some time passed before I got away from the office. Drove up to her gate, no answer on the intercom, so I climbed over. Her door was standing open, found her stretched out in the hallway. She . . ." He shook his head. "Looks like she walked in on a burglar. Looks to be some jewelry missing from her bedroom. Some drawers in her office were tossed. She'd been hit across the head with a heavy object."

"Oh my God." I sat on the sofa and stared into the room, but I was seeing Clarissa standing at the end of the bed with her hands folded, smiling down at me with that look of sappy contentment on her face. "My God."

"She's not dead, not yet, anyway. She didn't have the heart problems Julia did, but her age is against her. She's in a coma right now. She comes out of it, we'll know who to look for. But it's a toss-up, no telling when—or if—she'll come around."

I saw another picture of Clarissa. Last Saturday—her ash blonde hair perfectly styled, the crisp lines of her suit, the sparkle in her eyes as she stood in the sunlight on her porch and watched Rico Santillanes drive up.

"Santillanes. He was with her when I left. Where is he?"

"Seems to be a run on disappearing acts. When Clarissa called me about you, I figured he was probably still there, because the way she phrased it was, 'we found her gone.' His fingerprints are all over the place, including the bedroom, but whether she was all right when he left there or not, that's what I'm looking to find out. I went by his house, wife said she didn't know where he was. I put out an APB, he tries to cross the border, they'll pick him up."

"While I'm thinking of it," he said, walking over and standing behind the chair across from where I sat, "I guess when you left you didn't want to be alone so bad you minded taking Rachael along with you. I guess she'll verify your desert story?"

We both glanced at the front door. Still no sign of her. She'd probably walked on back to my place to check on her horse. I'm no good at quick thinking, but I did the best I could, not wanting to tell him she'd been with me, though I didn't know why exactly.

"I went to the desert by myself, picked her up walking alongside the road out by the freeway on my way back into to town, said that old jalopy she'd bought from Dave died and left her stranded. I was bringing her back here, let her use my truck." I stared back at him across the coffee table. "Do you actually suspect me? Or Rachael?"

"You did disappear pretty suddenly, without explanation. Theoretically, supposing Santillanes didn't do it, it's possible you could have circled back after he left. Rachael, too, for that matter. But why would you? That's the thing, isn't it? No, I can't say as you're high on my list of suspects, but I got to ask the questions."

"And Rachael?"

He gave me one of those long, unfocused looks like he does sometimes. "You say you picked her up alongside the road? I didn't notice that old car of Dave's broke down anywhere. Not at your house either. Been there looking for you. She tell you where she left it?"

I shrugged, but I was barely listening. I was seeing myself flat on my back in Clarissa's guest room. Using my peripheral vision to look up at Clarissa and Santillanes and...*Morgan*. My recollection of being at Clarissa's and what had preceded it was very fragmentary. I remembered being in this house with Morgan, walking in and finding her here in spite of the doors being locked and the house belonging to a dead woman...a woman she'd told me she'd heard of, hadn't she? She'd mentioned Julia, that she'd covered that story of her mother's burning. I was getting goose bumps, looking "coincidence" square in the face again, and it was scaring me to death. Was it really just a coincidence, Morgan passing through Las Tierras. Just an accident that she'd been at that gas station when the earthquake hit? Or had she come here deliberately, on some kind of mission? I thought of all those fake IDs in her satchel, all that money. She was a strange woman, all right, no doubt about that. I could see her shooting some asshole right through the forehead, but I couldn't for the life of me see her robbing an old lady and knocking her over the head. And what was it she'd been doing just before I'd blanked out? Something I hadn't liked, but I couldn't remember what. And why had she taken me over to Clarissa's? Why not to a hospital? My head was spinning. None of it made sense, and the sheriff was still talking.

". . .don't have a clear motive at this point. On the surface of it, looks like Santillanes had a pretty good setup, why rock the boat, but who knows what happened. Could be Clarissa wanted him to leave his wife, maybe upset him. Plus, the missing jewelry looks to be very expensive, according to the log she kept in her account books, but if theft was the primary motive in her case, that doesn't seem to connect at all to Julia's death. "No, the way I'm putting it together, I see both cases related, and I see two factors they've got in common. One, the women lived right next door to each other. I find it hard to believe that that's just chance."

I didn't know where he was going with this, but I didn't like it. "You said *two* connections?"

"Found this along with your keys in Clarissa's laundry room. Must have taken them out of your pants pocket when she laundered your clothes."

Hammersmith pulled a plastic-wrapped paper out of his jacket pocket and tossed it on the coffee table. I'd forgotten about it, but now I recognized the last note I'd received from the poet, the one Morgan had given me just before I'd gone into the fugue state. The one I must still have had in my jeans when I went to Clarissa's.

"What about the computer disk?" I asked, reaching for the note. "An AOL floppy?" I remembered, for the first time, the disk I'd pirated from Julia's desk when I visited Sam Oliver at the newspaper office.

"Nope, nothing like that. Important?"

"Maybe," I said, making a mental note to ask him about it later. For now, my attention was riveted to the note as I slid it out of the plastic and read it over. I suddenly remembered reading it before I'd passed out, and now my blood ran cold and my head began roaring. Somewhere in the room, from a long distance away, the sheriff was still talking.

"...think that, besides their proximity to each other, you're the only other link between the two. One night you go by Julia's with those notes, and Julia's dead. You go to Clarissa's with a note in your pocket, Clarissa's in the hospital. You hear what I'm saying?"

I looked up from the note. "You think I did it?"

"I can't deny I thought you might have set me up for your disappearing act, but I didn't come over here to arrest you, I came over here when I got a call from the law down around King City saying you'd been spotted headed this way, figured you were coming back here, and I needed to talk to you. I think somehow you're the key to all this." He looked hard at me. "I think someone's watching you. I don't know why or who or what they want, but I think whoever's doing this is going to make another move, and soon. I'm putting a surveillance man on you, can't get it setup till in the morning, so till then, I'm going to drop you off at your place, and I want you to keep your doors and windows locked."

After the sheriff had pulled Julia's drapes and secured the house, I rode behind him on the purple motorcycle, down Julia's drive and up mine. Inside the barn, Morgan was busy with her horse. The sheriff escorted me into the house, checked every room, even stuck his head inside all the closets. Before he left, he said what movie-star sheriffs have been saying for decades: "Don't leave town." Then he blasted off on his hog.

Which was a relief because I couldn't have pretended to pay attention much longer. I waited till the sound of the hog had disappeared from the air, then pulled the note out of my pocket. Everything on it was a blur except the words:

It's time.

26

Morgan

OCTOBER 31: ALL HALLOW'S EVE

At twilight, the air is not air, quite. It is a sulfuric mixture of decay and resurrection, sent up from the earth's bowels. An obfuscation of day and night, light and dark. Being neither this nor that, twilight rises lambent through some infernal, infinitesimal, invisible crack between then and now. In this nethersphere, ordinary laws of the physical world do not apply.

There is a calendar's day celebrating such a time, a passing of the seasons from summer to winter, that occurs at the end of October. Midnight is its nexus. It is a time nearly come, when the dead walk among us, hand-in-hand with dreams and illusions and myths and other betrayals of the senses.

I see them as I start to leave the barn for Frost's house which, at this late hour, is still dark. They arrive in a single line, creeping up the driveway. Such diminutive goblins. Such determined vampires. They carry brown bags, squeezed tight by the neck. Behind them, a woman trails at a distance. I linger in the doorway of the barn, watch as they file up the stairs to the porch, knock at the door. When no one answers, the children return down the driveway, a knot of failed demons, the woman following.

I enter Frost's house. She is sitting in the dark on her sofa, the note in her lap. Even as I close the door, she seems not to hear me. Yet she speaks.

"It's him. Daddy," she says, sotto voice. "He's back. He's coming for me."

I could change the subject. I could talk of Clarissa, of the attack on her I discovered listening through the window to Frost and the sheriff. I could confide my knowledge about the culprit who murdered Julia, based on my reading of her unfinished exposé filed on her computer, a suspicion that has been borne out by the surveillance tape I have just finished watching, the one from a camera I planted at Clarissa's house while Frost herself lay in a coma. I saw the suspect enter Clarissa's patio door, stay briefly, leave in a rush. Or I could go to Frost, take her by the hand and lead her to the bedroom, make love to her as the spirits watch in the light of the moon at the window. But whether I could recall her, even then, from her own willing descent into distraction, I do not know. And not knowing, I therefore choose the other, safer way.

I sit beside her and she recoils, returning momentarily to the present. "You. What did you do to Clarissa after I left, before you came for me? She's been attacked, maybe dead by now...jewelry stolen. And the disk..."

"Disk?"

She tells me of the AOL disk she has removed from Julia's office desk, thinking that her friend's work is hidden there, that it is a clue to her killer. I believe she is correct. I saw it in the culprit's hand leaving Clarissa's house. It is what he came for.

I ask, "You think I am a murderer, then? And a thief?"

"Aren't you?"

I look into her eyes deeply. Only the truth will do for her. "No, Grace, not a thief. And I have not killed your friend nor attacked your neighbor." Her eyes return to their former state—unfocused, the pupils dilated. "Do you believe me?"

She looks down at the note in her lap. "It's time. That's his phrase. He took it from the Eliot poem, The Waste Land. He said it was not simply a convenient bartenders' phrase, but words carrying great and eternal importance for us all, for me and him."

"Yes, Grace. So they do." I take the note from her, hold her hand which is ice cold. "It was his key phrase, his trigger, wasn't it, Grace? What he said when he wanted you to come to him, to have sex with you. When he wanted you to stay calm enough to hold out your arm so he could give you the injection. It didn't matter, did it, if you were in the kitchen cooking, or in your nurse's uniform and tired after a tough day, maybe watching *television. You might have been at a party, and the night was young, and you were having a good time.*

"Later, after you were institutionalized, there were probably coincidences when the command series—the whispering of 'It's time,' the touch on the shoulder—occurred accidentally, maybe a nurse giving you instructions, a friend reminding you of something. That would have triggered your escapes, thinking DeWitte had called you to him. He apparently got a kick out of it for a while. When it began to wear thin, he told the VA hospital in Tucson to tell you he was dead. Which didn't mean you didn't still go there since it was the last place you'd known him to be. It's called a post-hypnotic suggestion, Grace. Whenever you experienced the precise combination of words and touch, you were programmed to behave a certain way. What happened to Mary Bess and Jesse wasn't your fault. None of it was your fault, Grace."

She turns slowly to me, whispering. "Who are you? Why are you here?"

Questions which have no answers. Such is my dilemma. I ignore her; there is no time for us, only for her. "That's right, isn't it Grace? He comes to you, doesn't he, Grace, and he touches your shoulder, your left shoulder, isn't it?"

"My right."

"Ah, your right then." I raise my hand to her cheek, stroke the line of bone, let my hand fall light on her shoulder. The right shoulder. "And he says to you—"

"No…"

"—he says, 'It's time.'"

• • •

It is late now. Nearing midnight. I have done to her what had to be done. I lead her out the door, up the path to the ridge top. It is within such twilight times as this that I once lived, working for Pasonombre, completing the assignments for The Company. In that nether twilight region, there is no right and wrong, no rational world with its relative, changing values, no morality imposed. The twilight realm is beyond morality, a place wherein one possesses such clarity of vision that the pith of legislated behavior is mere fool's dust.

We are transitory creatures, here on earth but for a blink in a galaxy's instant. Worth no more than that. Meaning, in this place, is hubris, as easily rotted as old flesh on a hot summer's day.

So it is to this twilight realm I revert now, a place outside human ken, for this work I must do with Frost so that, without my urging, she simply follows behind me without resistance, through the silted air of this twilit night. Walking silent as the dead along the ridge. Following the decline of the dirt path, through the corridor of wild undergrowth with the sound of the stream in the distance, growing louder as we continue our descent into the darkness below.

27

DARKNESS—IT'S THE BEST FRIEND A FUGITIVE can have. Walking the desert all those years ago, it was the nights that kept me cool, but it was the dark that kept me hidden.

So I didn't think much about following her along the ridge, having always been partial to a night walk. I watched for Daddy D, but the only living creature I saw on the ridge was the black cat, a bit of pointy-eared shadow against the dirt path, like he was on Halloween duty and posted as guard. Then, as we kept walking, he disappeared.

Morgan wore black. Barely able to see her, I kept close on her heels, pushing through the scrub brush as we wound down toward where the stream ran loud. When we entered a dense copse of trees without even moonlight, my night vision failed entirely. I was surrounded by pitch black, and the stream ran so loudly I could hear nothing above it. Morgan took my hand, led me through trees that I knew by the smell were eucalyptus. She stopped among the low-hanging branches, and I yelled loud to be heard above the crashing water.

"Where...what are we—"

Her hand clamped hard over my mouth, and her lips pressed against my ear. Her sudden, explosive movements sent a rush of fear through me, and I struggled against her.

"Shhh, Grace. Be quiet. You're going to have to trust me—"

I fought all the harder, but her grip was like iron. I felt a hand drop light as a bird on my right shoulder as she held me tightly and spoke directly into my ear, a whisper that seemed to cut through the sound of the water.

"Grace, Grace. *It's time.*"

I stopped struggling. Fear melted away. I was bathed in serenity and light as air because the anxiety had fallen away like October leaves from their branches. I knew in my intricate center that something heavenly was just on the verge of happening if I could only remain calm enough to get to it. *Remain calm, remain calm,* I told myself, reciting my mantra.

She clasped my hand and led me away from the stream, away from the water. I couldn't see her, but I felt her arm around me. I could smell her. The body of Cordelia Morgan was a garden of unfolding gardenia blooms. She stopped, and I stood in the circle of her arm, a pocket of night where the air hung perfectly still. And then, without warning, a gust of chill wind swept across us, shaking the trees, making the leaves rattle the night.

The sound overwhelmed me. It carried a familiar edge, though I couldn't place it. It was not applause, not the sound of crashing ocean waves, though it was much like those. Then I remembered it was Halloween. I imagined, just above, an airborne coven of cackling witches—such was the sound made by the wind.

I smiled and leaned toward the gardenias, felt my head nestle perfectly into the softness of her breast, the promise it offered. I remembered the desert and felt my breath quicken.

"Yes, Grace. You're safe with me..."

I had known her voice was deep, but not so deep as this. It was a voice sent up from the mystery inside the earth. From the mystery in the crowded sky above the trees—

"...you're safe and warm, floating at the center of a dark pool of consciousness, deep inside. Every thing you have ever seen in the world and every word you have ever heard from the time you were born until this moment, it is all there, floating inside this great dark center inside you."

My head nodded, and I shut my eyes. In the velvet darkness, I can hear the voices. Hear my mother calling me (*"Gracie, Gracie, come in"*) to come in from a rainstorm, hear the raindrops tapping against the window panes and turning in an instant to a great terrifying downpour. I feel a stinging wetness against my face, though I am inside my house, safe, a small child hearing the sound of a door closing downstairs, hear the sound of my father's footsteps climbing up the wood stairs, growing louder, my bedroom door opening, his voice (*"Gracie, Gracie, it's time..."*).

"Shhh, be quiet. Don't cry. It's all right, Grace. You're safe here, but there is one more thing we must do. You must listen, pay attention. I want you to hear these words again, this one last time." One hand was stroking my hair, the other touching my shoulder. "You remember *it's time*, don't you? *It's time*...But wait. There's more. Know that this is only the first part of the sentence, and now it's time to hear the rest of it..."

I listened and felt the smile on my face, and then we were walking through an open field lit vaguely by the canopy of stars. In the far distance was a square pane of yellow light. We waded toward it, through tall, damp grass, and stopped a few yards from a small cabin. While Morgan approached the glass and looked in, I waited and studied her silhouette, the way the light brushed her face, stroked her high forehead and her cheekbones and the hard line of her jaw. She stepped away from the window, back into the darkness, and I thought for a moment she'd disappeared and left me here, but when I turned to scan the clearing, I smelled the gardenias and found her beside me.

She took my hand and guided me around the side of the cabin. When we turned the corner, meager light shone from the front window across a rough path that disappeared into the darkness toward the stream. Morgan suddenly tightened her grip on my hand, quickened her pace. In three fast strides, dragging me behind, she hit the door with her shoulder and we were inside.

The cabin was one large room with walls of unfinished logs and a rough wood floor. There was a handmade table and two chairs and kitchen cabinets which were built square and unpainted and plain as a box. In one corner, a single bed with a quilt over it was pushed against the wall. There must have been electricity to run the small refrigerator and two-burner electric stove, but the figure sitting at the table with his back to us was using a kerosene lamp of the type my mother had always kept up high in a cupboard for when the wind blew out the power lines. Several more lamps were lined up along the wall, as though he were collecting them for such a time.

Even with his back to us, I could tell it was an old man. His spine had curled into a hump, and his hair, having lost whatever shape and color it once had, made a baby-fine halo in the meager light from the kerosene flame. He wore a red and black plaid shirt, and his head waggled oddly from side to side.

Every cell in my body knew it was Doctor Bruce DeWitte sitting there, even if it took my eyes and head a time to catch up.

Because there was nothing about him that looked like the man I knew. When his head jerked around, the eyes behind his glasses were rheumy and pearled over with cataracts. His face in the flickering lamp flame appeared so desiccated that the wrinkled flesh was in the slow process of collapsing inward on itself like a rotting apple. Long, glistening strands of spittle dripped from his open mouth. The mere effort of turning had set his tendons shaking, and cords stood out along his neck as they struggled to hold up a head too heavy for the shrunken body. Yet, in spite of his trauma, the old man seemed to sense my presence as much as I sensed his. His hands flew up from the table, and his fingers fluttered in the air like mad moths.

"Gracie..."

I didn't recognize it at first, my name was so misshapen by tremor. I edged around the table, facing him, my mind rushing frantic as a rabbit before hounds, unable to think or find cover, until I finally stopped and faced my nemesis.

"Grace." A new voice came from the open door. I looked around and saw Zoloman Willis.

There are times, I think, when shock takes the shape of a beast, snatches you up by the scruff of the neck, lifting you straight off the ground so that in spite of your terror you can see from a clearer perspective. What had once been my predisposition to hysteria disappeared forever in that one instant—I watched the unfolding scene with the dispassion of a neutral spectator.

Zoloman Willis stood in the doorway wearing his elegant suit, a soft dove gray, with his hands resting in the jacket pockets as though he were taking a leisurely stroll across an English estate. I remembered the sense of vague recognition I'd had the day of my visit, and saw now that it was the suit, moss green that day but still so much like this one—and something else, too. A certain fluid movement of the body, as though the joints of his long, fine bones had been oiled and primed like precision instruments. The same way Director DeWitte used to glide down the Evanston State Mental Hospital halls in that dove gray suit all those many years ago. The kinship between them was obvious, though it took Morgan spelling it out before I began to make sense of it.

"Daddy D..." she said, eyeing the old man. She pronounced the name as though it were an accusation. Zoloman had gone pale. His attention shifted from me to Cordelia Morgan, while the old man launched into a high-pitched keening. She silenced him with a look that must have frozen his blood.

"...and Zoloman Willis DeWitte," Morgan continued, shifting her gaze. "We're having a little family reunion here. Father, son, and..." She paused, smiling at me, "...and stepmother? Wife?"

I stared at Zoloman. Daddy D's *son*? I remembered all those sepia photographs on his walls, the blonde woman who'd resembled me enough to be my twin sister, and at that same moment I recalled what Morgan had told me in the desert about DeWitte's first wife. My twin.

"In fact," Morgan went on, "Zoloman here has quite a mother fixation, isn't that right, Doc? Maybe you better tell him what really happened to his mother. Because you and I both know Maria Elena didn't have a drug habit. So she couldn't have overdosed on morphine like the death certificate said, could she? How about it, Doc? You want to tell Zoloman how his mother had enough of your addiction problems, was leaving you and taking the baby with her? Heading back to Mexico to live with her mother and father in San Miguel de Allende where you first met her? But—what a coincidence—the day before she was to leave, she died."

The old man exploded into an incoherent fit of snarling invectives and flying spittle. Zoloman stood in the doorway speechless, looking confused, glancing back and forth from the woman in black to the cursing old man. Morgan seemed to be enjoying herself. Her upper lip rose slightly as she took a step toward the creature who, for all his palsy and cataracts, kept a sharp enough eye on her to clam up when she moved his way.

Morgan paced and talked. "Coincidence number two," she said. "Couple of years after the death of his first wife, he marries Grace here, dead ringer for Maria Elena. And how about this for stacking up the coincidences—" She stopped directly across the table from the old man. "Just so happens Grace was going to leave you too, wasn't she? You couldn't stand the thought of it, just like before. So you devised a plan. That Friday night when you'd made her promise to call you, you'd already left for Phoenix earlier that same day, arranged for somebody to be at your place in L.A. to take the call. That way you had your long distance bill for your alibi."

The old man glowered. She paced again. "You could have saved yourself the trouble—because there wasn't all that much of an investigation, was there? Between the politicos in Phoenix wanting the case closed quickly and the reading public wanting blood, the details got shoved aside and Grace got a death sentence. You'd covered yourself, set it all up. Using hypnosis, one of your specialties at the Institute, you engineered the frame up of Grace. Those two women, neither of them would have died without a little help from you, isn't that right? No, you killed them mostly to make sure Grace was either gassed or spent the rest of her life behind bars— you didn't care which, so long as she wasn't running around free. You probably would have killed her too, maybe came to Phoenix that night with that in mind, but walking in on the situation like you did, it was already under way and made to order, wasn't it? All you had to do was add the finishing touches..."

The cabin tilted sideways and my head swam and I struggled for breath as her words faded away. Behind Zoloman, a shadow was walking toward us out of the darkness. Mary Bess. Her hair was pulled up in the knot, with the soft spray of curls collecting around her face. She walked softly in that way she had, partly on tiptoe, and passed through Zoloman and came into the middle of the room to stand behind the old man. She smiled down at him at first, just like she used to do when she served us dinner, as though no time had passed between then and now.

But then, as I watched, she changed. Her knees began to bend. She sank slowly, wilting like a flower, until she was lying on the floor, her spine broken and her eyes wide, unable to speak as she watched DeWitte pushing me down on the bed and spreading my legs and forcing himself inside me. Her image began to evaporate and I looked away, to that old man, the mucous seeping from his mouth and nose, his eyes filmed with disease.

Through it all, Morgan paced and talked about the Doctor's use of hypnosis. How he'd used a post-hypnotic suggestion to call me to him each time I made my escapes, enjoying the control he had over me, but then finally growing irritated with it, the publicity, convincing the authorities to tell me he was dead.

Zoloman had seemed spellbound throughout, but suddenly he stepped into the cabin, in Morgan's path.

"You spoke of my mother, of her death. You said she was not a user of morphine?"

Morgan and Zoloman stood eye-to-eye—the tall, sleek woman in black and the man in his elegant, antiquated gray suit, even his language seeming to be of another era. Before Morgan could answer, the old man at the table unleashed a howl that ripped through the cabin. He grabbed the edge of the table and pushed himself up, toppling the kerosene lamp. Morgan and Zoloman made a dive for it—Zoloman, being closer, caught it.

That's when I noticed what I'd missed before. There on the table where DeWitte had been sitting was a sheet of colored notepaper, that familiar notepaper my poet had used. My curiosity succeeded in doing what the old man's caterwauling and Mary Bess's specter hadn't—drew me out of my immobility and back into the room. I went to the table for a closer look while the old man squared off against Morgan. Zoloman had righted the lamp, and as I approached, he looked at me with the same naked adoration I'd seen during that brief moment at his house.

"Grace, I am glad your friend called me this evening to come here. Although I have meant for a long time to reveal myself, the longer I waited, the more impossible it became. So I watched you, I sent the notes instead, wanting somehow to have communication with you, to let you know there was someone who admired and revered who you are—"

"The notes? You? But I thought—" I looked down at the note on the table and then at DeWitte. The old man, apparently in fear of

Morgan, was edging away from her, toward his son, keening under his breath and hugging himself like a small child.

"But you didn't send any notes this week, did you?" Morgan said to Zoloman.

"That is true," he said. "I am afraid my father happened to come across me writing the note I had meant to send a few days ago, on what would have been your thirty-fifth wedding anniversary. It was then I told him about sending them—they seemed harmless enough."

He smiled that blithe, witless smile, serenely unaware of the tension in the room, as though he were in a bell jar at the center of a lashing storm. He took a step toward me with such glowing tenderness in his eyes that I recoiled.

"You are the woman for whom my life was created. I treasured every picture of my mother I could find in my grandparents' home. As a photographer, I loved nothing more than to discover blonde women of a certain veneer and pose them against a background of my own creation. I knew I must find my father, for only he could add to the store I had already compiled about my mother. He was happy to know I bore him no grudge for his abandonment, and pleased as well that I wished to take him under my care."

DeWitte stood hunched next to Zoloman, his arms wrapped around himself, his eyes tightly clenched, and the keening sound emitted sporadically, like a child's whine.

"My care was in exchange for any and all information he retained about my mother. When I discovered the story of his second wife, as well as her tragedy, I became enthralled by her."

Zoloman caught himself speaking of me in the third person, as though I weren't standing in front of him. His face reddened like a shy teenager.

"I became enthralled by you, as though somehow I had come to understand for the first time where my obsession had been leading me all along. Not to my mother, but to you."

He looked from me to Morgan, as though he felt obligated to explain himself to her as well. "I knew every time she came up before the patrol board. I knew when Mr. Belli took her case. I had been for some time aware of Miss Simmons' involvement.

I knew that she was searching to find a place near her own family home to purchase for Grace. So when Miss Simmons purchased the one for you, I bought the other. It was all very easy. As things always are when they are preordained."

His eyes glowed. For all the affection in his expression, I recognized something even more familiar than the gray suit and the fluid gestures—the profound disengagement of true madness. He took a step toward me, and again I stepped back.

"By the time you were granted your freedom, I had been living here already a few months. My father, of course, knew of my obsession, but he could not dissuade me from moving here. I could scarcely resist some method of contact, so I undertook the notes privately, unknown to my father. I selected happy occasions: the date of your freedom, your wedding anniversary, Christmas, your birthday. I sent harmless notes, in secret. Until a few days ago."

Zoloman frowned at the old man, then shrugged in his graceful way. "When he walked in on me as I wrote the anniversary note, he flew into such a rage that I put the note away and decided I must not provoke him further. We will have plenty of time, worlds of time together..."

I glanced down at the note lying on the table.

Its time now that I confess
To Gracie Frost about Mary Bess
Most of her was laid to rest
Except for what's inside this jar

It seemed I had gone deaf to all but the drumming of my own blood. I picked up the note and stared at it until Morgan took the piece of paper from my hand. I barely noticed. I picked up the jar, held it to the wavering light of the lamp. Inside was a small brown object, the size and shape of a shriveled pear. Dimly, very dimly, I became aware of the old man watching me, his back grotesquely hunched and a sly expression stealing across his face. At the same time, that other figure began to materialize behind him—Mary Bess. She was changed yet again. Just as she had once held her platters of pot roast between her hands, delivering them to our table, she now held her own head, a silver tear searing each cheek and, just above it, a gaping hole was torn in her chest where her heart had been.

Beyond the open cabin door, the wind screamed and tore through the trees, and the flame of the lantern danced wildly. The meager light in the room palpitated, shuddered between bright and dark for a moment, as though inside the earth some gigantic creature were rousing itself. I stared into DeWitte's desiccated face. Like the light, it too seemed to be in the throes of some private convulsion, the withered lips stretching into a rictus that I suddenly recognized as a triumphant leer.

The jar fell from my hands to the floor, breaking. In horror, I watched the glass scatter and the object roll across the pine planks.

Zoloman leaned toward me, caught both my shoulders in his hands. "You see, Grace," he said in a voice as placid as a summer's lake, "everything is exactly as it should be. Look at you—frozen in youth! Time itself has stopped for you and given me a chance to catch up. We, the two of us, we exist beyond time, perfectly matched, divinely created for one another! It is a true miracle! The heavens, they have made it so, because otherwise, it could not have been. Do you see?"

What I saw was Mary Bess with the hole in her chest, DeWitte with spittle dripping from his mouth and his eyes leering in the quaking flame. I pulled away from Zoloman and knelt down, picked up the shriveled thing. I looked down at it lying in my palm. I walked toward the old man then, the hard, shriveled thing clutched in my hand. Suddenly the glint in his eyes was replaced with something else, with fear. And then something else again—a sly intelligence.

A sound began rumbling from deep inside his throat, and when the words arrived, they were familiar. "It's time, Gracie." He had not a tooth in his rancid mouth. *"It's time..."* and he took a step toward me, reached out a hand toward my shoulder.

I was paralyzed for a moment. And then, as I watched his smile broaden into a stretch of toothless gums, I heard the wind from a long distance away, carrying the rest of the words, finishing the sentence. *It's time*, said the wind, *"...that this shit stops."*

Before I even knew I was going to do it, I was airborne, throwing myself at him across the table, toppling the lamp as I grabbed for his neck.

The last thing I remember is the crack of bones between my fingers, a blinding flash of light, and the night exploding into fire.

28

Morgan

I was waiting for it.

When I saw Frost crouch and her muscles tense, I calculated trajectory and velocity, came up off the floor at the same time she launched herself like a heat-seeking missile across the table at the old man. I blindsided her, tearing her away from DeWitte as the lamp toppled sideways, kept our momentum flying out the doorway, so that when the explosion came we had already hit the ground yards away as the night lit up and the ground shook.

Kerosene will do that.

We spent a long time talking to the sheriff, watching the flames take the cabin, Zoloman and old man DeWitte put into bags and carried to the emergency vehicles that did not turn on their flashing lights when they left. Hammersmith believes DeWitte, in a fit of insane jealousy, killed Julia in order to frame Grace and return her to the safety of the mental institution. This is not the case, of course, although I did not provide him with proof of Julia's killer and Clarissa's assailant. Doing so would necessitate explaining how Rachael McKinley, a woman who owns a horse farm in Kentucky, has the means and expertise to enter a dead woman's locked house and access her encrypted files, not to mention placing professional surveillance cameras at Clarissa's place. Provoking such curiosity in a lawman is foolhardy—another phone call to the caretaker at the Kentucky farm inquiring about the particulars of Rachael McKinley will easily crack my identity. Later, before departing Las Tierras, I will leave Julia's essay with Frost, as well as the film from the surveillance camera. There is no hurry; the criminal will still be here.

The sheriff has gone, and Frost has just finished a shower and made tea. We sit with our cups beside each other, she in her white terry robe, her hair still dripping from the shower. We face the patio doors and the black night behind them, the glass reflecting our images. I look into their mirror surface and see that Frost is wearing a thoughtful expression. She looks very tired. When she moves, the black glass shivers—the white robe, the white hair, the pale face that is starting to looked lived in.

For my part, I do not move at all. My black is absorbed into the glass. I sense the magnetism coming off her. She leans slightly toward me, though she is not aware of doing it. It is a small thing. A significant thing.

We sip the tea, and I let the silence feed itself until, finally, she turns to me. I am amused but not surprised to see that her flesh is not so smooth as it had been before this evening. She is different from the woman I first met last Sunday, more intriguing—the ivory skin, the blue eyes not glass, but indigo. It is as though she has begun to acquire texture, depth. Age.

"Well, it's been a night," Frost says, reaching for words. She runs a hand through her hair, shorter even than my own. It doesn't look half bad when wet. She smells of soap. "So how'd you come to taking me down to that place to start with? How'd you know it was there? Or that that old man lived there and who he was?"

I am preoccupied, but I explain how I had gone to Zoloman's the day we'd climbed the ridge, how I'd found the trail to the cabin and discovered the old man inside, waited till he'd taken his pole and gone fishing along the stream. I'd found the note he was in the process of writing, the same one Frost had received with DeWitte's signature phrase: It's time. Yet even as I speak, I am thinking of the seven days Jerry Preston said to wait before traveling with the horse, tinkering with the notion of buying a new rig. Leaving. The road is calling me in the way it does when I have stayed too long. I cannot discover the why of this, though I know there is a reason. The call intensifies as we sit talking and looking into the glass at one another. I pull the flask out of my bag and unscrew the cap, drink deeply. When I finish, I set it on the table. Hard.

I am distracted. I let her talk, barely hearing.

There is something wrong. Every instinct I have is screaming inside my head, telling me to leave. Leave quickly.

29

I CAN BARELY BREATHE THROUGH MY DESIRE. I've been locked up in a bottle, some minor bug, captured and forgotten. And now the lid's open, and I sit here beside her at the table with her words coming at me, smelling the gardenia of her, hearing the deep velvet voice, both of us facing the patio doors with the night darkness pressed behind them, our reflections mirror clear.

"Well, it's been a night," I say, catching her eye in the glass, running my hand through my hair. Not knowing what to do with it, that hand with a mind of its own that remembers the desert, that wants to reach over and touch her, stroke her face. But I don't. Instead, I ask her how she knew it was DeWitte living in the cabin.

"When you were at Clarissa's and I was researching, I discovered DeWitte and his first wife had a child, a boy he'd shipped back to Mexico after her death. I remembered all those photos you mentioned of Zoloman's, with the woman who looked like you. It all started to add up," she says. "Zoloman's age. The old man's age. The different tone and content of the last note and the one that came with the snake." She takes the flask of vodka from her bag and drinks deeply. "You could argue that DeWitte passed on his abandonment issues to his son. Zoloman's obsession about his mother, and women like you who looked like her, may not have led him to murder, but he had his own way of keeping people from walking out on him. He kept the old man a virtual prisoner in that cabin, and he kept you under close surveillance for two years."

I stare at her image in the glass, trying to hold her eyes, but they've begun to shift erratically. Avoiding me. Staring out through the dark glass, scanning the corners of the room. Can she be so oblivious to me when I'm so aware of her? I compute the time. She's here for another week because there's the horse that can't travel. We have that, at least that. I've been secretly imagining what it would be like to lock up this house, travel with her. I'm shameless. These bizarre thoughts crowd me, sizzle mercilessly through my brain.

She has grown quiet, and I talk because I don't know what else to do. "All right. I understand all that now, about DeWitte, how he hypnotized me. And we know who was writing the notes. But there's no proof it was him who broke in on Julia that night. I'll buy that DeWitte was crazy, and Zoloman too, I guess, but what's the motive? Why kill Julia?"

She stands up and walks back and forth in front of the table. I can't take my eyes off her.

"So you don't believe Hammersmith's theory about the old man and his obsession with you?" Her boots strike the floor, her hands shoved in her pockets while her eyes probe the darkness outside. "That DeWitte was watching that afternoon when you picked up the snake note, waited to see what you'd do, followed you to Julia's? That he'd gone so far with it for so many years, just the notion of you having friends—men, women, whatever—set him off?"

I prop my chin in my hands. "I can see why the sheriff might think that. DeWitte caught his son writing those notes. His anger triggers the old mania about nobody else having me if he can't, pushes him over the edge. Writes his first note and ties it to the snake, follows me to Julia's and drops in on her after I leave. And the anger takes over. He's crazy, after all."

"Sure, I can see Hammersmith figuring it that way, but I don't buy it. For starters, I've lived just about my whole life with crazy folks. I know how their minds run. The truly insane, they've got their own logic, maybe more than the nine-to-fivers out here walking around free. It's the kind of logic runs on its own rails, makes them a lot easier to understand, in my opinion. Once you're on to that, they're a lot more predictable than you folks here on the outside.

"So, okay, let's say the doc was nuts, from all the drugs he took if nothing else. Have to be, wouldn't he, to do what he did to Mary Bess and Jesse?" My heart lurches, but I keep going. "Here's something else that doesn't wash. I know the Doctor. He might have sliced Julia's throat, might've shot her and then dissected her, might've done any number of other things to her, but I don't for a minute believe he just dropped in and scared Julia to death, then put her in a trunk without doing a little extra to her for my benefit. That's not the Doctor. More likely than not, he'd have walked in on us and done it with me standing there watching, saying that old hypnotic phrase because it would still have worked, and he knew it would work. In fact, if you hadn't figured out what he'd done and changed the combination—"

"He didn't do it." She stares through the glass doors. "Her death wasn't about you. Julia had stumbled across a local smuggling network. Probably got her first whiff of it through Santillanes, the prime activator behind the local Mexican political movement. He'd watched his people being shipped across the border illegally like cattle, sometimes in boxcars, left to stand in the sun and even, on more than one occasion, suffocate and die in the heat. Or used like slave labor, paid not even enough for bare subsistence. He wanted to expose the exploitation of his people by the Americans who were benefiting. Not only benefiting, but actively promoting the transport of illegals."

She approaches the table where I'm sitting, speechless, and toys with a piece of paper, the last note written by the old doctor. "Santillanes was working secretly to stop the importing ring, but he had to be careful to keep his work under cover because his people would have considered him a traitor. In fact, his wife clearly did. To her and most of the others, no risk was too great to follow their dream. And nothing anyone could say was going to convince them otherwise. But Julia and Santillanes knew better. Julia was going to champion their cause in her own way, by writing an exposé and spreading it across the front page, and Santillanes was helping her do it by getting the proof."

My mind feels like mud. "Well . . . but I don't see . . . why would Santillanes want to kill Julia?"

"He didn't. But Pandy Meyerson did. He was a big loser if Santillanes stopped the flow of cheap Mexican labor. In fact, Meyerson was the main instigator in shipping the illegals across the border, then paying them starvation wages to build his houses. He'd have lost millions without them. And Julia knew it. She had the goods on him, thanks to Santillanes, and when Meyerson went to her house that night after you left, trying to talk her out of writing the article, she must have gone into cardiac arrest, and he let nature take its course, even helped it along. Put her in the trunk to throw suspicion on you.

"Later, that day you were in Sam Oliver's office, Meyerson must have seen you lift the floppy from Julia's desk, suspected what was on it, then followed you. He knew he had to get the disk or not only was he going to lose his work force, he was going to get nailed for Julia's murder. He probably saw you tagging along after the sheriff, then waited for you to go home. You went to Julia's instead, and I was also there. So he hung around, but when you went into a coma and I took you to Clarissa's, still with the same clothes on and that disk in your pocket, he had to wait for his chance. He found Clarissa alone that day after you took off and Santillanes had gone. She must have caught him going through the house, and you know the rest."

Suddenly her eyes focus on the note she's been toying with. She seems to see it for the first time. "Those other notes, the duplicate set I made? Where are they?"

"I gave them to the sheriff to—"

She leans across the table, grabs my wrist. *"You gave the notes I wrote, the duplicates, you gave them to the sheriff?"* She lets go of my wrist and streaks across the room, shutting off lights, locking doors.

"What's wrong?" I feel the terror rising. "We figured out the dates, I thought Hammersmith might be interested in them, might help him figure out . . . what *is* it?"

The room is totally black. I hold onto the edge of the table to center myself in the darkness. I feel her beside me, then make out her shadow as she rushes to the glass doors and pushes them open, looks out into the moonlight. I walk over and stand behind her.

"What's wrong? What's going on?"

She raises her hand, and I stop talking. She waits for a while and then whispers into my ear. "I'll need your truck. I'll leave it in the parking lot in Tucson where I met you yesterday. I'll leave the key on the top of the tire, front driver's side. I'll contact you in a few weeks about the horse." She reaches into her bag, pulls out some papers and a floppy disk, hands them to me. "Give the sheriff these. Julia's exposé. It needs to be published, Julia thought so and I agree."

"But Clarissa—"

"Proof? No problem." She rummages in the bag, pulls out a small square object. "Here, the surveillance camera. Caught it all. Pandy leaving Clarissa's with the disk in his hand. Julia will get what she wanted after all. His ass nailed across the front pages."

She turns to me, and I feel the warmth of her breath on my face, her hand stroking my hair. Her lips linger on mine, and then she steps out onto the deck. When I start to follow, she stops me.

"This isn't a game, Frost. Stay inside. Lock the doors. Keep the lights out. There are people out here waiting for me, and they'll kill you without thinking twice. No matter what happens, *do not leave the house.*"

I'm suddenly terrified. I look around but see nothing, only the twinkling lights in the distance. When I look back, she's gone.

30

Morgan

I stand in the darkness and listen. Nothing. The trees bloom in the moonlight and harbor sleeping birds; the barn looms with its dark mouth, black on black. I wait on the deck for a long time, until every sound, every nuance of odor expands and drenches the air. I inhale deeply and know that the animals behind the barn have finished eating and stand along the fence line, watching. That the horse, blowing through its nostrils, is edgy and restless in its stall. That behind me, in the trees to the south, a man breathes shallowly, while another is posted by the barn.

I know something else too, knew it before I stepped onto the deck. Knew it in the Tucson desert. I have committed the sin forbidden all pros—in courting Frost, I have courted disaster.

As I wait, I chart the course of information that has crossed Cruz's path as though I traveled with it through the electrical circuits connecting state to state, nation to nation. I am aware from our first meeting that the sheriff senses something about me, some strangeness, but my story has checked out, and although he is interested enough to run the fingerprints, he wouldn't have given them a high priority. He had bigger fish to fry—a murder, an attempted murder, a vanished suspect, an earthquake, and the impending war between the business and Mexican communities. Still, at some point, the sheriff will have handed those duplicate cards to a deputy who fed the prints into the system which would have matched those Cruz had kept on file at all the information depots of the world. The red flag is up. Someone calls Cruz's office in Santa Fe. The rest is history. And I am living it.

I feel myself in destiny's crosshairs, know with absolute certainty of the man aiming a weapon at my back. I have no fear he will shoot, though, not to kill anyway, because Cruz will have forbidden it. If I die any but a natural death, the papers I have on him will be sent to Paso, and Cruz is a dead man.

So I wait. I can be patient as a spider.

The gun to the south shifts his weight. The curtain at the window beside me moves ever so slightly, but I do not tell Frost to move away from it.

I simply take in the night, considering the stars and the universe and tabulating my options.

I understand at this moment, at this time and this place, events have converged to bring me to this intersection of blind fate and mere chance, frozen at mystery's center yet constrained to act. It occurs to me that, like those contrived situations Paso invented at The School, this may likewise be a test on a more elevated scale: the human mind pitted against inscrutable planetary events. Or perhaps merely a prank, mindless entertainment for The One Who Watches. Or do I inflate the issue? Is this all intellectual acrobatics, the ultimate farce of delusion, utterly meaningless?

Thus I deliberate, letting fate wait, though at last I come full circle. For all the celestial plenitude above, there is but one option available here below. One. That's the rub. When you are backed against a wall, walking forward is just another way of standing still.

I walk across the deck, my boots pounding the wood. I descend the steps and take pleasure in the crush of gravel branding the darkness. I increase my pace, walk straight through the mouth of the barn and see by the padlock on the bunkroom that though the door is still locked, the room will be full of him. Of course.

I walk faster still. Hit the door and nearly without pause open it so that he has no time to prepare, looking startled in the purple glow of my laptop screen. I enjoy, in that instant before the curtain falls, seeing him off-balance. Momentarily.

"Cord."

"Cruz."

I approach the table, sit with one leg on the edge, next to the laptop. At the table's center is the empty dish where Frost once fed the cat, beside it a full pan of its drinking water.

Cruz watches me with pale eyes the color of pewter. He is a pewter man: the suit, the frames of his glasses which glint in the glow of the monitor. A lethal man, my former lover, as polished as a gun barrel. In front of him, on the laptop screen, familiar columns list the names and amounts and account numbers of the banks where I have deposited my money over the years. He has broken the code, can access the money, and we both know that without it I am caught, captured, pinned to the wall. Lost.

I place my green bag on the table next to the computer and slowly jiggle out the contents. I move slowly so as not to alarm him. Nevertheless, he glances through the open door, into the barn which is too dark to see the two men whom he knows to be there with me in their sights. I open the case holding the checkbooks and the back-up floppy disk on which I have copied all of the information now on the screen. I remove it from the case, all the while holding the eyes of this once-upon-a-king of mine. I place the disk carefully in front of him, on the keyboard of the laptop: his prize, his trophy, proof of his win. Proof that he has backed me into this corner of the western coast. I am in check.

He savors the moment, leans back in the chair, into the shadows and out of the computer's light.

In the surreal dimness of the room, he could be anyone. I could be anyone. The two of us, vaguely perceived strangers for whom all things are yet possible. No gunmen waiting beyond this door; no woman with platinum hair in the house, fluttering the curtains. Only myself and this Other.

And then, because he is so inconsequential to my essential being, the room around me grows darker still and I find myself alone at the hub. I am weightless and hovering at the center of some obscure world, aware that this almost lambent room is but flimsy gauze covering something else, something so familiar that if only I can tear away the veil, I will discover the path of my escape.

Thus I am suspended alone in this moment, an eternity of sorts. I have no prayers, no idols, no benefactors. I carry only my library of information acquired through experience. I sift, therefore, through my life's events, thumb its pages for clues, for direction. I recognize my guide, always the senses, and plumb the darkness for a sign. . .

A perfume enters through the door, the odor of horse wafting in from the barn, of fresh hay, the restless shuffle of hooves. I am led by them backward, into other pastures, other places. A Kentucky vista where horses graze the fields and a child rides along the pasture's perimeter, glancing homeward. And see her there.

She stands in the doorway, in the shadow of the broad portico behind the pillars. She watches me, her daughter riding a pony. Her hand is above her forehead, shading her eyes against the bright angle of morning sun, exactly like the last time I'd seen her, watching from the sidewalk as my bus pulls away, taking me to Chicago, to college.

The image of my mother fades. No, not fades, darkens. Her face turns a charred black, then lightens to ash, crumbling altogether and becoming dust blowing in the wind which is all that was left of her after the flames...

A slight breeze enters the bunkroom, prowls the corners, stirs something on the table beside me. When I look down, I see the shudder of pages, so slightly moving that perhaps I imagine it—pages protruding from the folder stuffed into an outer pocket of the green bag, Julia Simmons' file on the Indiana commune burning. Clues to the cause behind my mother's death by fire. The insubstantial sound echoes through my mind, reverberating and compounding and sounding like syllables, though distantly, a woman's breath: "It's time," she might be whispering, "to trust...

The neigh of a horse wakens me. I find I am looking into the pewter eyes of the man before me, his body moving slightly in the chair, his suit fabric shifting, rubbing against itself, seeming to repeat the briefest of syllables...

"... trust."

And in that syllable, that one condensed directive, I see in my peripheral vision the slightest movement of the veil, a shadow behind it of another whose image becomes clearer as the veil ruffles, parts—a woman whose hair might be on fire, so bright it shines when struck by the shaft of morning sunlight entering through the windshield of the old truck, the platinum hair exploding with light, and her words joining the others: "What about your matrix?"

Two voices, then—a choir of two, not whispering now, but singing high and pure as seraphs, so that in the cloistered darkness, another image is recalled—the old woman of the church: "Es tiempo!" she says, pointing to me, "Confianza! Confianza o muerte!"

I search for escape, for release, but there is none. There is only the here and the now, this moment. And therein, all we know of eternity. Salvation. Grace.

Trust or die.

And so I trust. How can I not? I trust myself to know that whatever happens, this man cannot, must not have the information before him which will glean him millions.

Before Cruz can stop me, I grab the pan of water, dump it over the floppy, into the keyboard.

A light flashes from the computer, and Cruz leaps back. Smoke pours from the keyboard, the monitor goes blank. And chaos, the lightning and thunder of lost millions: two men rush into the room, shouting, grabbing at me, at the computer. Cruz cursing, beating at the computer with his suit jacket, trying to stem the flood.

Too late.

Check.

31

Morgan

Any way you slice it, this looks like a No Win. Cruz is out of money, and I'm out of luck.

Because Cruz has been more careful this time. The two guns keeping me pinned aren't the jerk-off variety like the ones he'd brought along a couple weeks ago in Colorado. These are pros, probably Company Issue. He's put some thought into this one—written the script, hired the players, directing the performance on-site. He is a competent man, a smart man. Problem with men like Cruz, they have no imagination.

I wait.

Cruz is taking his best shot at saving the computer, but the water has run through the keyboard, short-circuited the motherboard, fried the hard drive. He's in the grip of something, though, probably thoughts of my seventeen million dollars down the tubes, because even when the laptop flashes again, zapping him with an electrical shock, he keeps working to pry out the keyboard. When he finally gives up, he launches into a screaming frenzy, kicking the table, hitting the walls, finally lifting the laptop, aiming it at the wall. Thinks better of it. Stuffs it into my shoulder bag still on the table. Thinks maybe there's still a chance. There isn't.

It's an impressive display of temper. I could use the time to set up a game plan, but I don't. That would take me out of the room, into the future. That has always been my strategy before, but not now. I am still mindful of the images and directives. I stay right here, in the moment, inside my own skin, watching the performance and waiting for events to unfold as though this were some kind of acid test I am being subjected to. That is the feel of it. The novelty alone is heady as adrenaline.

When Cruz is finished punching the walls and kicking the table, he walks our way. I feel the blow, the pain, then numbness. I hadn't anticipated that he was going to hit me with his fist, but I do know he won't do it again, not with the two men watching him lose it on a woman. Something to do with male conditioning, more to do with ego—the two men holding me and watching him.

Cruz's ego, it is going to be the death of him one day. He struggles for control, fails. In some ways, his plight is worse than mine.

"I don't fucking believe you fried the fucking computer!" he screams. His face is white. "Jesus Christ, Cord! I'd have shared the money with you. You think you've kept it from me, but you've just screwed yourself." He whirls away, talking to no one, to the room, to himself. "I can't fucking believe it!" He hits a wall again with his fist, then removes a gun from the ruins of his suit jacket. He shoulders my bag and storms out of the room, motioning us to follow.

The thing about The Bitch from Hell is, has always been, she doesn't play the fucking game. If there's a way to turn gold to shit, Cord Morgan will find it. She's a genius at it.

He's steamed, steamed so bad he can hardly think through black waves of rage. She wouldn't have made a hard copy, he thinks, groping around the door of the barn for the light switch. No, not Cord. He knows her better than that. The whole ball of fucking wax was right here, and now it's gone, trashed. He feels a fury so intense and staggering that he very nearly doubles over with the pain of it. He clenches his fists, thinks about what he could do to her—no, by God, not could but *would* do, as soon as he gets her ass back to the Lab in Santa Fe. In a private room. Very private, soundproofed, triple-locked.

He's still groping around for the fucking switch, thinking that even if the money is down the tubes, he'll salvage something. Yeah, no shit. Like maybe his life. Like maybe he'll find out where those papers are she's holding on him, the ones proving he'd tried to rip off Pasonombre, and he'd do it by God killing her inch by inch, minute by minute, nerve ending by nerve ending. And enjoy every bit of it. She is dead fucking meat, and worse. She's his.

He finds the light switch, flips it on. The brilliance is unexpected, mega wattage suddenly flooding the place. He squints and is blinded for a moment.

We are, the two guns and me, standing in the suddenly bright arena of the barn. I am aware of a dynamic energy that has collected here, as intense and pressing as the light burning down on us. It feels as though some apocalypse is at hand, some urgency waiting to happen.

Cruz motions the men to release me, to wait outside. After they have left the barn, he walks toward me. I feel the drizzle of blood seeping down my chin. I let it seep.

Cruz is a few yards away when the cat appears. The black tom jackknifes from the rafters with the speed of a hawk diving at a rabbit. He hits the center of the barn floor, landing with lean grace well clear of me or Cruz. He seems, in fact, not to see us. He streaks in a mad panic around the walls, caterwauling like a thing possessed. That is when I understand where the energy in the barn has come from, the same energy the cat is reacting to.

Cruz, struck by surprise, aims his weapon in his right hand, braces it with his left. He bends at the knee, moves in a circle, trying to get the demented, circling cat in his sights. The animal feints several times in our direction, as though considering an attack, but finally streaks out the barn door and into the night.

The men outside, following Cruz's example, have also taken aim, but with the cat gone they stand uncertainly, looking a little sheepish.

I understand all that has gone before, the images, their directive; why it has been crucial for me not to act before this moment, waiting instead, which will make the difference, if I am quick, between life and death. Because I sense what the cat has sensed. I see what is to be done now, clear and simple, and I have maybe sixty seconds at the outside to implement it.

I gauge the position of the two men outside the barn. And Cruz—he walks toward me, motioning me toward the barn door with his weapon.

I do not move.

When he is a few feet from me, close enough that I can smell the old familiar man scent coming from him, the unique mixture of chemicals that

*I have slept with and lived with for two years, would know anywhere,
I speak to him low, as though I do not wish the men outside to hear.*

"Cruz."

*I have always thought it an enigmatic name, a syllable spoken by angels
as easily as demons.*

*He stops, and we stand near enough to feel the other's heat. He detects
my odor in the same way I detect his. The auditory memory—it is a
potent, a most reliable weapon. It can evoke enough nostalgia to clog the
brain and send it reeling.*

*We exchange looks, stand toe-to-toe. We are the same height, the two
of us looking into one another as though we are looking into a mirror, seeing there the memories of a past shared life. His pupils dilate for an
instant, turning his pale eyes black. I can sense the change in his pulse,
though he does not allow the rhythm of his breathing to alter. His eyes dart
momentarily past my head, to the door of the barn where the men wait
outside.*

My cue.

*I spin around on my heel, walking toward the horse with his neck
arched over the top slat of the stall, his eyes glossy, curious. Thinking: the
key to a good performance is to act with your heart and your body will
follow, act with your heart and there is no audience who can resist your
illusion.*

*Letting myself be drawn to the horse, letting his eyes and their blood
consciousness shut out the presence of the three guns aimed at my back,
knowing the horse and I are alike: our bloodlines vanished, sire and dam
dissolved into the earth; anchored, the two of us, and sprung from the
same soil, the same bluegrass pastures of our lost homeland.*

*Hearing behind me, whisper faint: footsteps, the ones on gravel now
that I am far enough inside the barn to be removed from the men's line of
vision as I walk toward the far side of the barn, toward the horse; hearing
the other footsteps on the dirt floor of the barn, gaining on me.*

*Hearing before me, the soft breath of the animal: stretching his neck,
touching his muzzle to my palm, grazing my hand with his velvet, then
suddenly sensing (like the cat) with that special awareness animals possess, the electricity, the current coursing stronger now, sent up from the
earth, for suddenly his eyes distend, their whites showing; he tosses his
head, snorts, lunges sideways with a deafening neigh.*

Hearing that Cruz is almost upon me, the heat of him, the scent of him;
and the gunmen's footsteps no longer on the gravel but inside now, on the
dirt floor of the barn, and Cruz is close and reaching out for me because I
can hear the shifting friction of his shirt fabric.

I lunge headlong into the stall, feeling his hand graze my hair, hearing
his hiss, his curse, his voice low and moaning from some place deeper than
his throat, "You-goddamn-fucking-bitch." The horse whirling and rearing
in the center of the stall, the ear-splitting nickers that sound like screams.

"What the hell—"

He looks around wildly. Mel and Al are following him with
their weapons drawn, extended, waiting for his command. They're
in the middle of the barn, scanning it, but they see exactly what he
sees, which is jack shit. There's nothing there, but something's happening. Something big if he can only figure it out, figure what she's
set up for him this time.

Then that light, that fucking megawatt bulb, starts swaying on
its cord, the shadows swinging everywhere and he can't figure out
what the hell's causing it, but it's not just the shadows moving like
he thinks at first, but the barn, the fucking ground he's standing on,
and he hears it then, over the horse's racket, a sound like thunder,
but goddamn it, it can't be thunder, and he looks up, sees the huge
old rafter where the lamp cord's attached, the fucking weight-bearing rafter that's moving, splitting in fucking two as he stands there
under it in the swinging black shadows and watches it begin to
shatter and then he knows she's done it again, a real crash-and-
burn, all-holds-barred, tour de force, that The Bitch from Hell has
somehow set up the fucking end of the world, and before he knows
it or can stop her, she's pulling her bag off his shoulder while he's
standing there looking up at the fucking rafter that's splitting and
falling and the barn moving fucking sideways like it's made out of
cardboard—

He tries to recover the bag, looks around fast at her.

"Heads up," she says, the bag in her hand, crouched inside the
stall where the fucking horse is rearing up, going to kill her before
he can have the satisfaction of doing it himself. She's grinning,
pointing at the roof with the blood still running down her face

where he should have hit her twice as hard as he did and when he looks up again, the fucking rafter's split, falling in while the others are in the middle of the barn, no fucking way they're going to make it to the door before the roof caves in and the sides too....

I pull the horse by the halter, heading fast through the side door of his stall, out into the night as the earth, the barn, the trees seem to convulse. The night shudders, the black air itself ripped with cataclysm, deafening with the shriek of splitting wood and men's screams and collapsing walls.

The horse is rearing, whirling around in the dark, but I hang on to his halter and circle his neck with my free arm to avoid his flailing hooves. He lifts me off the ground, and I'm whipped through the air as he rears and plunges while the world splits apart around us. Still I cling to him, talk to him, am dragged by him down the incline toward the highway, away from the barn which is still collapsing. At the pavement he begins to calm, and I gaze up the driveway and make out the lines of Frost's house. The barn, structurally unsound and weakened by the first earthquake, has collapsed, but the house stands firm, still dark and untouched by the quake.

The earth has calmed. I lead the horse along the pavement. His hooves clatter against the asphalt, then crunch on the gravel as we walk up Frost's driveway. We near the house, and though the earth still briefly shudders occasionally and the barn is still falling in on itself and the horse is panting heavily in my ear, I hear it. The crack. In the interim instant, I duck and jerk the horse sideways, feel the wind split by my ear as the bullet flies by. The horse rears, and as I cling to him, I see a shadow moving our way. A broken shape limping out of the gray breaking dawn.

One arm dangles uselessly at his side. His white shirt is ripped and bloody. Miraculously, his glasses remain, though a deep gash runs from his forehead down across the side of his face. In his right hand, the gun is aimed directly at me. He is still coming, limping, close enough now that I can see his mouth is moving, but I can hear no sound.

He's never wanted anything more in his life than to see Cordelia Morgan dead. He doesn't care about the papers, he doesn't care if he lives or dies, he doesn't even care that he's not going to get to kill her slowly, though that thought is the last to let go as he drags himself toward where she is fighting with the horse, trying again for a clear shot at her. Not caring if he hits the horse but knowing if he does, he'll lose her. She's fast, too fast, and his leg is mangled badly and it's slowing him down. But he doesn't care, doesn't care if the fucking thing falls off because he's got her in the sights, the horse too, and he's squeezing the trigger to get off that one clear shot...

If Cruz had been a baseball and her shovel had been a bat, Frost would have hit one out of the park. I watch with more than a little awe as he drops to his knees at the feet of the platinum figure who has stepped from behind a tree and hurled herself at him.

Checkmate.

I lead the horse up the drive to where Frost stands leaning on her shovel, looking down at Cruz motionless on the ground.

Across from us, the barn is a heap of lumber which is still settling and crashing sporadically. The other men who were standing at the center of the building when the quake hit could not possibly have made it out, but I realize that Cruz must have followed me and the horse through the side door. I bend down to examine him and cannot help thinking, as I note the depth of the jagged cut across his face, that he is going to have a tough time reclaiming his GQ look or running for public office in the future. He's out cold, though his breathing is regular.

I pick up the gun and drop it into my bag, tabulating how much time I have here, how long it will take Cruz's men to arrive. I consider Frost. And how, having made the first mistake, I cannot afford another. I am lucky. Most are not given another chance.

I remove the bag from my shoulder, unsnap the strap, clip one end to the horse's halter and hand the other to Frost. I explain that before Cruz has access to a phone, I need to reach the Dodge Dart waiting in the Tucson VA hospital parking lot. Not only is the car a reliable, highly tuned racing automobile under its grimy exterior, but Cruz will not have a description or license number on it. I take the backup set of motorhome keys from my bag and hand them to Frost, tell her I will contact her later. In the breaking dawn, her hair is silver. I touch it and tell her she might want to practice driving the rig.

By the time I am getting into Frost's truck, the sky has lightened to the color of slate and Cruz is tied and still unconscious in her back room, an unidentified trespasser who is going to have to wait for the sheriff or a hospital room, whichever comes first, before he will have access to a phone. And given the large number of emergency calls, according to the local operator, he may lie there a good while. The horse, no worse for the experience, grazes among the geese and the goats.

I start the old shambling truck. If the earthquake has not made rubble of the freeway, I have some delicious hours of highway solitude ahead before I reach Tucson. The last glimpse I have of Frost is in the rear view mirror. She's standing on the porch, leaning against the railing with the black cat propped against her leg.

When I come off the onramp and hit the freeway, the sun is lifting above the Sierras. The freeway is a long stretch of open road, unscathed by the earthquake. I lean on the accelerator, and the old truck surges forward. A finger of sunlight comes through the side window, touching the shoulder bag perched on the seat beside me. I've left the ruined laptop behind. Excess baggage. The safest file backup is no longer on the disk drives one carries, but on those virtual ones found on the internet, as much storage space as anyone could want—available to anyone who can access a website. On more than one of them, I've stored all my crucial files.

The shaft of sun illuminates the manila folder still protruding from the side pocket of my green bag. Julia Simmons' research of the burning of the Indiana commune. More new information than I'd ever dreamed of having.

I follow a curve in the freeway, leaving behind the eucalyptus and heading into the open California countryside. Heading east, into the blinding glare of the morning sun. I squint and shade my eyes. At the center of the brilliance lies a darkness, some shape beaconing me eastward.

Perhaps.

Or perhaps not.